THE ONLY THING MORE DANGEROUS THAN THE SHADOWS IS FALLING IN LOVE WITH THEM

BLACK WING
and
SHADOWS

J. L. Rosenauer

Book One of The Sandorg Chronicles

COPYRIGHT

Published by Jerrica Rosenauer
Imprint: Jerrica Rosenauer
ISBNs: 978-1-969797-00-2 (ePub), 978-1-969797-03-3 (Kindle)
978-1-969797-02-6 (Paperback), 978-1-969797-01-9 (Hardcover)
978-1-969797-04-0 (S.E. Hardcover with Jacket) 978-1-969797-06-4 (S.E. Hardcover without Jacket)
978-1-969797-05-7 (S.E. B&N Hardcover with Jacket)
978-1-969797-07-1 (S.E. Paperback)
Author: J. L. Rosenauer
Cover & Map Design by Jerrica Rosenauer
First Edition, 2025
Printed in the United States of America10 9 8 7 6 5 4 3 2 1

CONTENT WARNING

This book contains depictions of violence, war, torture, death (including of young characters), grief, past sexual abuse, and sexual content. These themes may be complex or triggering for some readers.

Not every reader will be sensitive to the same things, but I want you to feel safe going in. Please take care of yourself first—if you need to set the book down, your well-being matters more than finishing the story.

Lastly, this book includes over 200 versions of "fuck" in some manner, now 201. As well as other explicit language, if this book isn't for you, that's okay, but I did *warn* you.

♥ in the Chapter Title indicates sexual content. You know just in case you're in public reading.

CONTENTS

Map of Yebel
NORTH
Veil of Vultures
"Drusearon Mountains"
Northhold Outpost
Ashen Vale
Ashwynd
Blackmere
Chalahana
Eastvwyth
WEST
EAST
Winterhand Stronghold
Woxweth
Hallowford
Camp Echo
Fort Nemlina
Flugblatt Forest
Glonia
Wicklowe
Sandorg Vale
Fort Sanda
Zion Outpost
Fort Daysn
Lakish Outpost
Eliana
Esten
Veskonia
Whisper Outpost
South Brudgipt Outpost
Fort Kalona
SOUTH

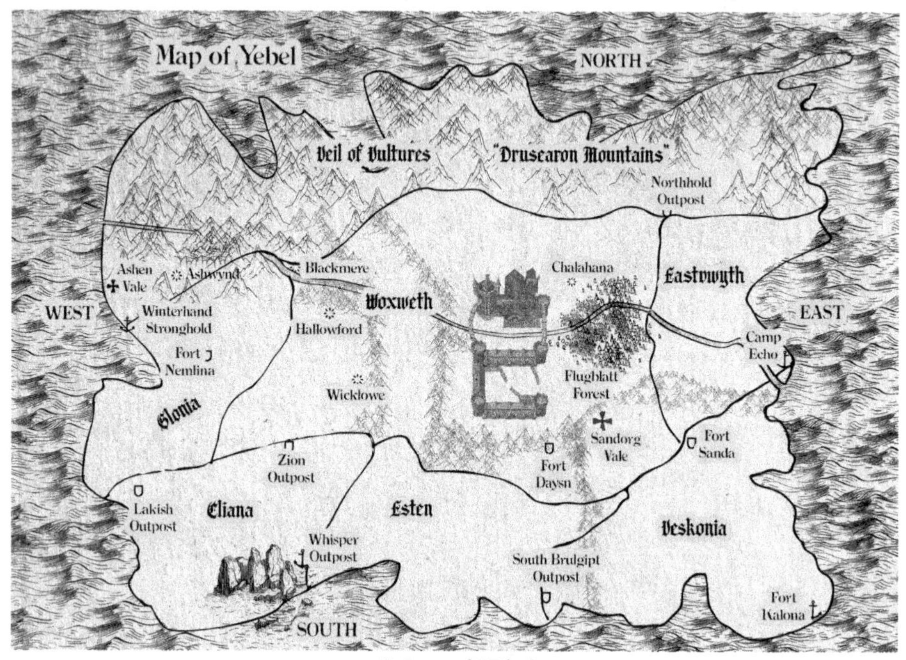

Map of Yebel

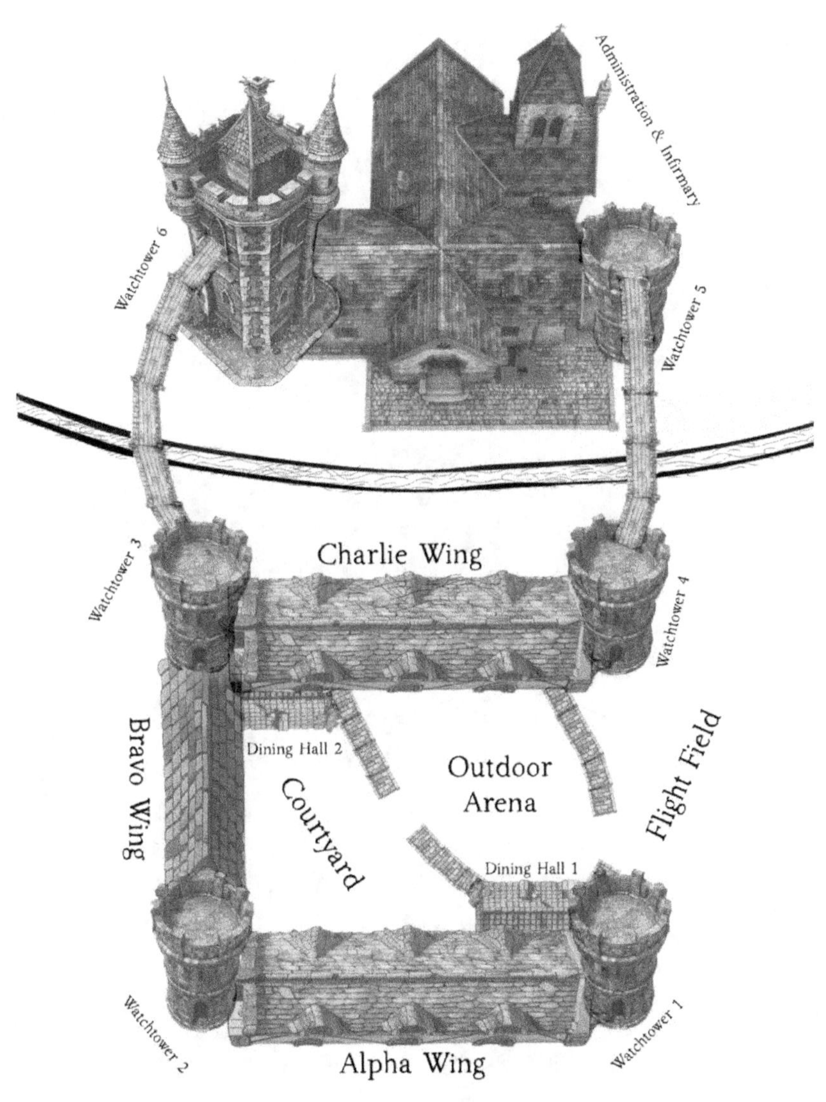

Map of Sandorg

Some bonds are forged in blood, others in birth. The rarest are written in love.

CHAPTER 1

Thousands of cadets before me had climbed these stairs, and thousands had failed. What made me think I was different? Nothing. Except I refused to go home and admit my father was right. Some cadets sprinted as if four hundred and fifty steps didn't wait above, shoving bodies aside in their rush. Others dragged their feet, dread written in every slow step. A few looked like prisoners, pushed into this climb by conscription, each motion reluctant, heavy.

Sandorg Military War College was massive, far larger than the drawings I had seen. At Sandorg, regardless of which of the seven branches, everyone started from the same point. The same hellish training lasted for eight weeks for each cadet. My dad tried his best to prepare me for what I would face, but I felt he was trying to scare me away from going.

"Move out of the fucking way!" one guy shouted as he hauled up the stairs.

Like we weren't all going to the same place. Chill the fuck out, man.

"What's your name?" The voice came from behind me.

The female cadet had been consistently following behind me the entire time. She appeared nervous, her breathing slightly heavier due to the pace. Meanwhile, my mind raced with numerous thoughts, as it always did. I told myself I didn't want to make any friends. I didn't want any weaknesses or become attached to anyone who might end up going somewhere else—or dying. She picked up her pace a little more, walking alongside me.

"Auriella, yours?" I paused for a second to look over at her. She had beautiful black hair and the perfect little points on her ears. Her pitch-black lashes framed her eyes, making them stand out. She stood about five feet six and had a nicely toned body.

"Torvi," she said. Her voice was shaky. "What branch are you going into?"

"Does it matter until we actually get there?"

It really didn't, if we didn't survive basic. I don't want to make friends. We probably wouldn't be in the same branch.

She grinned. "Of course it does, if you are looking forward to a goal, you will fight to see it. I am going to be a Rider."

"Same," I said. She wasn't taking the hint.

"Maybe we will be in the same wing."

"Maybe."

Maybe—Maybe we wouldn't, if either of us survived the first few weeks here. Even if we did, what was the point of making a friend that might die in the next four years, or won't make it beyond Judgment Day. Fuck. I might not make it. Her green eyes were too bright, too hopeful. I couldn't afford that kind of light in my life. Friends got ripped away. Better to keep my distance now than mourn later.

We continued to climb in silence. My dad didn't want me to pursue it, and although he was a Rider, I was the only child and wasn't obliged to go. However, I chose to attend. My mother supported me from an early age, enrolling me in courses to enhance my agility and teach me how to use weapons effectively.

Ahead, there was a lot of noise and shouting. My stomach started to churn, and nausea rose in my throat. In a few steps, I would be a cadet—and one step closer to bonding with a dragon.

"It's yes, instructor," a very loud, pissed-off instructor yelled ahead.

Fuck.

This was it. I wanted this. Right? Every seed of doubt my father planted came crashing into the back of my head. *They are going to yell at you nonstop. They will break you. You will be treated like scum for weeks. You're different—they're going to pick on you.* All the things he told me flooded into my mind as if he were standing right there. Shit, I hope he wasn't right.

I stepped onto the top of the stairs. A brown-haired Historian, dressed in sage green, sat at a desk and took our names. Six feet to her left stood the female drill instructor, whose dark eyes burned into us as we stepped forward. She looked ready to incinerate us alive with her gaze. Remembering what my dad told me, I reminded myself it wasn't personal. They were preparing us for war and molding us into warriors.

"Auriella Blackcreek, reporting for basic training."

"Leave your bag here to be stored, and report to Dining Hall One."

I turned, straightened my posture, and followed the other cadets, assuming they knew where to go. I crossed over the large bridge that connected the administration building to the watchtower. I passed by various drill instructors on the way, wearing caps that separated them from the rest, all standing firmly in place with no expression. Each one of them looked eerily as though they might take our heads off at any time. I wondered which of the seven branches they belonged to—Riders, Drusearons, Sorcerers, Shapeshifters, Infantry, Healers, or Historians—all of which played a vital part in our military, in wars past and future.

The dining hall was enormous, with space for at least five hundred of us. Row after row of stone tables lined the hall, some had benches and some had chairs, seating six to eight cadets. Cadets gathered in the hall upon their arrival. Some had been here for hours.

The bell tower tolled sixteen times, indicating it was sixteen hundred, and my stomach twisted inside out.

"Get your asses on the ground and give me twenty pushups," a deep voice roared, making my bones tremble.

Everyone in the dining hall dropped where they were and started doing pushups. I executed mine flawlessly. My legs straight, my arms locked straight, dropping my elbows to move my chest to the ground, and back up. Some of the cadets around me struggled, and I hoped none of the instructors noticed.

"What the fuck kind of pushup is that?"

I turned slightly to see the cadet the instructor shouted at, trembling on the floor. I tried not to be obvious, not wanting to draw attention to myself. The cadet—a small female with vibrant red hair—was clearly struggling to maintain composure, her body shaking violently.

"At-ten-SHUN," another instructor commanded. This one's voice wasn't as deep, but just as sharp. Everyone stood tall, hands to their sides.

"I am Drill Instructor Asselin. I am one of many who will be here pushing you to your limits for the next eight weeks. Let's cover some ground rules: One: Do what you're told, when you're told. Two: You should have nothing on you except the clothing you wore. Three: The next eight weeks will be hell, and some of you will not make it out alive—and a lot of you will wish you were dead instead. Four: If you have magic, you will not be able to use it. Don't even try. To my left, starting close to me: Instructors de Grignon, Minet, and Ramuel. To the right, starting close to me: Rivet, Pascal, Ossent, and Quillet."

The deep-voiced instructor was de Grignon, and the female I saw on the staircase earlier was Ossent.

"There will be eight hundred and seventy-five cadets starting training this year. If you didn't know, we hold one basic training session each year, which starts on May twenty-ninth and concludes on July thirty-first. Courses start tomorrow, you were the last group to arrive for this year's cadets. You will eat breakfast, lunch, and dinner here. Following dinner, you will stand in formation in the courtyard outside this dining hall. Now line up for dinner."

Asselin strode off, and the room broke into motion as boots scraped, and trays clattered against metal. The line surged forward, the smell of grease and stale biscuits clinging to the air. A hard biscuit was placed on my tray, with the meat that looked entirely too old to be served. Great. If we didn't die from training, it would be food poisoning.

I carried it to an empty seat, the wood sticky beneath my hand as I pulled the chair out. The first bite turned to paste on my tongue, chalky and dry, tasting the way damp cardboard might if left in the sun. My jaw ached with the effort of swallowing.

I kept my eyes on the plate, counting each breath to ten, using the rhythm to anchor myself. Voices rose and fell around me, chairs scraped, a spoon clinked against a bowl, but I forced the sounds into the background. I reminded myself not to snap my head at every noise, not to let the chaos peel my focus away from the food in front of me.

Clink. Clack.

Boom. Smack.

Chewing mouths.

A cadet sobbing.

Voices overlapping.

Tune it out, I told myself. Bite by bite.

The clock on us ticked, though no one had said how long. My father had warned me—they would return, and when they did, we'd pay for every wasted second.

"Get the fuck up."

"Whhhaa... whaaa... whatttt did I do?"

"You didn't eat fast enough."

"Was... was... was... was there a time limit I missed?"

"Was there?"

"Uh... uh... uh... no... no, sir."

The cadet, another female taller than me with dark brown hair braided down one side of her face, looked petrified. From her constant stuttering, I felt bad for her.

After that little show, every cadet finished their meal and rushed outside to the courtyard, falling into formation. Instructor Pascal paced back and forth in front of us, surveying us. He stood six feet even, with light brown hair. From my quick calculations, there were two hundred of us standing there—shoulder to shoulder, twenty across, ten rows deep. I stood in the second row.

He stopped in the middle of us, glanced at the other instructors, and announced that they would be walking us as groups to our barracks to join the rest of the cadets who arrived earlier. He would take rows one and two, Quillet would take three and four, and the other six instructors would each take one row. The row we stood in now.

Wait. What. The. Fuck.

My mind spun. They were not going to place us with our intended branches. We would be bunking all together. I swallowed the lump in my throat. We were not technically assigned to the branch we selected until we completed basic training, and even then, there was no guarantee we would graduate into that branch.

No branches. No certainty. Just strangers piled into barracks like sacrificial lambs.

The forty of us followed our instructor across the courtyard and into another building. We climbed seven flights of stairs, turned right, then left into a vast room filled with bunks. I scanned the room, doing the math. On each side stood twenty triple bunks, making one hundred and twenty beds in one room. At the opposite end, two doors waited—one marked "Male Latrine" and the other "Female Latrine."

"Attttennnnn-tiooonnnnn!"

The cadets already in the room immediately stood at the ends of their beds, creating two lines facing each other.

"This is the remainder of your platoon. Help them get settled into the empty beds." Pascal turned and left us in the room.

We stared at them, and they stared back. My eyes moved from person to person, taking in the other cadets. Then, down at the end of the room, my eyes widened, my eyebrows lifted, and my heart dropped into my stomach.

Huge black wings.

CHAPTER 2

I knew that the children of Drusearon warriors had to attend Sandorg, but I hadn't considered that I would be sharing a space with them. The Drusearon tribe, mostly residing in the northern part of our continent, was born with wings. From a young age, their children learned to fly, fight, and handle weapons. Their wings were similar to those of a dragon, lacking any feathers. Each Drusearon developed their magical abilities between the ages of eighteen and twenty-one, depending on various factors. Some of them had potent abilities, while others had simpler ones.

I heard nothing good about any of them. Growing up, I had been told stories of their barbaric ways—not to mention what happened to me at fifteen. I didn't want to think about that. That day had been the worst day of my life. Even losing my mother hadn't been comparable.

I claimed an empty middle bunk and dropped the assigned duffel onto the mattress. A tall shelf loomed beside the bed, stacked with the other duffels above and below. I pulled mine open, sorting through the issued gear before sliding it onto the open shelf.

Voices tangled around me. One cadet laughed, another muttered low, two more argued over something I couldn't catch. The sound pressed in from all sides, sharp and constant. My pulse kicked faster. My fingers twitched against my thigh, restless and tight. My jaw ached from how hard I clenched it, and every breath scraped shallow. My focus snapped from one thread to the next, jerking toward every word that spiked louder than the rest. My chest tightened until it felt like the whole room was trying to squeeze me out.

The day had wrung me out, every nerve stretched thin. I hauled myself into the bunk and rolled onto my side, knees pulled tight to my chest. The blanket came up over my head, muffling the voices and blocking the light. My muscles throbbed, heavy as stone, and my eyes burned each time I blinked. A dull buzz filled my skull, fading only when my breath slowed. The mattress caught my weight, and I let it drag me down into sleep.

"Waaaaaakkkeeee uppppp," someone screamed, followed by a deafening bell that sounded like it came straight from Marzana. I rubbed my eyes, trying to figure out what happened.

"Get the fuck out of your beds and stand at attention."

The haze cleared, and I realized I wasn't at home—Pascal was screaming—and I needed to get up *now*. Like the rest of the cadets running around me, we all scrambled out of our beds, any dexterity gone, and formed a line in front of our bunks. I wasn't even sure what time it was, wondering how many hours I had slept.

"Now that I pulled you out of your slumber, make your beds!"

Was.

He.

Fucking.

Serious.

He ordered us out of bed in the middle of the night and demanded we make them again. We spun around, scrambling to tug sheets tight. The cadet above me fumbled from the floor, knocking into my rack and ruining my corners.

Three bunks down, Pascal stopped at a bottom rack. The bed looked perfect, but he stripped it bare, flinging the blanket and sheet to the ground.

"Again," he snapped.

That's when I understood—it wasn't about the beds. It was about him showing us we had no control. One by one, Pascal tore our work apart. We remade them. He shredded them again. The hours dragged, our hands raw, our nerves stretched thin. By the time he barked for us to lie back down, every one of us knew he could strip us bare and force us to start over as many times as he wanted. The beds had never mattered. Only his power did.

And in less than two hours, he indeed came back, waking us in the same manner as before. This time, as we stood at the ends of our beds, he started at the beginning and had us count off—one hundred and ten of us in this platoon. He told us to put on our uniforms immediately and stand at attention again. He went up and down the line, screaming profanities at each cadet, making sure we all knew he was in charge, as if any of us questioned it.

He escorted us to the dining hall, where we ate a speedy breakfast, all while listening to the instructors yell at various cadets for anything and everything they deemed annoying or wrong. After we ate, we stood outside at attention for what felt like an eternity. The sun was blinding, and my skin felt on fire. Every single sigh, cough, twitch made my brain race to see who else was restless. I wanted to remain still, trying not to draw any attention that might result in me getting yelled at.

After what felt like hours upon hours, the instructors returned and led us into an enormous stadium classroom built for thousands of cadets. We all piled in, instructed to sit with our platoons, each instructor sitting behind us, waiting for the opportunity to pounce on anyone who interrupted. A tall, pale, blue-eyed female with jet-black hair fashioned into two braids that merged into one walked into the center of the classroom and introduced herself as Professor Melamora. As she stood in the middle, her voice projected so loudly and gracefully that it had to be magic.

She told us we were in the elite college of special forces, and that some cadets came from legendary family lines. She studied each of us as she rotated in the middle of the classroom. She flicked both of her fingers, and above her, two projections snapped into place, allowing both sides to view. The map of our continent, Yebel, showed all seven provinces and the many bases across it. The Veil of Vultures spanned the northern part of Yebel, also known as the Drusearon Mountains. My eyes stopped at the western side, where the Veil of Vultures met Glonia, where a star marked Winterhand Stronghold. My breakfast turned in my stomach, and my chest tightened and burned. It was one of the outposts where my parents had been stationed—the one where I lost trust in the winged Fae. I reminded myself I needed to calm down before my breathing became ragged and people noticed.

I looked to the northeastern province of Veskonia and focused on Fort Sanda, which was in the northern part of the province. My favorite fort to date.

I drew five deep breaths—in through my nose, slow out through my mouth—forcing myself to settle, to hold the rhythm. Every sound pressed closer. Beside me, a cadet panted, his ragged breaths loud enough to trip my own.

I shifted to smell. Gods, we needed another shower. Sweat clung sharp and sour, heavy in the air. Taste came next—the thin tang of orange juice lingering from breakfast, faint but steady, something I could hold on to. Last, I pressed my palms to my lap, fingers dragging over the thick canvas of my dark-green uniform pants. The rough cloth scraped my skin, anchoring me. Calming me. But I gripped tighter than I needed to, because if I let go, I wasn't sure I'd stay steady.

After Professor Melamora finished reviewing Yebel, she moved on to discuss what college would look like for the next four years. Every cadet, no matter the branch, had to complete basic training because, whether you came to be a Healer or a Historian, you could be in a combat situation at some point. Basic training consisted of eight weeks of intense training, during which participants learned how to survive without magic or special abilities. While not every cadet would make it to the end, death was not encouraged in basic—unlike some of the branches, which sorted out the weak. All the second-, third-, and fourth-year students left for summer leave. Every cadet had to return by July twenty-eighth to check in, and courses began on August first, regardless of the day of the week it fell on.

She explained that some cadets didn't leave for the summer, and some arrived back much earlier. However, we shouldn't see them, as they were only allowed to use Dining Hall Two and stayed in their respective wings of the college. We were in the Bravo Wing, which contained the Instructors'

Chambers, where the instructors could choose to sleep if they wished. Their section of the college was warded and off-limits to all cadets. On the other side of Bravo Wing were the barracks for basic cadets, located on floors four through seven. The Historian's quarters occupied floors one and two, with the library extending four floors underground.

Professor Melamora's tone changed, and she said sternly, much louder, "no cadet except Historians are allowed below sublevel one without explicit permission from the Historian professor." Well, okay then.

She clarified that our location was between the instructor chambers and the barracks, in the largest classroom on campus. In Alpha Wing, three sections were dedicated to Drusearons, Healers, and Riders. Charlie Wing contained the other three branches: Shapeshifters, Sorcerers, and Infantry. Each wing used the third floor for classrooms, and cadet leadership occupied the first and second floors. Once we completed basic training and became first-year students, we would be on the seventh floor.

"Quit fucking talking!" One of the instructors yelled, startling the absolute shit out of me, making me jump so hard I almost lost my balance.

"Start running up and down the stairs, now!" I turned to see Instructor Ossent screaming at a group of cadets, who immediately stood and began running up and down the stairs beside their section.

Professor Melamora raised her voice louder. "The rest of you, pay no mind to them and direct your attention back here."

We all turned back toward her. She continued discussing some common laws and college etiquette. I tried hard to focus on her, although I already knew most of it—a perk of growing up in the military. Despite trying to focus—the cadets running up and down the stairs dragged my attention away.

"Turn the fuck around, Blackcreek, or you will be next," Pascal said. His voice dropped low, but had a tone that went straight to my soul. My heart stopped for two beats, making my stomach queasy for a moment.

"Yes, sir," I responded, snapping my attention back to the front.

Fuck, get it together.

Later that evening, after a day of having our brains overloaded with information, standing in endless formation, and eating food that was questionable. We wound down in our barracks. Some cadets were sleeping, while others found camaraderie in each other. I lay on my bed, trying to relax my body, willing my muscles to let go. The group of cadets near my bunks were chatting, every part of me said not to engage and get involved, but I couldn't tune them out either. The nosy part of me. The part of my brain running rampant.

"I bet most of us won't make it halfway." One cadet shot out.

"It sucks they have taken our magic away," one said.

"What magic?" one asked.

"Some of us have magic... your flummadiddle if you don't," another said.

Wow. Worthless if we don't have magic. Clearly, some of them think they are better than the other.

"My brother said week five will be the hardest," another added.

"Yeah, mine said that too. He said he couldn't tell me details, but that a bunch of us will die," one said.

"At least we've got each other," one cadet said. "Fucking is a great way to take the edge off."

My head snapped sideways before I caught myself. I should have kept staring at the slats above me, but the voice came from the bunk to my left, bottom row. The cadet wasn't bad-looking—brown hair, dark blue eyes—decent enough if you were into reckless mouths. He grinned at me when I looked.

"You look like you would be fun in bed," he said, nodding his head my way.

I shot my left eyebrow at him, cocked my head to the side. "In your fucking dreams..."

I turned my head back and continued staring at the slats. Closing my eyes, forcing myself to tune them out and get some sleep. We never knew when Pascal would barge through the doors, demanding something.

CHAPTER 3

The first week hadn't been as bad as I thought it would be. It felt like the days repeated—over and over. Most nights, we got woken up by a screaming instructor. Sometimes it lasted for ten minutes, and sometimes it lasted for hours.

We began each day with physical exercises, though I was sure some of my fellow cadets considered it torture. Having trained for years beforehand, I found it manageable. After that, the dining attendants served us breakfast. Afterwards, we went to the lecture hall to review more expectations during basic training, the history of the college, and Yebel. We took a break for lunch, and oftentimes we spent the afternoons standing in formation in the courtyard for several hours. Sometimes, the instructors allowed us to go back to our barracks.

Most of us chose to get some sleep in, to catch up on the hours missed through the evening. After dinner each night, we received a rucksack filled with seventy-five pounds of gods knows what, and we ran around the college perimeter with it on our backs.

They told us that week two would be different from the previous week, and hell would actually start. When I awoke that morning, I could feel my nerves rumbling, anticipating the worst. I remembered all the warnings my dad gave me, telling me how horrible it would be. Like clockwork, Instructor Pascal came in and called for us to count, and we counted off, all one hundred and ten of us intact.

We marched into the dining hall and split into lines. I grabbed my food fast, ate the same way, shoveling it down like I had all week. When the plate emptied, I pushed outside to stand with my platoon.

Minutes later, the yard brimmed with bodies, rows locked in formation. The air pressed heavy, thick enough to taste. My gut tightened, warning me of something I couldn't name—was it because I expected worse to come, or because it had already begun?

A low thrum rolled across the distance, faint but steady. Wingbeats. The sound bled into my bones, each pulse louder, closer, rattling the air like an oncoming storm. The sky above felt lower with every beat, shadows dragging longer across the yard. My chest clamped down. Not one—several. I forced my stance still, but tension rippled through the lines. Boots scuffed. A cough snapped sharp. Cadets shifted as if the ground itself waited to break beneath us.

"Stand at attention and maintain control of your fear!" Pascal shouted.

I hoped it was dragons, though the military called on more than dragons for war. To me, they meant home. I didn't fear them, not truly—but I never forgot how fast one could turn on someone they weren't bonded with.

The wingbeats drew closer, each stroke pounding the air until it pressed against my chest. They roared loud and furious... Gods. The ground shook beneath my boots, the tremor climbing through my bones, a sound so immense it swallowed breath and thought.

Chaos erupted. Cadets shrieked, bodies crashing into each other as they bolted for the walls. Stone scraped with the stampede of boots. The stench of sweat and fear thickened the air, sharp and suffocating. Lines shattered. Formation broke like glass.

Eight hundred and seventy-five of us had stood there moments ago. Now maybe two hundred held their ground, shoulders locked tight. My stomach lurched, my ears rang, my pulse screamed against my throat. Gods—

"Get back in formation cadets!" an instructor yelled.

"Don't show them fear," one yelled.

"Why are you here if you're going to be a pussy," another shouted.

"I said get back into formation!" the first instructor yelled again.

Cadets ran back to their places in formation just as one of the red dragons in the drift swooped down closer and blew out a huge puff of steam over us, before lifting its head back into the air, letting out a roar, and blowing out a large stream of fire. All the cadets who had been running back now hit the ground on their stomachs. More cadets screamed in pure fear. I could hear faint crying from some of the cadets still near the wall. The wingbeats started to fade away, and the instructors continued screaming at all the cadets who ran. Slowly, they all began to re-form.

I grew up around dragons, with a parent who rode one, but my stomach threatened to empty breakfast onto the floor. Red dragons were the most temperamental and unpredictable of all dragons. Though I knew they weren't supposed to judge or incinerate anyone in basic training, my brain was not rational about it.

After everyone got back into formation, we headed into the outdoor arena. I stared at the various obstacle courses set up that looked like we might die on—and I *thought* they weren't trying to kill us. We all stopped in front of four walls that stood about eight feet tall.

"You will go in squads of ten, you will be timed the first time as you learn what is expected. However, the time won't count today. After your squad is complete, you will wait on the other side for the other squads to complete theirs. It is advised that you help everyone. Your only goal is to reach the end as a team. First squad, go!" Pascal stated.

I stood fourteenth in formation, making me in the second squad. I looked ahead at the three people in front of me and six behind me. It looked almost evenly split—four females, including me, and six males. We looked like a fit squad of ten. Surely we could do it.

"And go!"

The ten of us rushed forward. One cadet who definitely stood over six feet jumped to the top and pulled himself up and over like he wasn't part of a team at all. Two other guys walked up the wall, stood on either side, and motioned at me and the other females.

The one on the left stated, "ladies first."

The four of us moved to the wall. The girl in front of me got to the wall, and they lowered their hands. She stepped on their palms, and they pushed her up. She grabbed the top as they continued pushing her, she finished pulling herself over—merely seconds later, we all heard a loud thump and "FUCK!"

"Are you alright?" I shouted over.

"Yep, merely a hard landing on my ankle," she said.

Next, it was my turn. I stepped onto their hands, and they lifted me as I pulled myself up. As I got to the top, I straddled it before swinging onto my stomach and lowering myself to the ground. I looked forward and didn't see the cadet who took off. Guess he wasn't a team player. The other cadets made their way over. We repeated that for the next three walls, moving faster and smoother.

As I got over the fourth wall, I looked forward to the next part of the course, and my mouth gaped open. Fuck. In front of me, there was a twenty-foot balance beam, no more than twelve inches wide, crossing over a muddy pit with strands of barbed wire stretched across it. On each side, instructors with hoses gleefully sprayed it down. Falling off this would surely cause some damage, or even death if you hit it wrong. As I stood there in shock, the rest of the cadets made their way over, most of them also staring at it.

One of the wall spotters volunteered to go first. We nodded—fine, he could be the test dummy. We watched close, ready to learn what not to do. He stepped out slow, balanced, moving like he'd done it a hundred times before.

"Damn it!" he yelled just as the instructors started to spray him with water on both sides. "Are they trying to kill us?"

"Take a breath, refocus, and tune them out," I yelled to him.

He edged forward, steady breaths pulling through his chest, until the instructors hit him with a spray of water. He kept going, slow but stubborn, and when he'd cleared a few feet, I called my turn.

I stepped onto the narrow beam, dropped low, and straddled it, inching forward on my hands and legs. The spray shifted to me, water pelting hard against my shoulders, soaking straight through. Ahead, the first cadet picked up his pace, forcing the instructors to blast him again. That gave me space to move quicker, sliding another few feet.

I glanced back and yelled for the next cadet. One after another, we pushed forward, the instructors alternating streams, trying to knock us off balance. Water hammered us and the beam shook under our weight, but we adjusted, each of us pushing faster whenever the spray shifted away.

At last, I dropped off the end, boots hitting solid ground. A shout ripped out of me, a wild whoop that carried all the way back across the line.

"I'm Callum, what's your name? Figured we have been leading this squad, should know it?"

"Auriella, nice to put a name to a face."

The rest of our squad made it across. Another wooden wall was set up for us to climb, identical to the first set of walls. Callum and the other guy staged at the sides of the wall. This time, I went first, doing it entirely as I had before. I reached the bottom, pivoted to look at the next obstacle, and stopped in my tracks. My stomach lurched, and I felt my heart stutter. Being raised around fliers didn't mean coming across one unexpectedly wasn't alarming. I knew how fickle they could be.

"Hey guys, when you come across, do it nice and easy, there are two small-sized dragons... and they aren't happy."

"What"

"Uhhh"

"Fuuuuuuck!" The word tore out, tangled with gasps, voices blurring so I couldn't tell who shouted from where I stood.

I briefly closed my eyes, took a few deep, steady breaths, then reopened them to evaluate the scene. We faced a mud pit identical to the one we had crossed earlier, but this one was deeper—oh fuck. I understood why the dragons were so enraged. The eager ass who had started running, laid in the middle of the mud pit, his back pant leg caught on jagged, charred barbed wire. The cadet was visibly trembling, and I suspected he had vomited, based on the food clumps scattered nearby.

"Did you learn your lesson?" I asked.

"No. Yes. Um, um, um. Can you help me?"

"Maybe. Stay still, ground yourself, and don't look them in the eyes."

Two smaller dragons stood on each side of the pit—one silver, the other grey. I had never seen dragons this small before, standing only about ten feet tall, nor had I seen a silver dragon. They exhaled steam and occasionally spat streams of fire across the pit, so I kept my distance to avoid provoking them. I kept my eyes lowered, avoiding their gaze. The rest of the squad smoothly climbed over the wall, appearing relaxed and at ease.

"What are we going to do?" Callum asked, looking around the squad.

"I believe we are supposed to crawl through the mud pit, stay under the wire, or we become dragon lunch..."

"You...you... you think they will eat us?" the timid, shy girl stammered.

"I can't say they won't, dragons do what they want, although dragons don't typically pass judgment during the basic portion. Like this morning, it's to toy with us, work our nerves."

Callum turned around, looking at the cadet stuck. "What's your name?"

"Beau."

"Alright, I am going to go first and untangle Beau's pant leg, and then once we start moving, two people can crawl in and start across. Don't lift anything above the barbed wire, or they will burn you."

Callum got on the ground and started crawling through the mud toward Beau. He reached out to him and pulled his leg free. "You're free, maybe you will stick with the team for the rest of the course."

Beau and Callum continued through the mud. Another cadet and I climbed into the pit and started, and just as we got fully in, I heard a loud grumble and felt blazing hot heat go over my body. My entire body froze, and I realized I held my breath. When the fire ceased, I turned my head to see if the other cadet remained in the pit with me. I drew a breath and decided to get the hell out. I crawled as fast as I could. Cadets sounded behind me, and I closed in on Callum.

We crawled out of the pit on the far side. The silver dragon turned its head, eyes narrowing, and exhaled a heavy blast of sulfur straight at me.

The stench scorched my throat, the heat blowing my hair back in a rush. My skin prickled under its stare. It wasn't random—it was measured, deliberate, like it wanted to see if I'd flinch. A test.

The rest of our squad climbed out of the mud pit. Another wall stood ahead, about eight feet tall. We crossed as before, except the cocky cadet stayed with us this time. I climbed over and exhaled in relief. No living surprises waited on this side of the wall. Instead, a twenty-foot wall rose with boards for climbing up, and on the other side stood another wall with three ropes for climbing down.

One by one, our team made it over the wall. By this point, we were cheering each other on to keep going. The following section involved logs placed in a muddy area, just like the others. An instructor watched as we did it. A few of the guys started running and jumping over the logs smoothly and in coordination. The four of us girls finished it, though not quite as fast as the guys.

My legs were aching, my arms throbbing, every single joint screaming, my stomach roaring, and my throat parched. I silently prayed to anyone who would listen that we were near the end. I thought lunch might be over at this point. We came to another wall to climb over. This time, I let the shyer, calmer cadet, Ophelia, climb over first.

"Ahhhhhh!" She screamed, startling me, startling all of us.

"What's going on?" Callum called over, now motioning for Beau to go next.

"I... ummm... I... I... I..." she stuttered out.

"Oh Shit," Beau let out as he made it over the wall.

"Well, don't leave us hanging over here?" I called over, preparing to go next.

"Griffins," he shot out.

"Shit," we all said at once. I knew three types of creatures served in the Rider's branch. Dragons were most prominent, but griffins and firebirds also flew among them, though I knew far less about those. Griffins carried the head of an eagle, the body of a lion, and wings that spread wide. Most stood seven to nine feet tall at the hindquarters. Unlike dragons and firebirds, they didn't breathe fire, which gave me some comfort. They could, however, manipulate the weather, as well as being extremely fast and having a beak that would snap your head off.

We all made it over the wall and took a look around. Four griffins stood there, two on each side, all four of them making chuffing sounds at us. Between them was another extra-large, muddy pit with two ropes spread out about five feet apart, spanning the pit. I wasn't familiar with this either. Shit.

Callum confidently led our squad, immediately stepping onto the rope with purpose. He leaned forward, gripping one side firmly while balancing on his ankles on the other, inching steadily forward. The air grew frigid as sleet began to cascade down, intensifying the challenge.

I studied each griffin carefully, while I waited. One was solid black, while the other had black feathers faded into shimmering gold. The third was light brown, and the last was a deep, dark blue. Interesting. I had only seen shades of black, brown, and golden griffins before, but I hadn't spent much time around them, following my dad from fort to outpost. This was going to suck, but I had no choice but to keep going.

I climbed up and imitated Callum, my bones aching as if they might crack from shivering. My hands felt raw from all the wall and rope climbing. I sensed my body stretched to its limit, balancing between two ropes as I shimmied across, gripping as tightly as I could. I reached the midway point, took deep breaths, and tried to stay grounded.

Moving one arm over, then the other, I shifted my ankles over, falling into a rhythm. But when I tried to move my left arm again, it slipped. My right arm slipped, too. I tumbled into the cold, icy mud below. It hit like solid ground, and damn, that hurt.

"Damn it!" I screamed out.

"What did you tell me earlier? Take a breath and refocus."

I inhaled deeply, climbing out of the mud on the other side to start over. Instantly, the sleet turned to rain, and the sun rose.

BOOM!

Lightning and rain with the sun. Nice touch there, griffins.

I climbed back onto the ropes and made another attempt. My arms and ankles were screaming from rubbing on the ropes. *I would do this. I was doing this. I had this.* I repeated these three lines to myself over and over as I kept going. I crossed over and stood with Callum as we waited for the rest of our squad.

"So what branch are you planning to join?" I asked him.

He let out a little sigh and low laugh all at once, which made me raise one of my eyebrows at him.

"Are you going to keep it a secret?"

He sighed again. "It's just that the day you walked into our platoon, you saw some of the Drusearons and your eyes nearly bugged out of your head—"

I cut him off, "are you Drusearon?"

"No... I am a Shapeshifter," he said with his voice low.

I stepped back and observed Callum. He was handsome, standing at six feet two with golden-brown skin and jet-black hair tousled from the challenges. A deep scar ran across his right cheek, matching his stubble. His eyes shined vibrant green streaked with light brown, contrasting against his dark hair.

"Oh, okay, no problems there."

"Wait, so you're telling me that a Drusearon gives you worry, but someone that can transform into a wolf doesn't startle you?"

"Well, when you put it that way..." I let out a sigh. "Can you transform now? Orrrrr?"

"Wouldn't you like to know," he countered.

The last of our squad made it over the ropes. We made our way to the next wall.

"Please don't be a firebird, please don't be a firebird, please don't be a firebird," I chanted to myself quietly.

I decided not to be the first one across the wooden wall this time, because I didn't want to see any more surprises. Beau decided to go first this time, and within a couple of minutes, he yelled over, "we're done!"

I went over the wall, and about twenty feet forward, a female Historian sat at a table, writing down our time and completion as a squad of ten. She motioned us forward to the large squad across the field.

After all the squads in our platoon finished, Pascal stood in front of us and told us that our squad was the only squad that finished as a group, but we were the slowest. For the next four days, we would be running this obstacle course in the same squads. With eleven squads, the slowest eight to finish as a group would be rucking up Watch Tower Two, down the hall, and back down Watch Tower Three.

I looked towards our squad in a *"we have to get faster"* look. Callum nodded at me, like he knew what I was saying. He dismissed us for dinner—wait, what the fuck? We skipped right over lunch. Did this mean we would skip lunch the whole week? Damn, that fucking sucks.

***

The next day, our squad placed fifth, and we rucked up all those stairs. The griffin obstacle decided it. I fell three times, and Ophelia fell four. She stood an inch shorter than me, and I struggled because I was short. We rucked the ten flights of stairs in the towers with fifty-pound packs on our backs, and it left my body raw. When they dismissed us for the night, I climbed into my bunk, and the moment my eyes closed, I drifted into sleep.

The only positive aspect of running these courses was that the instructors did not wake us in the middle of the night. Our third run went more smoothly, and we made progress. The other squads also improved. We secured third place this time, which spared us from rucking that day, thank the gods. We missed second place by twenty seconds. First place came with an unexpected perk—the instructors dismissed them right after dinner without requiring them to form up. This meant longer, more refreshing showers and rare moments of peace in the barracks, where only ten cadets occupied the space instead of one hundred and ten.

The next day arrived. As our squad prepared to begin, we gathered in a huddle. We exchanged glances that conveyed—*We would succeed*. One rule was that we had to finish the entire course together, but we agreed that three of the guys would go first, followed by all four of us girls. After we crossed, we'd start tackling the obstacles. Once everyone got past the griffins, we would wait until most of us were across so we could cross the wall together.

We all stood in formation waiting for them to announce the winner.

"In the first place, securing their spot by five seconds... Second squad!"

"Yessss!!!" Our squad shouted together.

"Let's fucking go," Callum shouted.

Pascal's face turned solemn, and he looked towards our very cheering squad. "Get back in formation, before you lose your prize."

We snapped back to attention, faces locked, before he even finished the order.

"Second squad, dismissed. Eat first, skip formation. Everyone else—chow, then back here."

We funneled through the dinner line fast. I dropped onto a bench and shoveled food into my mouth like someone might yank it away.

"Think they'll steal your tray?" Callum asked, one brow arched, a crooked grin tugging at his mouth.

"No. I just want that shower and the silence that comes with it."

"Want company?" He leaned in as he said it, elbow nudging my side before a laugh broke out of him.

Whatever showed in my eyes made him stumble into an apology. Years earlier, I would have taken it without pause, no thought of what it meant. I had buried emotions under reckless intimacy, chasing escape until the tangle turned into attachment. Now anxiety prowled close, a tightening in my chest and a restless churn in my gut. I shoved it down, sealed it tight, locked the box before it could spill over and drown me.

I took my food tray back to the front and headed back to our barracks. I grabbed my shower bag and went into the shower, and took the most relaxing, peaceful shower I had taken in weeks. I made it back to the barracks, and it was still only our squad in there. They were all sitting around in a group on the bunks, chatting.

***

The next day, our squad prepared for the final day of the course.. We repeated the previous day's routine, but this time it felt like we moved faster, and none of us fell off the obstacle courses. We completed the usual drills and stood in formation.

My heart jolted, as if it skipped a beat. I took a deep breath, unaware I had been holding it. My eyes fixed on a five-foot-ten, tanned guy leaning against the wall with one leg bent. Blonde, short golden waves, and his pale blue eyes felt like windows into his soul. His gaze met mine, and I couldn't look away. Electricity surged through my body. Fuck. He was beautiful.

My heart felt as though it would beat out of my chest. My eyes dropped from his eyes, down to his lips... Good gods, his complete, gorgeous lips had this ornery smile across them. My stomach knotted, and I felt tingling in all—

"Second squad is our winner for the day, but Fifth Squad is our overall winner for the week, having the highest average time. Although had second squad not placed fifth the first time, they would have won by a landslide. Both squads will be granted a weekend of rest. I am proud of you, cadets, for working together..."

He kept talking, but the words slid past me. My pulse pounded too loud, my palms slick, my breaths coming sharp and shallow. Gods, who was this man?

At last, he broke our stare, and the spell snapped. I blinked hard, only then realizing how long I'd been caught in him. Minutes gone, stolen without me noticing. He turned and strode out of the courtyard toward the outdoor arena, and I stood frozen, breathless, like he'd taken the air with him.

"Earth to Auriella... Hello?" Callum caught my attention. I clearly had been in a daze and totally missed him releasing us.

"Uh, yeah?"

"You were in left field, you good there?"

"Yep, peachy keen."

"Well, let's get to dinner and enjoy the quiet time."

CHAPTER 4

ZANE

She was exactly as my aunt had drawn her—absolutely perfect. She stood there, staring at me, her hair a captivating blend of blonde and light brown, braided into two strands that fell down her back, stopping right above the small of her back. Her long hair, when loose, probably reached beyond her butt. Tiny points at the tips of her ears hinted at her Fae heritage, though they weren't as sharply pointed as some others. Her vibrant, emerald-green eyes sparkled with life and curiosity. Her skin appeared fairer than mine, dotted with the perfect number of freckles on her face and arms. Her dark brown eyelashes were full, long, and striking. She looked just as I remembered from six years ago, only slightly taller.

Thank gods for my sharp Fae sight and keen hearing. I absorbed every single detail, as I had six years earlier. My Fae senses caught more than they should sometimes, taking more than it should sometimes.

My aunt and uncle met when they were twenty-five, and their love was both magical and lasting. They shared a connection that no one else understood. Sometimes I would visit their home and stay with them, and she would tell me that someday I would find my Anam Cara. She had drawn her for me once. My aunt was special, with a gift of precognition, but it only worked on our family line, and it came and went. Her gift wasn't strong enough to be used for anything significant, but to me, she was extraordinary.

She was killed during an attack when I was thirteen. She had been like a mother to me, and I felt like a part of me broke that day. She and my uncle had tried to have children for years, but they never succeeded.

Fae children were special, and occasionally, families had only one child. My parents had seven children, which I believed must involve some kind of magic. Still, I thought they would have shared that magic with my Aunt Nemina—she truly deserved at least one child. She would have made a fantastic mother.

She left behind a journal I received after her passing, which described my Anam Cara and included her drawings. She told me that when I found her, I would feel an electric shock in my body. She urged me not to run from it but to accept it. I should treat her with respect, avoid being cruel, and love her unconditionally.

"She won't be who you think she should be. You won't find her in our villages. Love her anyway, let your dam break, and let her in. My dearest boy, she will be the greatest gift you will receive in life. Treat it as such. My vision shows that the two of you will be one of the most powerful couples to exist in the last century. You can't fuck this up. Our world needs you two."

She thought her ability was weak, and Gods, I envied her. The moment my ability manifested, I knew her simple ability was better than what I manifested. Every day I mourn her, wishing she could be here to guide me through all of this. Guide me with my ability. Guide me with my Anam Cara. Part of me broke the day I lost her. She told me to love her unconditionally, but it didn't tell me how to handle any of this. Would she predict all of this?

CHAPTER 5

I showered fast that night—twenty of us had beaten the rest back to the barracks. Inside, the room pressed tight, cadets huddled shoulder to shoulder. A few slipped out, probably chasing the same water. I claimed a seat, the chatter swelling like we were all supposed to start bonding. Fantastic. I had no plans to get close. Basic ended with graduation, and after that we'd scatter into different branches. Why bother tying myself down?

"Going around clockwise, what's everyone's name and intended branch? I am Callum and... a Shapeshifter."

"Beau, Infantry." I chuckled, figures.

"Vivian, Sorcerer." Fifth squad.

"William, shape shifter." Fifth squad.

"Blaze." He motioned his head to his back, where his wings popped out. "Drusearon." Fifth squad.

"Ophelia, Healer." Second squad.

"Asher, Infantry." Second squad.

"Auriella, Rider," I said.

"Selene, Historian." Second squad.

"Finn, Healer." Fifth squad.

"Thora, Rider." Fifth Squad. I looked at her, locking eyes with her, and we smiled at each other.

They continued around the room, I heard a few more Infantry, another Drusearon and a couple of the others. Thora and I remained the only Riders in this small group. I often drifted into my thoughts, lost in memories. I recalled the earlier encounter when I saw that intense, attractive male, who left me eager to see him again. Who was he? He wore plain black attire with no visible rank insignia, suggesting he might be a cadet, possibly one of the few who didn't leave for the summer.

Wearing all black didn't give me any solid clues, as Riders, Shapeshifters, and Drusearons all wore black. Professors wore khaki pants with their branch color as their top, Infantry wore navy blue, Healers wore baby blue, Historians wore sage green, and Sorcerers wore dark purple. The real question was, why did he cause such a physical response when our eyes locked?

Ow.

I felt an elbow nudge my side by Selene, bringing me back to the conversation.

"Sorry, what?" I asked. Callum chuckled as he looked at me.

"I was asking what type of Rider you and Thora are planning to be. Thora said a griffin."

"Oh, yes, um, a dragon. I hope to be a fourth-generation dragon Rider."

"That makes sense, as you were unfazed by the dragons when they flew overhead and during the courses."

"I mean, I wouldn't say unfazed, I was nervous. It is important to show confidence and respect them. They can be beautiful, but also ruthless."

"Good to know." He looked at William and began asking questions about where he lived and which bloodline he belonged to.

The last five days had beaten us raw. Relief came with the promise of a few days off—no drills, no runs, only rest. I slipped away to my bunk, pulled the blanket over my head, and let the weight of it press me down until sleep dragged me under.

****

He stood over me, and I gasped hard. He was here. No, he couldn't be. This was impossible. Run. Roll and run. I rolled off my bed and ran out of the barracks and down the hall. I could hear him coming for me, his wings moving alongside him. This couldn't be happening again. He caught up to me so fast.

"Come on, Auri, I only want to have some fun. You can't run from me…"

He had me pushed against the wall, my heart beat out of my chest, and my breath ragged.

"Please, no. Please don't touch me. Please. Please."

I pleaded with every part of my life. This couldn't be real. He was dead. I killed him. *You're dreaming, Auriella*, I told myself.

Wake up.

Wake up.

Wake up.

"Wake upppppp!" My eyes flashed open, and I gasped in a hard breath as I saw Ophelia next to me.

"It's merely a nightmare," she said.

My chest pounded so hard, I felt like my heart might burst out. I felt like I was struggling to catch my breath. She placed her hand on mine and reminded me to breathe in and out. I did precisely that. I took five deep breaths and realized I was beginning to calm myself. It was a dream, one of many I had over the years. I was safe. I was okay. I was alive. He couldn't touch me again. She gently removed her hand from mine and gave me a soft smile.

"I am sorry if I startled you," I said.

"It's okay, I heard something and looked over and saw you thrashing and breathing fast."

"Do you know what time it is?"

"I think the grandfather clock reads four fifty."

"Thank you."

It wouldn't be long before the platoon would be rising for morning formation and breakfast time, except for the two winning squads. Although it was clear that if we didn't make breakfast within the time the dining facility was open, we would indeed not be eating until lunch. I slipped off my bunk, slid on my uniform, and decided to take a tour in the quiet hours. I also wanted to learn my exits and places to hide.

I left our barracks room, which was on the seventh floor. Turning left down the hallway led to the stadium classroom and the instructor's chambers. Turning right would take me to Watchtower Two and the stairway. I chose to go right. I went up the stairs. Although the building only had seven stories, the watchtower extended two more stories higher.

The four sturdy watchtowers at the corners of the cadet housing and classrooms were staffed by cadets on rotation. During summer, students who chose to remain on base stayed as long as they took turns on watch. As I reached the top of the stairs, I saw two cadets standing and chatting, overlooking the sprawling campus and the lush valleys.

I made a slight coughing sound to announce my attention. "Hi," I said.

"Hello... are you lost?" the taller one in navy blue said.

"No, I haven't been here before and wanted to enjoy the view."

"Oh... Um... Okay." He gestured to the wall.

I stepped forward and placed my forearms on the sturdy wall, gazing out over the expansive campus. The view was breathtaking at this moment. I admired the deep indigo sky, fading into the vibrant hues of sunrise. Golden and pink streaks pushed through the horizon, helping me refocus, as they had done over the past several years.

I heard faint wingbeats, a sound I often listened for, and turned my head to see a delicate silhouette of a dragon and its Rider soaring high above. They appeared to be on patrol. I watched in awe. Their majestic figures moved gracefully through the sky. They performed a daring barrel roll, seeming to enjoy themselves during their duty. I let out a soft giggle, then remembered I was not alone in the tower. I looked over at them and smiled.

"Thank you for letting me have a view, I needed that fresh air."

They both nodded, and I made my way down the tower. I heard the bell tower signal that it was now zero-five hundred, and I knew the halls on the seventh floor would soon be filled with cadets heading to formation and the dining hall. I headed straight down the stairs to the third floor. Among all the wings, the third floor had a connecting hallway.

The third floor of the Alpha and Charlie Wings housed classrooms, whereas the Bravo Wing was dominated by two large gyms primarily used for sparring. Although we hadn't begun sparring yet, I was aware it was upcoming during basic training and would be a significant part of the Rider's branch training. I was also curious to see the overall gym and sparring mats. I pushed the door open, stepped inside, and froze in surprise. Shit.

There was the guy from the courtyard yesterday. Fuck. I expected to be alone in the gym, coming at this hour while most others were lining up. I noticed I hadn't shifted since walking in, my eyes fixed on him. He cleared his throat, which made me lower my gaze from the floor.

"Um, I'm... I'm... sorry. I didn't think anyone would be here." Shit. I was stuttering. This was great. Fan-fucking-tastic.

"No need to apologize, I am only trying to get some weight training done." Gods, his voice was deep and had that perfect amount of roughness to it.

"That was my plan. I think we will start sparring next week."

"Yeah, that usually happens during weeks three and four. Although if you want to spar, I am a good sparring partner."

"Um, what are the rules around here? I don't want to die during basic, that would be humiliating." I let out a soft laugh, but the reality was that sparring caused some of the highest numbers of injuries within first and second-years.

"No kill blows, period. I also don't want to die. No weapons, no intentional bone breaking. First to tap."

"Sounds easy enough."

"I am Zane, by the way."

"Auriella."

We both stepped onto the mat nearest the gym equipment. I offered my hand out to shake, and he shook it. I bounced on my heels a couple of times, feeling the mat becoming one with it. This was simply like every other sparring I had done. I threw out a right punch. He backed up just enough to miss it and moved to throw a half-right back towards me. I bounced a little closer, watching his shoulders, waiting for a strike. I took a step forward at the same time I threw a right hook, which he moved his shoulder back just in time, which was exactly what I wanted. I immediately threw a left punch and connected with his chest.

His face gave him away—he hadn't expected me to swing. He countered fast, driving a right into my left side. Pain flared, but I sucked in a breath and fired back. Two rights, then a left. The second right barely grazed him. He was quick, already picking apart my combos.

He struck again, fist slamming into my solar plexus. Air tore from my lungs. My body folded forward, chest burning, desperate for breath that wouldn't come.

I knew I needed to take a breath and straighten the hell up fast. The moment I stood straight up, I felt his legs curl around my ankles, and down we went, him pinning me under him. Shit. Shit. Shit. I didn't want to be in this position, not after we basically eye-fucked in the courtyard yesterday. Why did I even agree to spar?

"Now what are you going to do?" he grumbled at me.

"I'm going to work on the problem... in my head." I lifted my shoulders off the mat by pushing my head backwards, I worked my right arm in between us and did a hard hip thrust and rolled myself onto my stomach. I tucked my chin into my chest and rolled out and jumped to my feet.

"Like that..." I countered him.

"Nice." He was already on his feet, moving side to side.

I threw a series of precise body shots, landing a few accurately. He countered with a few punches of his own, but I let one strike my shoulder and moved closer to him. I swept my leg, aiming at his feet. He staggered, and I pushed him, causing us to tumble to the ground with me straddling him.

"Now, what are you going to do?" Like, I didn't realize he was much stronger, holding back on me, and could flip me with ease.

He let out a low growl. "I am going to let you soak in this moment, and I am going to enjoy the view."

My eyebrows shot up high. He caught me off guard with that. I shifted my gaze from his chest to his eyes, something I had been avoiding. Our eyes locked once again, and my entire body tensed with a tingling sensation I couldn't explain, something I had never felt before. What about him made my body react this way?

"Your eyes are stunning," he muttered.

"Thank you." I shot to my feet before I did something I'd regret. I had promised myself—no random hookups, not here, not at the school where I'd spend the next four years. But gods, he was handsome. His eyes caught the light, pulling me in like a bee to a flower. I told myself to run, but my legs wouldn't move.

He rose, and I struck first. A right, a left, another right, another right, and a left that cracked hard against his cheek. Dammit—I hadn't meant to hit that hard. His eyes flared with fury.

I dropped low, grabbed his leg, braced for the next move. He hooked his arm under mine and yanked me sideways, wrenching me off balance and slamming me onto my back. His weight crushed my collarbone, pinning me. I jammed my forearms and elbows up into his ribs, sharp and fast. He grunted, shifted his grip, and rolled us over. Suddenly I was face-down, his chest pressed to my back, his weight driving me into the floor.

This was a fucked position. I tucked my chin tight, fighting to keep him from locking my head. His breath skimmed my skin, his lips brushing the back of my neck. Heat shot through me, sharp and wrong and wanted all at once.

Trouble—more than sparring trouble. If he pushed, if he took me here on the mat, I knew part of me would yield. My body betrayed me, aching for it even as my mind screamed no. I couldn't give in, not here, not like this. I thrashed, elbows snapping back, but the strikes hit weak, barely a distraction. The fight tangled with the pull inside me, every move caught between the need to resist and the dangerous want rising under my skin.

"You know I have you, right?" He growled in my ear.

"Ha. I am fighting until the very end." I snapped back. He didn't know how bothered I was at the moment. And I was hot and bothered in all the right places.

He brushed my hair aside and leaned in close to my ear. "Does my presence bother you as much as yours bothers me?" He gently pushed himself up, as if admiring me. I heard him take a deep breath, as if he were startled.

"What?" I didn't know if that was in response to his slight gasp or to the question.

"That is an interesting mark…"

"Oh, it is a birthmark, my dad has one too." My father had a similar one—a delicate crescent of five tiny dots positioned behind our right ears.

"I… um… got to go." Before I could even respond, he was on his feet and shuffling out the door.

What the hell was that about? Maybe he realized we were starting to cross a line and hesitated to go further. I was glad he pulled away. My self-control often flailed, making my reactions unpredictable. I stood upright, wiped the sweat off my forehead, grabbed my sparse belongings, and headed for the busy dining hall to get breakfast. My stomach ached with hunger, as if it agreed with my decision.

CHAPTER 6

The rest of the weekend was boring and restful. Most of us in the second and fifth squads wandered the halls and outside grounds. Taking everything in. Monday arrived too fast, and we resumed our formations and physical fitness training. We spent the majority of weeks three and four in the sparring gym, sparring with each other.

We also received basic medical training. While we had potential Healers among us, they communicated with the rest of us to stabilize the person. During one match, two male cadets were competing against each other when the larger one executed a gnarly armbar that I had never seen before.

I was standing at the edge of the mat when the snap cracked through the room. A scream ripped after it. The cadet with the armbar let go at once, dropping to his knees with apologies. We steadied the injured arm, hauled him up, and they rushed him to the infirmary.

Later, another cadet locked a leg, and the pop of a knee blowing out made my stomach turn. The joint bent wrong, clear out of place.

Over the next two weeks, I sparred seven times. I won four, lost three. The victories felt sharp, a rush in my chest, proof I belonged here. The losses stung deeper. Each tap burned with the reminder that no matter how much I trained, someone could still choke me out or twist me apart. I always chased the throat, because oxygen ended fights. Still, every time I wound up on my back, chin jammed tight to my chest, I knew how close I stood to the edge. Winning fed my pride. Losing kept the fear alive.

Week five arrived, and everything began to fall into place. I wasn't sure if I had been assigned to a platoon with a more lenient drill instructor or what, but Pascal didn't yell at us nearly as much as some of the other instructors.

I wasn't complaining. He still shed tears and tossed our bunks, but over the last few weeks, his behavior had become much calmer. Our small second squad stayed close, sticking together during the various demanding drills we completed.

Week five, according to my dad, was expected to be another brutal and exhausting week. So far, it hadn't been as challenging as he had warned, but his motto remained, *'Prepare for the worst, and when it isn't so bad, you'll feel victorious.'*

We stood in formation, prepared for our tasks that day. Pascal was in front of our platoon, which now had ninety-eight members.

"Welcome to the Pass of Bête Noire, you have fifteen minutes to pack your rucks, preparing to be in the field for the next four days," he yelled across our platoon.

Four fucking days. What were we about to endure? We all rushed to our barracks and started packing. The room was chaotic, filled with various conversations and questions.

"What do we need to pack?"

"What are we going to be eating for four days?"

"This sounds like it will be a miserable time."

I could hear the worry of some of the cadets, and frankly, I was a little worried too. They all rushed back down to the courtyard and formed up again.

Pascal looked us all over, gave us a worrisome smile, and afterwards he turned and shouted, "Forward March".

We followed synchronously behind, five cadets in a row. We made it through the courtyard and the outdoor stadium and outside the college walls.

"Right turn," he shouted. The first row turned and moved forward. The second row marched forward, then turned right and moved forward. I wondered what the view would have been like from the sky. Formations had a unique beauty of formality to them.

"Right turn!" he shouted again as we headed toward the rugged mountains behind the Bravo Wing. The mountain pass was breathtaking, equally mesmerizing both during the day and when illuminated by moonlight. As I looked out early that morning, I could see the narrow pathway carved into the steep mountain that zigzagged upward. It dawned on me that we would attempt to climb this challenging slope.

"Halt, fall in," Pascal shouted.

"Over the next four days, you will be marching up this mountain. It will take nearly two days to reach the top and two days to return. There are traps along the mountain. You will need to watch your steps and work as a unit. You will be released with your squads staggered based on your obstacle ranking. There are twelve caves spread out around the midway region. They are first-come, first-served. You can choose to take the first one you came across or the seventh. Choose wisely how long you rest. You can pass other squads on the mountain. While this is a competition, do not intentionally cause harm to any other member. However, not all of you will return alive. Watch your steps. You are due back down here by twenty-two hundred, Thursday evening. Fifth squad, you're up first. The rest of you, rest."

Everyone broke into their groups and started chatting amongst themselves. We ranked second, which means we would start next.

"Hey, squad two, we want to keep a nice pace. If we go too fast, we will burn out. We also don't want to go too slow and risk falling too far behind. Let's aim for cave eleven or twelve, depending upon which one fifth squad takes. This will put us further up the trail to start after resting. I'll take the lead. Beau will take up the rear. We stick together." Callum told us.

"Second squad, you're up."

"Let's go," Callum marched forward, and we all followed, forming a single line.

We started about fifteen minutes after the fifth squad, but we were unsure of the timing for the other groups. We continued to march forward and appeared to be making good progress.

When someone from the eighth squad shouted, "excuse us," behind us, we all turned our backs to the mountain to let them pass, sticking to our plan to avoid overexertion. Moments later, a loud BOOM rang out, followed by frantic screaming.

We increased our pace a little to figure out what happened. As we got closer, the screaming grew louder, followed by shouting. That was when we saw one of the cadets from the eighth squad on the ground with both of his lower legs blown off. He looked unconscious, probably not surviving. I heard soft wing beats approaching. I wasn't sure where they were coming from.

Within seconds, Pascal landed on the edge. He tucked his wings in so fast that I barely had time to realize he had wings. Holy shit! They disappeared.

My mind raced in every direction. Within seconds, he grabbed the injured cadet up and took off into the sky. I knew Drusearons had magical abilities, but I didn't realize they could go without displaying their wings.

"Let's keep going, second squad. I am watching out for land mines. I am sure there will be more," Callum shouted back at us. We continued, passing by a shocked eighth squad.

"Also watch for the traps that send arrows shooting out of the cliff," Beau called up.

"How do you know that one?" I asked.

"My brother went through a couple of years ago," he said.

"Yeah, my dad totally left out this entire mountain quest, while he was trying to scare me not to join."

"Land mine," he yelled. "Wide step over it, and you'll be fine."

We all moved forward cautiously. I stepped over it, as wide as my legs would go, and marched ahead.

BOOM.

I closed my eyes. It wasn't loud enough to be the one I just crossed, but I turned around and looked anyway. I think the sound came from above us—fuck—fifth squad. Callum and I shared a look, which told me he thought the same thing. Overall, our two squads were the closest.

"Fifth squad, are you guys okay?" Callum shouted as loud as he could, with his head tilted up."

"We're intact. Finn has a nasty gash. We're okay." William shouted back.

Whew. A gash was an improvement over what we saw earlier. We kept moving forward, avoiding numerous land mines along the way. We also passed by a few wall traps, which required us to drop to the ground and crawl underneath.

Night began to fall, and we still hadn't reached the caves. We heard so many land mines explode and arrows whizzing through the air. The screams around us made me wonder how many more cadets had been lost on the first day. The sky was filling with stars, and a nearly full moon lit our path. We reached a section so narrow that we had to move sideways. I prayed Callum would spot any traps, especially with the low visibility, and hoped they wouldn't be cruel enough to set traps in such a thin passage.

"Ahhhhhh." I heard right beside me, from Nadine.

I turned my head her way, and she was hanging off the side of the mountain.

"Fuck" I yelled. There wasn't enough space or room to move down and assist her. I crouched down the best I could, with my back pressed against the wall. Asher was on the other side of her. He crouched down as well.

"Nadine, you're going to have to pull yourself up," I said.

"I can't. My... My... Hands are slipping."

"Auriella, if we both grab her hand, do you think you can pull her up?" He looked over at me.

"I can try." I reached out and grabbed her wrist, and he did the same on his side. Her hands were so sweaty, it felt like gripping baby oil. Fuck, I wasn't sure we could do this. We had to. We couldn't lose someone.

"Nadine, you're going to have to work with us here," I said.

"I can't... I can't." She whimpered.

"Yes, you fucking can!" He snapped back.

"You can do this. We can do this," I told her.

But I knew her grip was slipping from my hand. I tried to pull her up, but it felt as if she hung there, as if she had given up.

"I am losing her." I glanced at Asher. His eyes filled with sorrow, as if he felt he was losing her too. We couldn't lean forward much on the narrow path without risking a fall. Finger by finger, she slipped from my grasp.

Within seconds, she fell and disappeared from sight. Her scream echoed loudly enough to make my ears vibrate.

"Damn it," Callum roared at the front of the line.

Tears sorrowfully fell down my cheeks. We weren't close, but she was a part of our squad, and it was my hand that dropped her.

"We have to keep moving, yes that fucking sucked, but we can't stop."

We continued marching forward. I pressed my back and the heels of my feet as close to the wall as they could get. We continued moving through this pass. The pass widened up where we could walk regularly, thank the gods for that. We came upon the first cave, thank the gods for that too.

We stuck with our original plan and traveled to the last of the caves, continuing along the narrow, winding pathway. As we passed by the sixth cave, we saw the fifth squad busy preparing their mats for sleep. We nodded to them and moved towards the twelfth cave. We wouldn't know our place in line tomorrow because squads could leave at any time. Inside our cave, we found a large wooden crate and an open space illuminated by several flickering candles mounted to the wall.

On the large crate, there was a lock with a three-dial combination. Next to it was a rolled-up paper with a ribbon beside it. Selene moved over and opened it.

"I am a three-digit number, my hundreds digit is eight less than my tens digit, my tens digit is five more than my one's digit. Figure me out and food awaits." She read to us.

"It is entirely too late to be doing riddles..." I said.

"Zero-eight-three or one-ninety-four," Ophelia said quietly. She had barely spoken since Nadine fell.

"Not zero-eight-three." Callum continued to turn the dials on the lock, twisting the last dial in and then a click. He opened the crate. "One-ninety-four, beautiful job Ophelia."

He threw a sack to each of us, leaving one remaining sack. The one for Nadine. We all looked at it with sadness, knowing she probably wasn't alive anymore. We all sat down and quietly ate. In our sack, there was a peanut butter sandwich, an apple, an orange, a granola bar, some plain crackers, and a can of juice.

"Hey squad, I don't know about everyone else, but I am going to save my apple and crackers for tomorrow. Who knows what meals we will get tomorrow?" I said.

"Do you actually think they won't feed us in the morning?" Ophelia looked at me with concern.

"I am not sure, given that our departure time from the cave is our choice, I am guessing probably not," I said.

"I was going to suggest the same, actually. My brother warned me that I should ration out my food," Beau added.

"This is really going to suck. We have to remember by the end. We can't get snappy on each other. We will be tired, sore, and hungry by the end of this," Asher stated.

"We are a strong team, we proved, we can work well with each other during the courses. We have to stick together," Callum said, like the leader he'd been. "My guess is it's near two in the morning, we should leave before sunrise, is everyone good with that?"

We all nodded in agreement. Everyone took their rolled mat out of their ruck and laid it on the ground, crawling into it for the few hours we would get.

Before I realized it, Callum was waking all of us. I was uncertain whether I had dreamed. I still felt extremely exhausted. We all rose swiftly, rolling our mats and securing them to our packs. As before, we fell into the same order behind Callum and began climbing the rugged cliff. I could hear sounds from below. I wondered if we were now in the lead or if someone was ahead of us.

Within a few minutes, Callum was yelling "land mine" at us again. Damn, I guessed it would be like this the entire way up and down. Every so often, we dodged land mines or crawled under traps. We reached a point where we had to crawl up a wall to get onto the higher path. Luckily, the base of that path had a wider, circular area, which allowed us to help each other.

Once we climbed the steep, winding path, Callum advanced past us, taking the lead with confident strides. I fell behind him, my calves burning fiercely like they were on fire. Every step sent sharp aches through my knees, and our journey ahead seemed endless. My shoulders pulsated painfully from the weight of the heavy rucksack, each movement reminding me of the brutal climb.

BOOM!

I startled so bad, I almost lost my balance. It came from beneath us and shook the mountain. The screams coming from below didn't sound good. We were all frozen in place.

"Let's take a moment to gather ourselves for the loss of another cadet, and afterwards we carry on."

After about a minute, we moved forward and continued up the rugged mountain pass. We reached a long corridor where the entire wall was lined with dangerous traps, forcing us to crawl a considerable distance. Just as we were about to stand and walk, we approached another wall to climb. This one was steeper than the previous, with fewer sturdy stepping stones to use.

My height worked against me, but it never stopped me before. Beau and Asher pushed ahead, offering hands to help the three of us climb. That was when it hit me again—we'd lost someone. One of ours wasn't with us.

I forced myself upward, careful, steady, stretching as far as I could to haul my body higher. The top loomed close. I lifted my right leg toward the next stone, toes brushing its edge. The rock gave under me, crumbling, my foot slipping out from under my weight. My stomach lurched as the wall bit into my fingers.

Fuck. Fuck. Fuck.

It was only one foot. I hadn't fallen yet. I still had this. I adjusted my left foot outward and placed my right toes on it. Both hands clutched tightly on the jagged ledges in front of me. I looked down to find a place where I could bring one foot up. I spotted a more stable rock to my left, so I lifted my left foot and stepped onto it, leaving my right foot hanging for a moment before finding a nearby rock to use. I pulled my right foot up and reached above me for the next rugged rock, trying to pull myself forward. Beau reached me and offered his hand, helping me pull myself upward.

Selene chased close, closing the gap, already halfway up. I glanced forward to check the path—and her scream tore through the air.

I snapped my head back. She lay crumpled on the ground, Jeremy pinned beneath her. My chest tightened. Shit. Not good.

"How bad is it?" I shouted down.

"I think she has a dislocated shoulder, which is going to make getting up this harder..." Callum said.

"What about Jeremy?" Beau asked.

"I am fine, my leg will be sore," he said.

"Any ideas on how we are going to get her up here?" Asher asked.

"Anyone pack a rope?" Beau looked around. "Didn't think so."

"Ophelia has the most Healer training. Anyone have an undershirt she can make a sling out of?" I asked. I also received extensive Healer training, as my mom was a Healer, but I was on top of the wall.

"I do." Asher pulled out a shirt and dropped it.

Ophelia motioned to Callum to hold Selene in place, as she came to her side and did a quick pulling motion with her hand on the top of her shoulder. She got her arm wrapped into place.

"I have an idea... it is probably crazy but it's the only one I got," Callum said.

"Um, okay," Selene said through soft tears.

"I am going to put you on my shoulders and climb. I'll need you to lean towards the wall and be steady, so we don't fall backwards. Once we get up enough, they will lift you up," Callum said.

I certainly hoped this would work, because it definitely wouldn't end well if it didn't. My mind raced through all the ways this could go badly. He knelt down, and she perched on his shoulders, then leaned forward against the wall, using her uninjured hand to steady herself. He started to climb with a slow place. Moving his feet one by one, rather than maintaining a wide stance. He moved his arm up and pulled himself up, and I saw her sway back slightly. I gasped, my stomach dropping.

"Damn it, you need to hold steady and keep the lean forward."

She caught a rock and hauled herself higher. He paused, drew a breath, then climbed on until Asher and Beau could reach down and pull her the last stretch. Once she stood with us, I checked her wrap, tugging to make sure it held, then pressed my fingers to her wrist—pulse steady, strong. Callum came up right after her. The other four scaled the wall without trouble and joined our line. The sun bled toward the horizon, shadows stretching long, and my stomach growled loud enough to make my mouth water.

I pulled food from my rugged pack and started eating, sparking a chain reaction as everyone else followed suit. Each of us had saved something from our sacks the night before. We kept moving forward, our steps steady and purposeful. As we walked, we heard a low murmur of voices behind us. Damn, another squad was catching up. Everyone in our group noticed the squad gaining on us, so we quickened our pace to stay ahead.

CHAPTER 7

We reached the summit of the mountain, which was a vast, open field. A flood of emotions surged through me: victorious, joyful, exhausted, sad, and excited. It was a bittersweet moment. My knees buckled as I sank to the ground, and tears silently spilled down my face. We weren't the first to arrive. Tenth squad had beaten us. Did they sleep? I looked around the mountaintop to take in the scene. Tenth squad sat in a circle a short distance from the path. The sky was dark, illuminated only by the moon and the stars shining brightly. Torches dotted the field, casting enough light for us to see each other and move freely. Eleven crates sat nearby, one of which was already open, and I guessed that it contained our food.

"Hey guys, food is over here," Beau yelled. He noticed them at the same time I did.

We all walked over to the crates. None of them were locked or had notes, so we opened one and grabbed sacks one by one. We moved away from the path and sat down in a circle like the other squad had. It was the same meal as the night before. At this point, it was better than nothing.

"Same as before, save some for tomorrow. I know we are starving and barely functioning, but rationing is key," Asher said. I nodded in agreement.

I was starving but knew I had to save some food for tomorrow. The hike down would not be any easier, especially with Selene's arm wrapped tight and the need to descend two treacherous rock walls. By the end of the evening, we moved at a much slower pace than we started, with complete exhaustion. We lay on our mats, trying to get some much-needed rest. Periodically, we heard another squad arrive at the top, grab their food, and settle in. In minutes, my eyes got heavy, my arms twitched, and I drifted off to sleep.

Wingbeats pounded, followed by a screech so sharp it split my dream in two. For a breath I couldn't tell if it was real—until the ground shuddered beneath me. My eyes snapped open.

I shot to my feet, scanning the dark. Shit. A firebird. She towered nine feet, feathers blazing orange-red, each plume lit like flame. Her cry ripped through the air. It was deafening, rattling my skull until my vision pulsed.

Around me, cadets scrambled upright. More wings approached, the sound lighter, quicker than the firebird's heavy strokes. Pascal dropped from the sky, landing beside her, and the truth hit hard—he was Drusearon. I hadn't processed that before. Ramuel slid from the firebird's back and moved to stand shoulder to shoulder with him. "If you are standing here, you made it halfway through the pass. Now, everyone, drop and do pushups until I tell you to stop," Pascal yelled over the field.

Was he serious? I had hardly any energy left to walk. People around me started collapsing. Yes, he was for real. I also fell and began doing pushups. They were slow and, frankly, untidy.

I counted aloud: one, two, three, four, five, seven, eight. No, five, six, eight. The pain was overwhelming. I wondered how many repetitions I had completed. I needed to focus on something other than my screaming arms, aching legs, and strained core muscles. Everything fucking hurt intensely. My eyes throbbed, urging me to shut them, but I knew if I did, I might collapse.

"Stop. On your feet," he said. I didn't know how much time had gone by or how much I had accomplished.

"Now fall in a single line and run," he commanded.

I thought they were trying to kill us. We hiked up a rugged mountain with little food and less sleep. Now we ran around the rocky summit. I looked up at the clear sky and admired the brilliance of the stars and the glowing moon. I couldn't focus on the burning strength in my calves. Everything in my body threatened to give out.

"GET UP, CADET!" Ramuel yelled behind me. I turned my head to see what was going on and saw a cadet from the third squad lying on the ground. We all came to a stop, observing the situation. Most of us moved to a bent-over position, trying to catch our breath.

"Everyone else, keep going," Pascal said. We all resumed running. Increasing numbers of cadets collapsed, most of us vomiting at least once. After about thirty minutes, they ordered us to stop. I suspected my ankle might be sprained. It throbbed painfully with each heartbeat.

I stepped wrong earlier, but I couldn't give it the attention or focus it needed, or I wouldn't be able to keep going. It was screaming for help.

Our group returned to our area and collapsed onto the mats. I sat down, pulled my ruck closer, and took out a wrap I had packed in case one of my joints failed. I wrapped it firmly around my ankle, lay back, and aimed to fall asleep. My entire body shouted negative thoughts, so I forced myself to think of something positive. I looked up at the night sky, trying to drown out the crying and vomiting across the field. I focused on the stars, the moon, and the sounds of nature.

***

I made it to the end, and there stood the handsome guy I couldn't keep my eyes off of when he came near. I made my way to him, and he walked toward me, closing the gap. We stood inches apart, staring into each other's eyes. His right hand grabbed the back of my neck, and his left reached around, pulling me into him. His gorgeous, full lips crashed into mine, sliding his tongue into my mouth for me to suck on. He drew it out and sucked on the bottom of my lip. Fuck me, his kiss was glorious. He pulled away from my lip to start kissing down my neck. His hand moved to the back of my hair, before gripping a handful of it, and then he playfully nipped at my neck. He moved both of his hands down to my ass, gripped my hands so tightly before pulling me up into his arms and carrying me into—

"Wake up, everyone... We gotta go, everyone else is sleeping," Callum said.

"I was dreaming *soooo* good, though..." I cried out. "Yeah, it looked like it," he said, looking over his shoulder at me. My face tightened, wondering what that meant.

We all quietly got up, grabbed our things, and put them in our bags. The other squads were still sleeping, and our best advantage was to get ahead. We started down the mountainside, moving slowly and quietly for the first twenty minutes or so to avoid waking anyone. My body just wanted sleep and food—lots and lots of food.

I also wanted to revisit that dream because it was incredible. I hadn't seen Zane since that night in the sparring gym, even though I looked for him while walking the hallways. I didn't know which branch he belonged to, as we didn't ask personal questions. He was dressed in black, and his name was Zane... yet I found myself dreaming about kissing him.

The third day unfolded much like the previous ones. Our group moved steadily, avoiding land mines and deadly arrow traps. Other squads weren't as fortunate. Explosions from land mines echoed with screams nearby. We couldn't tell which units had triggered them, nor had they passed us. We reached the caves and proceeded toward the one closest to our destination, just as we had on the ascent. Inside, we found a cadet standing beside a sturdy crate, a sight that filled me with a sense of absolute dread. We paused, eyes fixed on him, too exhausted to voice any objections.

"In order to get the crate, someone will have to spar with me and win."

"Is he serious right now?" I said, looking over at my squad, back at the cadet, blinking my eyes slowly.

"Are there any rules to this?" Beau asked him.

"No, I was just—" Before he finished, Callum, Beau, Asher, and Jeremy rushed the cadet and tackled him to the ground, pinning him within minutes, leaving him to tap.

"Four against one is hardly fair, but I guess I didn't make that a rule." He motioned to the crate for us to eat, turned around, and headed out of the cave.

Asher cracked open the crate and passed out bags. Mine held a foil pack of circle-cut spaghetti, an apple, and a hunk of crusty bread. Lighter than the meals before, nothing to stretch into tomorrow. We were already running on scraps.

Grumbles moved through the squad—low, tired, the same hunger biting all of us. We chewed what little we had, unrolled our mats, and sank down like the first two nights. One more night of this grind. One more night before real beds. The thought beat through me like a drum. One more night.

We got up early and moved along the trail. We weren't moving nearly as fast as the previous days. We were all tired. Many of us were groaning with every step, every crawl. Callum was leading, as he had been for the past three days. I was right behind him. The sun was high in the sky, telling me it was midday.

More land mines and arrow traps exploded today than any day before, exhaustion dulling our reflexes. The journey stretched endless ahead, but all I could think about was the stale bread tucked in my pack. My stomach clenched as I pulled it free, chewing slow, forcing each bite to taste like something more than it was.

I nearly walked straight into Callum. He stood frozen, eyes wide. A dozen sharp whizzes cut the air around us.

"Ahhhhh!" he screamed out.

I was in shock, unsure if I could produce a sound. Pain shot through my entire body. I sank to my knees, pressing my hand against the wall for support, praying I wouldn't fall off the mountain. I was destined for more, and this wasn't my end. I had to fight. Callum had collapsed forward, tears streaming down his face. What the hell just happened? How did this occur?

"Are you two alright?" Ophelia cried out behind us.

"I... don't... know," I cried out to her. The pain was all around, and I was seeing stars.

"Let's figure this out." Asher was next to me.

"He's not going to make it. One of these is in his heart, and the other is in..." Ophelia said before she faded into the distance.

"No, no..." I cried out before everything went completely dark.

"Hey there, stay with us," Ophelia said softly, as I tried to open my eyes.

"How bad is it?" I asked her.

"Mostly flesh wounds, nothing life-threatening. You will likely experience pain and need a Healer. An arrow went into your calf, which is the worst one. You have one in your back, but it only pierced the skin. You also have one lodged in your hip and upper arm."

"Fuck. Everything is burning."

We need to set one of the arrows on fire and cauterize the wounds to stop the bleeding so we can move on.

"Shit." All I had were curse words, plenty of them. "Is Callum... is he?"

"He didn't make it..."

Oh gods. No... Why? My heart broke in two. He and I had grown close over the past few weeks, and now he was gone like that. This was the reason I didn't want to make friends or get close to anyone. People die here. Tears streamed down my face as I mourned the loss of my friend. I knew I had to stand and move. We could not sit here. I did not know how long I was unconscious or if other squads passed by us while they triaged me. I pulled myself into a sitting position to gather my thoughts.

"Where is Callum?" I asked, confused.

"Instructor Pascal already came and took him, wherever they take them to," Beau said.

I surveyed the remaining members of my squad, checking each one to confirm they were okay. Our group now consisted of eight: Beau, Ophelia, Asher, Selene, Jeremy, Theodore, Atlas, and me. I pushed myself upright, using the wall to steady my balance. I wasn't sure if I could walk. My calf throbbed painfully, unlike anything I had felt before. My left ankle still ached, and I struggled to bear weight on my right. My legs trembled uncontrollably, and eventually, I collapsed back onto the cold ground. This was really fucking bad.

"I think you guys might need to leave me," I told them.

"Absolutely fucking not," Beau shook his head. "Someone will need to take the lead, checking for land mines and trip wires. I will carry Auriella on my back."

"I'll take the lead. I've been training for Infantry since I was a child," Theodore said.

"We can alternate carrying her. Let me know when you need a break," Asher added.

Theodore stepped to the front of the line, with Jeremy behind him and Asher after. Beau knelt before me. I extended my arms over his shoulders, and he grasped my thighs and lifted me onto his back. Soon, I sensed my eyelids growing heavy, my stomach uneasy, and the world spinning around me.

"I think... I might... Vomit," I barely got the words out.

He paused and sucked in his breath.

"Sorry," I muttered.

"It's okay, take some deep breaths. The nausea comes from the blood loss and pain. What do you always tell us? Refocus yourself."

"Okay... I smell your hair, and you need a bath." I inhaled deeply. "I tasted the bland bread I was eating earlier." Another deep breath. "I see the back of your head. You definitely need a bath." Another inhale. "I feel your warm skin under mine." I took in the largest breath. "I hear all the rocks crumbling under our boots."

He let out a small chuckle. "Good, keep breathing, you're going to make it down this mountain, we all will."

I started to doze off again, my eyes feeling heavy. I leaned my head forward onto his shoulder. I felt so weak. I hated this. I hated feeling weak. I hated slowing my squad down. I hated for them to see me vulnerable and weak. I drifted into sleep.

"Hey Auriella, Asher is going to take you now," he said, tapping my thigh to wake me up.

"You can call me Auri..." I said. The words came out slowly. The world spun, everything was blurry, and my head pounded. I believed I was somewhat worse than what Ophelia claimed.

Beau knelt carefully, gently placing me on the uneven ground. He swapped places with Asher, who confidently reached down and lifted me just as Beau had earlier. The setting sun cast a warm, orange glow as we appeared to inch closer to completing this. My eyelids drooped, my body ached with exhaustion, and a strange sweat broke out on my forehead.

If you feel like your body is on flames, while also in an icebox, you have an infection, Auri. It's important for you to get the wound tended to before it spreads. Wound infections are the top reason we lose cadets at astronomical rates.

I remembered my mother's words—an aggressive infection was spreading fast. If I didn't see the Healers soon, my condition could worsen dramatically. Tears welled up and traced down my cheeks, some entering my mouth and tasting salty. It finally dawned on me that I was crying.

"Hey, you okay back there?" Asher whispered.

"I have an infection that's spreading fast, and I need to get to the infirmary soon."

"It's okay, you're okay. Close your eyes, I got you." He kept this voice low and steady.

"Hey squad, we need to pick up our steps a little faster. Auri isn't doing so well."

I could feel our speed increasing slightly. I needed to remember to thank all seven of them for this. The bouncing of being carried reminded me of when I was a little girl, and my mom would bounce me to sleep. I drifted off into darkness.

"Hey Auri, we've made it..." Jeremy was tapping my thigh. I was currently on his back, but I wasn't exactly sure when I had shifted from Asher's to him. I gradually opened my eyes. It was dark outside, illuminated only by the stars and the moon. We were now at the base of the mountain, the starting point of this journey four days prior. I could see a mix of blurry figures standing near the college, my eyes struggling to stay open, vision coming and going..

I caught sight of the striking light blue eyes that had mesmerized me from the very first moment I saw them. He locked eyes with me, but my heavy eyelids made it difficult to keep my gaze on him. His worried expression puzzled me, yet I couldn't quite figure out why. He didn't entirely know me. I felt a strange chemistry between us that I couldn't explain. My head jerked forward, and my eyes shut.

"Instructor Pascal, we need your assistance. NOW!" Beau shouted.

I felt shifted from one arm to another, I felt us through the air. I thought we were flying, but I wasn't sure. My bones ached, muscles burned, vision cloudy, the arms that held me were warm.

"Please don't die Blackcreek, your father will..."

My eyes sealed shut.

CHAPTER 8

PAIN.

AGONY.

SADNESS.

An overwhelming nausea and pain coursed through my body, overtaking everything within me. My knees weakened under me, heart beating faster each second, it was like she was siphoning *from me.*

I felt a wave of emotions that didn't exactly belong to me, which I recognized as my Anam Cara. I was aware that her platoon was heading toward the mountain pass of terrors. When I experienced it two years earlier, I barely made it out alive. An arrow struck my right wing, almost causing me to fall off the cliff. While having wings was usually an advantage, Drusearons were forbidden to use theirs during basic training—not that we could.

I still felt the silver string that linked us. She was alive. I couldn't help her, and that devastated me. My fist locked tight, my fingernails dug into my palms. Wings twitching to open. Every part of me wanted to fly up there. If I leapt now, if I gave in, they'd ban me from ever staying here during leave. But I couldn't do that, or I risked getting kicked off campus. Hell, there could be worse punishment for involving myself in the pass challenge. But gods, it would be worth it if I could reach her. If I could bleed for her instead. I couldn't leave her. I just found her. She was my Anam Cara. I never understood what my aunt meant about our connection until I experienced it myself.

Six years ago, I saw her for the first time but didn't feel it. She didn't know I was there, nor did she see me. I was about to approach her, but a grey, dappled dragon lifted her into the air. She raised her arms as the dragon swooped down with its sharp talons. My stomach dropped into my chest. I initially thought she faced danger. Instead, she let out a joyful yell as the dragon tossed her playfully into the air and swooped underneath, gently settling her onto the saddle. Her laughter and delighted shouts filled the air, swelling my heart. Within moments, she disappeared into the sky. I returned to that spot many times over the following months, but I never saw her again.

Nine months later, my two uncles were killed in an attack, and I felt confused and angry. I was furious at everything and everyone. It changed our family's dynamic and brought on responsibilities I didn't want.

The last two years at this place were marked by the necessary growth. Focus was placed inward, and anger eased through sparring sessions. Genuine friendships were formed, and sincerity was finally experienced. In my village, friendships were found, but motives often remained hidden.

Her unexpected appearance really disrupted my plans for this place. I'd intended to graduate, return, and find her again—determine whose dragon it was to track her down. It was obvious it wasn't hers, since she was too young to be bonded, implying it was one of her parents. Here, I learned that dragons can be selective about their bonds, though occasionally they form smaller bonds with their Rider's children.

I sensed her approaching, feeling intense pain ripple through my body. The agony overwhelmed me, inducing nausea as if I myself endured the torment. I stepped outside and pressed my back against the cold, rough stone of the college wall. I observed movement descending the mountain pass, the tension mounting as her presence drew near.

"What are you doing out here, Cadet Braegon?" Professor Pascal asked in a low voice.

"Just watching the new cadets complete the mountain of hell..." I said, completely lying.

He glanced at me sharply, raising an eyebrow as if he sensed there was more to the story. I had known Pascal since childhood, long before he became an instructor here. He had been stationed at Winterhand Stronghold and shared a bond of brotherhood with my father. Among the professors here, he was one of the few who truly knew who I was.

"Don't get yourself in trouble, please," he pleaded to me.

"I won't—"

"Instructor Pascal, we need your assistance, NOW!" one of the cadets yelled.

Auriella was on one of their backs, and my heart sank into my stomach. I straightened against the cold, rough wall. I fought every urge in my body. My bones begged me to run to her. No one truly understood what she meant to me, definitely not her. My stomach didn't just twist—it collapsed. My ribs felt as if they collapsed inward, my lungs burning for air that wouldn't come. I pressed myself back to the wall, nails biting into stone, fighting the animal urge to rip her from Pascal's arms and take her myself.

She looked like she was knocking on death's door. Fae usually outlived humans, but we were not immortal. The silver thread in my mind, which I believed connected us, felt faint—like it was slipping away. I closed my eyes, delved deep inside, and thought of that shimmering strand, pulling it back to me.

She couldn't fucking die.

We had hardly begun our journey yet. My aunt was rarely wrong, and she said we would share a fantastic connection and love story.

Pascal hurried to them, grabbing her. In an instant, he shot up into the sky. He would take her to the infirmary, and of course, there were no damn menders on staff during the summer. That seemed ridiculous considering there were just as many deaths and injuries. The ward that suppressed magic was only for the college itself, unless you had runes or was a professor. Once you crossed the river, magic was available. Most of the cadets didn't realize that—hell, most of them didn't even know how to wield magic properly yet. Thankfully, my wings didn't require magic.

I launched into the sky and flew directly to the infirmary moments after Pascal did. I landed in the watchtower, nodded my head at the alert cadets standing guard, and made my way inside. Only a few dedicated Healers stayed during the summer, and some experienced instructor-Healers were present.

The busy unit buzzed with cadets and seasoned Healers moving rapidly around. In the center, a rectangular area held the busy discussions of Healers monitoring their patients. I leaned against the cold counter outside the room where they had taken Auriella. Four Healers worked inside, efficiently cutting off her uniform and assessing her condition. Pascal looked at the desk, made eye contact with me, furrowed his brows, and expressed stern disapproval. He scrutinized her closely before confidently walking toward me.

"What the hell are you doing here?" He seethed at me in a quiet voice.

I leaned in close to him and whispered, "Anam Cara."

He pulled away from me, turning his head completely toward me, his eyes looked like they were about to fall out of their sockets. "What the fuck do you mean?" He had never used that tone before, making me drop my eyes to the ground.

"You know what I mean... and she doesn't know yet."

"Fuck... Do you know who—"

"You need to get in here. I need some extra hands," one of the Healers yelled.

Pascal rushed in, clamping both hands over the wound as blood poured through his fingers. I dropped to the floor, stripped bare of any strength I thought I had. My composure shattered.

Please, Marzana—don't take her. Please, Betha—stay with her, breathe life into her. I had never begged the gods for anything. Now I pleaded like a broken man, promising them blood, wings, my very life if they would just leave her with me. Pitiful, but I would kneel forever if it kept her breathing.

Blood was pouring out of her leg, arm, and back. They were pulling pieces of wood out of the wounds and tossing them on the floor. So much fucking blood. The silver strand flickered. My body leaned forward before my mind caught up, the pull of her blood calling to something in me I had buried. I clenched my fists until nails drew blood in my palms. If I gave in, if I touched that power, they'd know what I was. I couldn't. Not here. Not with her. My anger surged, desperate to tap into it. There wasn't a mender anyway, so it wouldn't do her any good right now.

Gods, I thought they might lose her. This was not our story. They kept adding gauze to her back, pulling out the arrow fragments and reopening the wound. My heart pounded faster than ever before. It felt like it broke into two.

Hours later, they finally stabilized her. She remained unconscious but continued to breathe steadily. With each passing hour, the silver strand felt stronger in my grasp. I was unaware of her awareness, yet I could feel her presence, smell her scent. When she arrived weeks ago, a tingling sensation had rippled through me. I thought my twin sister Aeliana was here. I glanced around the courtyard but didn't see her. That was when I spotted her—the face my aunt had sketched for me. She appeared older than I remembered from six years ago, but unmistakably her.

I stared at her, watching her chest rise and fall. Her face was pale, and even though she was resting, dark circles appeared under her eyes.

One of the Healer professors knocked twice, then walked in and gave me a slight smile.

"How is she?"

"You tell me, you're the Healer..."

"She is resting and healing. Only time will tell."

"Can't we get a mender here?" I grumbled at her.

"By the time they would get our message, she will be awake and making progress."

"I could fly and retrieve one—"

"No. She will be fine, trust the process."

I just rolled my eyes at her because, trust what fucking process? The one where she looked like she kissed Marzana's door? We had menders in other forts, and I could fly. The tone in which she said no suggested there was more to it. She checked her bandages and temperature. She adjusted the fluid bag that ran into her vein. She gave me a sorrowful look and left the room.

She joined the group of professors who were engaged in a deep conversation behind the counter. I tried to listen, but I heard nothing, which was unusual because I had excellent hearing. This wasn't the first time I witnessed a meeting while sitting in this chair, watching Auriella breathe. Several professors from the college met here a few times a day, speaking softly. I pretended not to pay attention, but I was very aware of what they were doing, just as I was observing her.

Three days had gone by, and I hadn't left her side except to use the restroom. Her chest rose and fell steadily. Sometimes, she would twitch as if her dreams were tormenting her. I would put my hand on hers, and she would settle back into sleep. I didn't touch her otherwise, not without her consent. It took her a minute to open her eyes and adjust to the room. Her usual emerald eyes had changed to a more bluish shade. They were wide open when she saw me sitting at her bedside.

CHAPTER 9

My eyes flickered, struggling to open, and it was bright as fuck. Where was I? It was hard to keep my eyes open for more than thirty seconds. Every time I tried to look around to see where I was and who was there, my vision blurred. There was a bright window to my right, next to my bed, which made it tough to keep my eyes open. I was in bed, but not in my own, so I had to be in the infirmary. I slowly turned my head to the left, and my eyes opened wide, both eyebrows raised. It was Zane.

"Hey..."

"Hi." I gave him a small smile. "How long have I been out?"

"Three days, it's Sunday."

"I guess I took the whole 'rest on the weekend' literally."

He let out a small laugh. "Yeah, yeah you did."

"Why are you here?"

"Should I go?" he asked, raising his eyebrows.

"No, I guess I just don't understand why you're here with me. We aren't friends."

"I'd like to think since we sparred, we're friends," he shrugged.

"How long have you been here?"

"Not too long, in and out." He dropped his gaze, but something told me that wasn't the full truth.

"Is the rest of my squad alright?"

"I believe so, other than the two lost on the mountain, I am not really privy to that information."

"Where did we place, do you know?"

"First." He gave me a big smile.

"When can I get out of here?"

"You've been unconscious for three days, and you're trying to hit the floor running?"

"I can't miss much in basic. I don't want to repeat. What did the Healers say?"

"The arrows that shot out were old and rusty, one pierced your calf. When they removed it, a fragment remained embedded. Cauterization prevented it from draining. Your calf muscle will take some time to heal, but they expect a full recovery. The arrow that went into your back scraped your kidney, but it should be fine. The one that hit your arm also had debris left inside. It went through your bicep, which, like your calf, will need time to heal. The arrow that hit your hip was the least damaging, leaving a puncture wound. Your squad members did what they could with what they had, and for that, you survived."

"Okay, that is a lot to process."

I figured I was alive, and that was what mattered. I still felt exhausted, like I could sleep more, but I also knew I needed to start moving to heal. I lifted my eyes and locked eyes with Zane. I felt a spark in my chest. He felt like home, yet I didn't know him. My eyes began to feel heavy, and it became difficult to keep them open. I drifted into sleep again.

"Please don't die Blackcreek, your father will..." *"He didn't make it..."* Callum collapsed, his pain was with me here. My pain unending, pouring through the dream, the arrows whizzing out hitting me, hitting Callum's heart.

I gasped awake, and it was dark outside. My dreams confused me. What did Pascal mean? I looked around my room, and Zane was no longer there. I saw a note on the table next to me.

Auriella,

I have to report for watch duty in the tower. I'll be back to check on you soon. With most of the cadets and staff gone for the summer, you might have to yell for someone if you need help. Rest up.

Zane

He wrote me a letter. Gods, if his eyes weren't already so captivating... A knock came at the door, and my stomach fluttered with butterflies. I looked up and saw my squad mates entering. A flicker of disappointment washed over me but elated to see them safe. As I took in all seven of them, it reminded me we had lost Callum and Nadine.

I wasn't close to Nadine, but Callum... Gosh, he led us so fearlessly and effortlessly. Over the past five weeks, I felt the closest to him. Tears rolled down my face, mixed with feelings of happiness and sadness. Damn it. I wasn't usually a person who cried easily. My emotions felt all over the place.

"How are you feeling?" Beau asked.

"I'm alive," I said, smiling at him.

"You scared us coming down the mountain, it was touch and go," Ophelia said.

"Thank you all for looking out for me. Thank you, Beau, Jeremy and Asher, for carrying me. I wouldn't have made it without you."

"We wouldn't have it any other way," Asher said, nodding his head toward Beau.

Ophelia motioned toward the door. "The senior Healer says you can go for a walk around the infirmary floor. It would be good for you."

"I am willing to try," I said. I moved to the side of the bed, which took longer than I expected. My body was still sore. Beau came to my side, wrapped his arms around my back, and helped me stand. My legs felt wobbly beneath me, but thankfully, my ankle wasn't hurting anymore. My calf was on fire, but I could do this. I had the support of my squad with me. Step by step, we made it to the hallway. With each step, the pain seemed to dull, like I was working a knot out of my muscle.

"What's the deal with you and the blue-eyed cadet?" Jeremy said.

"What do you mean?" I said, dropping my eyes to the floor.

"On the field, he didn't drop his gaze from you. He looked worried, and I could feel your pulse rising..." Jeremy said.

"There is nothing with us."

"Nothing? Hmmm, if you say so," Beau said.

"The last time I saw eyes lock like that, with that twinkle, was when my aunt and uncle—" Jeremy said, then stopped as Zane rounded the corner. He looked at each of my squad mates before he locked onto me.

"And you said there is nothing going on..." Beau mumbled under his breath before I elbowed him to shut up.

"It's good to see you up," Zane said.

"I'm Asher, and you are?"

"Zane," he said with a flat voice, giving Asher a straightforward look.

"How do you know Auri?" Beau asked.

"From around." He turned his eyes back to me. "I can take over the walk from here. Pretty sure you all need to get back to your barracks."

Asher, Beau, and Ophelia swung their heads to me. I nodded to them, letting them know I was fine. Beau moved from my side, letting Zane move in next to me.

"We'll try and stop by tomorrow. We start weapon lessons tomorrow. But you know, sometimes we get tasked with bullshit." Asher told me.

They all nodded or smiled at me as they left me in his arms. I turned my head to meet his gaze. His piercing blue eyes appeared darker than in the sunlight. His hair was tousled and slightly messy, as if windblown. He looked utterly stunning. He gave me that mischievous smile he first flashed when we made eye contact.

"What does that mean?" I asked.

He sucked his teeth and smiled at me. "Nothing, at all."

"Oh, it's definitely not nothing."

"Do you want the truth or some muddied version?" He looked down at the ground.

"Honesty, always."

"Are you familiar with mates?"

"When two people are destined to be together, completing their—wait, you're not saying that we are—"

"I don't know... Growing up, my family talked about mates or Anam Cara. I didn't take it too seriously. They said some people never find theirs. It was like a fairy tale, when your eyes meet for the first time, you will feel—"

"Electricity shooting through your body?" I finished his sentence. He lifted his eyes to meet mine. We stared at each other, letting minutes pass. I looked forward and started walking again.

"Yes. I don't know what any of this means, but I did feel an electric current course through me the first time our eyes met. The last day you were on the mountain, I felt a pain and dread I couldn't explain. That had to be yours, and moments later, they came in with one of your squad mates who didn't make it."

"This is a lot to take in..." I said. I wasn't sure how to handle this information or what it meant. Were we mates? The only genuine bond I believed in was with a dragon. I might marry and have children someday, but I never imagined someone becoming a part of my soul, someone I was truly meant to be with. I didn't even know him, yet I felt a strong desire to. After nearly dying, I didn't think I should be making any choices.

"I am tired, can we go back to my room?"

"Of course," he said.

We started walking back to the room, and something lingered on my mind, why didn't they save me up there? What did Pascal mean?

"Why didn't they take me off the mountain like Callum or the guy with his legs blown off?"

"Policy states they only remove cadets who have died, neither survived. It's sadistic. If I wouldn't have been kicked off this campus or charged with treason, I would have gone up there myself."

"I think Pascal told me I couldn't die and something about my dad..."

He shot his head my way, staring at me, confusion in his eyes. "Hmm, interesting. What do you think he meant?"

"I have no clue." I mean I had an idea, but I don't know. I was confused, maybe he didn't really say that.

We made it back to my room, and I got into my bed. Zane sat in the chair next to me, just as he had been when I woke up that morning. I raised an eyebrow at him, saying, "I know you say we may be mates or Anam Cara or whatever you want to call it, but that doesn't mean you're obligated to me or to babysit me."

"I want to. Plus, there are tremendously few Healers in the infirmary and many other injured cadets."

I simply nodded at him because I had no energy to argue. Exhausted in body and mind, I closed my eyes and slipped into a restless sleep. I dreamt of losing Callum once more, which caused me to toss and turn throughout the night.

***

The next morning came sooner than I expected. Zane slept soundly in the chair beside me, his messy, tousled hair framing his handsome face. I felt a strong pull toward him. I didn't believe our destiny influenced it, or at least I didn't think so. I wasn't sure what to think—being destined to be together didn't mean we had to be. I was only twenty years old, with four years of college and training still ahead of me. As a Rider, I knew I had to commit to the military as long as my dragon lived, assuming I bonded with a dragon.

Zane's eyes opened, and he jolted slightly. "Good morning."

"Morning, don't you have cadet stuff to do?"

"Nope, I'm on summer leave. I'm rotating through the watch towers in exchange for staying here instead of leaving. Otherwise, I'm free to do as I please. Would you like me to go?"

"No, I didn't say that. Sorry, I'm just confused."

"Anything I can clarify?"

"I don't know. What branch are you in?"

"I'm a Drusearon Warrior. I don't like to call it a branch."

My eyes probably showed everything I thought—the fear that overwhelmed me.

"Does that change things?"

"I um...um. I have some biases I haven't fully sorted out. You've been amazing to me, so I'm just trying to separate the two."

"I see. I'm sorry for whatever happened to you. I promise I'll never hurt you."

"So, you have wings? But I haven't seen them?"

"Yes, I use magic to hide them."

"Why?"

"My village is near the border, and we're often treated differently and shamed for our wings—so I hide them. I hide them so I don't get the look you gave me when I told you."

"I was never afraid before, but something happened—can I see them?"

He closed his eyes for a few seconds, then, peeking over his shoulders behind him, were his black wings all tucked in close to his body.

"Open them?"

He shook his head. "Not in here, but if you were willing to walk to the infirmary Watchtower?"

My eyebrow arched up. "Bribery for me to exercise?"

"Yes."

"You didn't have to bribe me. I wanted to walk anyway. I need to get out of here sooner rather than later."

"This wouldn't be an issue if there were a mender here," he grumbled.

"I didn't realize we didn't have menders on staff. I actually didn't think of them."

"Well, we do, during the school year, but almost all of them went home, and the others went to the battlefields where they were needed. If you had been mended, you would be fully healed, just a little sore."

I pushed my feet to the side of the bed. My legs buckled, trembling under me, the floor tilting for a breath before I steadied. Zane rose fast, ready to catch me. His presence hovered, tense, until I held my balance. He eased back a step, though his eyes stayed fixed on me.

Pain tugged at my calf with each shift of weight, not the sharp blaze of yesterday but a stubborn throb that dragged with every movement. I rolled my shoulders, stretched my arms—fire lanced down one, raw and biting. My breath hissed between my teeth. The ache clung deep in the muscle, refusing to let go, reminding me how far I still was from being whole.

I thought he was trying to fucking kill me. Climbing the watch tower from the seventh floor of the infirmary involved way too many steps. When we finally arrived, I leaned against the wall, needing a moment to catch my breath.

"Are you ready for this?" He vaulted up the rugged ledge and unfurled his wings—enormous, solid black, dragon-like in their stretch. The sight punched the air from my lungs.

He winked, then let himself fall backward. My chest seized, panic clawing up my throat—until he surged skyward, soaring with impossible strength. He rolled high in the air, wings cutting the wind, before sweeping down to land on the ledge in a single, fluid motion.

My pulse thundered, rattling in my ears. My skin buzzed like it carried static. He had revealed something wild, something untouchable, and the shock of it left me reeling. Then the wings vanished, gone in an instant, leaving me trembling, the image seared into my vision, etched so deep it felt carved into me.

"Do you like flying?"

"Yeah. It gives me peace and joy. I feel free."

"How are we going to navigate this?"

"Navigate what exactly?"

"The whole mate thing..."

"Before our eyes met in the courtyard, I had seen you upon your arrival and on a few other occasions. I immediately realized you were the most beautiful female I had ever seen. I was on overwatch when dragons flew overhead to scare the cadets, and you stood there so brave. I knew I wanted to get to know you. Later, standing in that courtyard and watching you, when you looked at me, I felt something I've never experienced or could even put into words. It was as if half of me was on the field, observing myself. I don't want to impose anything on you or rush this—this is all new for me too."

I nodded, "I am going to miss so much in weapons yielding."

"Deflection. Nice. The first week is about learning more about daggers, swords, and when to use each. For what it's worth, walking here means you should be able to return to courses tomorrow with some physical restrictions. You would need to get the senior Healer to agree, of course."

"I would like that." I pushed off the wall, stood up, and made my way down the stairs. Going down felt a little harder than going up, but I did it without any help other than using the wall.

CHAPTER 10

I returned to my squad and bunk the next morning. I had physical limitations that I worried would annoy my platoon. The week wasn't physically demanding, which I needed. We mostly learned about various military weapons. By the end of the week, we practiced throwing daggers. Since my right arm was still recovering, I swung with my left hand. Strangely, my left arm needed this practice. I hadn't noticed that my left arm was much weaker than the other.

Ophelia and I were walking to the dining hall for lunch. She kept giving me this smile like she wanted to say something, but wasn't sure if she should.

"Come on out with it?" I said.

"Oh, I don't know if it's my place." She reminded me how quiet and reserved she was.

"You saved my life, we are friends."

"You and... Zane... What is the deal?"

"Oh," I swallowed, taking in a deep breath, "I am not sure, honestly. He believes we are... Anam Cara?"

"Mates?"

"Yeah, I guess other places have different names for it."

"Hmm, what do you think?"

"I think he is an exceedingly good-looking male, and when I first locked eyes with him, it felt like lightning shot through my whole body. I didn't grow up being told about this."

"As a family of Healers, we learned early on that true mates are meant for only one person to complete their soul. Most people never find theirs, but that doesn't mean they can't love others. When two souls are destined to be together, both feel it the moment their eyes meet."

"What if one of us doesn't want it? We don't accept it."

"You will always be drawn to each other, even if you're not physically together. You'll feel and sense each other. Some people have rejected the bond of a mate, and it takes a part of their soul."

"Why do people reject the bond?"

"I only know what I was told, but my grandma mentioned that sometimes people find their soulmate after they're already married with children. In a few cases, it happens because they couldn't get along or because one partner wasn't a good person."

"What do you think?"

"When I saw you both in the infirmary hall, I knew by the way your eyes lit up for each other. I also think it's better for fewer people to know. A mating bond can be used against one of you. The stronger the bond, the more vulnerable you are."

"Oh... what should I do?"

"OH, I can't help you there. You have to figure out the path you're on. I can only walk alongside you."

"My mom was a Healer, though she never discussed it. When I arrived here, I wasn't eager to pursue a relationship, as I tend to fall deeply for people too fast."

"You don't have to, if you don't want to."

"When he's around, it feels like home. I want him, but a part of me is screaming we don't really know each other."

"Maybe, just take it day by day, see where it goes."

"Yeah... Thanks for this."

We entered the bustling dining facility, grabbed our food eagerly, and found seats with the rest of our squad. A chill ran down my spine as I looked behind me. There he was, standing against the back wall, watching me intently. He wasn't supposed to be here. All other cadets ate in Dining Facility Two. I raised my eyebrows in surprise, and he winked at me.

Did he just fucking wink at me? I was sure I was about to fall hard for him. I felt it deep in my bones. He turned and left the dining hall, glancing back over his shoulder.

I pushed to my feet, gave my squad a nod, and hurried to put my tray away. My calf burned with every step, a sharp reminder I wasn't fully healed. I slipped through the exit door—and a hand caught me, yanking me aside.

Lightning tore through my arm, racing straight into my chest. He pulled me in, and I dragged a breath deep into my lungs, forcing my eyes down. Lavender and pine clung to him, sharp and clean, and the scent tangled in my head. My heart hammered double-time, rattling my ribs.

His fingers hooked under my chin, tilting my face up. My gaze collided with his—ashen blue, unyielding. Another jolt ripped through me, my skin sparking. His hand slid to the back of my neck, steady, insistent, drawing me closer. Our mouths hovered less than an inch apart, breath brushing breath.

Everything inside me urged me to kiss him, to taste him, to feel his lips against mine. He took a deep breath and growled softly. Oh gods, this would wreck me. I wrapped my arms around his neck and moved my lips to his. I only lived once.

He kissed me slowly and passionately. He pulled back slightly and sucked on my bottom lip, then pressed his tongue into my mouth, caressing my tongue with tender intensity.

I had goosebumps all over, and my hair stood up on my arms. Every part of me wanted to rip his clothes off, but I held onto the tiny bit of self-control I had right now. He reached down, grabbed my ass, and lifted me. I wrapped my legs around him. He spun us around, pressed me against the wall, and started kissing my neck slowly and so gently. He gently set me down and stared into my eyes.

"I... we... can't." He let out a low growl.

"I mean, I am not saying no..." I whimpered to him.

"I want to, trust me, I want to rip the clothes off your body, lick every part of you. I want to make you scream my name over and over again."

"But?"

"You need to get back to class, and I really want our first time to be more than what I can offer out here. I want privacy."

"Fair... maybe we should date first?"

He let out a chuckle. "Yeah, maybe."

I gently pushed him away and headed back to class.

***

Week seven was about to begin, and we would be expected to spar with weapons. I was a little nervous, to be honest, since I was still healing. My right arm was still tender, but I was able to use it.

Our weekends involved less training and more freedom. I was sure that freedom did not include fraternization. Still, I was sure many cadets in our platoon hooked up—they did not hide it well. It was obvious when you entered the same bathroom minutes apart and emerged shortly after.

Growing up on different forts, reckless as a teenager, I picked up tricks fast—ways to get by, ways to get what I wanted. Maybe everyone knew back then, but I wore them like armor. My father couldn't control me, no matter how hard he tried. I shut him out, stubborn and set on chasing my own wants. Every time my off again boyfriend was on, he was relieved, though his disapproval never softened.

Day two of sparring began, and I was not called to spar the previous day, but I knew I would participate today. Despite my restricted training, practicing with a weapon remained essential for passing basic training. Our squad gathered around a single mat. Jeremy was called to spar against Blaze from the fifth squad, who had also encircled the mat to watch. Jeremy removed his shirt, revealing his toned, attractive physique. He stood six feet tall, had light brown skin, and short black hair. A stunning wolf tattoo covered his left pectoral muscle, with tribal symbols extending from it onto his shoulder and upper arm, symbolizing his Shapeshifter heritage.

Blaze followed suit and removed his shirt, revealing all of his majestic wings. His physique was more defined than Jeremy's, which didn't surprise me because Drusearons began training as soon as they learned to walk. Blaze stood about three inches taller than Jeremy. He had pale, luminous skin and long, sandy blonde hair that reached his shoulders. On his back, tribal tattoos wrapped around his wings.

They both stood on the mat facing each other, dancing around while holding a dagger in each hand. The daggers we used for sparring were dull but still sharp enough to cut. During our lessons last week, we learned how to inflict both lethal and nonlethal wounds. It was clearly emphasized that sparring should be nonlethal.

Jeremy extended his arm, and his dagger struck Blaze's left wrist, causing bright red blood to start oozing immediately onto his hand and the mat. He still held his dagger, though not as tightly as before. He moved forward and aimed at Jeremy's upper arm. Jeremy quickly dodged, spun around, and ended up behind Blaze, striking his calf. Fuck, that looked like it hurt. It definitely made my own calf ache in sympathy.

Blaze dropped to his knees. For a breath I thought he'd faltered, but Jeremy only stepped back, waiting for him to rise. Wrong move. Blaze sank lower, body spinning quick as a strike, and his dagger drove straight into Jeremy's foot.

Jeremy roared, the sound raw and animalistic. My stomach clenched, eyes going wide as the blade punched deep. He crashed to the floor, clutching his foot, blood already pooling beneath his grip. Blaze didn't give him time to breathe. He sprang up, slipped behind Jeremy, one bloody hand braced across his chest, the other pressing cold steel to his throat. Jeremy froze. Both daggers slipped from his grip and clattered to the floor. Surrender.

My heart pounded hard in my ears. It sucked watching a squadmate drop, but gods, the move had been brutal—clean, decisive, merciless. Impressive.

"Auriella Blackcreek & Arya Smithden."

I was called to the mat for a fight against a female from the third squad. I had only seen her briefly and mainly in our barracks. Because my right side was weaker, I adopted a stance with my left side leading. Everyone in my platoon knew I had been out for several days due to injuries sustained during the pass, so they knew how to target me. What they didn't know was that I had undergone extensive training in weaponry. Both of us received two daggers, as in previous matches. Over the past week, I focused on improving my skills with my left arm. She was a few inches taller than I was, but I was used to my shorter height and made it work to my advantage.

She pranced around. I threw out a fake strike with my right hand. She jumped back and to her right, and I immediately threw my left out, contacting her right arm above the elbow. She winced but instantly threw her right arm out toward my left to counter the move. I swayed back to dodge the strike. She stepped closer to me. I threw another strike with my left, giving her a warning. She moved back, and I advanced with her, this time throwing my right arm out, striking her hip. Red blood oozed down her leg and onto the floor. She hissed, nose flaring at me. She countered with a strike using her left hand. I dodged it, but she threw her right hand and struck my right arm, just below my healing arrow wound.

FUCK.

Pain shot through my wrist and up my shoulder. Blood dripped down my arm, making my grip on the dagger slippery and sticky. Unlike Jeremy, who paused to give his opponent a moment, she was attacking me again. I took a quick breath and shifted to avoid her invading my space. Then I went back to the center. She approached as I had expected. She threw two more strikes, which I dodged, then I countered with a left punch that caught her off guard. I hit her forearm hard enough that she dropped her dagger.

Perfect, just what I wanted. Once you dropped it or the dagger slipped out of our hands, we were not permitted to retrieve it. The rules of defeat stated that the person either tapped or lost both daggers. Like all the other matches, there was blood everywhere, making the mats slippery. I stepped forward, squatted down with quickness, and struck at her thigh. She was quick and moved back. As I stood up, my right foot slipped a little. She took advantage of that and moved forward to strike my left bicep. I let out a scream that even surprised me.

Shit. Shit. Shit.

Both arms throbbed with every heartbeat, each pulse a hammer of pain. My daggers stayed clenched tight, steel biting into my palms. I lunged, snapping three quick maneuvers with my right. On the third I pulled back, then drove my left across her stomach. The blade tore flesh, and blood welled fast, dark and slick. Her eyes burned with fury, something feral breaking loose inside her.

She switched her dagger to her right and slashed in a frenzy, steel cutting the air with vicious speed. I couldn't let her unravel. I had to end it. I circled, sprang onto her back, and locked my legs around her waist. I drove my dagger into her shoulder, the blade punching through muscle. Hot blood surged over my hand, spilling down her arm as she roared beneath me.

I swung my arm around, ready to press my second blade to her neck—when her dagger punched into my left calf. White heat exploded up my leg. Gods. Stars burst behind my eyes. Focus. I had to stay locked in. Pain could come later. I shifted hard, drove my blade into the back of her right arm to stop her from striking again, then dragged the steel up to her throat. She twitched, angling for my leg again, and I pressed the edge deeper against her skin.

"Fucking submit, or I'll drop my legs and drive this blade into your neck," I snarled.

Her second dagger clattered to the floor. I pulled my blade away and slid off her back. My right calf screamed from the fight alone, but the left poured blood, warm and fast. She hadn't struck deep muscle, thank the gods, but the pain ripped through me sharp enough to twist my gut. Nausea surged. Old wounds, new ones, all burning together—if I didn't choke it down, I'd paint the mat with vomit on top of blood.

I tore a strip from my sleeve and bound the calf tight, pulling until the flow slowed. My opponent stepped over and offered her hand. I gripped it, hauled myself up, and we shook. If you walked away with a nonlethal stab, the Healers could patch you up. I'd already spent days in their care—I wasn't going back. My arm was cut too, shallow but bleeding. It had already started to clot. I'd be fine. These scars would stay. I'd wear them like medals.

The rest of our squad wasn't called. Some of them had been called the day prior, and we still had three more days of sparring. Everyone had to be called at least once and ideally win at least once. Hopefully, my winning would allow me to continue recovering. The Riders' branch would be another brutal journey in a completely different way. I had some upperclassmen friends that I was so very eager to see and hug.

After afternoon sparring, we went to the dining facility. Thankfully, we stopped doing evening formations after the pass. Once sparring was over, we were dismissed for the day to eat and relax around the campus.

After I finished my meal, I headed back to our barracks because I was in desperate need of a shower. While climbing the stairs, I was pulled into the third-floor wing. For a moment, I was startled, but then I knew it was him. As soon as his hand wrapped around my arm, I felt a shock pass between us.

"Are you okay?" he said, his jaw tight and his words clipped.

"Um... Yeah, I am standing in front of you."

He let out a low growl. "With quite a bit of blood all over."

"Some of it is mine, and some of it was my opponent." I gave him a little smile.

"I felt your pain course through me..."

"You did?" I tilted my head slightly, raising my eyebrows at him.

"You're my twin flame, remember... When you have overwhelming emotions, I feel them. I don't fully understand how it all works. I sensed you on the pass. I sensed you today. I was on watch duty, or I would have come after you sooner."

"I prefer the term Anam Cara, mate." Giving him a wink, like he had done to me.

"Deal, Mate." His smile melted me, sexy and disarming in the same breath. He caught the back of my arms and drew me closer. Pain flared, sharp enough to make me suck my teeth and wince, but I let him pull me in.

He released me quick, eyes narrowing as he caught it. His hand slid to my right arm, gentle now, checking the damage.

"They got you right below your wound, smart move, but also what an asshole."

"I got her back," I blurted out. He leaned down and kissed my fresh wound.

"Where else did she get you?" he asked, looking at me.

"My left fucking calf, so now both calves are aching, little bitches."

He let out a small laugh. "What a dirty little mouth you have." He squatted down, pulled my left pant leg up to inspect it. "It looks nasty, but nowhere near as bad as that right was." Then he placed another kiss there.

"It'll buff," I shrugged.

He stood up, placed his hands on my hips, and pulled me in. He pressed his lips to my forehead, giving me a long, delicate kiss. Then he lifted my chin and gently pressed his lips to mine. Instead of a frantic kiss, it was a slow, intimate one. He stepped back and looked at me all over again.

"I may not be able to see you again. Cadets will be returning soon, and it will be chaotic for a bit. Please make it through the Riders' Judgment, I don't want to regret not taking you to my room sooner."

"I need to shower and tend to these wounds." I rose onto my toes, ignoring my burning calves, and kissed his cheek. "I'll see you soon."

Once I got in the shower, I assessed my cuts and the healing of my wounds. My new cuts weren't as bad as my previous wounds, which was good, but they were going to feel worse the next day. I cleaned them, applied ointment, and rewrapped them all. I headed back to the barracks and relaxed in my bunk. Throughout the evening, fellow cadets came and went. I drifted off into sleep.

***

The rest of the week proceeded smoothly. Our spirited squad performed exceptionally well, with only three members submitting to the formidable opponent. However, they were summoned to face another challenging adversary and managed to redeem themselves. By the end of the week, nearly every member of our platoon bore some form of bandages, proudly displaying our battle scars.

The week blurred as we processed through the stark barracks. We turned in worn uniforms and issued gear, trading the old for the new. As a platoon, we wrestled with the mess of crammed bodies in one room, the constant fight to keep it clean, but we managed.

There was no graduation. Instead, we reported straight to our branches to begin the real path. Each had its own way of breaking in first-years. Witches clashed in duels of magic, sparks and curses flying until only one stood. Infantry crossed steel in brutal sword matches. Shapeshifters raced across the college grounds to determine their speed. Healers bent over fake triage, forced to prove who could save the most in chaos. Drusearons stepped off ledges into free fall, testing whether instinct or terror would win. Historians locked horns in word battles, knowledge thrown like blades. And Riders—Riders faced Judgment Day.

While July thirty-first concluded basic training, we weren't released until the first day August. Marking the first day as first-year cadets. All the trainees stood in neat rows in the expansive courtyard, with stern drill instructors positioned confidently at the front. Instructor de Grignon stepped forward and expressed pride in our determination and the progress we had made.

"Out of eight hundred and seventy-five cadets who started, only seven hundred and eight remain. Seventy-two of those losses occurred during the pass."

Holy shit. We lost one hundred and sixty-seven of us in eight weeks. The pass took out seven of us in just our platoon.

"If you are a Drusearon, you will report to the Pass of Bête Noire. Healers will report to the infirmary. Historians to the first-floor library. Shapeshifters will meet in the outdoor arena. Riders will meet in the flight field. Infantry will meet in sparring gym one. Sorcerers will report to the river's field. You are dismissed."

CHAPTER 11

Rider's Judgment had been a dream of mine ever since I decided to become a Rider. My dad's majestic dragon, Kim, was a striking grey with black dapples along her powerful wings. She was a decent-sized dragon, standing nearly sixteen feet tall. She was my first experience with a dragon, and she always watched over me intently. Without her, I believed every dragon would frighten me.

"I am Major Bhatta, and I will be your instructor, teaching you about all the fliers. We have three majestically beautiful creatures that you can ride: dragons, griffins, and phoenixes. Today, you will face the Rider's Judgment. If you're not familiar with that term, let me explain. You will be given a serum that lasts during the walk among the fliers. They will pass judgment on you. If you have bad intentions or they feel you are not worthy, they will incinerate you or take your head. You also get to see your options. You will walk a single line among the fliers. When you reach the end, you will return to the outdoor arena. There are thirty dragons, twenty griffins, and eighteen phoenixes ready to bond with Riders."

I looked ahead and saw all the fliers lined up about two hundred feet in front of me. They were so beautiful that I thought all the color options were there. They stood facing each other, leaving an aisle for us to walk through. My dad always told me never to look them directly in the eyes, but to observe all the fliers during judgment. He said to appreciate their beauty, stand tall, and not show any fear.

We all moved into a tight single-file line. I wasn't sure how many Riders there were, but I believed we outnumbered the fliers, which made sense because the judgment usually took several of us. My stomach clenched as I remembered that not all of us would make it out alive, and I braced myself for another encounter with death. Thora, who was in my platoon, moved behind me, and I caught sight of Torvi up ahead. We had exchanged greetings here and there, but she belonged to a different platoon than mine. About fifty feet before the aisle where the fliers awaited, a stern Historian sat at a sturdy desk. She meticulously took names and handed us a vial of glowing serum. We advanced slowly, each step heavier than the last. Up ahead, the growling and stomping of the fliers echoed loudly, stirring my stomach into a painful churn. My breakfast threatened to resurface, but I clenched my jaw and refused to let it.

"I am so nervous..." Thora whispered behind me as we took another step forward.

"You have to get it in check. They will sense it," I said.

We moved forward. I was now at the desk with the female recording our names.

"Auriella Blackcreek." She lifted her eyes at me and raised her eyebrows. "Gen—"

"Yes," I cut her off. I didn't want people to hear. She nodded her head, like she understood. She handed me the serum. I poured it down my throat and moved forward. I was now between two dragons, five feet behind the male cadet in front of me. It felt like we were moving slowly. I was observing him, and gods, he was nervous. I saw the shake in his legs. With that, I fell back another foot, because I wasn't sure this was going to go his way.

The first two dragons facing each other were stunning. The one to the right of me was a solid black dragon, standing about fifteen feet tall, which was about average in size. The one on the left was a beautiful red that had various shades of red throughout her scales. I made a point not to stare them in the eyes, nor to show fear or avoid them.

Next to the black and red dragon were two griffins, followed by another group of dragons. One of them was also red, but more vibrant. I watched her twist her head at the cadet in front of me and quickly pull it back. Oh fuck. I knew that look, and before I could even yell at the kid in front of me—

Whooooosh.

She threw a perfect flame at him. Before I could react, the ground turned to ash beneath my feet. The air reeked fiercely of sulfur and not solely from her. I kept walking at the same steady pace, observing the beautiful creatures we could be bonded with. About a quarter of the way through, I spotted a group of stunning phoenixes, which slightly intimidated me—strange because dragons surpassed them in size. They shimmered in shades of vivid red and fiery orange. The one to my right tilted her elegant head toward me, causing my entire body to freeze in place.

"You're a small one, are you sure you don't want to ride a phoenix?" said a voice that made my head spin around to see where it came from.

"It's me..." and the phoenix on my right bobbed her head, but her mouth didn't move. Wait, that was in my fucking head.

"How did you do that?" I said. I knew fliers could communicate with their bonded Rider, but I was not bonded. My mind spun.

"What?" Thora said, her brows knitting as her head tilted.

"The serum you took let us read every cadet's intention, and mind speak without a bond."

"Nothing," I said to Thora.

That was crazy. I didn't even know how to respond. She was gorgeous, but I had always seen myself as a dragon Rider.

"That's a shame, you will make a fantastic Rider when the time comes."

Shit, she was in my head. They were all in my head. I smiled in her direction and kept moving, trying not to think about anything, but my mind had never not thought about anything. It always went down so many rabbit holes. After the phoenixes, there was another set of griffins. They made a chortling sound at me, but I pressed on.

"You're the young Blackcreek," a young female voice said inside my mind, but I wasn't sure who it belonged to. I stood between the two smaller dragons I met during the courses, the silver and the grey one. The silver huffed a steamy breath at me, and I turned my head toward her.

"Yes, that was me. You're a brave one, I like you," The voice said.

"Is that why you blew your breath at me?"

"It's better than incinerating you, isn't it?" Before blowing another breath at my face.

"I do appreciate that."

She really was a gorgeous dragon, but she was pretty small, but so was I.

"Yes, I am small."

Shit. I forgot they were in our heads. *"I said you are gorgeous too."*

"Remember me on bonding day."

Up ahead, I heard another dragon breathe fire, followed by screams. My stomach dropped, and my heart skipped a few beats.

"Don't worry, you have worthy intentions and are a worthy Rider." The silver reassured me.

"Thank you, I guess."

I kept walking, stepping over many charred spots, and I wasn't even close to the end of the judgment line.

"You don't want a baby dragon. I would choose you if you chose me." I heard a deep voice this time, and to my left, there was a dark blue, silvery dragon. His scales shined at certain angles. Goodness, he was a beautiful dragon. I'd never seen a blue like that before.

"Babies can't bond…"

"I am not a baby, and I may be more powerful than you." I heard the silver's voice, and at the same moment, I heard a small roar from down the line.

"Well, no, but she is young, never had a dragon Rider. I have the experience and power you need," he quipped.

"Ohhhh—you have a big ego too." I smiled while still looking to his side. He stood about seventeen feet tall, which was on the larger size. He blew a small puff of fire at me.

"Sorry, didn't mean to offend you," I said.

"Hmm. I think you did. You aren't wrong, though. I do have an ego."

"It seems I have a lot to think about," I told him before nodding my head and moving on.

I continued down the path, admiring all the various dragons, phoenixes, and griffins.

"Did you know they can talk to us?" Thora asked.

"I knew bonded fliers and Riders could, but not unbonded ones. Did they talk to you?"

"One, it truly startled me at first."

"Same, I wasn't expecting that."

I made it to the end of the Rider's Judgment, and I was still alive. I also had three fliers talk to me, which meant I had options—assuming I made it to bonding day. There was another desk at the end with another Historian. She asked for our names and gave us another serum. I lifted the vial to my mouth and poured it in. No more fliers in my head. That felt so violating. I guessed I should get used to it because once I bonded with my dragon, there would be open communication with them.

"Head to the outdoor arena," she said.

Thora was close behind me, so I slowed my pace so we could walk together. We both headed towards the arena.

"Still going for a griffin?" I asked her.

"Yes, and a beautiful dark blue spoke to me. What about you?"

"I had a phoenix and two dragons speak to me, but I am leaning towards a dragon."

"Which one?"

"I am not sure yet. I don't want to make an impulsive decision about this."

"That's fair. Super cool that three fliers wanted you."

"I am honestly not sure what to think about it."

We both entered the arena. There were two large gates for dragons to pass through, one on the flight field side and the other in the courtyard. The entire perimeter had a twenty-foot-thick stone ledge to support landing and perching fliers. There were seats lining the walls, similar to a stadium classroom. In the center was a large open field. In the upper corner, where it met the dining facility, there was a stage with twenty high pedestal chairs overlooking the arena. Officers occupied the area.

On the ground, numerous cadets gathered, most of them clad in black uniforms. The seating area near the stage was sectioned off, with signs reading "Feather Wing," "Dragon Wing," and "Eagle Wing." In the center, a sign marked "First-Years." Looking around, I saw that the seats for upperclassmen were filled, while the first-years stood together, mingling among themselves. Standing there felt awkward, as we were the center of attention for all the commanding upper-class students and officers. I scanned the sections, searching for my friends, but I couldn't find them.

An hour passed, and it looked like most of us first-years who went through judgment were here.

"Fall in, first-years!" an officer shouted.

We all moved into formation, standing at attention. Since we hadn't been assigned to specific platoons or squads, we created a line of ten across and filled it in. Loud wing beats approached. It didn't sound like just one, but I couldn't turn to look. I heard them land on the arena ledges behind us. A tremendously large yellow-gold dragon landed on the edge near the stage, causing the ground to shake. At that moment, I saw an average-sized grey dragon circling to land. As it drew closer, I noticed the black dappling in its wings—Kim. My father had to be there. I shifted my gaze back to the stage, where he sat in the front row. I was pretty sure he glared at me. I kept my face neutral and stayed at attention. Kim touched down between the yellow-gold dragon and the stage. All around, we heard other powerful fliers landing.

"At ease," an officer yelled.

I finally looked around and saw all the fliers up top, looking down and watching us. These belonged to officers and leaders. Next to the yellow gold, there was a significantly large, beautiful phoenix. As I looked around, I counted ten dragons, ten griffins, and four phoenixes.

"Congratulations and welcome, new Riders! I am Major General Kamban. I command all Sandorg. Above you are the fliers bonded to the officers sitting here, as well as the Wing Commanders for your wings. Ninety-four of you entered the Rider's Judgment. Seventy-nine of you made it through alive, making this one of the smallest years to start.

Now, I'd like to introduce some of the fine officers joining me. General Blackcreek, who oversees the military, has joined us. Brigade General Scullin oversees the Rider's branch. For instructors, we have: Captain Vindex, Captain Pascal, Captain Wormald, Captain Gile, Captain Rivet, Major Fogg, Major Duft, Major Bhatta, Major Melamora, Major Quillet, and Major Hildegard. Now I will turn this over to Brigade General Scullin."

"I also want to say congratulations and welcome to my command. There are three wings: Feather Wing, Dragon Wing, and Eagle Wing. Each wing has two platoons: Electric and Fire. In each of those platoons, there are two squads. Breaking it down further, each squad has four flights representing their academic year. In one wing, there are twenty-four cadet leadership positions. The only position not filled is flight guards for first-years. This will be filled in a couple of weeks, chosen by the leadership of your wing."

A Historian walked up the stairs to the stage and handed Captain Wormald a thick, rolled-up paper. He took that paper and gave it to Brigade General Scullin, who nodded his head in thanks.

"Let's assign your new roles. Wing Commander of the Feather Wing is cadet Nikolai Corson. Wing Commander of the Dragon Wing is cadet Casey Verlander. Wing Commander of the Eagle Wing is cadet Arya Cusick. When I call your name, please move to the section with your new wing. Feather Wing, Electric Platoon, First Squad, first-year cadets: Auriella Blackcreek, Lorenzo Carnethon, Sadie Devins, Akira Faraday, Clara Heston, Micah Riggins, and Jackson Zardes."

The six other cadets and I moved out of formation and headed toward the Feather Wing section. He kept calling out names, and cadets broke off, moving swiftly to their assigned positions. I saw Thora heading toward our section. Thank the gods, someone I recognized! She was in the same platoon but in the second squad. I looked up into our wing—my heart thudded with joy—Lili. She looked just as stunning as I last saw her a year ago during summer break. Her dark brown hair was braided and pulled into a neat bun. Her light golden eyes gazed at me, filled with genuine joy. She had been my best friend since birth. She was a year older than me and had arrived here when she was nineteen, while I started at twenty. Both of her parents were skilled fliers—her mother rode a majestic griffin, and her father bonded a fierce dragon. Our parents served at many of the same forts during our childhood. Our mothers had been best friends until my mother passed away.

"Wing Commanders, they are now yours," Brigade General Scullin said.

At the exact top row, a quite handsome guy stood up. Shit, he was tall too. Standing easily about six feet three, he had medium-brown skin with eight tightly woven braids. His eyes were the real showstoppers—they were green. It was a little hard to tell down here, but I thought there were flecks of brown in them.

"I am Wing Commander Corson. Welcome to the Feather Wing. I will have the first-years move into four lines, based on their platoon and squad. Electric platoon, First squad all to the right, then Electric's Second squad. Fire platoon First squad next to them, and Fire's Second squad all the way to the left."

We all shifted and moved into four single lines. As we did that, seven other upperclassmen stood up.

"For our entire wing, my Executive Officer is Aelina Kasteel. Electric Platoon, your Platoon Leader is Lilian Beverli, a third-year cadet. For the First Squad, your Squad Leader is a fourth-year, Persephone Emmen. For the Second Squad, your Squad Leader is Victor Corzine, a third-year cadet. Fire Platoon, your Platoon Leader is Eleanor Kapel, a fourth-year cadet. For that first squad, your Squad Leader is fourth-year, Adrian Holmstock, and the second squad's leader is second-year, Josephine Nieman." Corson told us.

I stood there with pride and joy, knowing that my best friend was a Platoon Leader and was in charge of my platoon. She had done well for herself while here.

"It is important to understand rank structure. If you don't come from a large military family, you might not know. The basics are that I trump everyone in this wing. When I am unavailable to make decisions, Kasteel stands in my place or makes decisions based on the best interests of the wing. Platoon Leaders outrank Squad Leaders and then Flight Guides. However, the Fire Platoon Leader can't discipline or command the Electric Platoon's cadets, and vice versa. However, it is recommended to follow their guidance. Any questions?" Corson looked around at all of us, taking us in.

"Now, Squad Leaders will be taking first-year students to the first-year chambers on the seventh floor. As first-year students, you will all have to share rooms. Each room contains a Military Manual and a Code of Ethics, as well as a Riders' Code of Ethics. If you aren't familiar with these, make sure to study them. All branches will host a celebration evening in the courtyard and arena. The gate between the two will be open. Food and refreshments will be available at dining facilities on both sides. You are now dismissed to your Squad Leaders. Kasteel, Kapel, and Beverli will be with me. We need to set up for this evening's festivities."

I guessed I wouldn't get a big hug from Lili until that evening. Emmen motioned for our squad to follow her. She led us out of the arena into the flight field, circled to Watch Tower One. We climbed seven stories and went through the door to the first-year chambers.

"Each room has three beds. Rooms one through twelve are for Feather Wing, thirteen through twenty-four are for Dragon Wing, and twenty-five through thirty-six are for Eagle Wing," she told us.

The second squad joined us, and Corzine stood next to Emmen. They looked at each other and whispered among themselves.

"Cadets Blackcreek, Devins, and Stoot are in room one, and cadets Aamir, Heston, and Faraday are in room two," Emmen said.

"Cadets Leon and Sulivar are in room ten, cadets Zardes and Zufall are in room eleven, and cadets Carnethon, Nanda, and Riggins are in room twelve. Due to lower numbers, some people will only have two in a room," Corzine stated.

"Place your things in your room and meet back out here, as we will be doing a tour and getting your uniforms," Emmen said.

Sadie, Thora, and I all entered our room. The size of the room matched my expectations, given how close the doors were. There were three twin beds spaced about five feet apart, each with a small nightstand beside it. At the end of each bed on the opposite wall, there were three wooden armoires, one for each of us. A tall window on the far wall offered a view of the dining facility roof, the flight field, and the arena. I bet room two had a beautiful view of the fields and woods. I placed my bag on the bed closest to the window.

"Can I take this bed?" I asked my new roommates.

"Yeah, I'll take the middle, if that's good with you both?" Thora said.

"That leaves me here, which is good with me," Sadie said.

Thora and I both nodded. That was simple enough. They both set their bags on their beds, and we headed back out into the hall with the rest of our platoon.

"First squad, line up behind me," Emmen said.

"Second Squad, behind me," Corzine announced.

Everyone lined up. The Fire Platoon began to enter the wing and receive their room assignments.

"We will go this way," Emmen said, pointing down the long hall. Corzine told his group that they were heading toward the watchtower. It made sense to keep the tours in smaller groups. We continued down the hall. Suddenly, Emmen stopped.

"There are bathing rooms located every four bedrooms, for any gender." She motioned us inside one.

We all moved inside. The bathroom looked nice. There were eight sinks along one wall, followed by six doors. She opened one of the doors, and inside there was a toilet and a square shower big enough for one person. There were hooks on the opposite wall to hang your items.

"All the bathing rooms on floors seven and six are the same."

We left the bathing room and continued walking down the dim, narrow hall. Each door was numbered and had a small light outside to illuminate the dark corridor. When we reached room thirty, she paused.

"You're all used to the large sparring gym in the Bravo Wing, but your floor has a smaller sparring gym available. There is also some workout equipment in there."

She opened the door for us to look in but didn't go inside. On the opposite side, she opened another door, revealing a laundry room with washers and dryers.

"It's pretty self-explanatory, but if your parents washed your clothes before you got here, this is where you should do it. Nobody wants to smell your funky asses." She looked back and smiled.

We all let out a small laugh. It's good to know she had a sense of humor. At the end of the hall, a door led to a staircase that descended.

"On the other side of this wall are the Healer's quarters. The only way to reach their chambers is to go down to the third floor and enter their stairwell. The third floor is the only level that connects all the chambers."

She motioned for us to follow and went down the staircase. She gestured toward the door, which had writing saying "Sixth Floor."

"This is where the second-years stay, minus any that are in leadership roles," she told us.

She continued down the stairs, motioned to the fifth floor, and told us that was where the third-years slept. We kept going down. She said the fourth floor was for fourth-year students. That was what Professor Melamora told us on our first day, so many weeks ago. We reached the third floor and entered that hallway. She motioned to the left and said there were two classrooms down there.

"Major Hildegard is our flying instructor. He's specific to the Riders and Drusearons only. His room is on the left. Major Bhatta, whom you should have met, teaches us about the flier type. His room is on the right."

She turned right and walked down the hallway. She told us the classroom on the right was for the Healers, so we wouldn't be using it. She motioned for us to enter the room on the left, across from the other. When we entered, we saw a room with beds, each separated by curtains.

"This is the clinic room, meaning if it's not life-threatening or doesn't require a mender, you can come here. They can stitch you up, give you medicine, whatever you may be needing," she told us before turning around and walking out. She pointed to another door, saying, "This door is for the stairwell to access the Healer's quarters, set up like ours." We continued down the hall toward the Bravo Wing. There were two more large classrooms.

"The one on the right is Captain Vindex's classroom. He teaches magic to all students. The one on the left is a Drusearon classroom, not relevant to you. Like the other quarters, the areas above and below us are for Drusearons."

It made me realize I had not seen Zane for several days, and I began to miss him. I did not know which room he was in or which floor he occupied. At the end of the hall, there was a door directly ahead.

"We are entering Watch Tower Two. There are landings on each floor that lead into the quarters for the Drusearons. We will go across, staying on level three of the Bravo Wing."

We all kept following her. As we moved along, another group of new cadets started their tour in the opposite direction. This wing we knew better because we had lived in it for eight weeks.

"Most of you should be familiar with this wing since you lived here. The barracks where you stayed are converted into guest quarters during the school year. Floors one and two contain the Historian's quarters. The sublevels are the library, and you are only permitted on sublevel one. Most of level three in the Bravo Wing consists of two large sparring gyms, where you guys sparred. Captain Gile and Captain Rivet are our sparring instructors. The classroom before is Captain Wormald, the Historian professor. You will have him once a week."

Unlike the hallway for the Alpha Wing, this hallway was closer to the courtyard rather than in the middle. It had large windows overlooking the courtyard. There was one large sparring gym, followed by a door that led into the stadium classroom.

"You all have been inside, but the stadium classroom is where we hold our current events lecture, discussing what's happening in our military. We review war strategies and recent developments there. The class is led by Major Fogg, Major Melamora, and Captain Pascal. You might recognize all three from drill instructions during basic training. Of course, there are doors for all levels, as it spans the entire seven floors."

We kept moving forward and arrived at the second sparring gym, nearly identical to the one on the opposite side. We pressed on until we reached Watch Tower Three. We crossed over on level three of the Charlie Wing as before. She gestured toward one of the spacious classrooms and explained that was where Major Duft taught wielding once students gained their abilities. She signaled with her hands and clarified that the other classrooms were explicitly designated for Shapeshifters, situated directly above and below us. The middle section was reserved for Sorcerers, while the end area was for Infantry. She pointed toward the far end and identified it as Watch Tower Four, then turned us around to head back to Watch Tower Three.

Once inside, she climbed to the eighth floor, pushed open the sturdy gate, and we crossed the narrow bridge that connected the campus to the administration building. Watch Tower Four also had a small bridge connecting it to Watch Tower Five, which led into the busy infirmary. A ground-level bridge crossed the rushing river. Watch Tower Three had a long, steep bridge leading to Watch Tower Six, the tallest of the towers. It also served as the check-in point when we first arrived. We crossed over and entered a reception area set up from my initial arrival for basic training. A desk sat near the entrance, opening into a spacious room filled with racks of uniformed clothing, mostly black.

"You'll report your name, then you'll be handed your uniforms. You'll receive five black tees, five black leather pants, two black leather jackets, one black leather field coat, and black combat boots. Your tees, jackets, and coats will have your last name sewn on the upper left side. On the right arm, there will be a small gold Feather Wing to show you're a first-year in the Feather Wing Rider's branch. There are many symbols, but the number on the right side indicates the year you are. Go to each person to collect your items. I'll be here on this wall waiting."

The bustling room crowded with cadets eagerly collecting their uniforms. I approached each station, announced my name, and received pieces of my uniform from attentive staff. Each stop took some time due to the large number of cadets collecting their gear. This likely prompted many cadets to return early for an advantageous head start. Once I had my uniform, hands full, I made my way back to Emmen. Once all seven of us were with her, she motioned toward the door, and we crossed the bridge again. We took a left and went down Charlie Wing to Tower Four, then went down to the ground floor, cut across the flight field, and returned to Tower One. We went up to the seventh floor.

"That concludes our tour. You are all free to do as you please. The first day is chaotic with everyone running around. Some people are seeing menders to heal from basic injuries, which, if you are in need, is an option. Most people tidy up their belongings in their rooms and prepare for this evening's celebration. Most wear a nice dress outfit. If you don't have one, you can wear one of your uniforms, or there is a lending closet of clothing back at the admin office, a floor below where we got uniforms. There are fancy suits and ball gowns."

She turned to walk away but quickly turned back. "Oh, also, I recommend always having at least two daggers on you. People are cutthroat, and without powers, you are sitting ducks. That said, per the code of ethics, no one may cause harm to another within the same wing." Then she left.

Thora, Sadie, and I headed into our rooms. I started rummaging through my bag, which I had just accessed that morning after basic training. I packed a few books for reading and studying. I brought six of my favorite lightweight, sharp daggers. I also brought two elegant formal gowns and a pair of flat shoes to match them.

Additionally, I brought some sleek black leather pants crafted with durable Kevlar, along with armored shirts also made of tough Kevlar. I heard stories about how ruthless others could be—not just Riders but members of various branches. My father was a military general, which meant he had made fierce enemies along the way. Since our names were sewn into our uniforms, other cadets would likely piece together my identity.

I chose a single black dress that reached down to my calves. It was tight around my torso and flared out at my thighs. The dress shimmered with constant reflections from its jeweled surface. I fastened both of my thigh dagger belts and sheathed two sharp daggers. I let my hair down, allowing the natural sandy blonde curls to cascade freely. My hair extended about four inches beyond my buttocks and appeared to grow an inch during basic training. Usually, my hair stayed in a braid, except when I washed it.

Thora also brought a sleek black gown that was floor-length and semi-tight, accentuating her figure. She stood a couple of inches taller than me at five feet five inches. She left her dark brown hair down, letting it cascade to her mid-back. Her olive skin complemented her light brown eyes, enhancing her natural beauty. I paused to admire how stunning she looked.

Sadie didn't bring a gown with her. Instead of going to the lending closet, I offered her my second gown. It looked stunning on her. The dress was floor-length for me, but for her, it hit mid-calf, since she was five feet seven inches tall, making her four inches taller than I was. Thora handed her a pair of black heels because they had the same shoe size. She chose to wear her light brown hair in a sleek bun, though I noticed it was slightly past her shoulders before wrapping it up. Her light skin with pink undertones contrasted strikingly against the solid black gown. She had piercing dark blue eyes and lengthy eyelashes, which immediately caught my attention.

CHAPTER 12

All the cadets headed into the courtyard. The six of us females in the electric platoon decided to walk in together. The courtyard looked beautiful. Floating orbs of light hovered overhead. Gentle music played, and groups of people gathered. The dining area doors were open for us to grab food and mingle. Maybe this was the college's way of helping us become friends before we turned against each other.

While going through basic training and being in a diverse squad with members from all branches, I couldn't imagine wanting to hurt anyone simply because they chose a different path. As we passed the outdoor arena, vibrant floating light orbs danced in the sky. Groups of cadets gathered nearby. The six of us gradually separated, each finding friends to talk to. I found Ophelia and embraced her warmly. We had grown close during basic, and of course, she had saved my life, which meant a great deal to me.

Suddenly, I heard shrieking, and before I could turn around, someone pulled me into the biggest, warmest bear hug I had ever experienced. I didn't need to open my eyes. I knew it was Lili, her frantic shrieks and tight hugs revealing her identity. She held me so firmly that I struggled to breathe. I coughed, and she finally released me, still gripping my arms. She stepped back to look at me, her height towering over mine. I stood at five foot three and never caught up to her.

"Oh Auri, I have missed you so much," she exclaimed with a wide smile.

"Me too. I can't believe I am in your platoon!"

"I know, out of six Platoon Leaders, you got me!"

"And you made Platoon Leader, that's amazing."

"Thank you. How was basic?"

"It was an experience. I got severely injured during the pass, but I made it out."

"Oh Auri, I didn't know. I am glad you are okay."

"I am good, you know me, I am a survivor."

She waved at someone behind me, and as I started to turn around to see who it was, I was pulled into another big embrace—Alexander.

"Ella, I've missed you so much. Gods, I dreamt of holding you again." His voice dropped, and warmth filled his eyes as he pulled me close.

I pulled back from him and looked up. He reached down, and before he could kiss me, I looked down, offering my forehead for him to kiss. He withdrew, sucked his teeth, and furrowed his brows at me. "What's wrong?"

"We are not—" I started, but a cough cut me off, and a familiar tingling crawled through me.

He eased away slowly and smiled, a look that revealed his annoyance yet masked it from others—an expression that sent chills down my spine. He turned sharply toward the source of the cough. My stomach clenched tightly, and I wrestled with how I would introduce him. *Oh, hey, mate, these are my childhood best friends, who are twins—oh, and we used to date.*

"Zane Braegon, this is Auriella Blackcreek." Alex introduced him to *me*. I was so confused.

"We've met," he said with a smile.

I felt an overwhelming sense of anger rush through me. It startled me for a moment, then I realized it was not my anger, but his. Why was *he* angry?

"Oh?" Lili said, raising an eyebrow at me, then turned to him. "Well, Auri is our childhood best friend."

"Alex has been one of my closest friends for the past two years," Zane said, keeping his gaze fixed on me.

Anxiety spiked, drying out my throat and locking my tongue. My mate—destined, bound—was best friends with the man I'd dated on and off for five years. The same man who had taken my virginity. Fantastic. My stomach twisted, and I forced down a hard swallow.

"Let's all get some food and sit down," Lili said with an empathetic look, as if she realized Zane was more than just a casual acquaintance. She was well aware of Alex and my relationship and had witnessed all its ups and downs firsthand.

"Yes, let's," Zane said, his face very neutral, but also looking like he was about to throw daggers out of them.

I let the three of them lead, and I followed behind. My mind raced, and honestly, I was on the edge of a full-blown anxiety attack. Zane slowed his pace to walk beside me.

"We should talk." His voice cut low between us, the words heavy enough to press against my skin.

"Not here," I said, looking at the ground.

"First floor, room two. Come in through Watch Tower Two. I will leave here in an hour or so," he told me before he picked back up the pace and stood next to Alex.

Shit. He was somehow in a leadership role, positioned on the first floor. I refused to let it bother me. It wouldn't kill me, and I told myself it would be okay. I hadn't seen my best friend in over a year. I increased my pace and moved to stand beside Lili. We all grabbed some food and headed to the expansive arena, where large, glowing bistro tables had been set up for cadets to enjoy a meal under the bright light orbs. I sat down between Lili and Zane, with Alex sitting across from me.

"So, how do you all know each other?" Alex asked, glancing at me and back to Zane.

"Ah, simply around. We sparred once, and she's a hell of a sparrer," Zane said, looking at me.

"Yes, she is. We used to spar a lot when we were growing up. Of course, it always ended in something more." He shot me a big smile, and I rolled my eyes.

The anger I felt earlier came over me again. I looked at Zane, who didn't look angry. I placed my hand in my lap, then slid it onto his knee and squeezed it. I was hoping he'd understand that I was silently letting him know I could feel him. I didn't keep my hand there long. I didn't want either of them to notice. He shot me a side glance and a slight smile, as if he understood.

"How did a dragon Rider become best friends with a Drusearon?" I asked, trying to change the subject.

Alex let out a light laugh and looked over at Zane. "We were in the same platoon in basic, we simply clicked. We have had each other's asses over the last two years. We both fly, only in different ways."

Zane looked unimpressed with this conversation, or perhaps that was his regular expression, because neither Alex nor Lili seemed to act otherwise. Every time we spoke, he was giving me subtle, devious smiles, or he displayed worry because I was on death's door.

"How has the ice wielding been going?" I asked Lili.

When she came home for summer break after her first year, she beamed with happiness that she got the ability to throw ice. Alex could wield fire making them a deadly combo. It was also ironic as they could balance each other out, as they had their whole lives.

"It is going really well. I always have to have some sort of water in order to manipulate it."

"I love to hear that, that first summer home was a little rough."

"My fire wielding is going great too. Thanks for asking—" Alex added.

"I mean I didn't, but that's *great* for you." I said to him. Lili let out a laugh.

"Hey man, are you good?" Alex asked Zane. Well, maybe this wasn't his usual expression.

"This is the face you usually give your wing, the unimpressed, unfazed Zane," Lili added.

"Your wing?" I looked over at him.

"I am fine, merely have a lot of things going on in here." He looked between them and tapped his head. He turned and looked at me. "I am the Executive Officer of the Black Wing."

"Oh, that's cool," I said, smiling.

"I am going to go get another drink. Want anything?" Zane said, looking over at us.

"I'll join you," Alex said, standing up. Both of them strolled back towards the dining facility.

"What the hell is going on between you two?" Lili said, in a lowered voice.

"I mean, it's nothing new. He broke my heart over and over again. I refuse to go down that path again."

"I didn't mean you and Alex, I mean—"

"Nothing," I cut her off, before she could finish.

"MmmHmm, yeah, that's what you said about you and Alex at first."

"Alex broke parts of me that I am still trying to fix. What happened to us five years ago really messed with me, especially since I arrived here."

"I understand what you mean. When I arrived here, the winged Fae—I mean Drusearons—triggered my anxiety attacks, all of them were him. I've learned that there are so many incredible Drusearons here, and we shouldn't judge them based on the actions of one."

"Yeah," I said, looking down at my plate and pushing my food around.

Zane and Alex rejoined our table, drinks in hand. Zane handed me one, and Alex handed Lili hers. I took a sip and realized it was a sweet mixed drink with a strong pineapple flavor. It was delicious, but I knew I should keep it at one.

"Let's dance," Alex said to us, "I get Auriella first."

Great, I was a possession.

"I'll spin Zane right on around," Lili said, afterwards grabbing Zane's hand and pulling him to the center where everyone else was dancing. A twinge of jealousy ran through me. I'd never been jealous of Lili before, but I mostly dated her brother.

I walked beside Alex as we approached the dance floor. We faced each other, and damn, this felt so awkward. To make it worse, the music changed to a slower song. Alex reached for my waist and pulled me closer. I wrapped my arms around his shoulders, and we began dancing slowly.

"Now that you're here, maybe we can give this another shot?" he told me softly.

"No. Please, let's remain friends. We are better as friends," I pleaded with him.

"You weren't saying that last year when I was home on leave."

"And as soon as you fucked me, and I told you I was still going to become a dragon Rider, you told me you couldn't do a relationship."

"I didn't want a long distance."

"You just wanted a good fuck."

"I didn't want you to join the military, but you did. I still love you."

"I don't."

"Have you moved on? It's only been a year."

"A year is a long time, people grow and change, but you left me crying…"

The song changed into another slower one. Fuck me.

"Let's swap," Lili said as she moved over and took her brother's hand, seemingly sensing where it was headed.

"Can I have this dance, *Auri*?" Zane asked, smiling at me and clearly enunciating my name.

I simply nodded my head and smiled. He grabbed my hand and pulled me closer before wrapping his arms around my waist. My heart skipped a beat. It always felt like home when he was touching me.

"That was sounding a little tense," he said, looking down at me, but I was avoiding eye contact.

"Yeah, it always is with him."

"Look at me," his voice dropped low and sounded so stern.

I looked at him, my eyes meeting his, and electricity coursed through me, as it had done so many times before.

"Good girl." He growled at me. My heart skipped a beat or five. Fuck. I wanted to kiss him so bad right in that moment and I couldn't.

"Do you feel a shock through your body when we look at each other?"

"Yeah, I am guessing you do as well," he smirked.

"Will that ever fade or stop?"

"I don't know, but I do know I am holding every restraint from kissing you and caressing that beautiful tongue of yours."

I immediately felt my cheeks flush with heat, wetness seep between my legs, and my thighs tingling.

"That's the response I like to see," he said, giving me that beautiful, devious smile.

"Let's dance!" Lili shouted as the song jumped into an upbeat rhythm. She seized my hand and Zane's, yanking us toward Alex before spinning free and breaking into motion. Her body flowed with the beat, loose and wild, every step daring the rest of us to follow. I lingered at the edge, shy, my feet heavy while hers seemed made for music.

"I'm actually going to head in, I need to do some paperwork," Zane said. Gave us a nod and walked towards the courtyard.

Lili held my hands, and we continued dancing. For a brief moment, I forgot about the dire situation I was in. Alex left at some point. I didn't notice when or where he went. We danced to several songs, and then I realized I needed to find Zane. I was certain he had questions. I knew I did.

"I am exhausted, so I'm going to head in," I said.

"Yeah, yeah, it's been a long day. If you need me, I'm on the second floor, eighth room."

"Thanks."

CHAPTER 13

I knocked twice, softly against the door. It flew open, and before I could speak, he grabbed my arms and pulled me inside. My back hit the wood, his hand locked at the base of my head, and his mouth crashed against mine. The kiss burned—hungry, demanding, stealing every thought I had. Leather clung low to his hips, nothing else. Gods. My breath hitched. His chest was tan and perfect, golden hair tousled. Black ink curled tribal across his shoulders, flowing down his back and tracing his arm to the elbow. He looked untouchable. Too much.

His hands slid up under my dress and gripped my ass. Heat roared through me as he lifted me, my legs wrapping tight around him before I could think. My dress rode high, pooling at my waist, leaving me bare. It was too quick. Too much, too fast. My heart rattled, torn between wanting to sink into him and the voice screaming that I should slow down. Gods help me, I didn't know which part of me was louder.

My underwear was getting soaked. No doubt he felt that on his stomach. He let go of one of his hands and moved it up my back, to the back of my head, before he grabbed a handful of my hair. He pulled my head back and started kissing down my neck. I ground myself against him as I leaned my head back. I let out a soft moan. Fuck. I wanted more. I wanted him. I needed him.

I let go of my legs, bringing me back down to the floor. I stood on my toes, nipped his lip before drawing it into my mouth, sucking on it. He let out this growl moan combo, and my gods, it almost undid me. I reached my arm down between us, feeling in between his legs, pressing my hand onto his thick hard cock. He clearly wanted me just as bad. I rubbed my hand up and down against him, doing circular motions through his pants. He let out a deep moan.

"If you keep doing that, I will take you to my bed and fuck you," he growled.

"Maybe I want you to fuck me, like there is no tomorrow," I moaned.

He reached behind me, unzipping my dress. He moved his hands to my shoulders and pulled the straps down my arms, letting my dress fall to the side and drop to the floor. My breasts immediately tingled when the cold air hit my nipples. I reached down and unsnapped his pants, but before I could start pulling them down, he grabbed me up into his arms and took me to the side of his bed.

He gently laid me onto the edge of the bed, following me down, kissing my neck. He moved down my neck and down to my breast before taking my nipple in his mouth. He sucked my nipple before gently pulling it away from my body. I was softly moaning, breathing hard, and fucking soaking my underwear. He stood back up, not dropping his gaze from me.

"Mmmhmm, what a good girl getting all wet for me," he said in that deep voice that I think I would do whatever he wanted. I moaned in response. He reached down between us, placed his thumb over my clit, and pressed in and moved in a distinctly slow circular motion. If he took off my underwear, I was pretty sure I would come undone. It had been way too long, and gods, I might explode, and he wasn't even in me. I wanted to fuck him so bad.

I leaned up on my forearms and reached for his pants to finish removing them. I unzipped them, afterwards moving my hands to his sides to push his pants down. They started to move down his hips, but he grabbed my hands and gently pushed my back down on the bed. He reached down to the sides of my underwear and pulled them, stepping back, taking them down my legs.

"Are you sure you want this?" I asked him.

"I have never been so sure about something as I am right now, but if you have doubts, we can stop."

"No doubts. Just want to make sure you won't regret fucking your best friend's ex. I have wanted you for weeks."

"One, I prefer you not bring that up while I am about to feast on you. Two, I don't care about that. Neither you nor I can help our fate. Three, I have wanted this from the moment our eyes locked in the courtyard."

He didn't give me time to respond before he pressed his lips in between my thighs. He took a finger and drove it down one side, up the other side, and back down. Oh, fuck me. This felt so good. I didn't think anyone had ever touched me this way. He slid one finger in gently, moving it in and out. He took his tongue, slowly moving it up and down the middle of my folds. I could barely breathe between moaning. Every time he came to the top, he did a circular movement with his tongue, wrapping it around my clit. I was on the verge of losing all control.

"Oh gods, Zane, I am about to cum, and I might be loud." I managed to get out in between breaths and moaning.

He let out a devious little laugh. "My room has a sound shield, so let it go for me, my love. Fucking scream for me, Auri."

Just as he demanded, I let it all out. In between loud moans, I was saying fuck. I was pretty sure stars flashed into my eyes. I felt an entire surge of electricity shoot through my body, much stronger than I had experienced in the past. My legs started shaking, and my arms were shaking. He finished dropping his pants to the ground and began kissing up my body. I was still trying to catch my breath. He stopped to lick circles around my right nipple before moving to my left.

He moved up, kissing my neck. I grabbed his face and pulled it to mine. I bit his lip before opening my mouth and letting my tongue slide into his, crashing into his. He grabbed a hold of my tongue, before he let go and pushed his tongue into my mouth. I started sucking on his tongue. He let out a growl. He reached his arm down, under my back, and slid me up the bed some before climbing onto the bed with me. He let his body down closer, and I could feel his hardness pressed against my thigh. He felt so hard and thick against me, so fucking glorious.

"I probably won't last a long time. It has been quite a long time for me."

"Same... oh wait, you already made me cum with ease," I said, giving him a smirk.

He reached down and pushed himself in slow, savoring every second. Fuck I wanted all of him. He felt so fucking good. I could instantly feel more wetness flooding the area. My entire body rushed with heat. He moved in me more before pulling out. Oh, he was fucking teasing me. I was gripping his back as hard as I could, and I was nipping and gently sucking on his neck. He moved in a little more with this stroke before pulling himself almost all the way out and stroking just the tip in. He pushed himself all the way in, hitting every part of me inside. Tingles rushed throughout me. I was moaning again in between my ragged breaths. He was breathing hard, too. I could feel another orgasm climbing, and I didn't know how much longer I could hold out.

"You're going to... make me... cum again..." I barely made out.

He grabbed my sides and flipped us over, putting me on top of him. "I want to watch you cum all over me, my love."

I leaned over him. He had both of his hands on my hips, gripped tight. I was riding him slow, wanting to savor every single second. We stared into each other's eyes. One of his hands moved to cup my neck pulling me in to kiss him. He slid over to nip on my neck, and I nipped his ear. He let out a deep moan, almost sending me over the edge. I pushed myself into a sitting position, and he moved his free hand to cup my breast as I rode him slow and deliberate.

We locked eyes again, I stared into his pale blue eyes as they flared in excitement. I felt the electricity shoot through me again, just as it had, and I felt myself losing control. I moaned much louder, screaming fuck in between moans. He gripped my hips with both hands, moving me faster on top. My entire body felt like it was being electrocuted, in the most pleasurable way.

He was moaning and grunting, which was further driving my orgasm much more intensely. We both let out a loud moan, his much more audible than mine. The whole room vibrated from the roar he let out. He pulled me down, our chests meeting.

I felt my entire body flush with heat, hot and burning. Every single part of my body tingled. Static electricity took over my whole body. My mind felt tingly, like I was on a cloud, euphoric. I had never felt this before. I was not wholly sure what I had just felt. It was the most glorious, pleasurable orgasm I had ever felt. My breathing was ragged and desperate. I reminded myself to slow my breathing, get it under control.

CHAPTER 14

His warmth still clung to my skin, but silence was dangerous—it left me alone with my thoughts. My heart should be slowing, steadying. Instead, it beat harder, each thud sparking a hundred questions I couldn't turn off.

I wasn't exactly regretting it, but gods, I couldn't stop second-guessing myself. I'd promised I wouldn't hand myself over so fast. Every time I'd moved this fast before, I'd paid for it—little pieces of me shaved off in quiet, invisible ways. Sex meant control when I chose it. Only control never lasted long once the quiet arrived. Guilt poured into me, but giving myself to someone was a power I struggled with.

That old scar inside me whispered it was about control. About proving no one could take from me again without my permission. If I chose it and started it, then it was mine. Mine to give. Mine to end.

It was the same pattern that had followed me for years—one more impulsive choice, one more way to stay ahead of my own ghosts. For a heartbeat, it worked. For a heartbeat, I felt powerful, untouchable.

Now the quiet pressed in, and doubt crawled beneath my skin. Was this strength, or just another desperate attempt to silence the past? Was I moving too quickly? Was I letting him take pieces of me I couldn't afford to give?

The thoughts spun faster, chasing each other in circles until my chest tightened. I wanted to focus on the way his hand had steadied me, the way his voice had pulled me back into myself. But my brain never let me sit still—it tore at everything, tested every angle, demanded to know how this ended before I'd even caught my breath.

Maybe this time was different. Maybe he was different.

I pressed my face into his shoulder, letting the silence stretch. It was safer that way, safer than saying the questions that gnawed at me. But silence would never last with him.

"And I thought I came in here to talk," I whispered in his ear.

"I had plans to talk, I did, I promise. Once I saw you, I let all self-control go. I guess it's better to have fun before we talk about serious things."

"I hadn't wanted to move this fast either. My self-control has never been my strong suit."

He handed me a towel and helped me clean up. I stood up to grab my clothes, but he grabbed me and pulled me back into his arms.

"Let's cuddle while we talk. I want to feel you next to me."

"Where do we start?"

"Ella, huh?" he said, almost annoyed, maybe bitter.

I pulled my head to the side to look up at him, raising my eyebrows at him. "He told you?"

"What he told me was that he was in love with a girl that he had been off and on with. He said her name was Ella. He mentioned that it was complicated, but that when he went home last year, you two spent time together. He told me about your birthmark, which is why I ran that day on the mat. Later I thought, since it was a bloodline birthmark, maybe it was someone else because clearly you didn't go by Ella."

"He is the only one who calls me Ella. When we were little, he couldn't say Auri or Auriella, but he could say Ella. It's always been a nickname that he's called me. It's not one that I go by."

"I hate that he has a special nickname for you," he said. He slid my hair to the side, lifting my chin and placing a kiss on my lips.

"Is that jealousy I hear?"

"No, maybe I don't know. Can I be jealous?"

"Jealousy and possessiveness are two different things, as long as you don't confuse them."

"I'll try not to be both. My bond with you has feelings I didn't know existed."

"Alex and I were over a long time ago. If there was even a remote feeling left. The moment our eyes linked, it was gone. We are better as friends. He nearly broke me."

"What do you want us to be?" he choked out.

"Um. I guess I hadn't thought of that," I couldn't imagine being with someone else, nor him with someone else, but I didn't want to sound clingy.

"Look, I want to be honest. I don't think I can handle you being with someone else. In the courtyard earlier, Alex reached down to kiss you, and I nearly lost it. I put all the pieces together in those minutes that you were the girl he always talked about. I felt my temper rising, but I kept it controlled."

"I felt your anger." I told him, looking back up at him, placing my hand on his heart, "I felt it again when he mentioned sparring."

"Sorry," he said, kissing my forehead.

"I don't know what label, or if we need labels, but I want us to be exclusive."

"Am I allowed to kiss you in front of other people?"

"Is that allowed? Are there rules?"

"No rules on intermingling, and you are far from my chain of command."

"In that case, yes, but I think I should talk with Alex first."

"Can I talk to him first?" He asked, which gave me a sense of relief.

"I guess, if that's what you prefer. I am going to tell Lili, though. So, am I going to run into any of your exes here?"

"Um... No..."

"Alrighty then."

"So... There is something I need to ask..."

"That sounds ominous..." I put my head down.

"You're General Blackcreek's daughter?"

I furrowed my brow and looked up at him, "Yeah, why?"

"Fuck me." He rubbed his eyes.

"Does that change something? I guess I don't understand."

"Gods. I hate him."

"Oh… I'm not him, I mean, I do love him, but we aren't the same. Why?"

"Fuck, I know you're not him," he said, anger rising.

"Hey, I am trying to understand here."

"I am sorry, I know. I have a lot of feelings about him. Five years ago, he sent a drift of dragons and phoenixes to my town. They incinerated a building where a group of leaders was having a meeting. My two uncles died that day."

"Five years ago—near the Winterhand Stronghold?" I asked, a lump in my throat so big that I might stop breathing. I knew the answer, and I didn't want to hear it. This couldn't be fucking happening.

"Yes." He cocked his head to the side.

The floor tilted. I slid off the bed and vomited before I could even breathe. Cold tile bit my knees. My arms locked around my shins, and everything narrowed to air, then no air at all. Every memory from five years ago flooded into my head.

"Auriella… you're okay. You're safe with me. What happened five years ago, because I am missing something. The amount of fear that overwhelmed me tells me something happened."

I didn't realize he had moved to the floor beside me. I felt his arms wrap tightly around my body as he lifted me into his embrace. I kept sobbing, trying to breathe, overwhelmed by a whirlwind of emotion. My racing mind refused to quiet. He carried me into another room. Through blurred vision and tears, I saw we were now in a private bathing chamber, with water running. He brought us into the shower, still holding me securely.

"Breathe, love, breathe," he whispered in my ear.

He moved to sit down with me in his lap. He pushed my hair out of my face and lifted my chin to look at him. All I felt was sorrow. I was afraid to know what his uncles' names were.

"It's okay, love. I got you."

"I don't even… know… where or how…to tell this…" I managed to get out in between sobs. I was starting to get control of my crying. I couldn't let this control me. It controlled the following two years of my life. Alex, knowing this, made him look at me and treat me differently. I looked up at him. *Lili and I were raped!* I screamed inside my head. His eyes widened, his eyebrows shot up, and he moved back from me. Wait, did I say that aloud? He stared at me.

"Did you just talk into my head?"

"I... um... I... don't know? Maybe you read my mind, can you do that?"

"Not that I am aware of, one of my aunts told me that there were some unique bond abilities that happen for mates, I guess that would be it."

He pulled me in closer, kissed the top of my head, "I am so sorry that happened to you."

"Drusearons terrified me before coming to basic, because..." Tears started to flow down my face again, and he wiped my cheeks. "It happened five years ago. Lili and I were walking around when he stopped to ask us where this one store was..."

My chest felt tight, it was like I was right back to that day. Where we stood walking through town. Fuck. I don't know how I can tell him this. I definitely never told Alex all of the details. Then again when he found out and came to the sanatorium, he looked at me like I was broken—as if I was a different person.

"Before we knew it, he wrapped his wings around both of us and shot into the air. We landed shortly after into a field. He tied us up... he—" I gasped in a large breath. Do I really have to say it out loud? It's been five years, and it still consumed me.

"—He raped us. One at a time—making us watch. While he was raping her, I managed to get free, and I jumped onto him and tried to choke him, but I was weak and disoriented. He headbutted me and... I woke up and Lili was still tied to the chair, and I was on the ground. Blood everywhere. I untied us and we walked in the frigid air. I was convinced he had left us, hoping we would die out there. Kim, my dad's dragon, and I had a unique connection. She sensed I was in distress and told my dad, and they found us. We both spent days in the sanatorium, recovering. The guy told us a name when he first approached us, David. It didn't take my dad long to figure out it was indeed his name. He met with a couple of leaders, informing them that he needed to be turned in for punishment. After a couple of days, they responded and denied the request."

I took in a deep breath. Tears flooded my cheeks, leaving a salt taste on my lips. I tapped my fingers on my thumbs, my knee bounced as fast as it could. It felt as though an elephant sat on my chest. My head felt dizzy with a wave of nausea. I could finish. I said the hardest part. He sat in silence, not interrupting me.

"Several weeks later, intelligence suggested he was hiding out in that building. It didn't mention that a meeting was scheduled in the late hours. I rode on Kim with my dad to a village. Several other dragons and phoenixes rode out, including Lili's dad. Kim landed near the building, as well as Lili's dad. We moved in, and to our surprise, they were having a meeting of sorts. They were protecting him. My dad and her dad knocked them out. When we arrived, David was cowering under a table. My dad pulled him out, and I drove a dagger into his heart. I watched his life end, and afterwards, I pulled my dagger free. We got back on the dragons and incinerated the building…"

"I am truly sorry that you ever had to experience that."

He communicated directly into my mind, similar to how the dragons did that day. Holy shit. I looked up at him, and his eyes were brimming with tears.

"I am sorry that you lost uncles that day."

He kissed the top of my head, closed his eyes, and took a breath.

"David was one of my uncles, and don't be sorry, he clearly deserved to die. I didn't know any of that. We were told it was an unprovoked Rider attack."

Tears streaked my face—and his. The water cooled as he lifted me from the tub, carrying me into the bedroom with towels draped in his arms. He set me on the bed, wrapped one around me, and drew the other across his waist.

His eyes never left mine. My chest swelled until I thought it might break open. Gods, I already loved him.

I didn't want this. I hadn't asked for it. We barely knew each other, yet something in me had already fallen, sharp and deep, before I could stop it. The speed of it made my stomach twist. Love wasn't supposed to hit like this, not so sudden, not so complete. And yet here I was, already lost. He climbed onto the bed and pulled me back into his lap, and I let him—because even as fear clawed at me, I couldn't look away.

"Sooooo... we can talk to each other, in each other's fucking heads?" I wanted to run as far away from the previous conversation as fast as I could.

"Yeah... I sort of suspected. My aunt and uncle were mates. Both were warriors. She told me bits and pieces. Watching them was almost sickening as a kid. They couldn't keep their hands off each other. They seemed to be always having a conversation no one else could hear, dancing with their eyes. Years later, she told me that mated couples have unique bonds. I thought maybe she was hinting at that, but I wasn't sure. I guess some things about mates are kept secret."

"Ophelia says we should keep the mate part secret, that it can make us vulnerable."

"We can do whatever you want, but do know, if someone puts your life in danger, theirs may cease to exist. The fear you felt after five years tells me that the fear you felt during was insurmountable, and..." He lost his words, as if he held back tears.

"I am okay. I am strong now, and I will never stop fighting for my life." I looked up at him and smiled at him.

He placed his hand on my cheek, rubbing his thumb side to side, caressing my face, before leaning in and giving me a long, deep kiss.

"Please promise me that you won't treat me or look at me differently." I pleaded with him.

"Right now, all I see is the brave, beautiful female that fate put into my life. From what I heard, you didn't need saving. Which, honestly, is perfect because I love a strong, fierce female."

He gripped me tighter, holding me like he never meant to let go. I knew what I shared was heavy, what we did before that. Everything tonight felt heavy. My dad only knew the full details of what had happened out there, something he learned while Lili and I were unconscious. It was the only time I was happy for his ability, happy that I wasn't required to share it all out loud.

"I really rather not talk about it... beyond tonight. If that's okay with you. I still have nightmares every now and again."

"Anything you want. If you ever change your mind, I will sit with you however you need me to."

I nodded. I was not sure if I would want to talk about this again. I wanted to change the topic, move so very far from anything heavy.

"What is your middle name?"

He let out a little laugh. "Zane."

I furrowed my brow in confusion at him. "Wait, what?"

"Roarke Zane Braegon the second." He flashed his little mischievous smile.

"Waitttttt... as in... the duke's son?" My eyes widened. "Shit!"

"As in that guy... I mean, you're the general's daughter. I am the duke's kid. It's fantastic."

My eyes were blinking at him. When they said his last name yesterday, it didn't click, but the situation preoccupied me.

"So, is it a bad time to mention that I am the marquess, the first son in line?"

"Why are you here?" I blurted that out before I realized it even came out.

He tilted his head at me, giving me a smirk. "If that was the case, how would I have met you?"

"I mean, you don't have to be?"

"Well, if my history lesson is correct, you don't have to be either. As for me, I want to be here. I don't want to be the duke now or ever. Also, no one knows I am his son. I checked in under my middle name. Of course, my father knows and respects my wishes to be here quietly."

"But your last name?"

"If someone starts to put it together, I brush it off and change the subject. Although I am pretty certain most of the higher officers are aware of my presence here, they haven't outed me."

"Sooooo... don't call you Roarke?"

"I've never really gone by that anyway, because of my dad, but yes, please let's keep this between us."

I turned around to face him. Got up on my knees and moved to straddle him. I flashed him a devious smile, "Okay, Roarke."

"You got jokes, huh?" He sucked his teeth, giving me a big smile, and pulled me closer to him.

Children of novelty, only children, and those deemed not well enough were exempt from conscription, yet here we both were. We were going against what was expected of us. He should be learning about taking his father's place as a duke, should his father pass. I could be doing anything, but I chose to be here. It seemed as if fate wanted us both here—fighting against a destiny we denied.

We sat holding each other, giving room for every heavy moment tonight. I steeped in his presence and comfort, though I knew I needed to go as I had many different things to do.

CHAPTER 15

I made my way back to the courtyard. The party was still going on, although with way fewer people. Since the first day fell on a Friday, we naturally got the following day off. I slipped right into the Rider's stairwell and climbed up to the seventh floor. I slipped into my room—Thora sat on her bed, but Sadie's bed was empty. There was a large pack sitting on my bed. I raised my eyebrows in confusion as I walked towards it.

"Platoon Leader Beverli came looking for you, but you weren't here. So, she left it on the bed. She said it was from your dad."

"Oh... Okay."

I walked over to the bag to investigate it more. The bag was similar to a medical bag that my mom had. I rubbed my fingers down the side of the bag. Lili came looking for me, but I wasn't in here, as I said I would be. Shit. I needed to talk to her.

"Hey, I'll be back in a short bit."

"I'm not your keeper," she shrugged.

"Fair."

I headed out the door and down to the second floor. I walked down the hall. These rooms were a bit more spaced out than ours. I found the eighth room and knocked on the door four times, precisely like we used to do when we were younger. A minute passed, and the door opened. She looked a little disheveled—maybe she was sleeping.

"Hey, sorry I didn't mean to wake you."

"I wasn't sleeping... I um have company..."

"Oh... Oh... I can come back."

"No, that's silly. Come in." She motioned towards the room.

"I have some things I needed to talk to you about... without..." I nodded inside the room.

"He will be leaving."

I entered the room to see a five-foot eleven guy with dark hair, tossing clothes around. He nodded and left the room. I thought I recognized him, but I wasn't sure—too many new faces recently.

"I thought you were going to bed earlier?"

"Yeah... um about that."

"You keeping someone else company?" She raised her eyebrows.

"Yeah," I looked down.

"Ohhhh, girl... It's Zane, huh?"

I looked up at her... "Guilty as charged."

"Oh... Fuck. I was semi-joking... Alex is going to fucking lose it." She sucked her teeth, looking at me in that disappointed look she always had when I was bringing questionable guys home.

"I didn't know he was Alex's best friend, first off. Secondly, I am not Alex's possession."

"It wouldn't have mattered if he knew him or not. He's always acted jealous and irrational when it came to you."

"Look, I don't want to hash us out. You know we were toxic for each other, as a couple, so I don't know why you are trying to push us." I gave her a slight smile.

"Sorry. I have always struggled with loving you two but also hating it."

"So... there's more to Zane and me." The words slipped out low, barely above a whisper, my throat tightening as I said them.

"As in, it's more than a fling," she said, raising one eyebrow at me.

"As in, we are mates."

She blinked her eyes at me for what felt like forever. "Fucking, excuse me?"

"Yeah..."

"Like, metaphorically, right?"

"No, like destined to be together. Like when our eyes meet, electricity shoots through us."

"Oh... Wow. I don't know exactly what to say to that," she scratched her head.

"Did you know about mates? Or Anam Cara? That's what he calls it."

"I didn't, until I came here. It's briefly discussed in lectures. I didn't take much stock in it. I guess I do now."

"We aren't telling people that we are mated, simply a couple."

"I'll always keep your secrets." She stepped up to me and pulled me into a hug.

"My dad gave you a present for me?" I asked, giving her a look of confusion.

"Oh yeah... He was in the courtyard, looking for you, but he found me instead. I told him you went to bed. He asked if I could pass this to you and tell you it was from your mom."

"My... Mom?" I raised my eyebrows.

"He didn't look like he wanted to give details, therefore I didn't ask."

"That's weird... don't you think?"

"I was caught off guard as well."

"She's been gone for six years, and he gives me something from her now."

"You know I am always here for you, and now that you're here I am even closer. There are fucked up cadets here, but there are also some amazing ones. Don't push away the good ones, we need each other."

"Thank you. I am going to head back up to my room and check it out." This time, I pulled her into a hug, holding her tight.

I returned to my room. Thora remained on her bed, absorbed in a book, while Sadie lay nearby in her own bed. I approached my bed and stared at the bag for a moment, uncertain whether I wanted to open it. My mom had been gone for years, and he had dropped off the bag, claiming it was from her, but he had not waited to hand it to me in person. I unzipped the bag and looked inside. It was filled with medical supplies. I slowly removed everything and laid it across the bed. Most of it consisted of equipment to triage someone during a crisis: gauze, a sturdy belt, elastic wraps, soothing salves, various bandages, a fire starter, and medicinal medications in clearly labeled bottles.

At the bottom of the bag, I found an envelope with my name on it. Maybe it was a letter from my dad. I opened it, then dropped it on the floor, gasping. Sadie and Thora looked at me, puzzled. I silently picked the letter up again.

My Dearest Auriella,

If you are reading this, it means I am not there for your first day in the Rider's branch, assuming you stayed in that course. Either way, I packed this bag for you regardless of which path you chose. I am sorry I am not there for you, my dearest baby. I want you to know that I love you more than the moon, stars, and galaxies. I hope that when you look at the stars, you remember our nights lying under them. Your father and I spent years trying for you, and gods, I wanted you so badly—you are everything I dreamed of. You are courageous, intelligent, and beautiful. Please don't let anyone make you feel otherwise. I need to share some essential things that I never had the chance to teach you. When you were born, we took you to be blessed by a priestess, as is the custom for most families. The priestess told me that when she touched you, she saw a vision that you had a fated mate, one who was a year older than you and born of nobility. I don't know who it is, of course, but over the years, I've learned as much as I could about mates to prepare you.

When you meet him, you will feel something inside you that you've never felt when looking at someone. It's believed that if you accept the bond and it is consummated, the two of you will have a direct line of communication—the more prolonged and more intense the bond, the more distance it allows. Make sure it's a bond you want before you consummate it. That really seals the mating bond. It's believed that if you and your mate are separated for a long time, your magical abilities will start to diminish until you're reunited. Your father is considered one of the most powerful Riders, which means you will also be a powerful Rider when you are allowed to channel and bond with a flier. If you find him before you're bonded and haven't learned how to shield your mind, you will need to learn how to do so.

The emotions of your mate and a dragon can become overwhelming. You have always felt deeper than most. Once you find him, don't fight it or run away. And no, it's not Alexander. Hopefully, you find each other before it's too late, like some others. Some secrets aren't mine to share, and I hope, my dear, they won't crush you when you learn them. Another thing, and this is the most important part. Don't trust anyone, not even your father. Things are happening in the military that aren't as they should be. Magic is being twisted in unnatural ways. Experiments are occurring that shouldn't be. Don't dig too deep and get yourself into trouble. Stay to yourself, but don't join any elite squads doing special missions. Please, my sweet girl, don't be the hero. I love you so very much. I am so sorry I can't be there to tell you everything you need to know.

Love,

Your mama

Tears were streaming down my face as I moved to the side of my bed and sat down, holding the letter close to my chest. The tears started coming even faster. I didn't know what to make of this letter. She knew about mates, and not only that, she knew I had a mate.

"Hey, does this work?" My head tingled a little, and I heard him.

"It does, Roarke," I said. According to my mom, we could talk over distances.

"I am going to ignore that. I was sleeping, but this overwhelming sadness awoke me, and it's not me. So, are you okay?" He sounded slightly worried.

"I got a package and a letter from my mom... she passed away when I was fourteen."

"Oh, I am sorry, love. Do you want me to come snatch you up and make things better?"

"I do, but I am going to sleep. I am tired, and there was a lot to process in the letter. Are you busy in the morning?"

"I am hoping to be busy making you see stars..." Then I heard him laugh.

"Are you always this infatuated with sex?" If only he could see the smile it gave me when I said that.

"Ummm... sorry... I," he stuttered.

"I left you speechless, exactly how I like you," I teased back.

"You can leave me speechless anytime. And I am only infatuated with you, and you are the only one I have been infatuated with, for the record."

"I'll be there in the morning."

"Just come in. Sweet dreams, my love."

I was still clutching my mom's letter. Thora and Sadie were both reading their own books. It was as if they knew I needed to cry alone, without interruption. I folded my mom's letter back up, placed it in the envelope, and then placed it back in the bottom of the bag. I put all the med supplies back on top. I would hide it a little better later.

I climbed into bed and pulled the blankets over me. My mind was overwhelmed with a thousand thoughts. It had been a tiring day, and I was completely drained. My thoughts just wouldn't settle down enough for me to drift off to sleep.

Two show-stopping dragons, one young and one older. One beautiful phoenix.

I had this dreamy, perfect mate.

She surely couldn't mean I couldn't trust my dad, right?

My mom wrote me a letter.

I could talk to my mate without speaking a word. I had a mate.

I thought I wanted that gorgeous silver dragon. Something about her drew me to her, spoke to me.

My best friend was my Platoon Leader. Alex would feel betrayed by both of us.

I was mated to a winged Fae, and according to my mom, there was no going back.

Gods, I missed her.

Fuck.

I needed to shut my thoughts down.

As I had learned, I took slow, deep breaths through my nose, concentrating on expanding my diaphragm with each inhale, then gently exhaling through my mouth. I repeated this, allowing my muscles to relax. Soon, my eyes felt extremely heavy, and I sensed sleep approaching.

CHAPTER 16

Five o'clock arrived too fast, and I couldn't sleep anymore. My restless thoughts before sleep definitely didn't help. My roommates were still sleeping peacefully, so I quietly and carefully left my room. Instead of heading to the courtyard, I chose to go to level three, cross over, and then descend to level one.

The hall was lit with candles that seemed dimmer than during the day, which I took as a sign of magic. I found his room, quietly opened the door, and walked inside. I hadn't noticed it yesterday, but I definitely felt like I walked through some kind of shield. My dad had similar shields at our various homes while we were growing up.

Zane lay on his bed, sleeping on his side in only undershorts. I paused to take in the scene. Unlike before, his wings were visible. They were close to his body but not tucked in tightly. They looked just as stunning as the day he first showed them to me. I used to fear males with wings because it reminded me of that day.

When I looked at him, I did not feel fear. My stomach tingled, and my heart thumped faster. I smiled as I watched him breathe in and out. His blonde hair appeared darker in the dimly lit room. Like Blaze, he bore a striking tribal tattoo that descended his back and wrapped around his wings. I wondered if he used magic to fill in the intricate details while masking them.

I approached the side where he faced outward, walking softly. I knelt beside him, pressed my nose gently against his, and gave him a tender kiss on his lips. His eyes fluttered open as he stirred, and he pulled me onto the bed with him, both of us lying on our sides, facing each other. He returned my kiss with the same gentle tenderness.

"What if I were coming in here to assassinate you?" I smirked at him.

"You wouldn't."

"I mean, if I were someone else, you would've slept through me coming in."

"Well, it would be foolish for someone to try to kill me. But most importantly, my room is warded, and only I can grant entry. I spent some time working on it yesterday so you can come whenever you want."

He kissed me again and pulled me closer until my head rested against his chest. His heartbeat thudded steady beneath my ear, warm and grounding. One arm stayed caught between us, but with the other I reached for his wing. My fingertips brushed the edge, and he flinched—not in anger, but in surprise, almost tender.

I pulled my hand back fast, pulse stumbling. His wing shifted, uncertain, like he didn't know if he wanted me to retreat or try again.

"Sorry," I whispered. "Am I not allowed to touch?"

"Well, there aren't strict rules," he said, his tone careful. "But most of us don't let others near our wings. Those who try usually don't live to tell about it. Drusearons are territorial over them, much like dragon kind."

"Oh..." My stomach dropped. Shit. I'd broken some unspoken law.

"But," his voice softened, "in a trusted, committed relationship, we allow it. Wings are sensitive. Painfully so. I've never let anyone touch mine. Still—I've heard there are... places. Erogenous spots."

"Are we in a trusted, committed relationship?"

"I thought that's what we agreed to yesterday?" He pulled back a little, giving me a confused look.

"I mean, I said I wanted us to be exclusive, but you never really said anything. I can be insecure about relationships and where I stand with people."

"I want you, and only you. You are a part of me. I know you said you didn't want to label it, so you can call it whatever makes your heart happy.

Honestly, I would go to a priestess to have our mating bond confirmed today. Hell, I'd marry you and shout it to the world."

This time, I pulled back and looked up at him. Wow. I didn't realize he felt so strongly about this, about us, about me. Wait, what did he mean by a priestess? My mom mentioned one too.

"What does a priestess have to do with it?" I asked him.

"Priestesses have special abilities with mating bonds. They can detect a bond and confirm it. Having it confirmed means they wouldn't be able to separate either of us from each other—"

"Because our powers become diminished." I completed his sentence.

He raised his eyebrows at me. "Yeah... How did you know that?"

"My mom—how did you know?"

"In one of the courses we took, it was briefly discussed. It's a small section, and honestly, most people might not even pay attention or believe it. Your mom, huh?"

"Yeah... she wrote me a letter, and she's known I've had a mate destined for me since I was weeks old..." I pulled the letter out of my pocket and handed it to him. He sat up to open the letter and began reading it. I studied him, watching his face change from curious to a look of shock. He had to be on the *don't trust your father section*. Not that he did.

"That's a lot to take in..." he said, looking down at it before handing it back to me.

"Tell me about it." I shoved the letter back in my pocket.

"I guess you read that a little late, because we already had glorious sex and sealed the bond."

I huffed a little laugh. "Regrets?" I teased.

"Ha. Not a fat fucking chance. You taste as glorious as you smell."

"Mmmm." I kissed his lips softly. "Soon I'll taste more than your lips." I gave him a little devious smile.

"Before we start something, because gods know that I want to do more. What do you think your mom meant about not trusting your dad or anyone?"

"I don't know. I truly don't know what any of that means. My dad has always been my rock and protector. It's making me question everything I thought I knew—everyone in my life. I'm honestly confused. Do you know something?"

"My dad suspected something had been going on that wasn't above board, which is why he agreed for me to come here. He wouldn't give me any details, though."

"You're in your third-year and haven't seen anything?"

"Not really, when I was in the infirmary with you, there seemed to be a lot of secret meetings, which is odd during the summer. I also think too many instructors and officers know my true identity."

"Oh. Also circling back, I'm not sure I am ready for wedding bells and all that, but I would get our mating bond confirmed. I also don't want to call you my boyfriend. I feel like what we have is something much deeper and more intimate than that. I also know if I start calling you my mate, it will start raising flags that maybe we shouldn't be raising. I'll call you my partner or my love to others, until you formally propose to me. Lili knows you're my mate though..."

"You told her already?"

"Yeah, she actually dropped the bag off on my bed when you and I were, you know... and I barely told her."

"I guess I should find Alex and have that conversation today." He ran his hand through his hair.

"Want to take a shower together?" I said, changing the subject.

"Like an actual shower, or is this code for you to take advantage of me in there?"

"Is it taking advantage if you want it entirely as much as I?"

Precisely as quickly as I finished what I was saying, he was scooping me up, taking my clothes off, and leading me to his bathroom. I wrapped my legs tightly around him, my arms around his shoulders. I sucked on his thick bottom lip, switching between wanting to suck on it and biting it. He gave me his tongue, and I took it in and sucked on it. He pulled his tongue back in, essentially taking mine with his, and he started sucking on mine.

We made it into the shower, which was easily double the size of the ones in the communal bathing chambers. He let go of one hand briefly to turn the water on, gripped my ass again and pushed me against the wall. My whole body quivered.

He kissed me, trailing down my neck. This time, I would be the one giving. I loosened my tight legs around his body and came to a stand. I started kissing down his body. When I came to his nipples, I twirled my tongue in a circular motion around them both before gently kissing down his abs.

His shorts were soaking wet from the water. I pulled them down to his feet. This freed his cock, letting it spring up. Gods, it was glorious and arduous as fuck. I wrapped my hand around it, but my fingers didn't quite connect, and he was a perfect eight inches. He let out a groan and reached down to my head, placing his hand on the back of my head. I licked the tip, playing with it, teasing him in every way as he had done to me. I dipped my tongue into the slit.

He let out a louder moan. I swirled my tongue around the top, making a circle, before dragging my tongue down the length. He was groaning, letting me know he was enjoying it. He grabbed a handful of my hair, pulsating it. I moved my tongue back up before taking him wholly into my mouth.

My mouth was watering all around him as I took him deep, swallowing him. Even with the grip on my hair, he was letting me control every part of this. I reached down with my right hand and rubbed my two fingers right behind his balls, as I moved his cock in and out of my mouth in a perfect rhythm.

He was groaning faster and louder, and his grip on my hair got tighter. Water showered down on both of us. He never masked his wings. They were behind him, slightly drooping. He reached down with his other hand and rubbed my nipple.

I was trying to focus on him. Him touching me made me slow down and pause with him in my mouth, taking his touch fully in. I snapped back to it and drew him out, stopping at the tip to tease him with my tongue again. His breathing became more ragged.

"Fuck, Auri. I am about to explode in your mouth."

"That's exactly what I am counting on, please fill my mouth with your delicious cum. Let it go."

I picked up the pace a little. I swallowed him in as much as I could, causing me to gag a little. He let out a loud moan, and I knew that he was getting closer. I applied more pressure behind his balls, moving in a smooth, fast rhythm.

"Oh gods, oh fuck... fuck me... Auri... gods. FUCKKK"

He let out a loud roar, and I heard his wings spring open loudly. His cock started pulsing into my mouth, filling it with a salty flavor. I swallowed it down. I slowed down, still moving his cock in and out of my mouth. I felt his pulse pulsating against my tongue. I came to the tip and applied a little suction, getting every little bit of cum he had to offer.

He gasped, the sound breaking into a moan, and heat ripped through me. Gods, I loved pulling that from him. I did it again, slower this time, and he answered with the same sound, the same shudder that tightened every nerve in me.

I lifted my gaze, and his locked with mine. The charge hit hard—electricity pouring through my mouth, down my chest, sinking low until I burned for him. It wasn't the same raw blast as before, but it was enough to set my body on fire, every inch alive with wanting.

I stood up, and he quickly grabbed me and pulled me into a kiss. He pulled back, pressed his forehead to mine, both of us barely breathing, taking it in. He pushed my shoulder to spin me around, grabbed up the soap, put it on a washcloth, and lathered me. He did it so tenderly, taking his time. He moved to my front and did the same, moving from my shoulders down. He knelt, moving the washcloth down my leg, before using his free hand to place his thumb on my clit, softly moving in circles.

He rose in a sudden motion, a teasing glint sparking in his eyes. Warm, soapy water slid off my skin as I snatched the washcloth from his hand and worked up more suds. I pressed the cloth to his chest, scrubbing across smooth skin, tracing every line and curve.

I shifted behind him and brushed the cloth over his wings, careful with each stroke, studying them. I had seen them fully spread only once before. Earlier, they hadn't stretched as wide, not like on the tower when he had flown—then they had unfurled in a breathtaking sweep of black, vast and unyielding.

He turned his head to peer over his shoulder at me, and I smiled at him. I moved the cloth to my left hand and took my finger and ran it over the webs in his wing. His wings started on each side of his spine, right under his shoulder blades. I rubbed my finger down the webbing that was near his spine, and his entire body shook. I pulled my finger back, not wanting to push his boundaries.

"It's okay, I've never had anyone touch them before. You hit a damned sensitive spot, in all the good ways."

I continued rubbing my fingers all over his wings, taking mental note of all the spots that made him shiver. I finished washing him down, then came around to the front of him. He grabbed me up and started kissing me feverishly, like he hadn't just cum.

He turned the water off, then pulled me into his arms, carrying me back to the bed. As soon as he started kissing me, my arousal immediately peaked. Gods, his lips felt so amazing across my skin. He moved down between my legs, still gently kissing me. He stopped on my inner thigh, close to my clit, and sucked there for a few seconds, and repeated on the opposite side. He took his tongue and slowly moved it from my perineum to my clit, in one gliding motion.

I felt myself getting wetter and my body flushing warmer. He took his tongue and flicked my clit with it at a fast-teasing pace. It felt so glorious, I swallowed hard, biting back my moan. He inserted two fingers into my wetness, and I let out a loud moan, and my breathing became more uneven.

He sent me into another earth-shattering orgasm, my vision fading to black as twinkling stars danced before my eyes. I had many other partners, but none matched the intensity of ours. I believed the emotional bond we forged, or perhaps our destined connection, fueled it. Whatever the reason, I was not complaining.

We cuddled on his bed, my head on his arm, both of us out of breath. Everything about lying in his arms screamed home to me, and at the same time, something felt off overall. Not with Zane, but something wasn't settling right. My mom's letters had me overall concerned. She revealed things but didn't tell me anything at all. I was happy that she wrote about the bond, but most of it I had already figured out—I was living it.

Someone hammered on the door twice, as if there was a fire outside. Zane and I both jumped. Like what the fuck? We both were dazed, hugging each other as if time had paused for a moment.

"Zane. You're late!" the voice screamed.

"Oh shit!" Zane shot to his feet. "I need to go. They're running an exercise on the first-years—forcing them into it. I was supposed to be knocking on doors and wrecking what they thought would be a free Saturday."

He yanked on his clothes in a rush. Whoever waited outside pounded again, sharp and impatient. Zane cracked the door, lifted two fingers in a signal, then shut it tight.

He crossed back to me where I lay tangled in his sheets. He bent low, pressed a quick kiss to my lips, and the taste of him lingered as he pulled away.

"Leave whenever you want. The first week will probably be hectic for us both, but I am always here if you need me." He tapped the side of his head. "Love, I know you can take care of yourself but be careful out there. I'd hate to have to kill someone in the first week."

CHAPTER 17

Gods, my head spun fiercely. Last night didn't go as I expected. I genuinely wanted to talk with her before we had sex. I didn't regret it, but I had wished to lay everything out before taking the next step. I experienced joy. I felt anger. I was confused. I was worried. Any emotion I could feel coursed through me. Joy in Auriella—that was everything I'd ever hoped for, everything I'd ever dreamed of. Thinking about her and the passionate love we shared ignited earth-shattering feelings. Anger and confusion mixed within me. Why the fuck did my uncle do that? Did my father protect him? Gods, Auriella didn't deserve this. I saw it in her eyes—the spark stolen from her—something she would never regain.

My relationship with Alex might change forever. He had been my closest friend. For two years, we spent weekends together, often finding each other in the quiet evenings to unwind. I loved the girl he loved—more than merely love. She was my Anam Cara, the vital core around which my being revolved. She was unaware, but she held my soul in her palms. The fact that he had a nickname only he used for her ignited a surge of anger within me. Knowing he had seen and touched her fueled my jealousy. I had never experienced jealousy before, yet here I was. I felt furious that my best friend had been with my mate. Logically, I understood it made no sense, but my emotions overwhelmed me.

Cuddling with her felt entirely right and perfect. I loved her deeply, but I couldn't tell her because I feared it would scare her. I had loved her since the moment I first saw her. I also hadn't mentioned that having our mating bond blessed by the priestess would grant us matching tattoos. I wondered how she would feel about it, especially since she bore no tattoos. In our village, it was essential for all Drusearons to get tattoos upon turning sixteen, marking their transition into adulthood and accepting their fate.

The Temple of Freya—the goddess of love—was where most people went to confirm their mating bonds, believing it honored the deep love between partners. Priestesses in every temple could bless these bonds. I guessed it depended more on which deity people worshipped than anything else. Growing up as a royal child, we had statues of each god in our palace, and we were expected to worship all of them, each with its own special day. As a curious little boy, I often asked my parents why we had to worship Marzana. One day, my mother knelt down and explained that although Marzana might seem like an evil god, he was the one we should ask for forgiveness from and pray that he would not curse us.

I was cursing all of the gods when Remus knocked on the door, reminding me we had a wing to lead. The Black Wing had always been known as a tough unit among the Drusearons. Remus and I promised that we would lead it that way again this year. Of course, our Platoon Leaders and Squad Leaders knew about this, as we had discussed it in our leadership meeting—almost all the first-year students were not prepared. I suspected the few who seemed to know we would be coming probably had older siblings and received a fair heads-up that Black Wing started on Saturday, if we ended up starting the year on the weekend.

Most of them hadn't been able to fly since the beginning of basic training because of the strict rules and peculiar tinctures prescribed at the start. The tincture Drusearons were required to swallow, which blocked our ability to fly, was the most shocking and absurd experience I had ever encountered. Some cadets deliberately swallowed only part of it or attempted to vomit afterward to reduce the effects. It also prevented us from roving, if anyone had that ability. The tincture was intended to last only two months, coinciding with the duration of basic training.

By week seven, I could fly very short distances and rove at length. My father told me before I went that the tinctures they would give me probably wouldn't last the entire time because of our bloodline. Of course, I didn't test it early or go anywhere in fear of getting caught. I had never been to the brig, and I didn't want to learn about it firsthand either.

We took the cadets out for flying practice and flight maneuvers. Some had only learned the basics, which was obvious. A few of them excelled and were clearly well-taught. My siblings and I were homeschooled, and our father hired top teachers for our education. Growing up, I hated the isolation. Now, I miss the one-on-one lessons and quiet time. While my siblings could be wild, some cadets were more unhinged than I ever expected.

After training I knew it was time for a very awkward conversation.

I knocked on his door twice. Alex opened the door and signaled me to come inside. He looked upset, and I was sure Auri was the reason. I was about to make things utterly worse. No point in dragging out the inevitable, though.

"Hey," I said.

"What's up? How were the flight maneuvers?"

I let out a small laugh.

"It's clear who will need more lessons and who was well-trained. Overall, we're looking good."

"I am excited to see what kind of talent we gained and see who won't be making it to their second-year."

"Riders, always looking to off each other..."

"Like you all don't," he laughed.

"Naw, just other branches." I laughed with him. Changing the subject, because I might as well get this done with. "You look to be in a funk."

"Mmm. Yeah, I thought seeing Ella—I don't know—I thought we would start over..."

"Yeah, I need to talk to you about her—"

"Wait, don't tell me you fucked her?"

I glared at him. "It's more complicated than that."

"No, it's not. I have been telling you I love this female for a long time."

"Yes and no. You've been telling me about a girl named Ella. Not once did you call her Auri or Auriella."

"And I told you about her unique tattoo, which you must have seen if you were—gods, she just fucks anyone, doesn't she?"

"Do not be disrespectful towards her." I could feel my anger rising, so I kept my shields up. I didn't want Auri to sense me upset or feel my anger. I hadn't realized before how deeply connected we would be, or that we could detect each other's emotions when they became intense. There was much my aunt hadn't taught me.

"You don't know her, like I do. When we weren't together, she was out fucking anyone who would twinkle their eyes at her."

I took a deep breath. *This was my friend. This was my friend. This was my friend.* I kept telling myself over and over because I undoubtedly wanted to punch him straight in the jaw right now.

"Shut the fuck up. I don't give a fuck about the past. I care about right now. We are mated. You two—"

"Wait, what the fuck did you say?" His cheeks flushed, showing his anger rising.

"I didn't stutter, and before you cut me off, I was saying, you two don't exist aside from friends. She will never see you as anything but—"

"You mated with her?" He growled at me.

"You know it is more complicated than that. Mates are destined from birth."

"This is fantastic. Fucking fantastic. My best friend is fucking my ex, and he claims they are mated."

"No claims."

"Has it been confirmed?"

"Not yet."

"Then fucking claims."

I rolled my eyes at him. I had never seen him this angry, this uncontrolled. Even when we found ourselves in stressful situations, he had always remained calm. I was sure this sucked for him, and I couldn't say I had ever been here before. I had many female encounters over the years, but I never desired a romantic relationship. Knowing I had a mate was always at the back of my head. Loving her the moment I saw her six years ago, I never let myself gain feelings for anyone else.

"I actually don't give a fuck what you think. I am telling you, Auriella and I are mated. We are together. I am asking that you respect our wishes to keep this information to yourself, as we are not announcing it to anyone."

"If you want our friendship, then you will end it with her."

"Don't make me choose Alex."

"You can't be my best friend and my—"

"Please, Alex. I want to remain your best friend."

"Choose. Fucking choose."

"Then it's her..."

"Wow... I... Just... Wow... I can't believe you would choose some bitch—"

My fist connected with his eye socket. I didn't realize I did it until it was over. My hand throbbed with pain. He had a cut on his eyebrow that bled profusely. He staggered backward, his other eye wide and fixed on me.

"We are done."

"When you realize what a fucking idiot you are being and you are throwing a tantrum, let me know. You have been one of my greatest friends."

I left him standing there without saying another word. At this point, it was useless. He was lashing out and acting like a child.

There wasn't time for games. Things were happening behind closed doors that I truly wanted to start understanding this year. Having Auri here made it more complicated. I didn't want her to be caught in the middle, and it was a distraction I didn't need this year. I wasn't sure which professors were involved, but while I was at the infirmary and they held their secret meetings, I took note of who was present.

Thankfully, Professor Pascal was not part of those, which was another reason I believed they had something to do with whatever was happening. Auri's mom's letters mentioned some kind of experimentation and advised against trusting the General. Some of the professors in the group knew I was the duke's son, which made it difficult to find out information.

CHAPTER 18

The rest of the weekend went smoothly. Thankfully, our Wing Commander didn't decide to start early like the Drusearons did. They spent most of the day on the flight field, performing flight maneuvers and engaging in sparring. We all received our schedules for the week, which showed our mealtimes, lectures, and the period. We ate together as a wing. There were a total of seventy-nine in the Feather Wing. Twenty-six were first-years, twenty were second-years, sixteen were third-years, and seventeen were fourth-years.

Before leaving my chambers, I sheathed my favorite six daggers—one on each leg, one on each upper arm, and two at my sides under my arms, concealed by my tee. Our platoon sat together but remained near the other platoon to maintain wing cohesion. Naturally, all the first-years gathered in a tight group. The officers clustered nearby as well. Alpha Wing was assigned to Dining Facility Two, which was conveniently located next to our chambers, making it easy for the Riders to access.

We shared the dining facility with other wings as well. I passed someone with two silver dragon symbols, representing Dragon Wing, a second-year. Everyone seemed to be eating peacefully, and there didn't appear to be anyone trying to attack others, as I had expected. Maybe everyone was feeling things out, and chaos would come later. There was a reason my dad told me the Rider's branch was cutthroat, and Zane warned me to stay safe.

After breakfast, we headed to the outdoor stadium where cadets had already taken their seats. Our Squad Leader led us to a large section and explained that Riders sat there. Around seven sections were visible, based on how the seated cadets clustered. To our right, the Infantry group occupied a sizable section, which I believed was the largest. On the left, the Healers stood out with their bright, vividly colored baby blue uniforms. Beside them, the Drusearons wore sleek black attire. More than half of them had their wings tightly tucked in. Sitting on these chairs couldn't be comfortable, but they offered ample space for all of us. My gaze lifted toward the top, where leadership usually sat, and I immediately recognized the familiar light eyes that made my heart flutter.

"Hey there, beautiful. I see I finally got your gaze."

"Finally? And hey sexy." I gave him a wink.

"From the moment you walked in, my eyes have been locked on to you."

"That's stalkerish don't you think?"

"I guess when you put it that way."

"If you keep staring, people are going to think you're in love with me or plotting my death." I looked away, not to draw attention to our stare.

"I really could not give a fuck about what anyone thinks. I will eye-fuck you every chance I can."

I could feel the heat in my cheeks, realizing I was probably blushing a little. I pressed my tongue to the roof of my mouth and took a deep breath, trying to hide it so no one else would notice. The room kept filling up, and within the next thirty minutes, there were no more available seats. Some cadets were standing at the back and sitting on the stairs. Professor Melamora walked through the lower-level door and onto the stage in the middle.

"Attention, cadets," she said, her voice projecting all throughout the classroom. All eyes fixed on her, the room went silent.

"Welcome, first-year cadets, and welcome back to all the others." She told us.

"Hopefully, everyone has become familiar with each other over the past few days. You should all be familiar with our Military Manual and Code of Ethics, often referred to as the MCOE, as well as the Code of Ethics specific to your branch. I would like to reiterate a few key points that apply to all cadets. MCOE 3-14-1 states that there shall be no relationships between professors and cadets unless the relationship was previously established and confirmed. MCOE 2-12-1 states that no cadet may kill another cadet other than in sparring or in self-defense. Violating this is punishable by death. MCOE 1-13-2 states that all cadets, except those in leadership, must be in their personal chambers by twenty-two hundred hours. Any questions on those?"

"To clarify, if someone is in my squad and I want to call them for a challenge, can it be a fatal match?" a male sitting in the first-year area of the Shapeshifters asked.

"Yes."

"And if they aren't, I can walk up to them and cause harm as long as I don't actually kill them?" He came with another question, and everyone directed their attention to him.

"Technically... Yes..."

"Good—"

"But some branches have truces to preserve their cadets. These truces are as sacred as any Code of Ethics we have. As you can see, some branches are much larger than others. For instance, the Sorcerers have a truce with all the other branches to protect their decreasing numbers. Furthermore, remember, when you take a life without merited cause, a mark is made on your soul. You also might find yourself with another set of enemies." She cut him off before he could continue.

"Noted." He said, then looked over as if he was directly looking at me. I swallowed a lump in my throat. I stared back with my fierce, emerald-green eyes because I would not back down. He had blue eyes, light brown hair, and lightly tanned skin. He seemed to be of average height, but it was hard to tell.

"Any other questions?" She paused and looked around before continuing. "This year, we've decided to add a few more courses. We haven't finalized the details yet. Once it's complete, you'll receive an updated schedule. One significant change is that more courses will now include multiple branches. Over time, the gap among the branches has widened, and we aim to bridge it. This is the third year that basic platoons included all branches instead of being separated by declared branches, and it has been successful. We plan to extend this approach beyond the basic level. In the military, teamwork across all branches is essential to defend our borders, not division among ourselves. We have two branches that conduct air patrols, but they sometimes fail to coordinate effectively. I'll be honest, there's chatter about a coming war with Rudemont, the predominantly human continent. The king might be trying some power move…"

I felt a sudden dread in my stomach. This was new to me. My dad never shared any concerns about this. But why would he—he never bothered to tell me about the politics of our continent. Historically, students in their third and fourth years were enlisted into service earlier than others. This also explains why branches were calling truces among themselves—to build larger armies instead of killing each other off.

"Now, if you are a second, third, or fourth-year cadet, you are dismissed. All first-year cadets will stay here."

Cadets in the upper rows stood up and started moving toward the various doors to exit the stadium. I sat in the first row, nearest to the stage. I pulled my legs in as the cadets moved past me. I felt a hand on my shoulder, looked up, and saw Lili. She gave me a little smile. It wasn't her usual cheerful smile but more like her sympathetic smile. She often gave me that when we got into trouble, and I got a tongue-lashing from my father. A moment later, Alex walked past me and shot me a look of disgust. I knew that look—it was the one I'd get after I hooked up with someone during one of our many breaks. Fuck. That meant he knew. I was sure I'd get the cold shoulder for a while. The difference was that I wouldn't take him back when he came back, begging and crying, saying he was sorry.

I felt a tingle down my spine and looked to the left. I saw Zane walking down the first row toward me. He stopped right in front of me, gave me a sweet, tender kiss on the forehead, and smiled. When he stood, he turned his attention to the Shapeshifter who was eyeing me earlier.

"Oh, so you saw him giving me a death glare earlier," I asked him.

"I think everyone saw it. Don't worry about him, love." He told me before walking towards one of the exits and leaving.

Sadie did a slight cough next to me. "Damn, Auriella."

I shot her a look and gave her a smile.

"By the way Alex looked at me, I take it you guys talked, and it didn't go well."

"Eh, nothing we can't handle. He will get over it, or he won't."

The room got quiet as all the upperclassmen left. Professor Melamora looked all around at all the first-years, giving us a small smile.

"I like to review some general education with each group of first-years and have an open discussion. I understand that some of you may not be as familiar with the military as others, and some of you might know a little but not be familiar with all the details. If your parents were in or are still in the military, raise your hand."

The majority of us raised our hands.

"Look around and take stock of whose hands are raised and whose aren't."

Every Drusearon, Shapeshifter, and Sorcerer had their hands up. Infantry, Healers, and Historians were a little over half. Three-quarters of us in the Riders' group had our hands up.

"As you can see, there are three groups where every cadet has their hands raised. One can't join a Drusearon without having wings. However, a Drusearon can choose to join another branch, though that rarely happens. If a child is born a half-Drusearon, most are born with wings, but sometimes fate says otherwise, leading them to join a different branch. Statistically, they tend to choose to be a Rider to enjoy the freedom of flying like their ancestors. Like the former, you can't be in the Shapeshifter branch without the ability to transform. Unlike the former, they are not allowed to join the other forces. Could you imagine someone shifting into a wolf on the back of a phoenix? Well, really, a flier wouldn't entertain them as a Rider anyway because of that. To join the Sorcerer branch, you must be able to wield magic without channeling, which means that technically a Drusearon could join this branch if they were born of High Fae, meaning they have greater magical abilities without relying on runes. Sorcerers were often called witches in many other cultures. As a witch, I speak for all of us—most of us don't care either way. Any questions so far?"

It was dead quiet. We were all utterly staring at her, taking everything in.

"Good, let's continue. Infantry, Historians, Healers, and Riders are open branches. The conscripted cadets could have chosen those branches, minus the Shapeshifters, if they wanted, and some of you did. Some of you may not have a military background and joined because you wanted to make a difference. Some of you have parents who are considered High Fae, which means you will more than likely be able to learn and use magic. If you were born to regular Fae, you won't be able to use magic without runes, and even then, it will only be simple magic. The last branch, the Riders, often has a mixed group—some of you have parents who are Riders. Some of you come from a line of witches and choose differently. Some of you were born to regular Fae and want to be different, riding a flier. If you were born to a High Fae, a witch, or a dragon Rider, you will be able to learn and use magic, if you haven't already. If not, once you bond, your dragon will channel magic to you, but your unique abilities are usually ordinary."

A couple of the Riders near me snickered.

"What are runes used for?" she asked the group.

"It is a type of stone that magic is placed in that allows lesser Fae to yield basic magic," a quiet girl sitting in the Sorcerer's group said.

"Less Fae, huh?" Professor Melamora sighed, "Yes, that's essentially correct."

"It can also amplify a Higher Fae's magical abilities," Atlas said, who sat next to the quiet girl.

"Yes, also that. To imbue a rune, you generally have to spend some years practicing your abilities. In the military, one task the witches do is imbue runes for other branches." Melamora stated.

"They aren't on the battlefield?" the cocky guy in the front who locked his eyes on me earlier asked.

"They can be, depending upon their abilities. Like all High Fae, we aren't all treated equally in what nature gives us in terms of magical abilities." She turned her body towards me and glanced in my way, "For instance, the daughter of the military general would be considered High

Fae and is expected to have great power. Not just because he is the general, but because his bloodline is unique."

I instantly felt my cheeks flush. I shifted in my seat and took a sip from my steel bottle. I hadn't sensed any power—I hadn't really attempted to, honestly. I didn't realize I was born with such incredible strength until now. Why hadn't my dad told me? It made no sense. But what Zane and I shared was some kind of magical ability.

"Say we are of High Fae, but haven't had any inkling of power?" Thora asked, as if she read my mind.

"Oh, you have power, but you haven't fully unleashed it. Some parents, though frowned upon, have given their children tinctures to suppress their abilities. When you arrived here for basic training, a ward was also activated to suppress your powers, helping us manage with fewer staff and preventing magical flare-ups. Now that we've removed that ward several days ago, you might begin to show or feel your power. Otherwise, Vindex will enjoy messing with you."

She told us, looked at me again, and gave me a gentle smile. It was almost like she was trying to tell me something. Would my dad really suppress my powers? Between my mom's letters and what I was learning here, I started to question things. My dad had always protested me joining the military altogether, but why? There were so many questions I wanted answers to, and I didn't feel like my dad would give them to me anytime soon.

"The funny thing about magic is there is always balance in check. If you are a Rider, your flier helps balance that check. They can and will stop the flow if they believe you are being too reckless. Conversely, they could incinerate you as well. Speaking of fliers, each flier also has different special abilities, and like High Fae, some dragons are more powerful than others. The more powerful ones are known for seeking out more powerful Riders to bond with."

"Does the size of a flier mean anything?" a female sitting in the Infantry area asked.

"Sometimes, most Riders and flier types don't really disclose that. Riders can't share flier secrets, and sometimes the fliers don't reveal information either. That said, General Blackcreek's dragon is decent-sized, and we know they are both powerful. Griffins aren't as vastly different in size, but some of them have incredible magical abilities. In short, don't underestimate any flier, even smaller ones. I like the questions. Let's keep them coming."

"If a High Fae decided to join the Infantry, would they have powerful magical abilities compared to us, who have none?" one of the Infantry cadets asked.

"Yes, don't see it like a competition, see it as complimenting each other. Don't see it as one is better than the other. Everyone here has something they will bring to the table."

"And if you don't, you'll die," the smartass Shapeshifter added. Half the class laughed while the other merely stared at him.

"We are in a time where we don't want to see cadets dying," she gave him a scornful look. "Let's do some critical thinking. Why do you think the chambers are set up the way they are?"

"Infantry is usually on the front line, so it makes sense to put them on an outer wing," an Infantry cadet said.

"Yes..." She looked around, waiting for more answers.

"Historians are positioned above the library and next to the instructor's chambers to assist with the retrieval of information," a quiet Historian said.

"Good..."

"Riders are positioned on the outer side, closer to the flight field. Healers are placed between the Riders and the Drusearons because they are historically the most severely injured in training. Infantry is also located at the end and next to the Sorcerer's chambers because they are the branch with the least exposure to fliers, winged Fae, and wolves. Therefore, they are more likely to be more alarmed by seeing us or our creatures. Historically, Shapeshifters aren't fond of Riders, so placing them the furthest away is an attempt to keep conflict lower," I said. At least my dad did tell me some of these things.

"Because the fliers took out multiple packs, because they wouldn't conform," one of the Shapeshifters shouted.

"Oftentimes, there is much more behind the scenes, as you will soon learn over the next few years," she said, before looking my way, "yes, to all of that."

She turned toward the Shapeshifters' group, "Now, you all know this, or I hope you do, so let's let them answer this one." She turned to the rest of us, "When do Shapeshifters start transforming into their wolf form?"

Everyone was pin quiet, just staring at her. She turned back to the Shapeshifters and gave them a nod.

"Most of us transform after we turn eighteen, which is why we have to come when we are eighteen, unlike some others. Some of us are seventeen but will turn eighteen soon, so we are allowed to join a little earlier. The goal is for us to transform here, guided by our professors. However, sometimes we do transform early at home, and our pack is really great at helping us through it," one of the female Shapeshifters said.

"Yes, good. Shapeshifters don't have magic in the same way some others do, and they don't see themselves as Fae. They have the ability to transform whenever they want, except for the first time, and are extremely strong in their wolf form. Their bite can be deadly if not properly treated. They can use runes like others to do things such as lighting candles, creating sound shields, and similar tasks. Their first transformation is said to be the most painful, which is why we like to be present for them."

"So, they don't transform only on full moons?" an Infantry cadet remarked.

She turned toward him and slowly blinked at him, which was comical as fuck. "I did precisely say they can transform whenever they want. Listen with your damn pointy ears."

Most of us let out a chuckle. The cadet sank into his seat.

"Let's shift the focus to the Drusearons. I have a particular interest in and knowledge of their clans, since my husband is Drusearon. As I mentioned earlier, you can't be part of that branch unless you have wings, for obvious reasons. We had four wonderful children, and three of them were born with wings, while our youngest was not. She is as special as the others. She chose to follow my footsteps and joined the Sorcerer branch, which we expected. What I didn't anticipate was that our second son, who has the largest set of wings among them, would choose the Healer branch. He's considered a mender because his abilities are stronger than a typical Healer, but he isn't quite a full mender. The point is that Drusearons aren't required to join their own branch. The only one they can't join, of course, is the Shapeshifters. Historically, no winged Drusearons have joined as Riders either."

"Wouldn't that be a sight—a winged Fae and a flier—falling off would be much easier," a Rider said behind me.

"Yes, that would be quite something. And you might actually see it. Sometimes, when we're in a battle, a Drusearon will ride a flier with its Rider and dive off for an unexpected attack. However, this depends heavily on the flier, its temperament, and how the Rider feels. Drusearons can have a wide range of abilities, from only performing simple magic to being very powerful. Similar to their abilities, their wingspans also vary in size. Speaking of their wings, when one can wield magic, some of them choose to keep their wings hidden. There are various reasons for this. It could be because, in their clan, it makes them a target for non-winged Fae. Wings can also be seen or felt as a vulnerability, so they only display them around people they trust. The most important thing is never to touch their wings without their permission."

She looked around and moved toward the Healers. "Healers are unique because most of you don't have magical abilities, and without a rune, you won't. However, you are one of the most essential branches we have. Most of us couldn't live without you. If you are truly High Fae and join the Healers, you will be able to use magic along with healing. Rarely do we see a high-level mender come from the Healer's branch. Generally, menders come from Riders or Sorcerers. Like my son, he is considered a mender. However, he is a medium level. That means he can mend flesh wounds, small fractures, and some poisons. High-level menders can heal larger wounds and broken bones."

"And let me guess, what about the nerds?" the cocky Shapeshifter said, looking at the Historian cadets.

"Watch your tongue before you find yourself out of my classroom. Historians are what keep the college running. They help professors and cadets with textbooks and document events that are happening so we can have an accurate record in the future. They may not be able to fight you hand-to-hand, but they can beat you in any kind of quiz." She turned to him. "And before you get any ideas, Historians typically don't spar, and killing one without reasonable cause will definitely land you in more trouble than you think."

"For any High Fae who joins as a Historian, they have the option to add wielding and sparring to their course load. Most only choose wielding. Oftentimes, if you are a High Fae Historian, you are assigned to battlefields to document the events that occur because they can protect themselves better. Does anyone know the duration of a military term?" She looked around.

"Regardless of whether they are conscripted or not, once you have entered, you are required to complete four years of college and two years of service, unless you're a Rider," I said.

"And what about Riders?" she probed.

"They are a lifetime service," I replied.

"Yes, but there are exceptions. All branches, except the Riders, can re-enlist and stay for various terms. However, if someone chooses to be a Rider, they will be committed for years to come. Fliers are dedicated to protecting their young and our continent, and when they take on a bonded Rider, it means they are fighting for the long term. A Rider can leave if the bond with their flier is severed. Doing so would take all the channeled magic with them, and often Riders can't bear losing their fliers, sometimes dying of a broken heart. Fliers often outlive their Riders, and some have had multiple Riders. They do feel the pain of losing a Rider, and it's common for them not to bond again for many years. There are cases where dragons bond so deeply with a Rider that they also die of heartbreak if their Rider passes away. A unique aspect of fliers is that they can form a bond with a second person, who is not a Rider." She looked at me and smiled. Did she know that Kim and I had something special? *Was* there a bond?

She continued, "It doesn't happen very often, and the bond isn't the same, meaning they don't channel power. We often think of it similarly to imprinting that can happen with wolves. In the handful of cases where it does happen, it is usually a mate or a child of the Rider. They sense each other and have a connection that fliers don't normally get with another Fae. Now that you've heard all of that, why do you think children of Riders choose not to become Riders?"

"That's easy. They don't want the potential lifelong commitment to the military, especially the daughters who may want a family," Thora, who sat at the end of my row, stated. I never saw it that way. I knew I wanted a family, but I also watched my dad navigate it with me in tow, even after my mom died. He had a lot of friends, mostly dragon Riders, who also helped take care of me.

"All students have their first hour here. Tomorrow, you will meet my co-professors. That's enough for today. Class is dismissed. You will go to your second class of the day. And remember, make good choices—a bad choice can leave you with more enemies than you're prepared for." She shot a look at the cocky Shapeshifter.

We all stood up and made our way out the exit.

"Why did she look at you when she mentioned a second bond?" Sadie asked me quietly.

"I'm not sure. My dad's dragon and I did have some kind of connection, but I wouldn't call it a bond."

We kept walking, and our second class was with Professor Vindex, who taught magic. First Squad stayed together for all lectures, while our platoon's second squad had many courses that overlapped with ours. My mind raced with everything I learned from Professor Melamora, or rather, all the things she was trying to tell me. I felt a strong connection with Zane. I spent yesterday reflecting on everything.

"Do you think my dad dosed me to keep my powers diminished?" I asked Zane.

"I think it is very possible if you haven't been exhibiting magic and you're already twenty," his voice sounded strained.

"But why? Are you okay? You sound—"

"I am not sure, love. I will come back to this in a bit, getting my ass handed to me on the mat, and you are the distraction they needed..." He told me, and then I felt a wall. It was weird and strange. It was like the connection went from stadium lights to a candle barely holding on.

CHAPTER 19

In our second class of the day, only our wing occupied the seats. I wondered how the situation would change over the next few weeks as we participated in more integrated courses. Honestly, it didn't matter to me. Being the General's daughter meant we moved between different forts and interacted with various branches of the military. Before I was attacked, Drusearons didn't bother me. Being here helped me begin to heal and remember that asshole didn't define all the other great Drusearons.

"If you have ever yielded magic, even unintentionally, move to the left side of the classroom. If you haven't, move to the right side. I want to be able to see what we're working with. Now, some of you may not yield magic until you channel with your flier because... well, you don't have parents of High Fae. Don't worry, once you start channeling, you will be considered High Fae—the perk of surviving as a Rider—and the only branch that can change your status."

Seventeen of our classmates moved to the left, leaving nine of us on the right side. I looked around at the others who weren't channeling. Professor Vindex looked at our small group. "Now, if you aren't capable of channeling until you bond, move to the back row." Five of the nine of us got up and moved. Thora was still sitting next to me, which I figured made sense since she had asked about it in our last class. I also knew both of her parents were Riders. She told me during basic. The other two were in the fire platoon.

"Alright, four of you, for whatever reason, should be yielding and aren't. The other five of you will go over to the others." He turned to the other seventeen cadets. "I want you guys to start working on building shields. You should practice having mental shields up."

"That's easy," one of the fire platoons' cadets remarked.

Professor Vindex gave him a look.

"Holy shit were you in my head?" the cadet asked.

"By practicing shielding, you might be able to keep me out someday. I am quite powerful, though. Everyone does it a little differently, but the most important thing is to go within and build a wall. Some people imagine building a wall with anything they want, some imagine building blocks, some use water to keep a door closed, and others imagine closing doors. Whatever feels right is fine. It all requires practice and focus inward. Even if you're not channeling, you can learn to lock your mind down. I will be able to feel you building them, and you will feel me glide over them," he told them.

I absorbed everything he said, remembering what my mom advised—I needed to learn how to shield myself from the overwhelming emotions of both my mate and my dragon or flier because it hadn't been decided yet.

Professor Vindex approached our small group. "Let's discuss where your powers are. First, let's talk about your parents, because that will reveal what kind of power you might be hiding." He looked at me, then at the name on my tee. "General's daughter, right?"

I simply nodded. I figured most people would probably connect the dots and figure it out if they hadn't already. Thora didn't seem surprised, but a couple fire platoon cadets shot me a look.

"This might be obvious, but you possess great power within you. We thoroughly need to understand the why." He glanced at Thora. "And yours?"

"Both parents are Riders. Dad is a fire wielder, and my mom's is classified," she told him. His eyebrows raised as he looked at her name tag, as if taking note of it. He glanced at the redheaded male sitting at the table. "And yours?"

"My mom is a Drusearon, and my dad is a Sorcerer. Neither has a specific ability I am aware of," he told him. Vindex nodded.

"And you?" Looking at the brown-haired male sitting next to the redhead.

"Father is a Rider. He can manipulate metal. Mom is a regular Fae."

"Alright. All of you definitely have the ability. Two of you should definitely be wielding. Thinking back to when you were ten to fourteen, did any of you experience anything that felt weird? You females would probably be on that earlier side."

"When I was eleven, I had a nightmare in which I woke up screaming and windows were shattered. My parents appeared really worried about me, and—oh my gods—my parents were keeping my powers under control. Professor Melamora mentioned that some parents give their kids tinctures. I couldn't believe they would do that. Afterwards, I took a tincture every night to *prevent nightmares*." Her face looked torn. She dropped her head, unsure of how to process the realization she had.

"That's okay to be upset, it is a lot to process. And yes, some parents choose to do that, especially if they believe their child's powers will be too great for them to manage," he said.

"I knew I was taking the tincture to reduce mine. When I was thirteen, I set the house on fire. My parents were horrified, and the air seemed to swirl through the house as I panicked. They sat me down, and I agreed to take it. I had actually stopped taking it months before I arrived here, but I haven't felt anything since," he said, he had a nervous tic of rubbing his palm with his finger.

Vindex looked at the other cadet. "I don't remember anything, and I don't remember taking anything daily?" the brown-haired cadet said. Vindex swung towards me.

"I also don't remember anything, and didn't think my dad was giving me anything, but I don't know anymore," I told him.

"Tinctures are the most popular method and the main reason we see delays in powers. I'm glad Professor Melamora shared that news. Sometimes it's a lot to take in. It's always important to remember that if a parent did that, they truly believed they were doing what was best for you. With all that said, I have a tincture for you—it's basically an antidote. While most tinctures should clear from your system, some last much longer and don't need daily dosing."

My head spun, and my mind raced. Wait. Every month I went to the doctor and got my fertility tincture. Was that it? Shit, I hoped so. Did they mix it up?

"What is it?" He asked me. My eyes always gave me away.

"Would they have mixed it into my fertility tincture?"

"They could, it is highly possible," he told me. He looked at the four of us. "This tincture tastes a little different once you swallow it. Within a few minutes, you may start to feel some tingling throughout. If you feel this, you have likely been given a tincture, and it was affecting you. If not, there is something else going on." He handed each of us a vial to take.

In near-perfect sync, we all lifted our vials and swallowed.

Across the hall, chatter from the other classmates had been rising, but it cut off at once, silence slamming into place. I flicked my eyes toward them, then back to Vindex. He didn't move, only watched. My gut told me he had struck them with his mind—a power both incredible and terrifying.

Did it work like our bonds with fliers? Or like the strange pull I shared with Zane? The thought needled at me, impossible to shake.

A sudden rush lit through me, tingling from toes to skull, a dizzy current that sent my pulse racing. Thora and the redhead jolted too, their eyes wide, their faces glowing with the same charge. My skin hummed, every nerve alive, my body thrumming like it might lift off the floor. Power surged inside me—wild, fierce, unstoppable. I didn't know how to shape it, but gods, I could feel it burning, and it felt incredible.

"I can see that the three of you are feeling different. You probably can sense the magic that's heightened in the college, but..." He looked at the brunette. "I can see that wasn't your problem..."

He turned toward us, "Stoot, Blackcreek, and Bosmini, you three can go over there to start practicing shields for now. Ludewuggin and I are going to troubleshoot some more."

The three of us approached the other group, and a few of them gave a quiet clap. It was almost embarrassing—our parents basically drugged us to keep our powers suppressed, taking a part of us away. At least Bosmini had a choice in his. I sat in a chair, closed my eyes, and focused on finding that wall.

"One of our Sorcerers may need to evaluate you to understand what's happening. Even if you weren't taking a tincture to reduce anything, that tincture also helps wake things up elsewhere. I know you said one of your parents is a regular Fae, and I know this is a hard question, but is there any chance that your father isn't actually your father?" I heard Vindex ask him quietly, but not quietly enough.

Holy shit, that would be such a crazy scandal. Our class kept quiet and focused on our mental work for the rest of the lecture. In the end, Vindex broke through each of our shields. I felt him push through mine as well, which was pretty strange. I had one advantage that others didn't—Zane. I could practice building blocks to block him out.

"*Did you shield me out earlier?*" I said, hoping he wasn't busy, as he had been earlier.

"*Yes, I damn near lost the challenge because hearing your voice caught me off guard. And that's not your fault. I just wasn't ready, and I love hearing from you.*"

"*Hmmm, well, I am going to practice shielding you out now.*"

"*Oof, I take it your second class was magic-wielding?*"

"*It was indeed.*"

"*Learn anything else insightful.*"

"*My dad has been dosing me to prevent my powers from coming out, using what he claimed was a fertility tincture. I hope it really was a fertility tincture—well, it really doesn't matter much now, since every cadet here gets it monthly anyway, but still.*"

"*That isn't the best way to start the day.*"

"*Nope, but it's okay... All is well. I felt a sense of power and tingling. And apparently, I am going to have GREAT powers, so they keep fucking telling me.*"

"*I wish I was there so I can kiss your dirty mouth and make all the things right in the world.*"

"Me too. I am now heading to Professor Wormald's class."

"I am in Professor Hildegard's class, which by the way, I have been flying since I was two."

"Want to trade?"

"Ha-ha, no. I can zone out in this class… Wormald is… um different."

"When can I see you?"

"Whenever you want…"

"Hmmm, you know what I mean…"

"Do I?"

"So, I can kiss all down your body, touch every part of you, feel your cock in my…"

"Hey, hey, hey, I don't need to have an erection in class."

"Easily bothered, eh?"

"Yes. You have that effect on me. Now, be a good girl and go to your next lecture."

Our squad headed into the Bravo wing and entered Professor Wormald's class. In his classroom, bookshelves lined the wall behind his desk with countless books. The room had a distinct, almost musty smell. We all found seats. This time, some of Electric's platoon joined us.

"Welcome to History. I am the mighty, wonderful Professor Wormwald, and clearly, I am a Historian, but I am of High Fae, so don't try any tricks in here," he told us.

"Yep, he's a weird one," I told Zane.

"I told you."

He went on to tell us about the history of our school and the continent. Most of us probably learned this in grade school. Come on, there must be something better out there. My mind drifted as he kept talking. I was trying to think of a time when I demonstrated power. I started the fertility tincture at thirteen, like most girls do. I didn't remember shattering windows. I felt like that would be memorable. Also, I hadn't set anything on fire, which I would remember. There was this thing about hiding in the shadows and manipulating my shadow to make shapes, but surely that was normal. I wondered what powers Zane had or what made Thora's mom's ability classified. I was no stranger to classified abilities, as my own dads was, which was why I assumed Vindex didn't say anything except to confirm he was my dad. My dad's abilities made it exceptionally hard to lie to him or sneak anything past him—a simple touch in the right spot, and he'd know everything.

***

The class ended, and I honestly couldn't remember most of what he said. Oops. My brain completely drifted off. Sometimes it happened when the content felt dull to me. It was lunchtime, and instead of going straight down to the first floor and into the courtyard, I decided to take a detour through the watchtower.

I rounded the corner of the tower to enter the Alpha Wing, heard footsteps behind me, and before I could fully spin around, I felt a dagger pressed into my back. Damn. I lowered my right arm and reached for the dagger on my right thigh. The dagger pushed deeper into my back.

"I wouldn't fucking dare," said the deep male voice. It was the asshole Shapeshifter who stared at me this morning. This bastard. I felt anger rise inside of me, crackling within. With my hand still on my thigh, I quickly spun to face him whilst pulling my dagger out at the same time. Before he could even react, I had my dagger at his neck. His dagger was now pressed against my stomach. We were both staring at each other with pure rage.

"What the fuck is your problem?" I snapped, my voice sharp enough to cut the air.

"You need to pay for your dad's debts," he shouted.

"The fuck I do. I am not him, and I don't owe anyone shit. If you're going to stab me, go ahead, I'll have this in your throat precisely as fast."

"I underestimated how fast you are."

"Look, I am not the fucking one... trust me." I pressed the knife harder into his throat.

Whoosh.

In an instant, Zane was there. I didn't know how—one blink, he wasn't, the next he stood in front of me. His eyes locked on mine, then he slipped behind the Shapeshifter. The name on his shirt read Elslurs.

"Is your boyfriend here to save you?" Elslurs drawled, his tone dripping with cocky disdain.

"She doesn't need saving... I am here because I enjoy inflicting pain on anyone who thinks of hurting her."

My eyes shot to him.

"Are there others?" I asked, down the bond.

"No, but he doesn't need to know that."

"I wasn't planning on killing him."

"Oh, but I was."

"Maybe offer a second chance."

"Well... I don't have all day, and I wasn't looking for a fight with two people," Elslurs said.

"Maybe you shouldn't look for fights at all," I said. Our knives were still drawn at each other. Zane was behind him, like a prey ready to attack his predator, and I was pretty sure he would enjoy it.

ROAARRRRRRR

I jolted, heart slamming so hard it hurt. The sound cracked behind me, too close, too sudden. My head spun. A wolf crouched low, teeth bared, saliva stringing from its jaws. A growl rolled deep in its chest, vibrating through the ground under my boots.

My breath caught sharp in my throat. My hands twitched, unsure where to go first. I forced my eyes back to the Elslurs—don't lose sight, don't turn away.

The air shifted, and Zane appeared at my back, his shoulders locking against mine. Solid. Steady. My pulse thundered, but at least I wasn't alone.

"I see you called for backup?" Zane snarled.

"I didn't... actually," he said. He genuinely sounded as confused as I was.

The wolf stalked around to the side and snarled at Elslurs. Interesting. The wolf turned his head toward me and gave me a wink. What the hell?

In a flash, Jeremy stood next to us. That was him? Holy shit. He could transform. I had so many questions, but now wasn't the time as I clearly had a knife pressed to my stomach, Zane wanted to end him, I wanted to offer a second chance, and now my basic squad mate just shifted.

"Asmoth, are you fucking stupid? Do you have any fucking common sense?" Jeremy asked him, giving him the death glare.

"I... I... only wanted to get my revenge. Her father killed our sister," he said.

Oh shit... they were brothers, and in the same year, they had to be twins. Oh, this was not good. Did I trust Jeremy right now? I mean, of course I did. If he wanted me dead, there were plenty of times for him. He helped make sure I made it down the pass alive.

"Yes, her father did. She did not. Auriella is a good person. I spent weeks with her. Her father doesn't define her. Drop the fucking knife." He scolded his brother.

Asmoth lowered his knife, and I lowered mine. Relief never had the chance to land. A sudden stab ripped into my left side, hot pain flooding down my hip as blood soaked through. I gasped, staring at the red spreading across me, brain lagging to catch up to what had happened. Zane moved like a shadow loose from its tether. In a blink his dagger sank into Asmoth's right arm, blood spilling fast down his sleeve. He wrenched the blade free, hand rising for a second strike.

Jeremy darted forward, eyes wide, his voice breaking without words. The plea was written across his face—mercy.

Zane froze, blade hovering. His chest heaved, eyes still locked on Asmoth, but he lowered the weapon. Then he turned to me, dropped to his knees, and pressed his hand against the wound in my side, his jaw tight with fury.

"Get him the fuck out of here, before I fucking snap his neck?" Zane growled at Jeremy.

"I might snap it myself." Jeremy grabbed his brother's arm and dragged him away.

"She fucking deserves it," Asmoth yelled.

"You fucking deserve to die," Zane snapped.

"Let's fucking go, you idiot," Jeremy growled.

The whole situation was a fucking mess. There was blood all over the floor—both mine and his. And for what, something my dad did. I had no clue why or when my dad apparently killed his sister. I didn't think my dad would do it without just cause, but I also didn't feel like I knew my dad anymore, either. Zane looked at me, his eyes filled with rage. They no longer had the pure, pale blue eyes that had once looked at me. Instead, their eyes had darkened to a deep indigo, a rich, intense shade.

"Let's go to the Healers and get you patched up," he said.

"I am fine, or I will be. I'll be stitched and continue on."

"I should have killed him the moment I entered the stairwell."

"So violent..." I said, giving him a little smile.

"I can be, and I won't be as willing to offer second chances anymore."

We went to the Healers, and they brought me in to tend to my wound. Two others were there, getting stitched up, but I thought they were upper-class students. I didn't pay much attention because, honestly, my side was throbbing, and my shirt was soaked in blood. Zane stood right next to me, watching everything the Healer did.

"I'll be fine, you can go to your next lecture," I said mind to mind.

"No, I will not until you are stitched, and they say you are good."

"You don't have to stare at them like they are plotting against me." He looked at me, our eyes locked, and for a brief second, I swore they flashed back to his light blue and then back to the indigo color.

"I don't think you realize the enemies your father has."

My eyes widened at him, eyebrows lifting. What did that even mean? Every time we were at a fort, it seemed like everyone liked my dad. He said it as if there were a lot. Of course, being the general, I figured there would be some.

"Yeah, I didn't think you did, and that shocked face you have confirmed it. I came into this place harboring intense hatred for him. You know the saying, the enemy of my enemy is my friend. I made a lot of friends here. Of course, now I have you, which complicates some of those friendships. I made it clear

that you were off-limits, or they wouldn't live to see the next day. That doesn't mean they like you or that others like Asmoth don't exist."

"I guess I didn't realize my dad was a villain in everyone's story." I dropped my head.

CHAPTER 20

The first week flew by. The lectures were mainly informational, and I already knew most of the material. I kept daggers on every limb and my torso wherever I went. I felt like I watched my back more than before. I had been trying not to dwell on what my father was truly doing or what my mom's letters contained. Honestly, I was just trying to survive. Week two began, which also meant we added sparring and obstacle training to our schedules.

We assembled into the current event class with Melamora, Pascal, and Fogg. Anyone that had the first meal block, often sat in here waiting for the rest of the cadets to arrive. Some cadets roamed the halls. For our wing, we had thirty minutes in between, but others only had ten minutes.

"Alright. Let's settle in." Professor Pascal said, his voice carrying through the stadium.

"Now that we have been in courses for a week, we will start discussing strategies during this class as well," Professor Fogg stated.

"Raise your hand if you are aware of the attacks from Rudemont along Veskonia's coast?" Melamora asked.

Over half of the room raised their hands. I looked around, taking everyone in. The realization of how shielded my father kept me. Maybe I should have paid more attention to his meetings and hushed conversations.

"How are they attacking?" Asked one of the Historians who sat in the upper leadership rows.

"That's a good question. They are sailing in from the east and sending hundreds of arrows through the skies onto land. Most of those arrows had an unknown substance, which injured and killed various troops," Fogg said.

The entire room went silent.

"How are they getting through sky patrol?" an Infantry cadet asked.

"Good question. However, we don't have that information. Keep the questions coming," Pascal said.

"Why are they attacking us?" someone asked.

"We also don't know—but generally, attacks and wars always come down to power," Melamora said.

"But they are human... we are Fae, clearly more powerful," another said.

"Don't assume they aren't powerful, because they aren't Fae. We also believe that they do have Fae amongst the ranks. That wasn't a question though," Pascal said.

"Did we attack back or rather were we able to?" I asked, the question had been burning in my throat.

"Great question. Yes, we did. Riders were able to seize the ship," Melamora said.

"Did interrogations happen?" I asked her. It seemed she wanted us to pry information from them, not giving us anything we didn't ask.

"No..."

I swore she was going to tell me, but after a few heartbeats, she didn't carry on, making me ask. "Why?"

"There were only two people on board, both were dead when the Riders boarded the boat. Both had self-inflicted wounds. There was a machine of sorts that assisted in launching the arrows in large scale," Fogg said, shifting under his feet.

I felt the swallow go down hard. What did that mean? Why? Murmurs amongst cadets started.

"Let's shift this, third and fourth-years please refrain from answering. What should we do to prevent the next attack?" Pascal asked.

Hands shot into the air. Pascal pointed to a male cadet in the back.

"Extend sky patrols farther out over the ocean," the cadet suggested. "Catch them before they reach land."

Professor Melamora tilted her head. "And how long do you think Riders can stay aloft before exhaustion? Patrols aren't infinite. Good start, but think broader."

"Line the coast with wards—something that flares when ships cross the boundary. We can't guard every stretch of ocean, but at least we'd know the moment they arrive," an Infantry cadet said.

A faint smile spread across Melamora's lips. "Better. Awareness before impact."

"Don't wait for them to hit the shore. Meet them halfway. Send Riders to intercept before their arrows ever reach us," Jeremy said.

Murmurs rippled through the rows. The idea was aggressive—dangerous—but it made sense.

"That's risky," Fogg admitted. "But perhaps necessary."

I felt my hand rising before I stopped to think. "Ships that sail across an ocean don't sail on air. They need food, water, and supply lines. If we cut those, they'll never make it here."

"You're beautifully brilliant," Zane said down our bond.

Pascal's gaze pinned me in place. He let the silence drag before answering, "Now that is strategy. Target what keeps them alive, not just the weapons they carry."

"How? How do you cut supply lines across an entire sea?" A Historian cadet asked.

Melamora's eyes flicked across the room, sharp as a blade. "That," she said, "is the question your generation will need to solve."

The air grew heavy again, tension sparking between cadets like storm light. The war wasn't theory anymore. It was on their doorstep—and none of us were ready. We continued debating strategy, shooting down ideas, elaborating on others.

***

The obstacle course was positioned at the edge of the flight field, near the mountain that stretched into the upper flight area, which led into the fliers' den. Up there, three dens belonged to the different species of fliers. Only fliers were permitted beyond that point. There were two entrances to the upper flight field. Stone stairs leading to the top, or the obstacle. Both options appeared unappealing.

"Feather Wing, Electric Platoon, first squad, this is the flier's Rite of Passage. This course is designed to prepare you to ride a flier without dying. You must pass this to move on to bond within a flier. You will practice this in your squad but complete it individually. Since there are twelve squads in total, each squad will get two hours twice a week to work on their skills. You have eight weeks to master this. For the first four weeks, there will be a barrier shield to catch you if you fall. After that, though, you're on your own. Cadets do die practicing. It is an unfortunate thing," Professor Quillet told us.

The seven of us stood at the base of the mountain, gazing at all six levels of the course. I was pretty certain our mouths hung open in awe. The mountain featured a perfect twenty-foot-wide section carved out of its face, extending straight up to the fifty-foot-tall summit. At the bottom right, stones rose about five feet high, followed by a sturdy wooden plank spanning across. After crossing the plank, ropes hung from another inclined plank, spaced roughly four feet apart. Once we navigated that, we encountered another slanting plank attached to the right side, also ascending. At the top, a small landing pad sat across a three-foot gap between the final platform and us.

You had more stones to climb, each small enough to grip tightly, none larger than a few inches across. These stones extended about eight feet upward, leading to another platform you needed to reach. My eyes widened as I looked up at the top, which appeared increasingly difficult, making the climb even more complicated.

Once on the platform, there was another plank starting about four feet from it. This plank differed because logs hung from the plank above, making it harder to cross. After crossing, you climbed a hanging ladder at the end to reach the plank with the hanging logs and crossed again. In the last fifteen feet, another plank was attached, forming a steep ramp upwards. It extended only eight feet, with a five-foot gap and a two-foot ledge to land on. The final part of the obstacle was a series of small ropes to cross, leading to stone ledges that brought you up to the bridge spanning the mountain opening. As you looked up the mountain, the obstacles swung more wildly as they rose higher.

This would not be an easy feat. I was one of the shortest females in the entire Rider's branch, standing five feet three, which I inherited from my mother. My father was six feet tall, and my mother was five feet two inches. I inherited most of my features from my dad—sandy blonde hair with streaks of platinum blonde, emerald-green eyes, paler skin with a peach undertone, and light freckles across my face and arms. My mom had a darker complexion, dark brown hair, and blue eyes. Why did I inherit her short height? I needed my father's height for some of this. I had never let it hold me back before, and I refused to start now, so I focused my thoughts.

"In eight weeks, every Rider will attempt this challenge. While you'll run it as a team, it is an individual event, meaning you won't be allowed to physically help each other. Each person will be timed, and the combined times of the squad will be recorded. Your timing will determine the order you're released on bonding day. The sooner you are released into the Flugblatt Forest, the sooner you and your flier can be bonded. You can practice in the evenings. However, there may be other squads practicing here, and I won't be here," he told us.

The seven of us walked closer to the obstacle together, all staring at it in silence.

"Well, I guess let's go practice our death," Micah said. He was usually the quietest member of our group. We all turned our heads and looked at him in unison.

"Well, I always wanted to be a groundbreaking artist," Clara said. We all lost it. I was glad my squad had a sense of humor. We could all die laughing.

"Alright, let's be serious for a minute—" Jackson started to say.

"I'm serious as a heart attack," Micah said. Now we were all howling.

"Are you all going to stand there laughing, wasting time, or practice?" Professor Quillet asked us. We all went silent.

"Alright, I'll go first, I have the height advantage," Jackson told us, and he wasn't kidding. He had a whole foot over me. He headed to the bottom and began climbing the stones that protruded from the mountain, moving at a smooth pace. The first plank was about eighteen inches wide and definitely required some balancing to cross.

He made it to the end, climbed up the first rope, and started swinging, creating momentum to reach the next rope. He almost made it to the end, and as he went to jump to the next rope, a gust blew the rope, causing him to miss, and he fell to the ground. It was a loud thump.

"Oops. The invisible ward is only after you get past the second level," Professor Quillet said.

We all took turns going. Once someone made it past the first rope course, the next person would take their turn. I fell so many times that my entire body screamed at me with every step I took back to my chambers. I never made it to level five. First, I struggled with the jump on level three. Once I got that down, the jump on level four kept taking me out. I made it across once, and then a log swing hit me right in the back, knocking me down. That wall that Professor Quillet was so proud of was absolute bullshit. Sure, I didn't hit the ground from twenty-plus feet up, but it was like hitting water. It hurt every single time. I guessed that beat having broken bones.

***

By the time I reached my room, my entire body was sore. Every joint hurt. On the plus side, I was so exhausted that my brain wasn't racing twenty miles an hour.

"I have good confidence that it's been a long day for you. You should sneak your way down here, and you can use my shower," Zane said mind to mind, in such a teasing tone.

"Only your shower?"

"I mean, you can use whatever you want in my room."

I didn't waste any time thinking about it. My muscles ached, and going down seven floors would absolutely suck. I also couldn't pass up the chance to touch him. The past week had been exhausting for both of us, as he was busy getting all of his cadets in line due to his position. We only saw each other in the mornings during current events and a few different times passing by. Somehow, the thought of touching him made descending the stairs feel less painful than I expected.

I opened the door and stepped through, feeling the tingle of the shield around the room. He sat on his bed, leaning against the backboard. He was shirtless, and damn, he looked so fucking incredible. The tattoos swirling down his arm, the messy golden waves, those baby blue eyes. Our eyes met, lightning shot through my body, and I was instantly turned on. I crawled onto his bed and moved toward him, never breaking eye contact. I slid over him and straddled his lap. He held onto my hips, pulling me closer. His hand moved to the back of my neck, and he pulled me in until our lips were almost touching.

We were both intently staring into each other's eyes. He tenderly pulled me closer before kissing me passionately, as if it was our last kiss. I felt a pulse of electricity run through my body, lighting me up from head to toe. My cheeks and neck flushed as we desperately swirled our tongues together. He reached down, gripping my tee on the sides and pulling it up, breaking our kiss to slip the tee over my head.

He flipped me over, putting me under him, and he started to kiss down my neck, gently biting it along the way. He continued down, stopping at my nipples, teasing them. Swirling his tongue in a circular motion, he then flicked it back and forth. My skin prickled with excitement, and I immediately felt wet between my legs. He moved down, kissing along my stomach, gently and slowly, building my want for him. He made it to my leather pants, unbuttoned them, and moved off the bed. He swung my legs towards him, putting me sideways across the bed, and he pulled my pants off. I propped myself up and pulled at his pants, because damn if he was going to take my pants off, he was taking his off too.

I unbuttoned his pants and pushed them and his underpants down to let them fall to the ground, freeing his beautiful and very hard cock. Before I could even start to touch, he pushed me back down onto the bed gently. He pushed himself away from the bed, my eyes watching him as he walked around to the other side of the bed. He gripped under my arms and gently pulled me to him, positioning my head at the edge of the bed, right under him.

I don't know what position this was, but I was undoubtedly looking forward to it. He reached forward and trailed one of his fingers gently down my stomach. I could feel everything getting wet in between my legs in anticipation of him. I gripped onto him, pulling his cock downward and towards my mouth. I swirled my tongue around the tip, slipping my tongue into the slit every couple of swirls.

He let out a desperate moan, moved his fingers down, taking his thumb and rubbing the most perfect circle on my swollen clit. We were both teasing each other with our tongues, both of us letting out moans, in between our ragged breathing. I reached back with my right hand, and I gripped his ass cheek into my hand as the perfect leverage to move him back and forth into my mouth.

POP

The noise startled me for a moment. He had unmasked his wings and spread them out. They weren't fully tucked in, but also not completely spanned out. Gods, I wished I could touch them too. Something about being vulnerable for me made my heart yearn for him more.

Instead, I reached my other hand down and cupped his balls into my hand gently. I alternated taking him all in my mouth and licking the tip and down his shaft. Each shift, he let out this guttural moan that nearly sent me. He, too, was playing a dangerous game. He slipped two fingers in while keeping his thumb right on my apex. Moving them in and out, putting the perfect friction on my clit.

"I want you to cum with me," he told me in my mind, *"and love, I am about to shatter."*

"Always with you, Zane." I felt myself building, the intensity was almost so much I could barely focus on him in my mouth, pausing every so often, letting his cock sit there so I could catch my breath. I took him in and really drew him in deep, causing myself to gag a little. I pulled him out a little before doing it again. He leaned more forward, started licking my clit, while finger fucking me. I felt like a volcano waiting to erupt. He was pulsing in my mouth, and he, too, was about to explode.

"Good girl—now Auri—fucking let it go," he growled in my mind, and just like that—on his command—I let everything erupt. It felt as if the earth stopped spinning on its axis. He pulsed and came into my mouth, and I swallowed. The taste was perfect, a mix of salty and slightly sweet. I heard him moaning, and his wings snapped open more.

"Oh fuck, Auri, fuckkkkkk. Your mouth feels perfect."

In between swallows, I was breathing raggedly and moaning loudly. I gripped his ass so tightly. It felt as though my hand was locked in place. He was still flicking me with his tongue, but he slowed down, leaving me to jolt with each pass. My legs and arms were shaking in response to our fiery passion. Gods, I hope it was always like this.

He pulled away from me gently, staring at me. He moved around the bed. I pushed myself upwards, putting my elbows behind me. He reached down behind me and pulled me up, lifting me into his arms. He kissed me so passionately, like we hadn't just had earth-shattering sex. He carried me into the bathroom and into his shower.

"I promised you a shower," he pleaded with me. He started the shower and carefully brought me inside, letting me stand. After turning me around, he started massaging my shoulders, back, and legs. I hadn't noticed how tight my muscles were or how wonderful a shower massage could feel. It felt incredible after falling so many times earlier that day.

CHAPTER 21

"Auriella Blackcreek—promoted to first-year Flight Guide of Feather Wing, Electric Platoon, First Squad," Professor Fogg announced. I felt surprised but happy because it meant I would get a private room on the second floor and a leadership role. Micah had worked hard alongside me, leading our group, so I had thought he would secure the position before me. Michalova Sulivar was promoted to Flight Guide for the second squad. Moving to the second floor brought me closer to Zane and Lili, but it also meant sharing a narrow corridor with Alex, who still hadn't spoken to Zane or me and avoided meeting my gaze whenever we crossed paths.

"Now I can sneak into your room and fuck you all wild," Zane sent down the bond.

"Pretty sure, my room is much smaller than yours, Mr. Big Shot," I teased back.

"True, but it will be fun anyway. Just means we have to be creative."

"Alex... will be on my floor too."

"Good mood, gone."

"Sorry, we just haven't really talked about it."

"Nothing to talk about, he is throwing a tantrum because he can't play with you anymore. He tried to make me choose his friendship over you, and I told him to go get fucked and I chose you."

"I hate that you had to choose."

"I didn't want to, but I will always choose you, if I am forced to choose."

"I will choose you too."

***

Professor Bhatta and Professor Vindex's lectures got combined for the first-years, covering topics such as fliers and magic. Since they were closely related, they co-taught us for a few lectures. Seventy-eight of us packed into the room. We were already down one Rider from when we started a week ago. Last week, we discussed the different types of abilities that could be manifested when you bonded with your flier. Most of us could use minor magic—lighting candles, closing doors, activating sound shields, warding rooms, or moving small objects.

Once bonded to a flier, we would manifest an ability. Most of us would get a common power, but few would develop an exceedingly unique one. Some common powers included elementals like fire, ice, water, air, or metal. Even among these, some became exceptionally powerful—just because a power was common didn't mean it couldn't be powerful, depending on the flier and Rider's bloodlines.

Psionics referred to powers of the mind, the rarest and most unsettling of the magical branches. Two in particular—those who could read thoughts without touch and those who could manipulate another's mind—were spoken of only in whispers. No laws named them, no decrees outlawed them, yet the handful said to have manifested such gifts never lived long. Their deaths were always described as accidents, coincidences, illnesses that struck too suddenly. No one admitted it aloud, but the message was clear. I just prayed I wouldn't develop one of those abilities.

Other types included memory readers—which, honestly, seemed nearly as invasive, though those at least required physical contact. That made them far less terrifying than a manipulator who could bend your will without a word. Beyond those came a wide range: short-term memory erasers, precognition, force-shield projection, telepathic relays, vision manipulation, teleportation, astral projection, and telekinesis. All of them sounded incredible—and utterly terrifying—and nearly all were kept tightly classified.

Some other unique abilities included menders, siphons, thermokinesis, lightning wielder, weather manipulator, or emotion manipulator. We usually only encounter a few people in a lifetime who possess the same unique power. Magic favored balance and only allowed a limited number of extraordinarily strong powers to exist at one time. Not only magic, but fliers also helped keep magic in balance, as they could control the flow of power if they believed someone was abusing it or taking too much. Of course, if you already had magic, they couldn't take that away.

"Today, we will start discussing the different types of fliers available for bonding. Dragons can be the most temperamental of them all, griffins are more tolerable overall, and phoenixes are a serious type all the time," Bhatta told us.

He flicked his finger and projected images of various fliers in front of the classroom. He stopped on the phoenix. There were three of them. All three looked different but still remarkably similar at the same time. "Phoenixes are the only type of fliers that don't have multiple different colors. They all have shades of red and orange that vary with each phoenix. Some start red and then graduate to orange, or vice versa. All phoenixes breathe fire, and while their beaks aren't as strong as a dragon's, they can snap someone in two just as easily. They are ruthless. You should never underestimate a phoenix."

"Is it true that if a phoenix's Rider dies, the phoenix will catch fire and die before they are reborn?" Jameson of Feather Wing, Electric Platoon, second squad, asked.

"Yes, and they are only granted to do that thirteen times before they aren't reborn," Bhatta said. "Oftentimes, we don't see a phoenix wanting to bond when they are in their last life. When they are ready to bond for the final time, that bond is usually significantly powerful."

Bhatta displayed a red dragon, then said, "fifteen red dragons are willing to bond this year. Red dragons are the most temperamental of all dragons. They breathe the hottest fire, and they also love their Riders fiercely." The projection cycled through different red dragons. While they all looked similar, they also appeared different. He stopped on one with a scar running down the right side of their face, over their eye. "This is Albalta. She is a beautiful, much older, and wiser dragon. If she chooses you, it would be an honor to bond with her. It is important to note that her bond with her last Rider nearly killed her when her Rider didn't make it. Some believe this bond may be the strongest she'll ever have."

He snapped his fingers, and a group of grey dragons appeared. "Ten grey dragons are coming forward to bond this year. Grey dragons are more levelheaded than other dragons. They also have the unique ability to blow poison gas. This means they have two forms of weapons at their disposal. Because of their calmer nature, they tend to choose Riders who are also reasonable. They are the quickest to stop the flow of magic if they believe you are not using it for the good of the continent."

The projection cycled through the ten dragons before stopping on the last one. It was the smaller one that I saw during obstacle training. "This is Lakung, as you can see, he is a smaller dragon. Just because he and some others are smaller, do not count them out. While most dragons aren't ready to take on a Rider until they are in their late thirties, sometimes for reasons unknown to us, some dragons choose to bond in their twenties. Dragons continue growing until they are around fifty. They experience their largest growth in the first three years, followed by another growth spurt around ten years and again around thirty years. It is believed that Lakung is twenty-five, making him one of the youngest dragons presenting themselves for bonding. Other than that, we don't know much about him, as he has been in the Flier Vale."

He moved on to show us the six yellow-gold dragons available. Each one was truly stunning. He didn't highlight any of them specifically. He did mention that the yellow-gold dragons were brilliant, often preferring Riders who were also intelligent. They don't care about the Rider's size. Statistically, they tend to choose more female Riders and can be particularly protective.

He flicked his screen and showed us four navy dragons, including the one that had a silvery tone. "Navy dragons are an all-around dragon. They have intelligence, humor, tenacity, and strength. They can also be frightfully ruthless. They tend to prefer warmer areas over colder mountains. Navy dragons are generally more reserved and less open.

They also tend to be excellent mothers and often raise other hatchlings, especially those from bonded dragons."

"What about the larger one with silver tones to it?" I asked. I wanted to learn more about him since he spoke to me that day.

"Ahh, that's Kekoa. He is truly a beautiful one. If any of you are lucky enough to bond with him, he would be a magnificent dragon to be with. He is among the top twenty largest dragons on the continent. Kekoa is also an older dragon and has had three Riders in the past—two of them passing from old age and one in an accident. He hasn't wanted to bond since his last one, and it's been over twenty years. Like Albalta, when his last Rider died, he nearly didn't make it," he told us.

"Is that how it is with all dragons? The more Riders they've bonded with, the lower the chance of surviving their deaths," asked one of the Riders from Eagle Wing.

"Sometimes, the bond between a Rider and a dragon, or really any flier, can be complex. Some dragons have had more than ten Riders and remain unfazed. This is said to be more common with reds and greys, but it doesn't exclude others. The more complicated part is when the flier passes before the Rider. Phoenixes will be reborn, but they have only a limited number of lives. This also means that just because they are on their thirteenth life, it doesn't mean they've had thirteen Riders. We know that the flier feels as though they lose a part of themselves when their phoenix dies and is reborn. It has not been recorded what happens if a flier passes away in their thirteenth life before the Rider does. For dragon Riders, when their dragons die, the Riders sometimes die too, and if they don't, they often feel like they want to. They lose magic that channels their abilities, which can feel like a huge loss. That said, several Riders do survive the loss of a dragon, but they seem to lose a part of themselves, which changes them. They can try to bond with another dragon. Sometimes, an offspring of their dragon will take them. For griffins and their Riders, their bond is unique. If either one dies, the other will follow within the hour. It is catastrophic to lose any flier or Rider, and regardless of the loss, it is felt by all of them," Vindex answered.

The entire class was silent. I didn't know how many of us knew that last bit of information he dropped. I knew I didn't. Of course, I had always focused on dragon kind.

"Now, let's get back to learning about who is willing to bond." Bhatta flicked his finger and showed us the three black dragons that were available. "Black dragons are ruthless and can be the cruelest of them all. However, some aren't as cruel as others. They are considered quite intelligent and manipulative towards others."

"The last two dragons willing to bond are silvers." He grinned before flicking his fingers, showing us the two silver dragons, one much smaller than the other. "Silver dragons are one of the rarest types of dragons and sometimes result from the breeding of other colors. They tend to be some of the largest dragons on our continent. Silvers have the unique ability to spray ice as well as fire. They have an incredible sense of humor, are quick-witted, great parents, and have keen eyesight. If you're lucky enough to bond with a silver, you should take it. They can be a distinctly selective breed."

"I thought you said they are large, but that one is much smaller?" a Rider from Dragon Wing asked.

"Yes, Esme hasn't had her last growth spurt yet, as she is the second youngest dragon willing to bond this year, at only twenty-eight years young. She is stunning, isn't she?"

Esme was her name. She spoke to me and expressed her desire. I found myself drawn to her because something about her felt strangely familiar and right. Kekoa was also incredible, but my heart told me Esme was the one.

"Now, we will move on to the griffins," he told us.

"WOOOT!" one of the Riders in the back yelled out.

"I am glad we have some excited potential griffin Riders here. Griffins are such beautiful, unique fliers. They love their Riders with all their hearts. They will fight for their Rider until their very last breath. Griffins usually appear around twenty to twenty-five years old, placing most of them roughly at the same age as their Riders. Unlike dragons, where colors often indicate personality types, each griffin is different. Nonetheless, they are all smart and curious. Their talons can easily tear someone apart. Because they are smaller, they can maneuver a little more easily than a dragon."

He flicked his fingers again, and light brown griffins appeared. "There are eight light brown griffins. Like the other fliers, every color has different shades and markings."

He continued to show us seven black and gold griffins, three golden griffins, and two dark blue griffins. Like silver dragons, the dark blue color was rare, which made sense, as the first time I saw one was during obstacles.

"Now that we have discussed the sixty-eight fliers willing to bond, more might join on bonding day. Similarly, some of those fliers may decide not to bond when the day arrives—"

A Rider in the middle interrupted him. "Wait, so there could be fewer fliers than that?"

"Yes, that is what I said. Now, before I was rudely interrupted, there might be fliers out there with the same Rider in mind. If that Rider doesn't choose them, they may decide not to bond after all and wait for another Rider they like. Like Fae, fliers can also have mated bonds. This can make things a little more complicated for Riders if your flier is mated. Usually, this means both Rider-flier pairs are stationed at the same fort or outposts near each other. If one of the pairs isn't bonded, the other flier usually comes along and stays in the nearby lair or vale. Mated fliers can be separated for a while without issues, but sometimes they can get more temperamental. Unlike Fae bonded mates, they don't lose their powers when separated."

"There are... you mean... we could have a...destined mate?" Erik Zufall of Electric's second squad asked.

"Yes. It isn't a common occurrence, and sometimes it isn't discussed in all the villages. I do believe it is something we should teach more about in lectures, as it appears every year, I have more students who are lacking." He rubbed his hand through his brown hair. "I am going to give a condensed version because I don't want to derail us off course. There are different terms used depending on what region you are from. Mates, soulmates, twin flames, bonded mates, Anam Cara, or forelsket are majority of the terms used to describe when two Fae are destined to be with each other. This destiny is something that occurs at birth, and when they meet, the bond begins, as both of them feel something incredibly unique. The key is that when the two consummate, they seal the bond. This means the couple's magic becomes more powerful. They possess unique traits that only bonded mates have, and they cannot be separated for an extended period without their power diminishing. Any questions?" Vindex said, answering the question.

"If your mate dies, do you also... die, like fliers?" Akira asked.

My heart skipped a few beats—a realization I had never considered before. Our lives were deeply intertwined.

"I honestly couldn't tell you. Most mated individuals don't disclose when they are, and it can be classified. I imagine, based on what I do know about bonded mates, that if they don't die, they probably feel like they want to. Another important thing is that priestesses have the unique ability to sense if you have a mate and when the mating bond has been sealed," Vindex told us.

CHAPTER 22

"Nellie Pitino calls Auriella Blackcreek," Professor Gile announced.

My eyes widened in surprise when I was caught off guard by being called out, but I shouldn't be. Exactly as Professor Melamora explained, week three would bring changes to our courses, and it also involved calling out other cadets during sparring. All cadets sparred three times a week. We trained with Gile twice and Rivet once.

Our first sparring class of the week was a mix of our platoon, some of Dragon Wing's platoon, a platoon from the Drusearons, and Infantry. The second sparring session included Shapeshifters, Healers, and a few Historians. The third sparring class had the largest mix of Sorcerers, Shapeshifters, Drusearons, and Infantry. I was sure that class would be intense.

Nellie stepped onto the mat, wings pressed tight to her back, her height shadowing over me. She pulled her black hair into a ponytail with one sharp tug, her eyes locked onto mine, blazing with abhorrence. That stare told me everything—I wasn't just fighting her. I was fighting another ghost of my father's past.

The fury inside me cracked open. My chest felt like a furnace, heat rushing through my veins. Rage bled into every corner of me—at my mother for not being here, at my father for his secrets, at Alex for being a dick at every turn. All of it fused into one storm, and I let it roll through me as I faced her.

I stepped onto the mat and bounced on my feet. I stared back at her with my green eyes narrowed, although I was sure they had changed colors, reflecting my shifting mood. I did not offer a handshake before we started, as she challenged me with mounting rage pouring off her. I moved forward in a provocative stance, throwing out my left fist to gauge her reaction. She dodged and threw a fist out with speed. I swung my head to the side and dodged it. I kneeled even lower and charged her. She fell backwards, and I quickly climbed on top to mount her. She was bucking her hips under me. I threw a couple of rights and lefts, and she threw her arms up to cover her face. I threw a right to the side of her face and made contact. She threw her right up and got my shoulder. She bucked at the same time, hard enough that it jostled me. She was able to slide out and jumped to her feet.

Before I could fully rise, she drove her boot into me with a brutal kick. The air ripped from my lungs, shock locking me in place for a heartbeat. I forced another breath in, scrambled up, and staggered back to carve some space between us.

She closed in, fist snapping forward. Her right hook cracked across my cheek, heat blooming along the bone. My vision sparked, but I didn't wait. I reached to my thigh, yanked free a dagger, and slashed. Steel bit into her arm, tearing skin. Blood poured hot down her pale flesh. She gasped, glanced at the wound, then ripped her own dagger free. I pulled my second blade, gripping it in my right. My left hand struck first, another swipe, and before she could reset, I flicked my right. The dagger buried deep in her shoulder, blood spreading fast across her leather.

Her response came sharp—she snapped her wrist and let her dagger fly. I jerked sideways, but not fast enough. Pain seared across my arm as the blade grazed past, slicing skin but sparing me from having steel lodged inside.

I felt a tingle alongside my spine, the familiar feeling I got when Zane was nearby. I couldn't exactly look around the room and divert my attention from Nellie. She pulled out another dagger and charged at me. I jumped to the left, getting out of her way. I flicked another dagger at her, hitting her ass. She let out an angry yell, reached back, and pulled the dagger out, throwing it off the mat. She flicked a dagger, and it landed in the front of my thigh.

Fuck.

That.

Hurt.

I felt anger wash over me, and over the past few weeks, I'd learned which feelings were Zane's. I had learned to build a mental shield. I hadn't been able to block him or his feelings out yet entirely, but I got close. I stacked the blocks in my head because I couldn't let his feelings distract me right now. I had a dagger sticking out of my thigh, which had blood oozing down my leather pants. Pulling it out would only make it bleed more. I reached for my side dagger, unsheathed it, and gripped it with my right hand. I was fucking done dancing around with her. I ducked low and charged her again. She hammer-fisted my back a couple of times. I reached with my left arm, hooked her legs, pulled her down, and mounted her. I gripped her right arm, locking it onto the mat with my left arm, and moved my dagger to her neck and pressed it to her skin.

"I don't know what your fucking problem is, but I am done playing, and it's time to submit," I growled in a low voice in her ear.

"It's bad enough that your father is a murderer, but you had to claim one of us. I've been trying for a year," she hissed back.

Oh *shit*. This wasn't only about my father. This was about Zane. My heart started beating faster, and I could feel the heat rushing to my chest. I pressed the knife into her throat harder. Any harder, or if I changed angles, she would be bleeding. I couldn't let her control my emotions. Those were mine to control. I inhaled deeply.

"I don't own anyone. You didn't stand a chance. Now submit before you start bleeding more onto that pretty porcelain face of yours."

She clenched her fist and knocked three times beneath my tight grip. I sheathed my dagger and sprang to my feet.

I narrowed my eyes and stared. "Don't underestimate me again."

Throughout my life, plenty thought that because I was short, I would be an easy target. What they didn't know was that I had been sparring and practicing with daggers since I was little. I looked around the room and saw him leaning against the wall with his arms crossed. He appeared unamused, so I lowered my shields. He locked eyes with me, then shifted his gaze to Nellie, who was standing up. I turned my head to look at her. As she rose, she looked at him before dropping her eyes. I looked back at him, and he stared at her with a glare that suggested he might actually kill her.

"Apparently, this little fight is about you—" I said down the bond.

"Oh, not your father?"

"Hm, yeah, she may have mentioned him, but she was angrier when she mentioned that I put some kind of claim to your kind, to you, and that she had been after you for the last year."

"I never gave her a single second of my time."

"Why was she convinced that I stole one of you?"

"Some Drusearon warriors, mostly the females, believe that we shouldn't go outside our clans. That we are creating a bunch of half breeds..."

"I guess she's one of those. She's been trying for a year, making her a—"

"Second-year."

"Blackcreek, Winner," Professor Gile stated, "what does that make for you?" He looked at me.

"In all of my sparring or since I've been here?"

"The latter."

"This makes seven to three."

"Nice, your mother would be proud," he said with a smile, before calling the next names up to the mat.

I guessed he knew my mom. I didn't remember him, but it was natural that I wouldn't recognize everyone my parents knew, especially since my mom, as a Healer, had helped many people over the years. Healers were usually well-liked. I looked down at the dagger in my thigh—here goes nothing. I took a deep breath, pulled it out on the exhale. It began bleeding again, so I tossed the dagger towards Nellie. I pressed my hand over the wound to stop the bleeding. Lili started walking toward me and grabbed a cloth from the shelf.

"Here, use this. You can go back to your chambers to clean up if you need."

"I am fine."

"You're always fine." She narrowed her eyes at me.

I just gave her a half smile. "I'll stay with our platoon, as a Flight Guide should." Then I gave her a genuine smile.

"Congratulations, by the way, you've earned it." She patted my back and moved to another mat to watch one of our third-years start to spar.

I moved back to the other first-years, and being a Flight Guide meant I helped direct them and kept them on track. Our Squad Leader was skilled at keeping everyone focused, but sometimes the lectures involved only the first-years. It was essentially a prestigious title for someone excelling in courses and sparring. Usually, I ignored it and disliked being in the spotlight. I preferred to stay in the shadows, watching everyone. However, becoming a Flight Guide felt like a selfish choice. I wanted space of my own. As an only child, I had never shared a place. I also hoped to get closer to Zane. Gods, I was already acting like a clingy, needy person. It irritated Alex when I was clingy. He used his need for space as an excuse to hook up elsewhere. I wasn't any better, often sleeping with newly graduated officers.

"Alexander Beverli calls Zane Braegon," Professor Gile said.

My eyes shot to him and around the sparring gym. Damn. Alex called Zane out. Fuck.

They stepped into the circle, both of them unsheathed their daggers, throwing them to the side. Something cadets did when they agreed to a weaponless spar. The air between them felt heavier than the humid heat. Alex struck first—a fast jab, then a hook. Zane blocked, the thud of bone on bone echoing. They clashed hard, fists and elbows snapping, boots grinding against the packed floor.

But Alex's eyes flicked toward me at the edge of the ring. His lip curled, and fire licked across his knuckles. Not a spark—flame. The gym gasped. Magic wasn't supposed to touch these fights, though sometimes magic did flare under tempers.

"Keep it clean," Gile said.

Zane didn't back off. He lunged in close, ducking under Alex's burning swing. His hand snapped to Alex's wrist. The fire stuttered. The bright flare guttered like a torch in the rain, drawn into Zane's grip. For a breath, orange light seared along Zane's forearm, veins lit like molten lines beneath his skin. Then it vanished, leaving only Alex's stunned face.

Alex staggered back, fists curling, breath rough. "What the fuck was that?"

"Control yourself," Gile snapped, but his eyes narrowed on Zane. "Both of you."

Alex came at him harder, fury twisting his face. He tackled Zane low, and both of them slammed onto the mat. They grappled, bodies twisting, grunts tearing from their throats as they fought for leverage. Alex tried to pin Zane's shoulders, but Zane rolled, using his weight to reverse. Alex's elbow caught his jaw—sharp crack, head snapping sideways. Zane spat blood, eyes flashing, but he didn't break.

They writhed across the mat, fists half-landing, boots digging for purchase. Zane shoved free, grabbed Alex's leg, and twisted. Alex snarled, lashing at him, but Zane coiled lower, locking Alex's ankle under his arm and falling back. His hips jerked, wrenching the joint.

Alex's cry split the room, raw and guttural. He clawed at the mat, face twisted in pain.

"Tap," Zane growled, voice low but steady.

Alex spat a curse, refused. Zane twisted harder, the hold cinched tight. Alex tapped the mat three times. For one more breath, Zane held the lock, eyes boring into Alex's—calm, unflinching. Then he released, shoving Alex's leg aside. Alex curled in, clutching his ankle, breath coming ragged. The gym stayed silent, the only sound was their harsh breathing.

Zane stood slowly, jaw tight, blood at the corner of his mouth. He didn't look at anyone. Not even me. For the Drusearons in the room, he was their Executive Officer, the second in command of their wing. Alex was in charge of his platoon that was in the room. The gym was still buzzing, but all I heard was the echo of Alex's cry. My stomach twisted. Zane hadn't just beaten him—he'd held him there, calm as stone, until Alex nearly broke.

Part of me wanted to flinch away from that steadiness, from the way his control looked colder than fire. Another part of me wanted to trust it, to lean into the one person who didn't seem shaken by anything. And yet...

both of them had been fighting over me. Just as Nellie had fought me over him. It seemed both of them were pulled into some jealous rage.

I pulled my eyes from Zane before he could look back. If I let myself get caught in that stare, I wasn't sure if I'd find safety there—or lose another piece of myself.

"Harlyn Cowens calls Sadie Devins," Professor Gile called out.

I jerked my head at Sadie. Maybe Zane and I weren't the only ones making enemies out here.

"You still aren't over this? I moved on a year ago," Sadie told Harlyn. Clearly, there was much more to this story. Harlyn was an Infantry cadet, distinguished by her navy-blue uniform. They both stepped onto the mat and started feinting at each other, throwing fake punches. Harlyn took a step forward and threw a hard right at the same time, connecting with Sadie. Her eyes widened, and she gasped. I thought that rocked her brain a little bit. Sadie unsheathed a dagger and flicked it at Harlyn, hitting her on the right side of her chest, right below her collarbone. I knew that had to hurt. She winced, jerked the dagger out and threw it back. Sadie ducked and missed. As she popped back up, Harlyn had already drawn a dagger and flicked it across, hitting the left side of Sadie's chest. Sadie gasped hard, reached for the dagger, with terror in her eyes. She dropped to her knees.

"Fight is done," Gile shouted as he ran onto the mat. I was right behind him, heading to Sadie. I hoped it had missed her heart. Lili and Persephone rushed to the mat too, and all four of us gathered around her.

"That's what you get, messing with other people's partners," Harlyn yelled.

"Get the fuck out," Gile yelled at her. He usually didn't look fazed when one of us went down.

"I'll take her to the infirmary," Zane said. I hadn't even noticed him move to the mat. One breath, he stood beside us, the next he scooped her up—and vanished.

My pulse lurched. What the hell? How did he do that? In the tower attack, he had appeared the same way, out of nowhere.

I glanced around. I wasn't the only one staring. Gile and most of the Drusearons barely blinked.

Teleporter. Was Zane a teleporter?

"Let's get back to sparring, next up…" Gile continued. I stopped really listening when I didn't hear anybody else in my platoon.

"How did you do that?" I said down our bond.

"Wouldn't you like to know?" he teased.

"I mean, yeah, I would. Can you teleport?"

"Yes, but we call it roving. Most Drusearons of Royal Fae can learn to do it. We have to have been to the place we want to go, and when we first start doing it, we can only go short distances. I have been doing it for a while so I could go quite a distance by myself. Carrying someone is about half the distance."

"What other abilities do you have?"

"Oh, my sweet love, I have so many. Most of them left for the bedroom."

"I got it, not sharing that information quite yet."

"I can't… I want to. I will, but not now. Please, my love, don't push."

"How's Sadie?"

"Nice change there, she will make it, it missed her heart by millimeters. She will be here for a day or so."

Sparring finally concluded, resulting in a few more injuries. Aside from Sadie, our platoon mainly remained unscathed. By the end of the day, I felt utterly exhausted, a typical feeling for me these days. The day grew more challenging because I had to carry my belongings from my seventh-floor chambers down to the second floor. My room was only two doors away from Lili's, which made me happy since I was closer to my friend. After finishing, I returned to the seventh floor, gathered the other first-year students, and led them to the infirmary to visit Sadie. When I was injured, my squad came to see me, and I made sure to visit them as well.

CHAPTER 23

I finally returned to my room for the evening, taking everything in. Fortunately, my room faced the field beside the college. The chambers on the other side lacked windows because they shared a wall with the dining hall. The room featured a full-size bed, larger than the small chamber bed upstairs. There was a high-back reading chair in the corner, an armoire opposite the bed, and a desk in front of the large floor-to-ceiling windows that overlooked the field. Black drapes could be drawn closed for privacy.

Flight Guides didn't get private bathing chambers. We used the common hall bathing room. Only Wing Commanders, Executive Officers, and Platoon Leaders had private baths in their rooms. Their rooms were also significantly larger—a benefit of their rank.

I hadn't addressed my cuts from sparring earlier. They weren't deep and really wouldn't require stitches. I pulled out my mom's med bag and started taking out the items, looking to see what I could use to take care of them. I pulled out a brown bottle of salve. It had 'wound care' written on it, so I set it aside. I pulled some gauze out and put it with the salve. As I felt into the bag, I noticed a small zipper halfway down. I opened it and pulled out another deep brown bottle. There wasn't anything written on it, and it was hard to see inside. I opened it and looked inside, finding a neatly folded paper. I gently pulled it out. It had definitely been in there for a while.

My dearest Auri,

If you're reading this, it likely means something has gone wrong. I wrote two letters for this bag—a general one in case something happens to me, and this one. I'm writing this before my meeting with your father, the general, and other senior officers. If I am not here to retrieve this letter later, assume I was killed due to what I found out. Auri, I really hope you reconsider and decide not to join at all. Your dad is in deep, with more secrets than I can share. We only stayed together for you. They are taking powerful cadets and experimenting on them. However, if you join the military, hopefully, your dad will finally change. A war is coming, and it might arrive before you actually enter, but they don't expect everything to fall into place for another eight years—by the time you're twenty-two, you should be graduating. The King of Rudemont is building an army, recruiting Fae to join him. Some of the dukes in our provinces are collaborating with him to stage a mutiny aimed at breaking away from Yebel. Our king is corrupt, and maybe joining the mutiny is what you need to survive. But all of this will come out over the next several years—pay attention, baby girl. I've taught you everything you need to know. Now you need to put it all together. Remember what I discussed in your other letter about your mate—they will always be loyal to you. You can trust Lili. Her mom doesn't know everything, but enough to try and keep you three safe. I have always loved you, and everything I have done is for you.

Love always, Mama

Tears streamed down my face, and I hadn't realized I was crying. My mother had been murdered, and my father was involved. How did this happen? My heart pounded fiercely, my chest felt scorching hot, and heat radiated down my arms as it climbed up my neck. I placed the letter on my bed and decided I needed fresh air. I fortified my mental shields block by block, certain he could feel my pain through them. A faint tingling ran along my spine as I ignored it. I didn't want to speak right then. I couldn't speak right then. I was shattered. I ached to set the entire world on fire.

I climbed to the top of Watchtower One, where two Riders sat on watch duty. I didn't say anything, simply moved to the ledge and sat on it, gazing at the sky. The moon was bright, and stars were scattered across it. Facing towards the Flier's Vale, I saw fliers circling overhead for overwatch. It was quiet tonight, and I appreciated that peace. I thought about my mom and the last year of her life. She was murdered the year before I was raped—were those events connected? I never believed so, but now I wasn't sure. My dad had enemies who, in some way, also became my enemies. Honestly, he only recently became my enemy. He was involved in my mother's murder, or so she implied. At the very least, he knew who did it and did nothing. Was that why he didn't want me to join?

Swoosh. Suddenly, he sat down next to me on the edge. I didn't bother to look at him because I knew it was Zane.

"You've successfully blocked me out."

"That was my goal."

He looked over his shoulder at the two Riders, nodded to the side, and they moved down the stairs.

"I felt glimmers of sadness and anger, but you have gotten good at shielding."

I simply nodded my head slowly and kept staring into the darkness. I was speechless at that moment.

"Auri, you've never been quiet. What's wrong?" he asked, reaching over to put his arm around my shoulders and pulling me close.

Tears streamed down my face faster than before. He pulled me close, reminding me he was my safe person. I smelled his lavender and pine scent, which made me feel at home. I didn't exactly know what or where home was anymore. It was a reminder of how chaotic things were at the moment. I let my shields lower, bit by bit. I couldn't shut him out. I wanted this relationship to be different. I wanted to trust him and let him in. I had to. Undoubtedly, every part of me wanted to run away.

"My mom was murdered..." I told him through our bond, knowing I couldn't say it out loud—not only because I didn't want to believe it, but because I couldn't let anyone overhear it.

"Shit... Are you sure?"

"I discovered another letter hidden in my pack. She wrote it days before she was murdered, essentially stating that if she didn't pull it out, it meant she had been murdered."

"Wow... I am so sorry."

"There is more..."

"I can't imagine how much worse this can be."

"Is the Veil of Vultures planning a mutiny?" He turned his head toward me so fast, his eyes wide.

"I... um..."

"So that's a yes..."

"I... Fuck..."

"It's just us here, literally and mentally."

"Saying it to you puts both of our lives at risk."

"I love this... I fucking love this." Anger surged through my body. My chest felt so tight, and my throat seemed like it was closing in on itself. I recognized that my anxiety was rising, and I needed to get it under control before it controlled me.

"I am in fact not loving this." He placed a kiss on the top of my head and hugged me tighter.

"My dad was involved in the murder of my mom, my mate's province is part of a mutiny I'm just learning about, we're apparently going to war soon with the other continent and the provinces within it. Oh, and somewhere, someone is performing experiments on... I have no clue who."

"Your dad—"

"Yeah, my dad—fucking killed my mom."

"Literally?"

"I mean, does it matter? She said she went to a meeting with him, the general, and other officers. He's here, she's not. He's now the general... sooooo not much to deduce there."

"I honestly don't have much information. I'm not certainly sure where I stand on everything. I know that my dad might be planning a coup. I don't know which other provinces are involved. I only know a few details because I listen and pay attention when I shouldn't."

"I want to crawl into my bed, cry, and not come out for days..."

"Not an option, you are strong. You have already overcome so much. We are a team now, and you will not falter."

"I can't think about this anymore. I have more questions, and neither of us has answers. My mom did tell me that I was safer joining the mutiny... so there's that."

"Tell me, Auriella Reyna Blackcreek, what do you want?

"I don't know, as long as I have you and my dragon."

"I forget that one day a dragon will be added to our dynamic."

"There are seven of you, right?" changing the subject.

"Yes..."

"Wow, what was that like?"

"Chaotic and loud, our home was filled with frequent arguments among siblings. Raised as royalty, we were expected to behave impeccably. As the eldest twins, Aeliana and I were supposed to set an example and guide the younger children. I was rebellious and resisted these expectations throughout my childhood, while Aeliana always kept me grounded."

"What are your other siblings like?"

"Theodora is after us, and she's the wild card. Then there's Arkin, quiet and shy, always following the rules. Helena, ah, I miss her. She's the calm in the storm, always reasonable. Adrian is the sixth, and we weren't prepared for him. Thea was wild, but Adrian was wilder. He climbed the walls and was generally into everything. Elizabeth, or Lizzy, is the baby. The first six of us were all under two years apart, most of us only a year apart, but Lizzy came five years after Adrian. Everything is her way or the highway." He smiled afterward.

"You miss them, huh?"

"Yeah, I do. Well, sometimes, I don't miss the bickering."

"The most bickering I have experienced was with Lili and Alex. They are the closest to me."

"That might make you lucky."

"Perk was that I was the center of my parents' attention, which apparently is the only reason they remained together."

"Being with me means you have gained six siblings, so welcome to the—chaos."

He pulled me in tighter. "Hold tight."

Lights flashed.

I heard a whooshing sound. I opened my eyes, and we were on top of the mountain—Pass of Bête Noire. I thought I was going to die when I was up here before. I remembered the view was beautiful. He had just teleported us—or roved, as he called it, which felt weird. One second, we were on the ledge, and the next, we were on this mountain top. He sat on the ground and pulled me down next to him before lying us back to stare directly into the sky.

"What's going to happen when you graduate?"

"That's almost two years away…"

"I get anxious about the future. I am constantly thinking about it, especially with all of the things coming up."

"I will graduate and be stationed somewhere, probably Fort Dasyn, because it's the nearest fort to the college, and we will need to be near each other. Assuming we have gone to a priestess by then."

"We will. How far of a flight is Fort Dasyn?"

"For me, about three hours, it is over the mountains on the Alpha side. Dragons fly a bit faster. I, of course, can be in your room in seconds. Let's worry about making it through the next couple of years here, though."

We lay on top of the mountain with my head resting on his shoulder and leaning toward his head. His arm was wrapped around me, curling under and up to my side, holding me close. We stayed there quietly, breathing in unison. I inhaled the crisp mountain air, listening to the cheerful chirping of insects as they sang. I heard the river rushing in the valley below. It was an incredibly peaceful night. My mind felt overwhelmed. I had endured many tough challenges. Fighting daily to survive and dealing with my parents' constant bullshit was exhausting. Every day, I was pushed physically and mentally. Cadets wanted to see me fail, secretly hoping and praying for my downfall. But I was determined to succeed. I aimed to prove to everyone who doubted me that I could overcome anything and rise above it.

CHAPTER 24

The week passed swiftly. Our squad held sparring sessions on Mondays, Wednesdays, and Fridays. On Tuesdays and Thursdays, we focused on obstacle training, while the remaining days were dedicated to our regular courses. We stayed active daily, which was better than some other platoons that combined sparring and obstacle training on the same day. When Friday came, after our all-branch current events class, our squad went to Professor Rivet's gym.

I hadn't looked forward to sparring since it often caused conflicts between branches. Many disagreements occurred. A cadet could only be called out twice in one day, and if they got seriously injured in the first match, the second was postponed. We started each session with callouts before random pairs. To make a callout, one had to notify the professor's assistant a day in advance. I was called out twice on Wednesday. I wanted to yell—*I fucking hate my dad, too*. Instead, I simply stepped onto the mat and did it. I lost the first match but won the second.

Our platoon was the only Riders. The rest consisted of Drusearons, Shapeshifters, Sorcerers, and Infantry. Each branch stood in its own group, separate from the others. Zane was among the Drusearons. Professor Rivet started calling out names as he walked around to each mat to start the matches. He had ten assistants helping him call the matches.

"Darla Cuzner calls Lilian Beverli," Rivet said. First squad moved to the mat to support our Platoon Leader. The second squad went to another mat to support one of their cadets. I watched as Lili stepped onto the mat with this Infantry cadet, who also wore black. Lili glared at her like she might set her on fire. I wondered what the hell happened between those two. The two of them were close in height, but Lili had an inch over her. Darla had blond hair and blue eyes, starkly contrasting with Lili's.

They both bounced around. Lili reached down with both hands, unsheathing two daggers, one for each hand. Darla's blue eyes flared in response, and she grasped one of her daggers, but before she could even get a chance to get the second one out, Lili was on her and started swiping left and right with both daggers. My eyes danced, watching her dominate. I didn't think Darla really knew what she was getting herself into. Darla dropped low and charged, but Lili dodged her with such quickness, leaving Darla stumbling.

Lili went on the attack, flicking her right dagger into Darla's calf and her left into her back. Darla dropped to the mat, and Lili hopped onto her back, pulling another dagger out and pressing it into her throat. Darla tapped the mat three times.

A wave of happiness washed over me. That was my best friend, and she had improved a lot over the past two years. She and I used to spar constantly while growing up—of course, we didn't use daggers or stab each other. All around us, cadets were sparring on different mats. You could hear punches, grunts, and growls everywhere.

"Asmoth Elslurs calls Auriella Blackcreek," Professor Gile announced.

Of course, this fucking prick again. I felt Zane's rage surge through the bond. He heard it from where he was. Our squad moved together toward the mat that Gile pointed at. I stepped onto the mat, pulling daggers into both hands. I wasn't holding back like I had in the past. I was done with this guy's bullshit. Zane moved next to the mat, standing by Lili. I couldn't focus on him or let his feelings distract me. I stacked those blocks in my mind, blocking him out. Asmoth stared at me with the same anger as before. He pulled out a dagger and charged forward. I didn't think he wanted to spar. I was pretty sure he planned to kill me.

He knocked me onto my back quickly. I wasn't surprised since he towered over me. I felt pain shooting up my spine, and my head hit the mat with a force that made it feel like my brain rattled inside my skull. My eyes fluttered in response to the pain. I couldn't die today. It wasn't in my cards.

Fuck him. Fuck this. He reached back to start landing punches. I covered my head.

"Get up, Auriella!" Zane's shout cut through me. Like I was lying there for fun.

I bucked my hips under him, straining for leverage, but his weight pinned me. He snatched my right hand, wrenched the dagger free, and shoved it aside. I swung my left at his ribs. He knocked it down like swatting a fly. My chest heaved, fury boiling hot. I refused to stop moving, refused to let him trap both arms.

He leaned in close, shadow filling my vision, eyes burning with the thrill of having me under him. My heart raced, pounding so loud it filled my skull. Rage lit in me—I hated that look, hated that I was losing ground. I snapped my forehead into his nose, bone cracking against bone. Blood gushed down, spilling across my face. For a second, I thought I had him.

But he roared, half in pain, half in triumph, and bore down harder. His grip clamped iron on my arm, his weight crushing the fight out of me. My calf burned where I twisted wrong, every breath ragged and shallow. The dagger point pressed at my throat—not deep, but deep enough to remind me how close I was to the end.

I thrashed once, twice, pure fury pushing me to keep fighting, but his strength swallowed mine. My muscles gave out. My vision blurred. My pride screamed louder than my lungs.

"Tap, bitch," he growled, low and certain.

"Fuck you," I hissed back. My nails dug into the mat, body shaking.

But in the end, my palm slapped down. Tap.

The sound cracked through the silence. He released me and rose, blood dripping from his nose. My chest heaved, rage clawing through me. I sat there shaking, humiliated, furious with him, furious with myself. The fight wasn't lost—it was stolen.

And I swore I'd take it back.

Zane stood over me, hand outstretched. I gritted my teeth and took it, hauling myself to my feet. My body ached, my pride worse, but I refused to let him see me broken.

I wasn't sorry for the fight. He'd pressed me hard, and I hated that I'd tapped. What burned wasn't the loss itself—it was how close I'd come, how easily he'd forced me down. Rage coiled tight in my chest, hot enough to choke. Let them all see it. Let them all know I wouldn't be underestimated again.

I met Zane's eyes. Worry lined his face as he searched mine. I dropped my shields, forcing the bond open, and let him feel the storm I held back—shame, fury, and the promise that next time, I wouldn't lose.

"I am fine."

"You're covered in blood."

"None of it is mine."

I lifted my shirt and wiped the blood off my face, then bent over to gather my daggers. I smeared the blades clean against the fabric before sliding them back into their sheaths. My legs carried me toward my squad.

Lili stared at me, brows furrowed, concern plain in her eyes. Savage—that was what she called me. Maybe she wasn't wrong. Maybe something inside me had always been off. I'd never grieved the way others did. Death didn't rattle me, not most of the time. Some losses cut sharp, like my mother's, a wound that never closed. But strangers? Enemies? I'd weep over a wounded animal long before a Fae. Animals had never shown me cruelty.

Still, a question gnawed at me. Why hadn't he finished me? He'd tried before, and no one would've stopped him. He could have driven the blade down, ending me with impunity. Instead, he let me walk away. That unsettled me more than the fight itself.

We had plenty of matches left. I forced myself to shake it off. No point in dwelling.

CHAPTER 25

It was the first day of autumn. Except for summer, each equinox was celebrated just like the first day of lectures. This year, the celebration was planned for September twenty-seventh, a Saturday evening. Over the past few weeks of lectures, we had been doing the same activities—sparring, climbing mountains, attending lectures, sparring more, and falling down the mountain. On October first, regardless of the day, the Riders would climb the Flier's Rite of Passage. We were only days away from that.

Current events class involved a lot of debating of the brewing war between Yebel and Rudemont. We all piled in there each morning, this morning was no different. As a Flight Guide, I had moved to the upper rows with the other cadet leadership. Today it was only Melamora leading the class, bravely taking all of us on. "Humans do not fight as we do. They breed armies by the tens of thousands, trained for lines and volleys. They rely on steel and powder, on ships and engines that can cross the ocean and fire upon us from distances even a Rider cannot close unscathed. In the last decade, they have perfected machines that launch storms of arrows tipped with alchemical fire—what the troops call iron rain."

She let the words hang, her eyes sweeping the lecture hall.

"Against us, they know they cannot match sorcery or dragon fire. So, they turn to numbers, industry, and endurance. Where a Fae soldier may fight for three centuries, a human army replaces itself every twenty years. When one wave dies, another rises behind it."

A Historian cadet raised his hand. "Then why are we not already invaded?"

"Because," Melamora said, "power is not only measured in numbers. A single bonded Rider with phoenix or dragon fire can break a fleet. A ward woven by a Sorcerer can turn aside cannon shots. But do not mistake our strengths for invincibility. The humans adapt. Every year they bring new weapons across the sea, and every year they press closer."

Professor Melamora's voice carried across the tiers. "Intelligence suggests the humans are experimenting with blood rituals—binding their soldiers to magic stolen from the land itself. These rites may prolong life, may twist humans into something that heals from wounds no mortal should survive."

A low murmur spread through the cadets.

"What are they making?" an Infantry cadet blurted.

Melamora's expression hardened. "No one knows for certain. Some call them Alp. Others, Strigoi. But the word appearing most often in reports—" She let the pause stretch, her eyes sweeping the rows, "—is Nosferatu."

The name hit the hall like a cold draft.

"That's just a legend," one Historian scoffed, though his voice shook.

"Legends," Melamora said sharply, "are only stories until someone decides to make them real. Do not dismiss what you do not understand."

The mutters grew louder, cadets leaning in to whisper the name under their breath *Nosferatu. Nosferatu.*

The word Nosferatu clawed straight through me.

I had heard it before. Years ago, when I was still little enough to sit on my father's knee while he spun stories by firelight. He'd told it like a camp tale, voice low and dramatic, letting the shadows on the walls dance as he spoke.

"They're men who traded their souls for blood," he'd said, eyes gleaming with the fire. "Bodies that don't stay dead, hearts that don't beat, but still they walk. Their teeth are sharp enough to tear through bone, and their thirst never ends. Nosferatu."

I'd pulled the blanket to my chin, wide-eyed. He'd only grinned, leaning close so his breath tickled my ear.

"If you ever hear one scratching at your window," he whispered, "don't look. Don't open. Once you meet their eyes, they'll never let you go."

Then he'd laughed, ruffling my hair, as if it was only a game to spook me before bed. But I still remembered lying awake that night, staring at the shutters, half expecting to hear the scrape of claws.

And now, years later, the word didn't sound like a story anymore.

The word lingered in the air like a curse.

"Nosferatu," one cadet muttered, the syllables sharp as broken glass.

"That's a ghost story," another scoffed. "Meant to scare children into shutting their windows."

"Exactly what you're acting like now," Melamora cut in, her voice flat. "Ghost stories are often truths wrapped in warning."

A Historian cadet leaned forward. "Even if it were true, why would humans need such abominations? They already outnumber us."

"Numbers aren't everything," Melamora said. "They fear our fliers, our wards, our lifespans. So, they create what they cannot be. Something that doesn't tire. Doesn't die. If they succeed, it won't matter how many troops we have."

Someone snorted. "If they drink blood, we'll cut their throats before they get close enough."

Melamora's eyes narrowed. "Arrogance is the first casualty of war."

I caught myself gripping the edge of my seat, knuckles white. My father's voice still echoed in the back of my mind. *Shadows on the wall. Don't open the window.*

Across the rows, I saw Alex shake his head. "Humans can't outmatch the Fae. Not in magic. Not in strength. Not in flight."

"Keep thinking that," Melamora said coldly, "and you'll be the first to die."

"Humans? Nosferatu? Stories to frighten children," Asmoth said, loud enough for the rows around him to hear. "If they come, they'll bleed like anything else."

A ripple of laughter spread through the hall.

Melamora's voice cut through it, sharp as steel. "Do you think I stand here spinning ghost stories?" She let the silence stretch until the last nervous chuckle died. "Ancient Historian records mention Nosferatu on Yebel centuries ago—creatures raised through rituals that drained the life of the unwilling. They fed on blood because their own bodies could no longer sustain them. Entire villages fell before a single one."

The laughter was gone.

"But they were destroyed," a cadet blurted, uncertain now.

Melamora's gaze swept the rows. "Destroyed... or forgotten. History has a way of burying what we don't wish to remember. If humans have rediscovered the process—or worse, improved it—then the war you're preparing for is unlike any your parents or grandparents faced."

A hush fell. Even the most arrogant looked uneasy.

I sat frozen, her words scraping down my spine. Nosferatu. I could still hear my father's voice from years ago, spinning it like a fireside tale to scare me before bed. *If you ever hear scratching at your window, don't look.*

Back then I'd thought he was teasing. Now, I wasn't so sure.

Had he known? Had he told it like a story because he didn't want me to see the fear in his eyes? He'd always been careful with what he shared—too careful. Every story I'd ever heard from him suddenly felt like a half-truth wrapped in a blanket of lies.

The hall was quiet around me, cadets shifting uneasily, but all I could hear was my own pulse. If the Nosferatu were real—if the humans had truly made them—then my father had kept far more from me than I ever guessed.

And gods, what else had he told me without telling me?

"What do you make of this?" I asked Zane.

"I've heard the rumors but thought they were rumors or stories... now maybe not."

"My dad told me stories of them when I was younger, but said it wasn't real."

"I am sure he didn't want to scare you."

"He left me unprepared instead."

Melamora led the class through more heated debates, some cadets challenging the news she shared with us. My head ran around circles. I don't know what I can even do about this, I couldn't let something I had no control over, control me. I needed to focus on today. I needed to focus on my training.

***

It took me three weeks to finish level five. The final challenge—swinging across short ropes in strong winds—was much more complex than I expected. I finally completed it at the end of week four, just in time. The following week, we lost our barrier. Lorenzo was the first to fall when it was gone, breaking his femur and tibia. His scream was so loud I felt like I still heard him the next day. He was stitched up and returned the following week. His fall reminded us to go more slowly.

Last week, I slipped while running toward the ledge at the end of level five, but I managed to grasp it and pull myself up. I kept telling myself, *'I can do this.'* Several cadets had already fallen and couldn't be saved. We wouldn't know the final count until all the Riders finished the Rite of Passage, but it seemed we had lost at least five cadets.

Clara and Sadie managed to complete the course by the end of the third week. Clara slipped once during week four but recovered quickly. Akira struggled with me, especially with the physical aspects. Despite being two inches taller, she was still shorter than most female Riders.

During sparring, she had more losses than wins, but she showed improvement every week. We went to the gym in the evenings to do more training. Micah, Lorenzo, and Jackson had been completing the pass since the second week, but when they tried to move too fast, each one made errors and slipped somehow.

It was our second-to-last day of practice before we finished, meaning we were just one step closer to the Rite of Passage. All seven of us gathered at the base of the mountain pass, forming a circle.

"I think our time is a little slow, but we are also graded on how many of us complete it as well as timing. If all seven of us make it, we should have good timing and not be in last place. Every time we tried to speed up, it cost us time because someone slipped. I know my height affects my speed, and I'm sorry for that," I told our group.

"Electric Feather's First Squad!" Jackson shouted.

"Electric Feather's First Squad!" we all echoed.

As fall approached, the weather began to change. The wind grew stronger, and there were more rainy days. That day was no different—there was fog in the air, with light rain. Standing at the base of the mountain, you couldn't see more than halfway up it. At that point, Professor Quillet was just there to babysit us. He didn't offer any guidance or advice. Instead, he timed us to let us know our individual times. Lorenzo decided to start us out. He climbed up the stone ledges and walked across the first beam.

Even at this low height, you could see him sway a little with the wind gusts. He held both arms out for balance as he moved smoothly across the beam. When he reached the end, he climbed onto the ropes and breezed right through. Once he pulled himself onto the start of level three, Clara decided to go.

Lorenzo had already crossed the second beam, which had a steep angle, jumping the first gap onto the ledge. Clara made her way across the first set of ropes, climbing onto level three. Jackson moved forward and started across. He moved the fastest across the beam, as if he had been born for this. Clara made it to the jump and leapt across, just like she had been doing. Jackson had already turned and was making his way across the ropes. Once he climbed up, I started across the beam.

Getting across the beams hadn't been a problem for me. My short height helped me move without much wind. Lorenzo should be finished, but looking up, I could only see the hanging logs. Clara should be at the last set of ropes, so I started making my way across the ropes—

"Ahhhhhhhhh." Clara's screams rattled through my ears. Please let her grip something before she falls completely. I couldn't freeze. In fact, I needed to move even faster. What if she didn't and fell, hitting me on the way? I was only about ten feet from the ground, so it wouldn't be as bad, but her hitting me wouldn't be great. I glanced up to see if I could spot her before I started moving across the ropes. She was still screaming. It was echoing off the mountain, and she got closer.

I was pretty sure I heard banging as she fell. I was on the last few ropes before the screaming was right there. I looked behind me and saw her fall to the ground. My heart sank into my stomach. Sadie's face immediately went pale. Micah vomited on the ground. I held onto the rope with all my strength. From my position, I could tell she was no longer alive. Her neck was contorted unnaturally, and her legs were bent at the knees. Her soul was now with Betha.

I couldn't just stay there hanging. I had to keep going. Losing a squadmate sucked, but we were at a war college that was preparing us for death. I climbed onto level three and walked the beam up. Sadie climbed up and onto the first beam.

I was quite sure I heard Micah crying below. I also suspected they had started dating, though they hadn't made it official. Most first-year students didn't get into relationships, mainly because our living situation was terrible. Unless you were sleeping with a cadet leader—third or fourth-year students—privacy was scarce. Still, that didn't stop anyone.

The Historians, Healers, and Witches all had their own private chambers regardless of year because they had fewer cadets than the other four branches. Cadets were also known for bargaining their rooms or making deals with roommates to stay away for extended periods.

Climbing the stone ledges to reach level four was quite challenging. They were slippery, and the top ledge was set apart from the others, requiring you to reach behind and let your legs hang before pulling yourself up. Fierce gusts of wind caused shivers to run down my spine. My leather jacket offered no help. It was soaked through. I jumped onto the beam with hanging logs from the ledge, then grabbed the logs and carefully crossed the beam. About halfway across, I heard a sudden scream below. Although the scene was hard to make out, I was sure it was Sadie.

My stomach twisted into a tight ball. I preferred Sadie because we shared a room and had grown close. Still, I couldn't focus on her. Focusing on her would distract me and slow me down. I kept moving across the narrow beam of logs and climbed up the ladder onto the next beam. This part was my least favorite. Half of the beam was flat and easy to walk on. The other half was a steep incline rising about ten feet. Then, I needed to jump across a gap onto a small, jagged ledge. A running start would be ideal, but the beams weren't broad and had become slick from the rain.

I took a deep breath. I was pretty certain I wouldn't make it across this time with the relentless rain and furious wind. If I could get a firm grip on the rugged ledge, I could pull myself up as I had done before. I reached the steep inclined beam and tried to walk up quickly, but the rain made it difficult. I had to adjust my approach because it was the first time we faced this challenge in torrential rain. I climbed about four feet before reaching the ledge, then sprinted toward it. I didn't quite succeed in jumping onto the ledge, but I managed to grip it firmly. Thank you, Parvaiz. The God of luck had always come to my side when I needed him.

The shorter ropes were flapping in the air with the wind, but I knew it wasn't about time. It was about making it across. I leapt onto the first rope and slowly made my way across. Thank the gods, when I finally climbed on top of the mountain.

Lorenzo and Jackson sat at the top, their eyes filled with pure defeat. Jackson had tears streaming down his face and was completely still. I sat quietly beside them. Sadie quickly followed and joined us, relief washing over me that she was okay. The rest of our squad settled on the ground, one by one. The original group included seven. Now, only six were gathered.

This was my squad, and I had lost one of them. I swallowed hard at that realization.

When someone died, their body was placed on a sturdy wooden raft, set ablaze, and pushed down the raging, tumultuous river. At the war college, the raft often carried more than one body as we burned it. Everyone silently prayed to the God they worshiped most. Marzana, the fierce Goddess of death, was the keeper of death—she embodied hell. She took life away when individuals proved unworthy of living.

Betha was the inspiring Goddess of life and water, revered as a sacred figure who granted us vitality. Some Fae believed worshiping Betha would lead them to peaceful heavens after death. Few worshiped Marzana, but many cherished Betha. I worshiped both Parvaiz, the fortunate God, and Freya, the enchanting Goddess of love. I was raised to believe that love and luck enabled you to conquer any challenge. Betha was vital because she provided life and sustained us daily through the nurturing forces of nature. She represented a perfect balance among the Gods.

Wymond was the fierce God of war, believed to be the primary source of constant conflict and chaotic upheaval. Panki was the witty God of humor, notorious for his mischievous and sinister ways that often sparked chaos. Pragyan was the wise God of knowledge, renowned for his vast understanding of everything in existence.

We were all sitting there together, silently letting the tears run down our faces as the rain picked up. The struggle between saying something and letting us all sit in shock and sadness was ripping at me.

We needed to start descending the stairs before Professor Quillet began yelling, as the next squad would be arriving soon. "Clara was amazing, and she will be missed. She would want us to take the moment we have taken and honor her life by kicking ass, moving forward. Let her soul rest with Betha," I told them.

"With Betha," the five of them said in unison.

The rest of the day felt like a thick fog as I moved through a space that hadn't seemed real. The past few months had worn me down, tearing me apart and overwhelming me. I felt sadness knocking at the door, eager to reveal its ugly face. I refused to let her in. Anxiety lingered with me every day, free of charge, but I didn't want sadness inside. Tomorrow promised to be a great day. We planned to celebrate and then enjoy a week off from lectures to do whatever we pleased, including visiting the charming nearby village of Chalahana. Rumors spoke of a fantastic tavern there, where we could all drink and relax.

I climbed into bed, gazing out the window, curtains drawn back. The sky shimmered with bright stars that usually brought me joy, but that night they offered no comfort. My mind was empty. Instead of racing thoughts, there was complete silence. My soul ached, exhausted and heavy. Every time I closed my eyes, a painful memory flashed vividly. Tears streamed silently down my face. Silence persisted. Eventually, my eyelids grew too heavy to keep open, and I drifted into a restless sleep.

CHAPTER 26

Zane knocked four times.

I wasn't sure why he knocked. He could walk in or speak into my head. I stood up from my chair, where I had been sitting since I woke up that morning, staring into the abyss. I didn't know how long I had been sitting there. My mind split in ten different directions all at once. The weight of it all overwhelmed me. Sadness knocked, and I refused to acknowledge her.

I greeted Zane, standing in the doorway with an unmistakably dapper appearance. He wore sleek black leather pants and a long-sleeved black tunic that clung to his sturdy frame. My gaze shifted to his arm, where a forest green item was folded neatly over it, adding a splash of color to his dark attire.

"Hi, beautiful," he said, giving me a wry smile. I was sure that my appearance caused that smile. My hair was wildly frizzy and unbrushed. I was only wearing a T-shirt and hadn't showered since the previous day.

"That's sweet, but I am anything but—"

"My Anam Cara, you are beautiful, especially with your messy hair." He reached out, cupped my chin, and lifted it, making my eyes meet his. Lightning coursed through my body.

"Tell me what's wrong?"

"Super tired... That's all. I'll be okay." I smiled at him. One, I was sure he could read right through.

"I brought you a gown for tonight if you're still planning to attend," he said, grabbing the green dress and unfolding it for me to see. It was stunning—a deep forest green. The top was made of a tight polyester fabric decorated with small diamond pendants. The skirt transitioned into a more sheer material, featuring slits on both sides that reached approximately mid-thigh. It was truly beautiful, and he had chosen this for me. It brought me joy, something I needed after last night.

Watching Clara fall had been painful but pushing her into the moat was terrible. Micah's cries were so intense that they made me cry alone. Being a leader was tough, and I had been trying hard to stay strong and lead them, but seeing one of them break was hard.

"It is gorgeous. I will shower and get ready. I lost track of time, as one naturally does. You can go ahead, and I'll see you out there," I told him with a small smile.

I grabbed the gown and my shower essentials and headed out the door. He grabbed my arm and pulled me back. His mouth crashed onto mine with fiery rage. He wrapped his arms around me and—

Flash. Darkness. Moving through space. Light.

I opened my eyes, and we were in his room. My eyes were wide.

"You can shower here, and I'll wait for you."

"I am so glad you didn't do that little trick into my chambers earlier. I think I would have perished on the spot. Warning next time, please," I pleaded.

"As you wish, my Anam Cara," he said, with that little devious smile that had captivated me from the beginning.

He sat back in his lounge chair. I shuffled into his bathing chambers. I couldn't deny that I preferred this much more than the shared chambers. I had thought his plan to bring me here for a shower was to get me naked, but I walked into the chambers alone while he remained in his chair.

The shower stall amazed me with its impressive design. It had two overhead rain showers from the ceiling and two showerheads positioned directly above my shoulders. All four of them drenched me with perfectly warm water. Showers always brought me a sense of peace and calm. I sank to the ground, sat on the floor, and pulled my knees to my chest, letting the water fully envelop me. I took deep breaths, reminding myself I was okay and that this moment would pass. I closed my eyes.

"Hey—"

Shit. Sleep had pulled me under, and his sudden movement jolted me awake, my heart slamming against my ribs.

"Well, okay then, you fell asleep..." he told me.

"Yeah, I guess I was tired. I'm gonna get out. Sorry."

"No need to apologize, I am the one sorry for startling you. You know we don't have to stay long, make an appearance, and disappear afterwards."

"It's alright, I am fine."

He smiled at me, then nodded and headed back into his chambers. I stood up and finished showering before stepping out. The shower was exactly what I needed. It was supposed to be a wonderful day and evening.

The Autumn Equinox celebrations started in the afternoon. We enjoyed a feast in the dining halls, and later, both the courtyard and outdoor arena would be vibrant with festivities. Like our initial celebration when lectures began, floating orbs hovered about ten feet above the fields. Bistro tables were arranged for eating and conversation. A bar was set up on both sides to serve the cadets. Throughout the yards, there were games for cadets to enjoy, some more individual and others for teams.

The dress that Zane got me was stunning. I wasn't sure where he found this gem, but it felt like it was made for me. The forest green shade enhanced my eyes, shifting them to a cooler, bluer green. I braided two sections at the front and pulled them back to form a braided crown. I oil-treated my remaining wavy hair, leaving it down to control the frizz. I strapped two dagger sheaths around each thigh, with side slits for quick access. I also wore black flats in case things went wrong.

I left the bathroom and stepped into the bedroom. Zane lounged with his feet up, but when his cloud-blue eyes caught mine, he straightened. He let out a low whistle that shot through me like lightning. I should be accustomed to it by now, but it still left me feeling exposed.

He swung his feet off the stool and rose. Before I could breathe, he stood in front of me, taller, shadowing my frame. His gaze locked on mine, heavy and unshakable. He reached for a strand of my hair, curling it around his finger, tugging just enough to send a shiver racing down my spine. He leaned in and pressed a kiss to my forehead—soft, disarming. His hand slid down, closing firmly around mine, grounding me while my heart hammered.

"You ready?" he asked.

"As I'll ever be."

"Whenever you are done, we can be done," he said, before guiding me through the door. I gave him a slight smile and nodded.

The great thing about celebrations was that we weren't required to eat at specific times or stay within our branches. We could mingle freely. Of course, there were always assholes looking for trouble, which was why I always kept my weapon handy. With Zane standing beside me, I doubted anyone would be willing to try anything. The facility resembled a buffet set up for the event, allowing us to choose our own food. I selected crispy chicken wings coated in a mild, spicy sauce and some golden-fried potato cubes. Alcoholic drinks remained unavailable until dinner. Meanwhile, there was water, lemonade, and tea. Zane and I found a small table and sat down to eat.

"Auri!" I heard a familiar voice yell out. Lili walked to our table and took a seat next to me. I gave her a quick smile.

"Although you're my Platoon Leader, I still feel like I don't see you enough," I said.

"That's because you don't. You spend way too many evenings in Zane's room instead of mine," she said, giving Zane a look. "Actually, I barely see either of you."

"Hey, don't blame me, she's barely in my room these days either." Which was true. I had been spending way too many of my evenings alone in my room.

"Hmmm..." She gave me that look I knew too well—the one that said she worried about me. A pep talk would follow. It always did. I had no siblings, but she had filled that space, equal parts steady hand and irritating older sister.

"Anyway, my flight will complete the Rite of Passage soon. We won't break records. The goal is to survive, not die fast. And we're down one." My gaze fell to my plate. Clara's absence dug like a knife. As a leader, it sat on my shoulders, heavier than it should, even though I knew it wasn't my fault.

"Your group looks strong, actually. I can't share times or details from the others, but your flight is doing well." She smiled, her golden eyes catching the light.

The grief stayed. It always would. But her words sparked something small and steady inside me, a reminder that I hadn't lost everything. Maybe I was leading them right after all.

"It feels like we have so much more to do and learn, and yet time seemed to be going by quickly."

"Yeah, when you're fucking a divine being..." she muttered.

"Oof, are you jealous?" I quipped back to her. Zane stared at me with this sense of amusement.

"No, not really, merely stating the obvious."

"Hmmm... Well, he is very, very divine to fuck and to be fucked by. Gods, the way his magical divinnnnee tongue works—"

Zane choked and spat his drink across the table, and Lili's eyes went wide. I started laughing because water was now all over the table, and several people turned to look at us.

"Point taken..." she murmured. He smiled at me while wiping his mess up.

"I simply wasn't expecting all of that... I can show you tonight precisely how—how did you say that—oh yeah, how that divine tongue works, tonight."

"Simmer down, love. You won't be able to stand up without showing the world just how divine you are." I shot him a big smile.

"Any who, it's not like you aren't getting laid?" I said.

Her cheeks flushed. "I was just giving you shit, and yes, I am in a situationship with someone."

"Oh, is that what that is?" I gave her a wink.

"Yes, dating in this place is hard."

"That it is."

"Hey! We are easy," Zane finally added to the conversation. Lili looked at him like she had almost forgotten he was at the table, like he hadn't just spat water at us.

"That we are." I gave him a wink, and he reached over and kissed my forehead.

"You guys make me sick."

I chuckled lightly, though it felt somewhat heavier inside. That was something she used to say to Alex and me. I didn't miss him—well, I did, but only as a friend. I realized long before Zane that Alex and I were toxic for each other romantically. I wasn't sure how we could move beyond this. Alex had always been my anchor when we were younger. When my mom died, he comforted me through my tears and panic. We hurt each other in ways I didn't think we could truly mend.

"I am going to go play bean bag toss. Would you like to join?" Zane asked me before standing up.

"I am good, I'll sit and catch up with Lili." He placed a kiss on the top of my head before walking off across the field to join some other Drusearons.

"Soooo, how are you really?" she asked me, in that knowing tone.

"I'm fine."

"Yeah... that's what I thought. Not so great."

"I am fine. Or I will be—"

"Famous words from the Savage."

I let out a little laugh as she said that little nickname she had for me, reminding me that I was a savage and strong.

I knew there would be death, and I knew teammates would die, but when it happened, it didn't mean it wasn't hard.

"To die in training is to graduate into legend." She recited a traditional Rider's saying, reminding me that each cadet was still honored.

"Honestly, death isn't the heaviest thing on my mind. It's the letters I found from my mom. They were confusing and left me with so many questions that keep circling in my brain, never shutting the fuck up."

"You have always struggled with shutting your mind down. Are you practicing your breathing and other coping skills?"

"Yes, always. A lot is going on, making everything I am learning harder to practice. I will be fine, I promise."

"Yeah, you have always said that, and somehow you end up doing reckless shit."

"I won't try to sneak into any dragon vales…"

"Or get into any unnecessary fights with bigger people?"

"Um, I can't promise that. Some people want me dead around here."

"Or get stumbling drunk and have a—"

"Hey-uh. I get it, you're worried. I survived when you left, I will be a-o-fucking-kay."

"You always say that." Lili gave me a look, the one that said she wasn't buying it for a second. Before I could answer, a shadow fell across the table.

"Some things never change," Alex said, voice edged with something I couldn't name. He stood there in his cadet blacks, a drink in one hand, eyes fixed on me like we were the only two people on the field.

My heart gave a stupid little lurch—memory and muscle reflex tangled up together. I hated that he still had that effect on me.

Lili's eyes flicked between us, narrowing to a sharp edge. "Alex." Her voice landed flat, heavy with warning.

"Lili." His gaze never left mine. "Can I sit?"

"Yes," she said.

"No," I said at the same time.

That old, dangerous mix of familiarity and unfinished business tightened around us like a noose. He sat down like he hadn't actually asked a question, his eyes darting from Lili to mine.

"Do you need something?" I asked, giving him a stare down.

"No, not really. I figured I would stop and say hello while your bodyguard isn't here—"

"He's not my bodyguard. Gods."

"Yeah, yeah, your mate, whatever."

"I feel like I should go get a drink and let you both get out whatever you need to say," Lili announced. I shot her a look, furious at how she could even consider leaving me here with him. Before I could say anything, she spun around and walked away, leaving us sitting across from each other at the table, staring in silence.

"Well, our buffer is gone... so that's fun."

He laughed. "Who are you kidding, with or without her, you've never cared to say what you want."

"That's fair..."

"Look, I am mad, and I am working on it," he said, looking across the field at Zane. "You are the first female I was with, the first person outside my family I loved. I hoped we would grow older and mature, eventually finding our way back to each other. I thought we would start anew when I returned from summer break, now that we're both here. But you rejected me, and my world shattered when Zane told me about you and him being mated. I will always love you, accepting that it will only be as friends."

His words sat between us like a live wire—dangerous to touch, impossible to ignore.

"Alex..." I hated how soft my voice sounded. "We were bad for each other. We burned too hot, too fast, and we both got scorched. You know that."

He gave a half-smile, but it didn't reach his eyes. "Doesn't make the fire any less beautiful."

My chest tightened. For a heartbeat, I was seventeen again, pressed against the cold rookery wall with his jacket around my shoulders. As quickly as those thoughts came, I also remembered every fight, every bruise we left on each other's hearts.

"Zane makes me better." The words scraped out at last, heavy on my tongue.

Alex nodded once, sharp, like he'd been expecting that answer but still hated hearing it. "And I make you worse."

"That's not what I—"

"It's fine, Ella. Really." But his knuckles whitened around his cup, and the muscles in his jaw worked like he was chewing down something bitter. "Please... don't disappear completely, alright?"

I didn't promise. I simply stared at him, and for a moment, we were both too stubborn to look away. The cheer from the field rolled over us, and my head turned before I stopped it. Zane was laughing with his teammates, cheeks flushed, hair wind-tossed. His eyes found mine—then Alex's—and the smile faltered hardly enough for me to notice.

Alex leaned back in his chair like he owned the space between us. "Here comes the bodyguard," he murmured, not trying to hide the edge in his voice.

"Don't start," I warned.

"Who's starting? I'm only saying... he looks ready to defend his claim."

"I'm not—" I stopped myself. This wasn't a conversation I wanted in front of others, but Alex's eyes were now fixed on Zane, as if he was watching a storm approaching and challenging it to strike.

Zane reached us with a grin that didn't quite reach his eyes. "Everything good here?"

"Yeah," Alex said. "Merely catching up. Been a while since I got to talk to her without you stealing all her time"

Zane huffed out a laugh, clapping a hand on Alex's shoulder. "I don't steal. She likes me better."

Alex's smirk twitched, but he didn't take the bait.

"Come on, Anam Cara," Zane said, tilting his head toward the field. "Walk with me. They're starting another round."

I got up, brushing my palms on my dress. "See you around, Alex."

"Yeah," he said, but his gaze stayed on Zane for a beat too long.

We headed toward the bean bag toss in an easy silence. Zane's hand brushed mine—steady, grounding, not a claim. "He's fine," Zane said at last, as if answering the question I hadn't asked. "We've got years between us. I know where we stand."

"And where's that?" I asked.

"He's my friend. You're my mate. That's not changing. It will all work out." His tone was warm, confident, but I could hear the layer beneath it—like he was shoring up a wall before the storm really hit.

The music drifted across the courtyard, lilting strings mingling with the rhythmic stomp of boots on stone. Lanterns swayed overhead, throwing warm gold light over the crowd. Zane twirled me beneath his arm, the grin on his face making my heart skip.

"You're getting better," he teased, one hand steady at my back.

"I've had a good teacher," I shot back, letting him spin me again. Across the courtyard, Lili danced with a pair of younger cadets, laughing so hard she nearly tripped over her own boots. Sadie was nearby, dancing closely with a female cadet. Alex was somewhere in the crowd, moving stiffly to the beat like he'd been dragged there under protest. The air was sweet with spiced cider and roasting meat, the kind of night where you almost forgot the weight of the day. Almost.

Then the shadow fell.

It swept over the courtyard like a cloud blotting out the moon—fast, silent at first, until the wind hit. A rush of air slammed into us, tearing through the lantern lines and sending them spinning wildly. Shouts rose as a dragon dropped lower, the glint of red scales catching torchlight. The dragon's wings beat hard enough to scatter tables and send mugs of cider crashing to the ground.

"Down!" someone yelled.

Zane yanked me in close, shielding me as a gust knocked dancers off their feet. The dragon banked sharply above, the force of its turn toppling a row of chairs. Sparks leapt from a shattered lantern, setting a nearby banner alight. Panic surged through the crowd—cadets shoving to clear the square, instructors shouting orders no one could hear over the roar of wings. Somewhere in the chaos, I caught a glimpse of Lili grabbing a younger cadet out of the path of a falling canopy beam.

Zane's grip tightened. "Stay with me."

The dragon wheeled once more overhead, and in its wake the courtyard dissolved into a storm of light, shadow, and the kind of fear that sat deep in your bones. The crowd surged as the dragon dipped low again, its roar splitting the night in two. Zane's hand was an anchor in the flood of bodies—until someone slammed into us from behind.

His grip tore free from mine.

"Zane!" I shouted, but my voice was drowned out by the noise. The crowd of cadets pushed me sideways, away from the courtyard's center. Someone fell in front of me, and I had to jump over them or get caught. The heat from the burning banner pressed against my right side, so I ducked instinctively while smoke stung my throat. A shadow from a dragon's wing flew over the cobblestones, and I looked up just in time to see the smaller dragon banking again—too close. Its powerful downstroke jarred my teeth and forced the air from my lungs.

I clattered to the edge of the courtyard, where overturned tables and broken wood created a maze. A Healer cadet—wide-eyed and trembling—was trapped beneath a heavy bench. Instinctively, I knelt down and scrambled my fingers at the wood.

"Push on three!" I yelled. She nodded once, tears streaking through soot on her cheeks. One. Two. Three—

We shoved, and the bench rolled enough for her to crawl free. The dragon's cry ripped across the courtyard again, closer this time, followed by the unmistakable snap of a tether breaking. My heart slammed against my ribs. This wasn't normal—something was wrong.

"Auriella!" The voice was faint but cut through—Zane's, somewhere on the other side of the courtyard.

I turned toward it, but the crowd heaved again. The younger cadet clung to my arm like a lifeline, and in the scramble, I realized getting to Zane wouldn't be simple. The dragon's shadow swept over us once more, and in that heartbeat, I understood—if we didn't move, it wouldn't matter if I found him. The dragon's cry split the air again, and the Healer cadet at my side flinched so hard she almost dragged us both down. The press of bodies shoved us toward the edge of the courtyard, boots skidding over spilled cider and broken glass.

"Stay with me!" I yelled over the roar, tightening my grip on her arm. A banner pole crashed to the stones ahead, splintering into jagged spears. We veered left, ducking under the cover of an overturned table. Smoke clawed at my throat as we crawled, the heat from the burning banner licking across my cheek. Through the chaos, I spotted a familiar figure shoving his way toward us.

Alex.

He reached us in three long strides, pulling the cadet to her feet with one hand while steadying me with the other. "This way—clear path by the wall!"

We ran, ducking low as another wingbeat slammed into the courtyard. I caught glimpses of the dragon overhead—red scales shimmering, eyes wide and wild. The far wall came into view, lined with a row of supply carts.

Alex pushed us between them, using their bulk as cover. "Stay put," he ordered the cadet. He shot me a look. "Go find Zane before he thinks you've been trampled."

I didn't argue. I darted out into the thinning crowd, scanning for him. My heart clenched when I saw him—shoulder to shoulder with two other cadets, helping an injured cadet limp toward the infirmary. His gaze locked on mine instantly.

He was at my side in seconds, eyes sweeping over me. "You alright?"

"I'm fine. Got someone out from under a bench." My voice was steadier than I felt.

He nodded once, relief flashing across his face before he set his jaw. "Command wants everyone in their chambers and leadership to do counts."

The square was mainly clear, but the red dragon still flew above, its wingbeats frantic. Lantern light caught in its eyes—bright, almost feverish—and I realized it wasn't looking at the crowd in general. It was looking at me.

"Zane," I murmured, "something is wrong."

He followed my stare upward. "It's young," he said. "Too young to be out of the vale."

The dragon descended again, a hot, gusty wind sweeping over us. The red wasn't fully mature—its talons were thinner than an adult's, and its movements were quick but still unpolished. It wasn't attacking, but it was frantic, almost desperate motions indicated panic. It landed abruptly on the courtyard ledge, claws sparking against the stone. Its sides heaved with ragged breaths, and its wings flickered as if caught between flying and falling. A deep, rolling, unsettling sound erupted—the beat of many wings filling the air. My stomach sank. Shapes appeared on the shadowed horizon against the moonlight. One, five, ten, more.

A dragon drift closed fast. The ground trembled as the first of them roared, the sound shaking through my bones.

What the fuck?

They burst into view and scattered just as fast. The group swept across the courtyard in a single wave, fading into the horizon—except for a blue one that dropped onto the ledge beside the small red dragon. A moment later both launched into the air, wings cutting the night before they vanished into darkness.

"Cadets, inside!" an instructor's voice cracked like a whip over the courtyard. "Chambers, now! Leadership, get your counts!"

Another shout from the opposite side. "Move! Lock it down!"

Zane's hand closed around my arm, firm but not rough. "You heard them."

I moved into the Rider's wing while Zane headed to his. Such situations had protocols. As a Flight Guide, my task was to ensure each cadet stayed in their room and then inform Persephone Emmen, our Squad Leader. She would escalate the report to Lili, who would then pass it to Corson, our Wing Commander.

Squad Leaders and Platoon Leaders stayed outside their chambers until they received reports from those below them. Sadie, Akira, Micah, Lorenzo, and Jackson were all accounted for, and no one was injured. After notifying Emmen, I went to my chamber on the second floor. During a lockdown, we had to stay in our chambers unless there was an emergency, you were in leadership, or on tower duty, until the bell tolled 12 times consecutively. There were no bells to indicate the time during a lockdown.

I sat in my chair, gazing out the window, wondering what had upset that little dragon from the vale—it looked so frantic. Knowing dragons, they didn't usually want to cause harm to any of us, all of us mutually protecting each other.

Dong. Dong. Dong. Dong. Dong. Dong. Dong. Dong. Dong. Dong. Dong. Dong.

Finally, not that it mattered, by that point, we were supposed to be in our chambers anyway. I could rest easy now, though, knowing we weren't on lockdown.

"Coming in." He projected down our mental connection and was in my room within seconds, standing before me.

"It's past curfew."

"And?"

"And you don't need to get in trouble."

"I can rove," he said, stepping closer, "and they'll never know." I swallowed but didn't move back when he reached me. The lamplight caught in his eyes, deep and dark, as he braced one hand on the back of my chair, caging me in.

"Zane—"

"I don't want to talk about dragons," he murmured, his voice low and rough at the edges. "I want to see you."

"You're impossible," I whispered.

"You like impossible."

Before I could argue, his mouth found mine—slow at first, a question and a challenge rolled into one. I responded to both, my fingers curling into the fabric of his shirt, pulling him closer until his knees bumped mine. He deepened the kiss, one hand sliding to the back of my neck, the other skimming down my side, leaving a trail of heat behind. The rest of the world—the dragons, the lockdown, the noise—faded away.

Zane's mouth moved against mine with a kind of urgency that was all too familiar, but that night there was an edge to it—like we'd both been holding our breath since the chaos outside and only now were letting it go. He kissed me like he needed the taste to keep breathing, his hands gripping my hips and pulling me to my feet. My chair scraped back, forgotten, as my chest pressed to his. The room was quiet except for us—uneven breathing, the faint rustle of fabric, the soft thud of his boots as he walked me backward toward the bed.

"Zane—" I started, but the way he looked at me stole the rest of the words.

"You think I'm here because I can't follow rules," he said, his voice low and rough. "I'm here because I can't stay away from you."

My heart pounded hard against my ribs, but before I could answer, his mouth pressed against mine again, deeper and hungrier. We'd been there before, too many times to count, but it never got easier—only more dangerous. Zane's mouth claimed mine again, but this time there was no hesitation. Each movement carried the weight of nights gone by—the ones that left me trembling, breathless, and craving more—and yet, that night felt sharper, hungrier.

He pulled me close as if he'd been waiting all day to touch me, his hands sliding over the familiar curves and planes of my body with the confidence of someone who knew exactly where I'd melt. I could feel his pulse against mine. The steady rhythm pressed to my chest as he guided me backward until my knees hit the bed. The room was dim, shadows cast by the low lamplight dancing across his face, softening the lines I'd only seen in quiet moments. His fingertips traced the edge of my jaw, then down the column of my throat, his gaze never leaving mine.

"You know I can't stay away from you," he murmured, leaning in so close his breath warmed my ear. "Not when you look at me like that."

Every gesture of his hands, every shift of his weight, was deliberate—teasing and certain all at once. His lips found mine again, deeper this time, the kiss building in a way that made my toes curl and my fingers twist into his shirt. When we fell back onto the bed, it wasn't clumsy—it felt like falling into a rhythm we'd never lost.

The heat between us flared, and I could feel every beat of it in the spaces where we touched and where we didn't, where the ache of almost was its own kind of fire. His forehead rested against mine for a breath, eyes locked on me as if he might finally say the words we'd both been dancing around. But instead, he kissed me again—slowly at first, then deeper, until thoughts were impossible and the rest of the world didn't exist. And in that moment, with his heartbeat thundering against mine, I didn't need to hear the words to know.

CHAPTER 27

Last night was blissful and, honestly, exactly what I needed. Zane stayed with me until the early hours before going back to his room. Filled with passionate sex, leaving me aching for more the next morning. Falling asleep in his arms was more than I needed. It was something I hadn't even realized I wanted until I woke up. I longed for more nights with him in my arms, and that thought made me wonder how I would manage without him nearby during my final two years. I couldn't let myself dwell on that because it was self-destructive. I needed to stay in the present.

A group of us were headed to Chalahana for the day, ending it at the lively local tavern. Sadie, Thora, Lili, and a few others from our wing joined us. Chalahana was about one and a half miles from the admin building, and we had to walk there and back unless you had wings.

Even the Riders with fliers weren't allowed to fly there. Zane, of course, came along. He brought a few of his Drusearon friends, some of whom I hadn't met before. I offered for him to spend the day with his friends, but he politely told me absolutely fucking not.

We all met outside in the flight field. Lili approached, looking like she was heading out to pubs back home, while I dressed ready for a fight. We were not the same. Maybe her confidence as the Platoon Leader didn't leave her as vulnerable as I felt.

Lili smirked at my boots and braided hair. "You planning to wrestle someone on the way there?"

"Perfectly prepared," I said, adjusting my jacket. "Not all of us can depend on charm and shin-high heels to keep us safe."

She rolled her eyes, yet I noticed how she scanned the field—automatic and assessing, just like I did. That was her strength. She could appear to be heading to a dance but remain three steps ahead of anyone trying to challenge her. The rest of the group arrived gradually, laughter and casual chatter filling the cool morning air. Zane showed up last, his hands in his pockets, flanked by two tall Drusearons. They carried themselves with quiet confidence, danger concealed behind relaxed smiles.

"Alright," Lili said, clapping her hands. "Let's get moving before the sun decides to bake us alive."

We had to cross the river bridge, go through the field, and then onto the dirt road. I could really use my horse back home, travel would be easier.

"Auri, this is Eli. Eli, this is Auri," Zane nodded to the six-foot-two-inch male on his immediate left. He had olive skin, dark black hair, and light brown eyes.

"Nice to meet you," Eli said while giving me a nod.

"Same," I said with a smile.

"And on the other side of him is Oliver."

"Hey," I said to the five-foot-eleven, pale-skinned male.

"Nice to finally meet you, Auri," he said.

Eli's handshake was firm, and his smile was quick but not overly warm. He was the kind of male who judged people before deciding whether he liked them. Oliver, on the other hand, had a spark in his pale eyes—perhaps mischief or the quiet confidence of someone who'd already decided I was worth knowing.

"You two causing trouble already?" Zane asked them with a smirk.

"Not yet," Oliver replied. "But the day's young."

Sadie, a step ahead with Lili, glanced back at the sound of our laughter. "If you three start brawling in the tavern, I'm not covering for you," she called.

"I'd never." I tilted my head and let the words drip sweet, my grin sharp enough to betray me.

The dirt road stretched ahead, shimmering in the heat. My boots crunched over gravel, and I found myself walking inches from Zane so that our arms brushed now and then. His presence, as always, felt like a shield and a challenge all at once.

"Chalahana also has a decent market," Eli offered, glancing at me. "If you're into that sort of thing."

"I'm into food," I admitted. "And maybe something strong to drink after the walk."

"That we can manage," Oliver said, grinning.

By the time the rooftops of Chalahana came into view, the conversation shifted to training stories—half boasting, half teasing. The kind of banter that made the walk seem shorter. But underneath it all, there was a quiet awareness between me and Zane, each glance and touch tinged with last night's memory.

The first stop was the outdoor market that sprawled across Chalahana's central square. Bright awnings flapped in the breeze, their shade spilling over stalls filled with everything from shiny fruit to brass trinkets and hand-dyed scarves. Sadie headed straight for a jewelry table, holding up a pair of silver ear cuffs to the light. Lili browsed with such confidence that vendors straightened up, sensing a big spender. I lingered at a leather goods stand, running my fingers over a row of well-made belts.

"This would suit you," Zane murmured behind me, and when I turned, he held a narrow leather braid tipped in silver. "For your dagger." I raised an eyebrow.

"Planning to buy me gifts now?"

"Maybe I am," he said, with his devious little grin.

Eli and Oliver went to the food stalls and returned a few minutes later with paper cones filled with spiced nuts. "Fuel for the shopping warriors," Oliver said, offering me one.

After an hour, the smell of roasting meat drew us toward a cafe tucked away off the square. Inside, the cool shade provided a welcome break from the sun. We settled into a corner table by the window, where the breeze carried faint hints of pine trees.

Lunch was substantial—plates of roast chicken, fresh bread still warm from the oven, and pitchers of chilled cider. Conversation flowed freely around the table, but occasionally, Zane's knee brushed mine beneath the table. Each gentle touch brought back memories of last night, where we spent hours alone in our world. I caught his gaze once while he was eating, and his look made my heart race. He didn't need to speak for me to understand what he thought.

After exploring the town and visiting several stores, we headed into the famous local tavern for drinks—one of those spots with a crooked sign and music spilling through the open door. Inside, the air was cooler, shadows gathering in the corners where locals sipped their mugs. A trio in the back played a soft, rolling tune on fiddle, drum, and flute. We took a table near the center, big enough for everyone to gather but small enough that knees bumped underneath. Zane slid into the seat beside me, his arm brushing mine in a way that might've looked accidental if I didn't know better.

"You're getting the first round," he said, passing me a couple of coins with a grin. "Show me you can order like a local."

I raised an eyebrow but headed to the bar anyway. The bartender was a broad female with an easy smile who poured generously. I brought back tankards of deep amber ale, setting them down with a dramatic flourish.

Eli tapped his mug to mine. "Not bad."

Sadie was already halfway through hers by the time we all took a sip, and Lili was scanning the room as if she were deciding whether to find a dance partner.

Zane leaned in close, his voice quiet enough for only me to hear. "You keep looking at the door."

"Old habit," I murmured, taking another drink.

His lips curved in that way that told me he knew exactly what I meant. "Mine too."

The music picked up, and a few people started dancing in the open space between tables. Eli and Oliver shared a story about a training mishap that made Zane laugh, but every so often, I felt his gaze on me—steady, deliberate, like a promise.

It all began with the music—speeding up now, the fiddler leaning into a wild tune that made the floorboards vibrate. Lili was on her feet in seconds, pulling Thora along before anyone else could react.

"Come on, you can't sit through this!" she called, spinning Thora toward the open space near the fire.

They moved with a reckless joy that made people smile, both of them struggling to find their rhythm but then syncing perfectly and moving flawlessly together. Lili's grin was so wide it could be seen from every table. A few locals clapped along, and one or two joined them, boots pounding on the wood. I leaned back in my chair, tankard in hand, letting the laughter and warmth of the tavern wash over me. For a moment, it felt like nothing bad could reach us here. That was when the shadow cast itself across the table.

"You're too pretty to sit alone," a voice said, and before I could reply, a rough hand landed on my shoulder.

I froze, my smile slipping away. "Not alone." My voice stayed even as I tilted my head toward Zane, the movement sharp, deliberate.

The male hardly looked at him before leaning in closer. "Bet you dance better than your friends."

Zane's chair scraped back. "Move your hand," he said, low and dangerous.

The male snorted, clearly more drunk than brilliant. "What, you her keeper?"

Zane rose, and Eli and Oliver shifted with him, weight forward, ready. The patron's smirk slipped, but pride held him in place—he shoved Zane's shoulder.

That was enough. Zane caught his wrist and twisted, precise, sharp, until the man hissed through his teeth. Chairs scraped, and someone at the next table lunged in. A shove snapped into a punch. Music cut off, replaced by shouts and the crash of a tankard exploding across the floor.

Eli vaulted over our bench to intercept another drunk lunging toward us. Oliver stepped in front of Sadie, who had half-risen from her seat, and I found myself yanking a stool out of the way of someone stumbling backward. Lili and Thora darted back to our side, breathless from dancing and now wide-eyed.

"You always pick the best places," Lili muttered.

"Not my fault this time," Zane shot back, as the barkeeper pushed us out the door.

The barkeep's voice cut through the chaos like a blade. "OUT! All of you!"

And just like that, we were slipping into the darkness, the sounds of the tavern closing behind us. The sun had set, leaving the world bathed in a silver-blue glow. The road ahead was barely more than a pale ribbon under the moonlight, with grass on either side whispering in the night breeze. The group grew quieter now. Lili and Thora walked ahead with Sadie, their voices low and tired from laughter and the lingering heat of the tavern scuffle. Eli and Oliver lagged behind a bit, speaking in murmurs that didn't carry.

Zane kept close, his stride falling in step with mine. Our shoulders brushed now and then, a steady reminder he stayed there. The air between us shifted—still charged, but softer than the tavern heat. Quieter. Heavier.

"You didn't have to step in so fast," I said at last, my voice cutting through the silence.

"Yes, I did." His reply came low, certain. "I'll always step in."

Something in my chest tightened, both infuriating and impossible to ignore. "I'm not helpless, you know."

He glanced at me, the corner of his mouth twitching. "I know. But he didn't."

We continued walking in silence, the steady sound of boots on dirt echoing beneath us. In the distance, a night bird called, and the faint smell of woodsmoke drifted through the air.

"You've got a look," he said after a moment.

I tilted my head toward him. "What look?"

"The one you get when you're thinking about things you won't say out loud."

I gave a half smile, keeping my eyes on the path. "Maybe I like the quiet."

His hand brushed mine—casual, seeming accidental, yet he didn't immediately pull away. I didn't either. When the towering college walls came into view, most of the group had settled into a relaxed, exhausted silence.

Lili and Thora were the first to head toward their chambers, with Sadie trailing behind them and giving a lazy wave. Eli and Oliver lingered long enough to chat briefly with Zane before they headed to the Drusearon wing.

That left only the two of us standing outside the gates in the flight field, the cool night air against my flushed cheeks. Curfew was near—too close for anything reckless—but neither of us moved right away.

"You should get inside," I said, tilting my head toward his side of the building.

"I will," he said, but his eyes never left mine. The firelight reflected in them, warm and steadfast. "I just... didn't want the night to end yet."

Something twisted low in my stomach, equal parts longing and warning. "We'll both get caught if we stay out here."

"Then come with me," he murmured, stepping close enough for me to feel the heat of him. His voice was quiet, meant only for me. "No one's watching right now."

I should've walked away. Instead, I found myself leaning in slightly, pulled by the gravity he always seemed to carry. He brushed his knuckles along my jaw, slow and deliberate. "One more minute," he said, like a promise and a dare.

And in the quiet beyond the torches, with the hum of the base settling for the night, I let that moment stretch until it was almost too much.

"You're stalling," I said, folding my arms.

He smiled in that maddeningly calm way. "Maybe I don't feel like saying goodnight yet."

"Curfew is in two minutes."

"Then we'd better take the fast way." His eyes glinted, and before I could ask, the brush of his mind against mine sent a clear image—his hand on my arm, the air folding around us.

"You're not serious—"

Too late. The world shimmered, and the crisp night air quickly shifted to the warm stillness of my room in the span of a heartbeat. The sudden quiet made it feel almost as if we had stolen it.

"One day you're gonna get caught…"

"Doubt it… what can they actually do about it? Most of the professors know who I really am."

Before I could come up with an argument, he took my hand and guided me toward the bed, sitting down and gently pulling me beside him. "I'm not here for anything else tonight," he murmured, the seriousness in his voice making my chest ache. "Just want to hold you."

Something in me melted at that—no teasing, no games—simply truth in his voice. I shifted until my body curled against him, his arm sliding around my waist, the steady thump of his heartbeat under my cheek.

"You make it very hard to forget you're here," I whispered.

"That's the idea," he said, and I felt the faintest smile against my hair.

Somewhere between one heartbeat and the next, sleep gave way to awareness.

The room was dim, with only the faintest hint of pre-dawn light spilling across the floorboards. My head was still on Zane's chest, his breathing deep and steady, one arm wrapped around me as if he had no intention of letting go.

For a moment, I didn't move. I simply listened to the steady rhythm of his heart, the soft rustle of the wind against the window. I wanted to stay right there, in that warmth, until the world forgot we existed. But a distant bell tolled once, low and hollow, reminding me that soon the college would be waking up.

"Zane," I whispered, brushing my fingers lightly against his side. "You need to go."

His arm tightened briefly, as if he could will me into silence. "Five more minutes," he murmured, voice rough with sleep.

"You said that five minutes ago," I said, but the smile tugging at my lips probably ruined any sternness I was going for.

He cracked one eye open, gaze locking on mine. "Then I lied."

Still, he moved—reluctantly—sitting up and running a hand through his hair. The air between us felt charged, full of things neither of us had the nerve to say out loud.

At the door, he paused, glancing back over his shoulder. "Tonight?" he asked.

I swallowed, nodding once. "Tonight."

He disappeared, the faint shimmer of his rove leaving the room colder and quieter. I counted the hours until curfew.

CHAPTER 28

Although it was Autumn break, all first-year students had to complete the Flier's Rite of Passage on October First, and the day had finally come. The mountain cut before us was twenty feet wide, fifty feet tall, and layered with eight weeks of blood, sweat, and bruises. Instructor Quillet stood at the bottom, his voice echoing through the cold morning air, with a stopwatch in hand.

"Feather Wing, Electric Platoon, First Squad—Sadie, Akira, Micah, Lorenzo, Jackson, Auriella. You know the rules. Each of you goes when the cadet ahead hits the third level. Don't waste my time."

Sadie stepped forward first.

She hit the rope climb hard, body flowing smooth with each pull. By the time she reached the plank and its angled ropes, her long arms carried her through the gaps with ease. She launched over the first gap, stone grips catching fast, hardly slowing her momentum. The swinging logs shifted under her weight, but she moved quick, braid snapping as she drove through the final ramp. Her boots struck the bridge, and the stopwatch clicked.

Akira lunged forward with sharp precision. She didn't waste motion—every climb and swing was intentional and measured. She wasn't the fastest, but she made no mistakes. The logs just grazed her shoulder before she ducked through and made the final jump without hesitation.

Micah was motivated by grace, pulling himself up the rope as if it owed him coins. He faltered on the inclined ropes, losing some seconds, but compensated with a nearly flawless ladder climb. His landing on the ramp caused the plank to shake, yet he pushed through the last ropes to reach the bridge.

Lorenzo had speed but lacked balance—his first plank crossing swayed dangerously. By the stone grips, he gasped but pushed through. A swinging log slammed into his ribs and almost knocked him down, but his stubbornness carried him onto the bridge.

Jackson was a natural at these skills. Rope climb? He did it with ease. Gap jump? Flawless. He navigated the logs as if he were born to them, ending with a burst of speed that made Quillet raise an eyebrow.

Finally, it was my turn. The rope burned my palms almost immediately, but I forced my legs into the rhythm Sadie drilled into me. The angled ropes were definitely tougher—each reach pushed me to my limit. The first gap? I barely caught the ledge, pulling myself up with a grunt. My fingertips screamed on the stone grips, but I didn't let go.

The logs swung erratically, appearing faster due to my shorter frame. I darted in quick bursts, heart pounding, and reached the ladder, climbing swiftly. The ramp's five-foot gap almost knocked me down as my boots slipped on the landing, but I pushed through the last rope lattice. When my hands gripped the final stone and I stepped onto the narrow bridge, my chest burned fiercely, yet I had completed the climb.

We didn't cheer or shout—just shared exhausted smiles. Eight weeks. One teammate lost. And each of us had crossed that bridge. Waiting at the top were all the Wing Commanders—Corson, Verlander, and Cusik. The three wing Executive Officers were also there. All of them had stopwatches, each timing someone differently. "Your overall squad placement will be announced closer to Bonding Day. Great job, Electric's first squad," Corson said.

***

The week off drifted by in a haze of late mornings and slow days. No drills, no lectures, no endless hours under the sun until your skin felt like leather.

Except for the time we completed the Flier's Rite of Passage. Otherwise, it was just... breathing space.

We relaxed in the commons more than usual, played cards until the pile of coins in the center of the table was more about bragging rights than actual money, and wandered into Chalahana again—this time without any brawls or bruises. Some afternoons, we sprawled out on the grass near the flight field, watching the dragons soaring high above, their wings catching the sunlight in flashes of gold and fire.

Every night, just before the barracks fell silent, Zane slipped into my room. Sometimes he'd rove in, sometimes he'd take the risk of the walk, but he always came. We'd talk about nothing and everything until our words blurred into yawns, and then he'd pull me close, his arm heavy around my waist.

It wasn't always about heat and tangled limbs—though there was plenty of that. It was how he grew still when I settled against him, his breathing slowing first, as if he trusted me enough to sleep peacefully. Perhaps, during the hours between midnight and dawn, I trusted him the same way. By week's end, I was more rested than I'd been in months—and more entangled with him than I liked to admit. The sadness that had been knocking at my mind's door had vanished.

Every cadet began the day in our first class, held in the stadium classroom. Professor Melamora stood in the middle of the speaking platform, flanked by Professor Fogg and Professor Pascal. Melamora's presence attracted all eyes to her, despite the room's size.

"I trust you all remember the events from a few nights ago," she started, her voice easily reaching the highest tier. "The young red that disrupted the courtyard."

A murmur spread through the room.

Professor Fogg stepped forward, his gravelly tone cutting through the noise. "That was no random disturbance. Two days earlier, the fledgling's mother—a veteran red—was killed in combat alongside her bonded Rider. Both died defending against another coastal attack."

Professor Pascal's voice softened Fogg's bluntness. "Dragons mourn. They mourn deeply. When a dragon dies, their lineage often feels this loss. In the case of a fledgling, the impact can be... severe."

Melamora's gaze moved from section to section, her expression unreadable. "This young red is back in the vale with the elders. Do not mistake grief for harmlessness."

I sank back into my seat, the image of the little red still burned into my mind from that night. Frantic, searching—not reckless, but desperate. And now I understand why. Melamora's words echoed in my mind, the murmurs of the other cadets fading into the background. Do not mistake grief for harmlessness.

I kept my eyes fixed on the pale wood of the bench in front of me, but my mind had already gone somewhere else. Somewhere colder.

When my mother died, the world didn't pause to explain what happened. There was no warning—just a sudden change from one moment to the next, her laughter still echoing from the night before, and then—silence.

I remembered the hollow ache in my chest, as if something had been scooped out and could never be restored. I'd stare at doorways, hoping she would walk through, and at shadows, thinking I'd see her figure. Alex and Lili had held me during the first nights, but even their comfort wasn't enough to silence the panic that awakened me in the dark.

The young red... she must be going through that same pain, but probably worse. Dragons didn't just lose their mothers—they lost the connection, a heartbeat shared so naturally it was like breathing. And I understood exactly what that was like.

"A final note before we move on," Professor Pascal's voice cut through my thoughts, smooth but easily carrying across the tiers. "General Blackcreek returned to campus the next day with his bonded dragon, Kim. As most of you know, Kim is an elder—one of the most experienced living dragons in the vale. Together, she and the other elders were able to subdue the young red without injury and place her into a deep, restorative sleep."

The low murmur that followed was immediate. My head snapped up before I could stop myself.

My father.

"She will stay in this condition for a while, giving her body and mind time to recover from the trauma. Since we don't get involved in dragon—or flier—affairs and they are secretive, we only know what dragons have told their fliers. She's no longer a concern," Pascal said.

I sat back slowly, my pulse pounding in my ears. The image of him—of them—flying together across the sky was almost too vivid. Kim's massive wings blocking out the sun, my father's steady hands holding on… and that little red, curling inward under the weight of grief she couldn't yet understand.

The pain in my chest persisted, now mixed with curiosity, unease, and unanswered questions. My father had been here for over a week—yet not a single word had passed between us. That realization struck me hard, like a stone in my stomach. It wasn't unexpected—he had recently mastered the art of absence—but it still hurt. He could cross oceans, calm dragons, and face chaos head-on, yet he couldn't spare a moment to meet my gaze. Part of me actually preferred it that way.

Because beneath all the formal respect and titles, I still believed he had been involved in my mother's death. Too many unanswered questions. Too many coincidences that weren't. Now he was back, walking these same halls, his shadow brushing mine without ever touching. And for the first time in months, the air felt too tight in my lungs. Then again, they didn't say he was still here. Perhaps he had come and left shortly after.

The remaining current events proceeded as the instructors reviewed protocols for managing another incident and our respective responsibilities. They covered the new schedules sent out this morning to all cadets, which modified some class times. Our platoon continued to spar three days a week on the same days. However, the groups and periods changed.

The gym was a cavern filled with echoing voices and scuffed mat floors, the air heavy with anticipation. This was our second class of the day—sparring—and Instructor Gile's rules were ingrained in every cadet's mind. Once called out, you fought until someone tapped, someone dropped, or someone didn't get back up. No exceptions.

"Kaelen Veyth calls Auriella Blackcreek."

The murmur that spread through the gym was instant. A few cadets leaned forward, eager for the show. I made my way across the mats, my boots striking the floor with deliberate force. Kaelen was already waiting on the mat, rolling his shoulders, that cocky half-smile set on his face.

"Been wanting to test you," he said, voice pitched to carry. "See if you're as good without your winged-boy watching your back."

I stepped into the ring and took a dagger from the mat. "You'll regret finding out."

"Begin," Gile said.

Kaelen darted forward, feinting with his bare hand before swinging his dagger in a swift slicing arc toward my side. I caught his wrist, twisting it forcefully to weaken his grip, and drove my knee into his gut. He blocked with his thigh, pivoted sharply, and in the next moment, his dagger vanished—shifted to his left hand.

The bastard was fast.

He swung again, the steel blade narrowly grazing my sleeve. I responded with an elbow blast that struck his jaw, causing his head to snap back. The crowd reacted with a subdued ripple, but Kaelen only grinned wider, a spark in his eye showing he was relishing this.

"You fight like a girl," he said, breathless but taunting.

That lit something inside me—sharp and hot. I pressed forward, dagger in hand moving in a tight, punishing rhythm: cut high, slash low, twist, strike. He dodged and blocked, but my blade found its mark across his ribs. He retaliated with a hook that rattled my teeth, forcing me back a step. We circled each other, both breathing hard, the weight of the crowd pressing in.

"Tap out," he said, mocking.

I lunged forward, and he met me halfway. Bone cracked loudly against bone, echoing through the dusty rafters. A final twist wrenched his dagger from his hand. I raised my knife beneath his chin, pressing firmly enough for him to feel the pressure. His chest heaved with rapid breaths. He held my gaze for three long beats before tapping twice on my arm. Gile stepped in instantly, but I was already lowering my dagger. Kaelen's smirk faded into a cautious expression—perhaps respect or curiosity. I turned my back before I could be certain.

"Theron Vargash calls Casimir Nanda."

The room quieted enough for the weight of the call-out to settle. Casimir—light brown hair damp against his forehead, blue eyes calm—moved from another mat with measured steps. He was reliable. Solid. One of the best hand-to-hand fighters in our class. Casimir had the predator's gleam in his eyes.

Gile's voice snapped through the air. "Begin."

They clashed in a quick, intense burst—Casimir opened with a precise diagonal slash, which Theron deflected and dodged. Theron then kicked low, unsettling Casimir, and advanced with precise, controlled strikes. Casimir blocked and countered, managing a light hit on Theron's shoulder. Theron adjusted—his movements subtle, yet faster than human limits. His strikes sharpened and became more aggressive, gradually pushing Casimir back with each step.

A flash of steel—Theron's dagger drove into Casimir's forearm, forcing him to drop his weapon. Casimir didn't hesitate. He tackled Theron, driving both of them to the ground. They rolled, fists and knees flying, until Theron finally wrenched free with a quick, fluid twist.

And then—

The dagger came down. Not flat, not a warning strike—the point, hard, brutal, straight into Casimir's throat.

The sound in the gym shifted. The crowd's noise dissolved into a collective, shocked silence, broken only by the wet, choking gasp from Casimir as he clutched his wound. Blood bubbled between his fingers. Instructor Gile moved, but not quick enough. By the time he reached them, Casimir's eyes were wide and glassy, and his body lay slack on the mat. Theron slowly rose, breathing heavily, his expression unreadable. He carefully set the dagger back on the floor and stepped away.

"Winner—Theron Vargash," Gile said. His usual finality in his voice now carried a hint of darkness.

They took his body so quickly. The rules hadn't been broken. But the air in the gym was different—heavier. The heaviness that didn't fade in a day. There were several more matches, some of which were callouts, and then it shifted to randomly matched. Thankfully, there were no more injuries or fatalities. A check-in with Michaelova would be needed later, since Casimir was in his flight. The feeling of losing a fellow cadet was already known to me.

***

The magical arts classroom felt nothing like the combat gyms. The air carried a sharp tang, almost metallic, as if it had been steeped in spell work long before we arrived. Sunlight poured through the high windows, striking the protective wards carved into the floor. The concentric circles glimmered faintly, alive with hidden power, as though the room itself breathed magic.

Professor Vindex paced at the center, his long coat brushing the tops of his boots, eyes sharp as he looked over us. "Today is about control," he said, voice steady but weighty. "Raw power will impress no one if you can't hold it in your grasp." His gaze flicked to me for half a heartbeat before moving on. I didn't miss it.

We formed a wide circle—Sadie on my left, Micah on my right, with Akira, Lorenzo, and Jackson arranged around us. Vindex's class recently seemed to combine magical discipline with physical exertion. This time, we were each assigned to hold a sphere of energy while performing a series of movements, including strikes, spins, and defensive stances.

I summoned the magic from deep within my core, just as I practiced, and it came effortlessly—fast, hot, eager. The air around my hands shimmered, and the sphere blazed to an almost blinding white-gold. My pulse raced sharply. It was so easy to let it grow, to feed it until the heat brushed against my skin and the sphere expanded beyond my control. I knew exactly what that felt like—the moment when the magic stopped being mine and began to own me. I crossed that line weeks ago. I had already burned past it.

A flicker of memory—the last time I didn't hold back, when the air cracked and the ground shuddered beneath my feet, when others looked at me as if I were something dangerous, something other.

"Focus, Auri," Sadie muttered under her breath, not looking at me. I realized the sphere in my palms started to hum, with its edges warping from raw energy.

I took a slow breath, forcing the heat down, narrowing the light until it was steady and small again. My body moved through the strikes, the sphere hovering perfectly between my palms as I shifted.

Vindex moved behind me, his voice quiet. "You can yield more than most in this room. That will either make you invaluable... or get you killed. Decide which it will be."

The words lodged deep. I could feel my squadmates pushing themselves, struggling to keep their spheres through the final sequence. Mine never flickered. And that was the problem. I had power inside me, but I hadn't been taught how to use it. It all came flooding in, and I was trying to take it one day at a time.

The day was filled with more lectures, and by the time I returned to my room for the night, I was completely exhausted. Zane wouldn't be joining me because he had watch duty due to a cadet being injured on the field. My eyes closed as I drifted into a deep sleep.

Initially, the sound was so gentle I thought I had imagined it—a faint scrape resembling leather against stone. My heartbeat quickened as I slowly pushed up, muscles tense. The second sound was unmistakable now—the latch on my window clicked loudly.

I reached for the dagger under my pillow, but before my fingers grasped the hilt, the shutters swung inward and something dark and fast flooded into the room. A sharp, chemical-sweet scent hit me, causing my vision to swim. I swung blindly, steel meeting something solid, but a hand covered my mouth, another held my wrist to the mattress. My heart thundered in my ears.

"Quiet, little Blackcreek," a voice rasped near my ear—low, male, carrying the faintest trace of an accent I didn't recognize. I bucked hard, but another figure was already there, binding my legs with practiced speed. The scent in the air thickened—my eyes watered, head feeling heavy.

Through the blur, I caught a glimpse, a pale scar curling from the jawline of one of them down into his collar and the glint of a silver clasp shaped like a wolf's head. Not cadets. Not instructors. The last thing I saw before the blackness dragged me under was the moonlight catching on a shard of glass where my window had been.

CHAPTER 29

The last thing I remembered was the taste of cloth pressed hard against my mouth and the pulse of wards thundering in my ears. Voices, muffled. Hands dragging. Then nothing.

I awoke to a darkness that felt heavy, almost physical. My head throbbed in slow, nauseous waves, and a bitter taste lingered on my tongue. Cold stone pressed against my cheek, damp enough to leech the warmth from my skin.

I tried to sit up. My arms jerked to a stop. Leather cut into my wrists. My ankles too—bound tight, metal weighing them down. I twisted harder. The rattle of chains cracked through the silence, loud and metallic, like a shout. My pulse thundered in response. Instinct drove me inward, searching for magic. Nothing. No flicker, no hum, not even a whisper. Panic clawed up my throat.

A faint lantern glow pulsed high on the wall, just enough to outline the cell: stone walls slick with damp, no windows, one iron door. The air smelled of wet earth and smoke—and something sharper, metallic, that prickled along my skin.

I braced my knees under me, testing the give of the bindings, but they didn't move. My breath came faster, shallow, too loud in the silence. That was when I heard them—boots on stone, measured and steady, drawing closer.

The iron door scraped open.

Two figures entered, hoods shadowing their faces. One moved with an easy, lazy gait, but the taller one kept his shoulders squared, steps sharp, a man accustomed to command.

"Awake at last," the tall one said, voice low but cutting. He stepped into the light, and my stomach sank. I didn't know his name, but I knew the clasp at his throat—the wolf's head I'd glimpsed before the world went black.

"You'll be quiet," he said, "or you'll regret it."

My voice came out steadier than I felt. "You drugged me, dragged me here, and think I'll just sit pretty?"

A slow smile curved his mouth. "We didn't take you to hurt you, little Rider. We took you because of what you are."

My skin crawled. "And what exactly is that?"

His smile widened, patient, cruel. "You'll find out soon enough."

They left me chained for what felt like hours, long enough for stiffness to set into my limbs and the cold to crawl beneath my skin. I tested the bindings again—no give. Tried for magic—nothing. Hopeless. My bond with Zane felt gone.

The door groaned open again. Only the tall one entered this time. He drew his hood back, revealing sharp cheekbones, storm-gray eyes, and streaks of iron threaded through his hair. He crouched, close enough that I saw the thin scar running along his jaw.

"Do you know why you're here?"

I kept my face blank. "Because you're an idiot?"

The backhand snapped my head sideways, sharp enough to sting but not to knock me out. Pain radiated through my jaw. I forced myself to meet his gaze, unflinching.

"You're here because your father took something from me. From all of us." His tone didn't rise, but the weight in it was worse than shouting. "We've been waiting a long time to make him bleed. And then—" his smile thinned, "—the gods handed us you."

Ice spread through my chest. "General Blackcreek."

His mouth curved again, not quite a smile. "So, you do know. Good. Then you understand how sweet this will be."

"You think he'll trade anything for me?" I forced the words through clenched teeth. "You don't know him very well."

"Oh, I know him." His breath brushed my cheek, cold and steady. "I know what he's done. And I know exactly how to make him watch while his precious daughter suffers for every drop of blood he spilled."

Fear spiked hard, choking, but I swallowed it down. "You'll regret not killing me now."

That earned me a sharper smile. "We'll see. In the meantime, you'll stay here. And when the time is right, we'll send him your screams."

He leaned in close. Too close. My pulse roared. Muscles coiled tight. In one lunge, I drove my shoulder into his stomach, twisting my bound wrists toward his throat. The chains bit deep, cutting my skin, but I didn't care—I hooked my knee and shoved.

He grunted, knocked back a half step. It was enough. I snapped my head up and slammed it into his jaw. Pain burst through my skull, hot and white—but when I tasted blood, satisfaction burned through me.

For a breath, I thought I'd won.

Then his hand clamped my collar. He yanked me up until my toes scraped the floor. "You stupid little—"

I spat in his face.

His control shattered. Fury sharpened his features, dangerous and raw. He slammed me against the stone. My lungs emptied in one violent rush.

"Lesson one," he growled, his voice venom and steel, "you don't touch me."

His fist drove into my stomach, folding me over with a sharp gasp. His hand caught my head, smashing it back into the wall. Light exploded across my vision. The cell tilted, smearing sideways

The last thing I heard—before blackness swallowed me—was the scrape of the iron door opening again, more boots entering. And his voice, calmer now, almost pleased.

"Now, we begin."

***

I came to with water stinging my face. My body jerked, lungs dragging in air too fast. My skull pounded where it had slammed the wall, and the taste of iron coated my tongue.

The bindings hadn't changed—wrists raw in leather straps, ankles locked. Only now I was upright, forced into a heavy wooden chair bolted to the floor. My shoulders ached from the unnatural angle. My spine pressed hard against the backrest. Three of them stood before me. The tall one, still calm, still watching with that thin smile. Another leaned against the wall, arms crossed, his hood still drawn. The third—a woman this time—paced slowly in front of me, her boots clicking against the stone.

"Wakeful enough?" she asked, tilting her head. Her voice carried the easy cadence of someone used to questioning, not shouting.

I spat blood onto the floor between us. "Why don't you come closer and find out?"

Her lips curved. "Good. Defiance makes the breaking so much sweeter." She circled behind me, fingers trailing along the back of the chair.

The tall man spoke again, voice as steady as before. "Tell us about your father."

My stomach clenched. "You want his strategies? His secrets?" I let out a short laugh that scraped my throat raw. "Then you dragged the wrong person. He never trusted me with anything."

"Lies." His eyes narrowed, sharp and storm-colored. "He shields you for a reason."

"He shields everyone," I snapped. "Because he doesn't trust anyone."

The woman leaned in close, breath warm against my ear. "And yet, he would burn the world for you. Wouldn't he?"

For a moment, I faltered. Images flickered—my father's warnings, his cold lectures, his hand resting heavy on Kim's scaled neck as if the dragon were the only one he trusted. Then I remembered he damn near set Ashwynd on fire when I was attacked. They couldn't know that.

I forced my face blank. "He'd never bend. Not for me. Not for anyone."

The tall man studied me in silence. Then, without a word, he drew a thin blade from his belt. Light caught on its edge as he lowered it to my arm. The steel pressed cold against my skin.

"If you're going to kill me, then fucking do it already."

The impact that hit my face happened so fast, so hard. Pain shot through my eyes causing black and white flashes throughout my vision.

Darkness swallowed me, then spat me back in pieces.

I was chained to the wall again—leather cutting into my wrists, iron shackles at my ankles. My head sagged forward, too heavy for my neck. Every heartbeat pounded through my skull, shaking my vision loose.

I couldn't tell how long I'd been here. A minute. An hour. Days.

The lantern high above blurred, its glow splitting in two, then four. Boots scraped nearby, voices low and steady. I caught fragments—laughter, a question, my father's name—before they slid away again.

Cold fingers gripped my chin, jerking my face upward. A man's features loomed close, sharp and storm-colored, but they swam in and out, like ripples across water. His mouth moved. I caught only a word here and there—blood—Blackcreek—scream.

I forced my eyes open wider. "Go... to hell." The words slurred, half-broken, but they still left my mouth.

The strike came fast. My head cracked sideways into stone, a shock of white detonation bursting behind my eyes. The room spun. My stomach heaved. Time fractured again.

I was slumped forward. Then I was upright. Then light flashed, and someone was laughing. I couldn't tell what order it happened in.

Another blow snapped my head back. Pain surged hot and sharp, then dulled into a roar that drowned everything else.

The silver thread inside me flickered faint, thin as smoke. I clung to it with what little strength I had left. Please. Don't let it break.

The next impact drove the world sideways again. Darkness pooled in the corners of my vision. My body wouldn't move, wouldn't obey.

The last thing I knew was the weight of my own breath stuttering, then slowing... and the cold certainty that I might not wake again.

CHAPTER 30

Current Events was a required course for all cadets, which meant Auri should be here—second row from the top, halfway toward the west aisle. Her spot was empty. I told myself she was only late. She'd stroll in, hair still damp from a too-long shower, muttering about oversleeping. Except... she didn't.

The room filled in around me, the low rumble of voices bouncing off the circular tiers. Still no sign of her. My gut tightened. I reached for our mental bond but hit a solid wall. I closed my eyes, focusing on breaking it down. She never shut me out this hard. It was as if the wall were empty.

By the time Professor Melamora started droning about shifting trade routes in the Northern Range, I was leaning forward on my elbows, scanning the tiers. Auri's squad was there—Sadie, Akira, Micah, Lorenzo, Jackson—all present. She wasn't.

Something cold settled in my chest. I pushed up from my seat, ignoring Melamora's startled pause. "I'll be right back," I said, not bothering to wait for permission. I tried to reach her again. Closed my eyes and really focused. Usually, I could feel her, sense her, but this time...nothing. My heart was beating double, now.

When I arrived at the Riders' wing, my heart pounded. Her door was closed but unlocked. Inside, the bed was unmade, and a dagger lay on the blanket. There was no sign she had prepared for morning drill. Her boots still sat there. Her window was wide open—perhaps not unusual in summer, but it was fall and had been freezing overnight. Plus, she was on too many people's hit lists, thanks to her father, to leave it open.

I didn't need more proof. Something was wrong. Bad wrong.

Corson came out of Current Events with the other Riders' Wing Commanders. "She's gone," I said.

That got his attention. They all froze mid-stride, eyes flicking between us.

Corson straightened slowly, his expression controlled in that commander's way that always made my teeth grind. "Zane—"

"No, listen to me. Auriella Blackcreek is missing. She wasn't in Current Events. Her bed was disturbed. Boots are still there. Dagger left. Shutters busted. She's been gone since sometime after lights-out."

He studied me for a beat too long. "And you're certain she didn't simply—"

"Don't." My voice dropped, low and lethal. "You know her. She wouldn't wander off without her blade. Someone took her."

His jaw clenched. "I'll order a sweep—"

"A sweep?" I stepped in, inches away. "We should already be beyond the gates. Riders in the air, trackers on the ground. Every minute you wait—"

"Protocol, Braegon," he snapped, steel in his tone now. "We lock the perimeter first. Then we search."

"I don't give a damn about protocol." My hands curled into fists at my sides. "We're burning daylight. If this is about who her father is—not to mention she IS the fucking general's daughter—"

"This is about doing it right," he said, though his gaze flickered, barely.

That told me enough.

I turned on my heel before I could say something that would get me permanent latrine duty and began sorting through who I trusted enough to join me, off the books. If Corson wanted to play it slow, fine. I'd find my way.

By the time I left the strategy hall, I knew who I could count on, not just people who were capable, but people who would move now, without questions or hesitation.

Lili was the first. I caught her before she headed into the sparring gym, twin daggers strapped to her hips. "She's gone," I said.

Her brow furrowed. "Auri?"

I nodded once. That was all it took. She didn't ask about Corson or demand details. She simply fell into step beside me.

We found Alex in the Alpha Wing Hall. He tensed the instant he saw us together. "What's this?"

"Auri's missing," Lili said.

His jaw worked, but he didn't waste time pretending not to care. "Where?"

"Don't know yet," I said. "We're going to find her."

Eli and Oliver were in the courtyard, mid-banter with some other Drusearons. I caught Eli's gaze and tipped my head. He joined without a word, Oliver right behind him.

Once we were clear of any ears, I spoke straight. "Corson's locking the perimeter and waiting on a sweep. That's too slow. We're going now."

Eli's mouth curved in a sharp grin. "Finally. Some fun."

Oliver frowned, but there was steel in his eyes. "We do this quietly. If they catch us—"

"They won't," I said.

We gathered gear in minutes—blades, light packs, enough water for a long day. Lili produced smoke flares from gods knew where. "If we find her and need a quick pick up," she said.

We moved to the flight field, Lili and Alex already summoning their dragons.

"Where first?" Alex asked.

"Tracks," I said. "If they took her on foot, we'll find a sign near the Alpha side. If not..." I let the rest hang. If not, we had no choice but to start guessing—and there wasn't time for that. The campus was already alive with sound—dragon wings beating overhead, instructors shouting commands, the metallic ring of gear checks. Perfect cover.

The flight fields were a chaotic mess. Cadets ran drills with their bonded fliers, taking off in staggered intervals, looping in tight arcs before landing hard and fast. From the ground, it was a cacophony of noise and motion. From above, a swarm that no one could track individually.

Lili had Veyra saddled and waiting in the shadows off the Alpha side of the flight field. Alex's Korven crouched beside her, restless, smoke curling from his nostrils.

"We slot in right after Corzine's group launches," Lili murmured, keeping her voice low. "Their formation breaks south for wind training. We peel off before anyone clocks us."

Eli adjusted the strap on his pack. "What if the watchtower spots us?"

"They won't," Alex said. "We're ghosts until we're out of range."

We timed it perfectly. Corzine's squad took to the air in a spray of dust and wingbeats, and we launched right behind them. Eli, Oliver, and I flew under the dragons, masked by their shadow.

We stayed tight in formation until the towers were only dots on the horizon. Then Lili signaled—two sharp hand motions—and both dragons banked hard east. The drills behind us continued, their noise covering our escape.

Once the campus disappeared into a haze, we dropped lower, skimming treetops. The smell of damp earth rose in waves. I scanned the ground for any sign of her.

A few miles out, Eli pointed toward a break in the canopy. Something fluttered on a low branch—a strip of dark fabric. I leaned down, catching it as Veyra eased closer. It was a torn strip of black cotton. Auri's.

"She's out here," I said, my voice tight.

No one argued. We turned the dragons toward the forest's edge and pushed harder, the hunt officially begun. The cloth was our first sign. We hunted and searched all the grounds. Eli tracked it to an animal den, and Auri wasn't there. Every hour that passed, my chest felt tighter. Like my heart was on the verge of disintegrating.

There were pieces of her clothing all over. We spent the entire day flying over the forest, searching the ground. I could smell traces of her everywhere, like they were toying with us.

"We need to call it a night and find a place to camp," Lili said.

I knew that was what we had to do, but I didn't want to do that. I will kill every fucking person for this. If she didn't live, I wouldn't either.

"I know…"

We found a clearing where we all rested for several hours until the sun started to rise. I dozed off a couple of times. Sleep would not happen for me. My mind wandered too much to settle into sleep. Every snapped twig in the woods left me jerking my head. My head throbbed in pain.

****

We scoured the underbrush, followed broken twigs and bent grass, until the trails tangled into one another. We searched the ground, while the dragons flew overhead. The sun burned overhead. Sweat stung the cut on my ribs, soaking my shirt. Every time I reached for our bond and found nothing, it got harder to breathe.

By midafternoon, tempers frayed. Eli cursed the useless trails. Alex snapped at him, and Lili shoved between them before it came to blows. My own patience was gone—I could feel myself one second from ripping into all of them.

A glint of iron caught my eye between the trees—ventilation grates set into the side of a rocky hill.

"That's not a hunter's camp," I said. "Too well hidden."

"Dungeon entrance," Alex said, drawing his short blade. "There's an old supply hold under these woods. Mostly abandoned, but… if someone wanted to disappear with her, this is the place."

We approached on foot, crouched low. The fall air was cold enough to fog my breath, but underneath was something else—damp air rising from below, laced with the acrid tang of torch smoke.

Eli found the entrance, a half-collapsed stone arch swallowed in ivy, a rusted iron gate hanging open on freshly oiled hinges. The entrance was a jagged mouth of stone and iron. Two guards sat outside around a low fire, dice scattered on a barrel.

Lili motioned, silent. Her dagger flew, burying in one man's throat. He gurgled, hands scrabbling, before slumping forward. Alex stepped from the shadows, blade punching into the other's gut. Both fell without a sound.

The arch glowed faintly with wards. Alex pressed his palm against the stone, fire crackling under his skin. The wards cracked and bled light before shattering.

The dungeon was a foul rush of damp air and old blood.

Inside, the passage sloped downward, and outside light faded quick. We moved in silence, boots crunching on loose stone. Faint echoes drifted up from the depths—footsteps, low voices. At the bottom, the smell of stagnant water and old stone pressed close. Across the corridor, behind thick iron bars, was a narrow cell.

The dungeon stank of stagnant water and fear. My boots splashed through puddles as we rounded the corner. That was when I saw her: slumped in chains, head down, unmoving. Something inside me went cold.

The first guard stepped forward. I didn't slow down. My blade punched into his chest, steel grinding bone, before I yanked it free. He dropped without a sound. Lili was on the next, dagger flashing under his ribs. Eli's sword caught another across the throat—a clean, wet slice that left him gurgling.

A shout came from behind the cell block, and three more males charged. Alex cut down the lead before his sword cleared its scabbard. I slammed my shoulder into the next, driving him into the wall hard enough to crack stone before plunging my knife into his gut. The third lunged at Eli, only to take Lili's blade to the back of the neck.

Three more came from the top, and another two came from down the hall. Lili and I pressed our backs against each other. I felt her power between icy rage. My body calling it, wanting it, needing it. I put up a block, no one could see that, not here, not now.

The four of them came at us rapidly, swords swinging. Alex threw out flames, incinerating two of them in seconds. Lili was summoning the standing water, throwing ice throughout. Our bodies still in contact, calling her power, a little bit steeped in turning my blade icy. I swung endlessly, slicing the male's head clean off his shoulders. I quickly tossed the icy sword, hoping no one saw. I put distance between us, looking all around.

Thirteen. That was all of them. None left breathing.

I shoved the last body aside and stepped into Auri's cell. Her wrists were raw and bleeding from the shackles, her face pale and still. I cut the chains in one brutal swing, catching her before she hit the stone.

"She's breathing," I managed, though my voice was tight. "We're getting her out—now."

No one argued. We left the bodies where they fell, blood seeping through the cracks. The stairs were slick with it on our way out.

Outside, dragons waited, wings shifting restlessly. I lifted Auri into my arms—her weight frighteningly limp—and vaulted onto Veyra's back, uncertain if she'd survive the ride but unwilling to wait.

"Let's go!" I shouted, and the world dropped away as we shot skyward, leaving the dead and their stinking pit behind.

The cold air lashed my face. Lili leaned forward over the pommel, wind tangling her hair, but my focus was on the silent weight in my arms. Auri's head rested on my shoulder, her hair whipping in the wind. She was so pale—too pale—and I watched for every shallow, irregular breath.

Ahead, Korven's grey scales glinted in the sun as Alex rode, with Eli and Oliver just above. We kept a tight formation. By now, the campus would be locked down. They'd know the moment we arrived.

Lili's voice cut through the wind. "We're pushing her as fast as she'll go!"

I didn't answer. Every second between here and the college was a threat. The dungeon's stink filled my nose, Auri's limp body pressed to my chest—a constant, gut-twisting reminder that I was too late to stop whatever happened. Roving a long distance with someone who was near death wasn't a risk I wanted to take. My father taught me it was something that should only be done if there were no other choices.

"You're not dying on me," I muttered for only her to hear. "Not now. Not ever."

The Watchtowers came into view. Veyra caught an updraft, and I pulled Auri closer, shielding her from the wind.

Beside us, Alex caught my eye across the distance and gave a sharp nod. No words—just that silent promise. We'd get her home.

"Almost there," Lili called back, but my jaw stayed set. Almost wasn't enough. She had to make it all the way.

"Land on the admin side, next to the infirmary. I can rove from there."

Lili banked Veyra hard toward the admin side, heading for the flat stretch beyond the infirmary courtyard. As we touched down hard, Veyra folded her wings tight. I leaped down with Auri in my arms, boots hitting the stone. Her limpness made my heart hammer—no flinch, no murmur, only a faint breath I kept checking for.

"I've got her," I said to Lili, though it was as much to myself. She dismounted, and Veyra launched skyward.

Alex and the others touched down, but I didn't slow. I roved us through the field in three strides, magic rippling around us, pulling us forward. In the next instant, we were in the infirmary, air sharp with herbs and steel.

Healers dropped what they were doing the moment they saw her. Hands reached out, voices overlapping—questions about her pulse, her injuries, how long she'd been gone. I didn't let go until a calm, steady senior Healer met my eyes and said, "We'll take her now. You stay close."

Like hell I'd be anywhere else.

The menders took her from my arms the moment we crossed the threshold, their hands already glowing with pale gold light. One began working immediately, magic threading into Auri's skin in fine, deliberate pulses, searching for damage beneath the surface. Two Healers followed close behind, arms full of warming stones, salves, and clean bandages. While the menders worked on what magic could repair, the Healers tended to the rest—wrapping her wrists, checking for fractures, coaxing warmth back into her chilled body. The air smelled of crushed herbs, hot stone, and the faint metallic tang of magic at work.

Minutes in, one of the menders went still, eyes narrowing. "There's intracranial bleeding," she said, voice clipped but calm. "Likely from a blow to the head." Her glow flared brighter, sinking deeper into Auri's temple. "You're lucky you found her when you did..." She flicked a glance at me, her tone heavier. "She wouldn't have seen the next sunrise."

My jaw locked. The urge to turn around and hunt down anyone tied to this was so intense I could taste it, but I forced myself to stay. "Then fix her," I said, my voice low and sharp. "Now."

They did. For hours, magic hummed through the room, weaving in slow, measured waves as the bleeding stopped and pressure eased. The Healers worked in tandem—cool cloth on her forehead, careful hands checking for other injuries. Little by little, the gray left her skin. Her breathing grew deeper. Steadier.

When the menders finally stepped back, the glow in their hands faded. "She'll be weak," one said.

"She needs rest. But she'll live."

I pulled a chair right up beside the cot, my hand wrapping around hers. "You're safe now," I murmured, thumb brushing over her knuckles. "And when you wake up, I'll still be here."

I didn't leave her side for the rest of the night.

Warm sunlight filtered in through the infirmary shutters, spilling across the cot in broken stripes. I stirred the moment I felt the faintest movement beneath my hand.

Her lashes fluttered first, a small sound escaping her throat as she shifted. "Zane...?"

I was on my feet before she could even try to sit up, one hand braced on her shoulder, the other gently cradling her head. "No. Don't move yet."

She blinked slowly, groggy from the menders' magic. "I feel... heavy."

"You had a brain bleed," I said, thumb brushing across her temple, wishing I could erase it. "If I'd been a few hours later—" I broke off, the words clawing too close to what I couldn't bear to imagine.

Her brows knit, a faint crease forming. "You found me."

"Damn right I did," I murmured. My voice caught. "And I'll always find you, Auri. No matter where you are, no matter who tries to take you from me."

Her gaze caught mine, still fogged from sleep, but sharper now. "Zane..."

I didn't let her look away. "I need you to hear this while you're awake enough to remember it. I love you."

Her breath hitched, joy flickering over her face.

"I'm not saying it because you almost died," I continued, leaning in until my forehead rested against hers. "I'm saying it because it's been true for a long time. I was afraid to scare you away. I've loved you from the moment I met you. I love you, Auriella."

Her fingers twitched weakly against mine, and though there was no strength to pull me closer, I went to her anyway, careful not to jar her as I pressed my lips to her temple.

"You don't have to say anything now," I whispered. "Just rest. I'll be here when you wake up again."

Her eyes drifted closed, but the faintest smile touched her lips before sleep claimed her. I stayed right there, hand wrapped around hers, steady as a promise.

CHAPTER 31

Light pressed hard against my eyelids, too bright, too sharp. The smell of herbs burned in my nose, but underneath it—blood, iron, smoke.

Hands dragged me across stone, my heels scraping raw. Voices bent in strange echoes, overlapping until I couldn't tell one from another.

"She's the proof."

"Her blood will open the door her father closed."

"Imagine it—Fae strength, shifter rage, Nosferatu hunger—one body."

Chains bit my wrists again, and I tasted copper on my tongue. I tried to scream, but my voice came out in someone else's throat, thin and broken. Another voice rose clearer than the rest, low and certain, the one I couldn't forget. "He began it. We'll finish it."

The words cut sharper than the blows ever had.

I jerked awake, heart racing, throat raw. White ceiling beams swam into focus above me. Linen sheets tangled my legs. The infirmary.

My head felt clearer—still sore and confused, but the thick fog had lifted. The first thing I noticed was Zane, still seated in the same chair, holding my hand as if he hadn't moved since I last closed my eyes. His eyes were closed now, head tilted forward so a lock of dark hair fell over his face.

"Zane," I rasped.

His head snapped up like he'd been waiting for that exact sound. Relief flashed through his eyes, tempered by something more profound I couldn't quite name—until the memory struck me.

"You told me you love me."

For a heartbeat, he didn't answer. His jaw tightened, but he didn't look away. "I did. And I meant every word."

A thousand emotions crowded in—shock, warmth, the fear of what it meant. I swallowed the lump in my throat. "You should know... I love you too. I think I have for a while. I—" My voice cracked, and I hated it. "I didn't want to risk losing you if I said it out loud."

His hand tightened on mine, steady and grounding. "You couldn't lose me if you tried, Auri."

I let out a shaky breath, closing my eyes before opening them again. "Stay. At least until I fall asleep again."

"I'm not going anywhere," he promised, shifting his chair closer so his arm rested on the edge of the cot. His thumb brushed over my knuckles—slow and sure.

A female in solid black robes—a mender, judging by the last traces of magic fading from her hands—came in quietly.

"You're a stubborn one," she said with a wry smile. "Most cadets don't come back from a brain bleed this severe, even with magic."

I swallowed, my fingers twitching in Zane's. "You... healed me?"

She inclined her head. "Completely. The damage is gone. But even with mending, brain injuries are unpredictable. They're... resistant. Magic can knit bone, seal skin, even mend muscle without a scar—but the brain is more delicate. The wrong spell, too much power, and we risk losing memories, changing personalities—even killing you. We had to work slowly, carefully. You're lucky he found you when he did."

Her gaze flickered to Zane, who still looked halfway ready to hunt someone down.

I glanced between them. "So... no lasting damage?"

"No," she assured me. "But you'll be monitored for the next few days—headaches, confusion, any changes in speech or balance. You're actually free to go, but you'll need to check in at your wing's infirmary. And Auriella..." She fixed me with a steady look. "You push yourself harder than most. Don't test the limits of recovery. You got a second chance. Don't make me regret giving it to you."

When she left, Zane leaned closer, his voice low. "Told you. I'll always find you."

The tightness in my chest eased enough to breathe finally. "Guess I owe you my life now."

He shook his head, eyes holding mine with unwavering intensity. "You owe me nothing. Please... don't scare me like that again."

***

Less than an hour after leaving the infirmary, we got word to report to Kamban's office. The command wing felt colder than usual. Tension crackled in the air of the conference room. Major General Kamban sat at the head of the table, posture rigid, eyes hard as flint.

We filed in—Lili, Alex, Eli, Oliver, Zane and me—and lined up along the far wall. The silence dragged out, sharp and oppressive.

When he finally spoke, his voice was quiet but dangerous. "You left this college without orders. You violated restricted flight protocols, exposed two bonded dragons to unsecured airspace, and engaged hostiles without proper support. That level of insubordination could've gotten all of you killed."

His gaze sliced across each of us—sharp as any blade. "Let me make one thing clear—this is not a fucking playground. There are no second chances out there. If you break protocol again—well, let's not."

The threat lingered over us like a storm about to break. As the air felt ready to snap, Kamban leaned back, his expression shifting—merely a fraction—toward something soft.

"That being said..." His tone softened just slightly, enough to notice the change. "You managed to bring back General Blackcreek's daughter alive. If we had lost her..." He exhaled slowly, the sound weighty and purposeful. "It wouldn't have only been a personal tragedy. It would have been a fucking political disaster. The sort that topples commands, fractures alliances, and leaves us open to every enemy willing to circle for the kill."

He looked me over, and for the first time, there was something almost—almost—real in his eyes. "You saved her. That's not something I can ignore."

The steel slid back into his voice. "So, here's how it goes: extra watch duty, no weekend privileges. Two weeks. And when it's over, you'll remember your goddamn orders aren't suggestions."

"Am I actually being disciplined for being kidnapped?" I cocked my brow.

Kamban's gaze pinned me—hard enough to bruise. "You were the objective, Cadet Blackcreek. You were the whole fucking reason they risked breaking protocol. Whether you like it or not, your presence raises the stakes. You don't get to be careless."

"I didn't exactly sign up to get kidnapped," I shot back, my brow going higher.

"Exactly," he snapped. "Which is why you will learn from this—how to never be a fucking liability again." His stare froze me. "In this world, being taken is as much a failure as not coming back. Do better."

The silence after was colder than the wind outside.

"Two weeks," he reiterated, rising as if the gods had decreed it. "Extra watch. No weekends. And if I have to rescue any of you from a situation like this again, you won't be standing in my office."

The office door thudded shut behind us, echoing down the corridor. The others peeled away in silence—footsteps fading—until it was only Zane and I standing under the shitty corridor lights.

I could still feel the weight of Kamban's words coiled in my chest. "Am I supposed to feel grateful for that?"

Zane's jaw flexed. "Grateful you're alive? Yeah. For him? Fuck no."

I stopped, making him turn. "You heard him—being taken is as much a failure as not coming back. Like I had a fucking choice."

He stepped close, his voice low. "That's the thing, Auri. In his world, there's always a choice. And you either make the right one, or someone else pays for it."

Anger flared in my chest. "I did fight."

"I know you did," he said, voice firm but not unkind. "I saw what you did to those bastards. That's not the point."

"What the fuck is the point?" I snapped.

He didn't look away. "The point is, you're here. And I'm not letting him—or anyone—use what happened to shove you in a corner. But you have to keep your head, because next time, I might not get there in time."

His words landed like a punch I wasn't ready for. My throat tightened, but I didn't look away. "You always find me."

His lips pressed into a hard line. "I always fucking will. But I'd rather not have to drag you out of another cell to prove it."

For a moment, the hall was all bristling tension and breath between us. He jerked his head toward the exit. "Come on, little Savage. Let's get out of here before someone else decides to chew our asses."

We stepped out into the cool night, Kamban's office still clinging to us. Zane stayed close, his eyes already scanning the courtyard like he was hunting the next threat.

After a moment, he asked, "Do you know how to ward your room?"

I shook my head. "Not yet. It's now on my priority list."

His jaw tightened, that protective fury flaring. "That's not good enough, Auri. Not after tonight."

I smirked. "You offering to teach me?"

"I'm not offering," he said, "I'm fucking doing it. Now."

Before I could argue, his hand found mine—warm, solid—and in the next heartbeat, all the air rushed out of my lungs as he roved us straight into my chamber. The world blurred and then solidified around us.

He didn't let go until he checked every corner, every shadow, every window with a warrior's caution. "Close the windows."

I moved, curiosity punching through my exhaustion. "So... what's the difference between a basic ward and yours?"

He shot me a sharp look over his shoulder. "Mine actually keeps some bastard out."

Concentration flickered across his face. I couldn't see a damn thing, but magic prickled in the air. "You'll learn this. Over the year, your magic will keep getting stronger. No one gets in unless you say so. Other than me—that's it."

"Well, that's fucking convenient."

He grinned. "You can pull anyone in, if you want, but you have to do it each time."

He stood by the door, staring at me, calm but dead serious, waiting for my next move.

Slowly, he crossed the space between us, likely teasing me. When he reached me, he didn't touch—not yet. Standing inches away from me, I felt the heat radiating off him, the steady press of his presence pushing out any negative thoughts.

"You scared the hell out of me," he murmured.

I tilted my chin up. "Not the first time you've said that."

"Not the first time you've made it true." His gaze dipped briefly to my mouth before finding my eyes again. "You could've died, Auri. And I—" He cut himself off, shaking his head like the words were too dangerous to finish.

The silence between us said it all. His hand lifted slowly, fingers brushing just under my jaw, tracing the faint line of my pulse. My breath hitched, but I didn't move.

"You're safe now and I'm not leaving you tonight."

The promise in his voice wasn't just about safety. I stepped into him, closing the last inch between us, my hands fisting the front of his shirt. His mouth was on mine before I could think about anything else, the kiss deep and consuming—like he was pouring all the fear, the fury, and the relief of finding me back into the kiss. When we finally broke for air, his forehead rested against mine, his breath rough.

"Ward's done," he said, voice low and heated. "Now you're mine for the night."

He moved closer, slow and sure, until my back met the wall beside the window. His palm flattened there, caging me in without touching. The space between us was thin, charged, pulling tighter with every breath.

"You've been through hell," he murmured, his voice low and rough, "and all I've wanted since pulling you out of that place... is this."

His fingers brushed under my chin, tipping my head up. The kiss started soft, but it didn't stay that way. It deepened, like he tried to erase every trace of the dungeon from my body—replacing it with the feel of his mouth, his hands, the weight of him pressing into me. My fingers curled into his shirt, pulling him closer. His scent—clean leather, lavender, and pine—wrapped around me, grounding me as much as it ignited something deep in my chest.

Zane broke the kiss enough to speak against my lips. "Tell me to stop and I will."

I didn't.

His jacket hit the floor. Then my boots. His hands mapped familiar paths over my hips and waist, every touch both a promise and a claim. We moved toward the bed in a blur of urgency, but not without pauses. Those brief moments where his forehead rested against mine, where he searched my eyes like he needed to see proof I was here, alive, wanting him as much as he wanted me.

When we finally hit the mattress, it wasn't desperation that guided him anymore. It was intent. He took his time, like he had all night, to remind me what it felt like to be wanted without fear, to be touched without violence. And when his mouth found mine again, it was slower—deeper—anchoring me to the only truth that mattered in that moment.

He reached between us, guiding himself into me. We both let out a moan in unison, my body letting him know exactly what I wanted. He kept the pace slow, letting us savor every single thrust. Both of our tongues entangled each other, breathing each other's air. Every few seconds, he trailed away from my mouth and gently sucked and nipped my throat. Leaving breathy moans coming out of my mouth. He bent his head down, sucking my nipple into his mouth, and gods, that was fucking amazing. His other hand was firmly gripping my ass.

He was grunting beneath the sucks. I could feel the flushing of warm liquid between us as my climax was building. He pulled himself off my nipple, ever so gently. Part of me yearned for more of that until he used his right arm to push himself up. He stared at me, watching, his eyes moving down my body. My cheeks flushing, I followed his eyes to watch where we met, him entering and pulling back every second. He reached down with his other hand, placing his thumb onto the bundle of nerves between my legs. He applied a little pressure by moving his thumb in a circular motion. My whole body was tingling, my vision was cloudy, and warmth was rushing over my entire body.

Zane was thrusting faster, thumb moving perfectly, his eyes locked onto mine. I was losing control, and by his low grunting, he was too. I could feel the slickness between us, his thumb getting slicker with each circle. I was under him, moving my hips, grinding on him, the urge for him to move faster. He answered by taking me deeper and faster, never letting off his thumb movement.

My entire body felt like lightning went through it, followed by flames. I moaned loudly with no care to who heard, within seconds of losing myself, Zane let out this loud growl and moan, followed by several "fucks". He plunged into me as deep as he could, his thrusts slowing down, his thumb much slower, both of us taking it in. My body felt like it was being electrocuted every deep circle he made with his thumb. Gods, I don't think anyone ever made me climax so hard and so loud. The way he knew my body, moving us into perfect synchrony.

Our breathing slowed in unison, the night stars twinkling out the window. Zane stayed half-curled around me, his chest rising and falling against my back, one arm heavy over my waist like he couldn't quite let go yet. His fingers traced idle, lazy paths along my hip, not demanding—just... there. Grounding. I could feel the steadiness of his heartbeat against my shoulder blade, the way each beat seemed to match my own until we were perfectly synced.

"You're quiet," he murmured, his voice low and still edged with that roughness that came after letting the adrenaline burn away.

I tilted my head back against him, catching the faintest hint of a smile in his eyes. "Trying to memorize this," I admitted. "The way you feel right now. The way it feels… safe."

His arm tightened slightly, and he bent to press his lips to my hair. "Then don't forget it. Because I'm not going anywhere."

We lay there for another long stretch of silence before the outside world began to creep back into my thoughts. But for that moment, with his warmth around me and the soft weight of his promise still lingering in the air, I let myself stay exactly where I was. My eyes felt heavy, my body feeling lighter than it had been.

CHAPTER 32

The wings closed around us, blotting out the sky. Lili screamed, and my own voice ripped raw as we were dragged off the ground. The field was gone. Stone scraped my back. Chains locked around my wrists, pulling my arms until my shoulders burned. My throat was dry, choked with the stink of smoke and blood.

"Don't bother," a voice hissed in my ear. Sour breath, hot against my skin. "No one's coming for you."

Another voice answered, colder. "She'll fetch more than her father ever did. His blood built this. Hers will finish it."

I thrashed, kicking, but hands slammed me down. Rope bit my skin, then shifted to iron. My knees buckled as weight crashed across me. My breath strangled.

"You thought you were strong?" The words twisted through the dark. "You're nothing without him. Without us."

Lili's cry broke through, but when I turned my head, it wasn't her tied beside me. It was me. My own face, bruised and bleeding, staring back with hollow eyes.

"No," I rasped, straining against the chains. "No, this isn't—"

Fingers tangled in my hair, yanked my head back. A mouth brushed my ear. "Stronger. Faster. Hungrier. That's what you'll be."

I screamed—

—and the sound broke into a gasp.

The chains, the blood, the cold stone—gone. Linen sheets clung to my damp skin. My lungs dragged in too much air, too fast.

Zane's arms were around me, his voice steady at my ear. "It's me. You're safe. It's just me."

I clutched his shirt with shaking hands, the phantom sting of iron still burning my wrists. My heart hadn't slowed. It felt like it never would.

Zane's warmth steadied me long after my chamber walls came back into focus. My pulse still thrashed, wrists aching as if the chains were real. He brushed a strand of damp hair from my face, searching my eyes.

"You're safe," he whispered again, as though saying it enough times would make it true.

But the voices from the dark clung to me. *His blood built this. Hers will finish it.*

I carried them into the lecture hall hours later, sliding into my seat as if my body weren't still trembling. Professor Melamora stood in the center tier, hands folded neatly behind her back. Above her, the map of Yebel shimmered to life. A dark mark pulsed on the western edge.

"Lakish Outpost was attacked two nights ago," she said, her voice echoing sharp in the amphitheater. "Four Riders and their fliers fell. Three Drusearons. One Shapeshifter. All burned where they stood."

The room went silent.

"They were veterans," Melamora continued. "Not cadets. Not green soldiers. Veterans. If you think being a fourth-year here makes you invincible, take this as proof otherwise."

A hand shot up from the row ahead. "By humans?"

"Yes," she said, "by humans."

Murmurs swelled.

"That's impossible," Jeremy muttered.

From across the hall, Asmoth's voice cut through, dripping with disdain. "If they fell, it's because they were careless. No human outmatches a shifter, let alone the others."

The air tensed.

Melamora's gaze snapped to him. "Carelessness? These were seasoned warriors. One rode into two wars before you were even born." Her voice hardened, slicing the silence. "Never confuse arrogance for strength. It is the fastest way to die."

The cadets shifted uneasily.

I stared at the mark glowing on the map. Lakish Outpost. My stomach twisted, the nightmare's whispers echoing through my bones. *Stronger. Faster. Hungrier.* Was that what they were making? Was that what killed eight veterans in a single night?

And why did it feel like my father already knew?

Melamora let the silence stretch until the whispers died down. Then she turned sharply. "We will not simply mourn. We will learn. Tell me—why was Lakish Outpost vulnerable?"

Hands hesitated in the air. Finally, a Historian cadet spoke. "It's on the western ridge. Limited visibility if the enemy came from the sea."

"Correct," Melamora said. "But visibility alone does not explain eight seasoned warriors dead. Pascal?"

Pascal's boots echoed as he crossed the front tier. His gaze swept the cadets, hard enough to cut. "They were flanked. Simple as that. Riders can't fight if their fliers are crippled first. Humans aren't fools—they targeted the beasts, not the warriors. Always remember—take down the wings, and the Rider falls. The same goes for Drusearons."

Uneasy murmurs spread.

Professor Fogg cleared his throat. "Reports suggest coordinated volleys. Arrows laced with a substance that burned through scale and hide. Likely alchemical in nature. Not like fire-oil but refined. The humans adapt faster than you give them credit for."

A cadet from the Infantry rows raised his hand. "Then what should have been done differently?"

"Good question," Melamora said. "What do you think?"

"More scouts in the air," Laderra said.

Pascal barked a short laugh. "Scouts don't matter if you don't know what you're looking for. The bastards hid their ships under heavy cloud banks. By the time the Drusearons scented them, it was too late."

"Then the answer is retaliation. Strike the coast, burn their fleets before they launch," Michalova said.

"Revenge without strategy is suicide," Melamora snapped. "You cannot burn every ship. And for everyone destroyed, two more will be built."

Fogg raised a finger, his tone calmer. "A layered defense is the only viable answer. Ground wards to shield the outposts, fliers rotating in tighter intervals, Infantry ready to intercept once the enemy makes landfall. We must treat them as an organized army, not as pests."

Pascal folded his arms. "And never underestimate desperation. Humans fight like cornered dogs. That makes them twice as dangerous."

I sat rigid, heart pounding against my ribs. The nightmare whispers crawled back—*stronger, faster, hungrier.* If this was desperation, why did it feel like something worse was coming?

***

We all piled into the sparing gym with Professor Gile, in which we had the largest mix of branches together. Everyone was still calling out grudges, which took up the first part. If you didn't get called out, you were matched up randomly with another cadet. Everyone sparred at least once during class. A lot of anger was released in here.

"No surprise... Elslurs calls Blackcreek," Gile said.

This mother fucker. He already stabbed me once, beat me on the match another time. Determination hit me, I had to win. There wasn't an option, humbling this cocky bastard was what he needed. I let the anger surged through my body, I checked all my daggers in place.

We both stepped onto the mat, Zane and my platoon posted at the edge, eyes locked on us. Noise swirled from the other bouts—blades clashing, cadets grunting, instructors shouting corrections—but the circle around us felt too sharp, too bright.

Asmoth grinned, rolling his shoulders as if he had already won. "Third time's the charm, Blackcreek. Or third time's the shame."

"Go!"

He came at me hard, all muscle and speed, his blade swinging in a brutal arc meant to rattle me early. I caught it, steel jolting up my arm, but I held ground. The small crowd around us roared louder, sensing the grudge.

I ducked under his next strike and drove in low, slashing for his ribs. He twisted away, fast, shoving his shoulder into me and knocking me back a step. The mat thudded under my boots as I steadied.

"Come on," he taunted, eyes glinting. "I thought you wanted this."

I forced air through my nose, anger sharpening into focus. No wild swings. No losing control. He wanted me reckless. Not this time.

We circled, blades flashing. He feinted high, came in low—I caught it, sparks biting from steel. My knee shot up, clipping his thigh, and he hissed.

"Better," he muttered, low enough only I heard. Then his blade snapped forward, nicking across my arm. The sting burned, shallow but humiliating.

"Stay tight!" Lili shouted from the edge.

I tightened my stance, parried another strike, then lunged. My blade caught his side—shallow, but enough to leave a mark. His grin faltered.

The crowd noise swelled. Even Gile had leaned forward slightly, arms crossed.

Asmoth snarled, shoving harder, his strikes faster, heavier. My arms shook under the force, but I met him blow for blow, refusing to give ground. My pulse thundered, every ounce of me screaming that I couldn't lose again. Not here. Not to him.

We locked blades, faces inches apart, breath harsh. His voice dropped, venom low. "You'll never belong here, Blackcreek. You're just blood with a name."

Rage flared white-hot. I twisted hard, ripping my blade free, and slammed my elbow into his chest. He stumbled, hit the mat, and I went with him, pinning his wrist with my knee and pressing the edge of my blade across his throat.

The gym roared around us, but all I saw was his face, twisted with fury.

"Tap," I snarled.

For a breath, he didn't. His muscles bunched under me, teeth clenched, eyes daring me to push harder. Then, with a hiss, his hand slapped the mat.

I shoved off him, chest heaving, sweat dripping into my eyes. The crowd's noise surged into a roar. Asmoth sat up, rubbing his throat, smirk crawling back onto his face though it looked thinner now.

"Enjoy it while you can," he muttered, low enough only I caught.

Not just a rematch. Not just a fight. A warning.

"Next call—Braegon. Match—Arkwright," Gile announced, his voice cutting over the noise of the gym.

A ripple of energy went through the mats. Beau was an Infantry first-year cadet, who also helped save my life, carrying me down the mountain. And everyone knew Zane—tall, dangerous, his temper a blade in itself.

The two stepped forward, blades in hand, facing each other across the mat.

Beau dipped his head once. Respect, not mockery. "Let's see what the infamous Braegon can do."

Zane's mouth curved, but it wasn't a smile. "Try to keep up."

"Go!" One of Gile's assistants announced.

They clashed fast—Zane pressing hard, his movements sharp, relentless. Beau held, blocking, absorbing the hits with steady precision. He fought like a wall—firm and unshaken—while Zane fought like a storm—driving and circling.

The crowd gathered closer, drawn in by the rhythm—steel meeting steel, boots scraping, the thud of impacts as neither gave ground. Beau shifted suddenly, sweeping low. Zane jumped, barely clearing it, then countered with a slash that grazed Beau's shoulder. Beau only grinned, blood beading. "Not bad."

Zane's eyes flicked, narrowing, and he drove forward harder, blade flashing in quick arcs. Beau blocked two, ducked the third, and shoved him back with his shoulder. The mat thudded under their boots.

"Strong," Beau said between breaths, "but you fight angry."

That landed sharper than any strike. Zane's jaw tightened, his eyes flicked toward where I stood at the edge of the mat.

The fight raged on—Zane hammering, Beau holding, neither faltering. Sweat slicked their arms, breath ragged, but still neither tapped.

Finally, Beau hooked Zane's ankle, and they both went down hard, rolling. Zane came up faster, blade pressed to Beau's throat. Beau's palm hovered over the mat, his grin faint even as his chest heaved.

"Tap," Zane said, voice low.

For a breath Beau hesitated, eyes meeting his evenly. Then, with a firm slap, he yielded.

The roar from the Drusearons was deafening. They clearly admired and respected him.

Zane stood, offered Beau a hand up. Beau took it without hesitation, their grips firm.

"You're as good as they say," he muttered.

"And you're better than most," Zane replied, almost grudgingly.

For once, there was no smirk, no gloating. Just respect between two fighters who knew the other wouldn't break easy.

The cheers still rattled in my chest long after the matches ended. Sweat clung to my skin, the sting of Asmoth's blade still sharp along my arm. I'd won, but the victory tasted strange—half bitter, half sweet.

Maybe I'd proved myself. Perhaps I'd only made the target on my back brighter.

The nightmare clung to me even now, whispering under the noise. *His blood built this. Hers will finish it.* My father's voice, the professors' warnings, Asmoth's sneer—they all twisted together until I couldn't tell which was worse. The enemies outside our gates, or the ones sitting beside me in class.

I looked at Zane, his hand still locked with Beau's, respect sparking between them. It should have been reassuring, seeing strength recognize strength. Instead, unease coiled low in my stomach.

We were all training, fighting, bleeding for a war that felt closer every day. But deep down I couldn't shake the thought that something else was coming. Something bigger than humans with fire-oil, bigger than our rivalries and grudges.

Stronger. Faster. Hungrier.

The words echoed in my bones. And I wasn't sure if I was preparing for the war ahead—or being shaped into it.We spilled into the courtyard after sparring, sore and buzzing from the fights. There was a downtime before our next lectures started. Laughter bounced off the stone walls, the air thick with sweat, and the tang of bruised pride.

Micah started it, as always. "Alright, ability bets. Bonding's coming. No one's escaping this without a guess."

Groans and protests rippled, but he grinned, leaning forward. "I'm calling wind manipulation, blowing everybody away."

"Then we might all smell you." Lorenzo wrinkled his nose. "Gods help us if that's your gift."

Laughter broke.

"Ice," Lili cut in, flicking a shard across the ground that hissed and melted. "Already sorted."

"Show-off," Micah muttered.

"Fire," Alex added, flames sparking along his knuckles before he clenched them out. "Runs in the family."

Sadie clapped, smirking. "Finally admits it instead of pretending he's humble."

Jeremy leaned in, his grin quick and sly. "Speaking of family, Sadie, you should know—I've got strong lines. Shifter blood, oldest son, destined for something powerful. Better odds than Beverli at least."

Sadie raised an eyebrow. "Is this supposed to impress me?"

Jeremy's grin widened. "Worked on half the girls in Charlie Wing."

"Too bad I'm not half the girls," Sadie shot back, making the group howl.

Asmoth shoved Jeremy's shoulder, laughing. "Gods, you're pathetic." His eyes cut to me, narrowing. "Guess your luck ran out, anyway. Braegon took the one you were eyeing."

The group stilled for a beat. My pulse thumped hard against my ribs, heat rushing to my face before I could stop it.

Zane's gaze flicked to him, sharp as a blade. "Watch your mouth."

Asmoth leaned back, smirk widening. "Just an observation."

Before it could tilt, Beau spoke up from the far end, calm and even. "Abilities aren't the only thing that matters. Half of you won't live long enough to use them if you keep fighting stupid."

"Always the optimist," Micah muttered, but the tension eased.

Lili elbowed me, grinning. "C'mon, Auri, you've been quiet. What do you want?"

Dozens of eyes shifted my way. My stomach knotted. What could I say? That I wanted power strong enough to silence the chains still burning my wrists at night? That I wanted something more than being my father's daughter?

I forced a smirk. "Professional napper."

The table erupted, and the moment broke into laughter again, though Zane's eyes lingered on me, unreadable.

For now, we laughed, but bonding was coming fast—and I knew nothing about it would be a joke.

CHAPTER 33

The following two months after the kidnapping felt markedly different. The wards in my chamber stayed vigilant—Zane ensured that—and he grew increasingly protective without explicitly saying so. I observed how his eyes tracked people intently as we walked through the bustling training fields. He lingered outside my door longer before returning to his own wing, if he left.

Training didn't slow down. If anything, it became even more intense. The instructors challenged my survival skills to ensure I would never feel that vulnerable again. Combat drills doubled in frequency. Obstacle runs faced harsher weather conditions. My sparring matches grew increasingly brutal. I didn't lose anymore.

The squad's morale had also undergone a change. Lili was more alert and faster to give orders—perhaps to avoid another mistake. Eli and Oliver now showed me a calm respect that wasn't present before, and even Alex... Well, Alex no longer looked at me with hatred. Instead, there was a sense of understanding.

I stopped waking up in a cold sweat most nights, yet I remained cautious. The dungeon haunted my worst dreams, but Zane's voice pulled me back each time. Beneath it all, the bond between us grew stronger than I expected. We didn't speak the words again since that day in the infirmary. Yet, words weren't necessary. Their presence showed in every glance, every scan across the field, and every moment he waited outside the door until I was safely inside.

The last two months bled together into a rhythm of drills, lectures, and the occasional night spent tangled in Zane's arms. But even the most disciplined routines couldn't hide the tension creeping into the air around campus.

Bonding Day was coming.

Every year, on December thirteenth, the Flugblatt Forest became filled with fliers and Riders—not for sightseeing, not for training, but for the rite that would decide the futures of unbonded cadets. That day, the forest became the stage for the most dangerous and sacred tradition we had, walking into the fliers' domain and either leaving with a bond... or not leaving at all.

It wasn't just dragons we would face. Griffins, with talons like forged steel. Phoenixes, whose flames can sear through armor. The fliers chose their Riders—if they wanted one at all. And they didn't always choose kindly.

Cadets had died in Flugblatt. The fliers themselves tore apart some, while others were cut down by rival cadets desperate to secure a bond. There were no referees or protective wards—only the understanding that entering the forest meant accepting the risk.

The air was thick with whispers of what might happen. Dragons had been spotted circling lower than usual. Griffins called out from the cliffs beyond. Phoenix embers had been found smoldering in the frost along the forest edge. The fliers knew. They always knew. Whether the forest gave me a bond or a grave, only the fliers could decide. And I couldn't tell if the thought made my blood sing... or turn to ice.

Training doubled. Professor Quillet had us in endurance drills at dawn, running obstacle courses until our legs shook. Professor Gile and Rivet followed with tactical sparring—blades, unarmed, and disarm attempts—reminding us with every strike that on December thirteenth, the threat might come from the cadet beside us just as easily as from a flier.

I wasn't the only one carrying bruises into the mess hall. Fights broke out during mealtimes, sometimes over petty things, sometimes over nothing at all. Everyone was sizing each other up, calculating strengths and weaknesses. You could almost see the unspoken thought passing behind people's eyes. If it came down to you or me in the forest, I'd make sure it was me.

One evening, as Zane and I crossed the courtyard, a shadow passed over us so huge it swallowed the light. An elder dragon—big enough to carry a siege tower on its back—circled once over the college before heading toward the forest. Despite the distance, I felt the weight of its gaze.

Squad Leaders kept us busy with survival drills—navigating without landmarks, finding water in frozen terrain, and moving silently through the brush. By the second night, I was falling asleep in my boots.

Zane kept a watchful eye on me, but he wasn't the only one. Lili's tone got sharper, her questions more pointed. Alex was quieter than usual, though his gaze lingered longer during practice matches. Friends could be possible opponents.

And through it all, the forest loomed on the horizon—dark, sprawling, and waiting.

***

The bell tolled before dawn rattling the frost off the barracks windows. My breath hung in the air as I swung my legs out of bed, the cold cutting sharply against my skin. It wasn't simply another training day. It was Bonding Day.

Four months of drills, bruises, and sleepless nights had led up to this moment, and now the whole college was awake before the sun, the courtyard buzzing with a mixture of excitement and dread. Cadets moved through their groups, some checking their gear, others acting as if they weren't watching their rivals.

A few days earlier, the final scores for the Rite of Passage had been posted in the mess hall. Our squad—Sadie, Akira, Micah, Lorenzo, Jackson, and I—ranked fourth out of twelve. That meant we would be the fourth group to enter Flugblatt Forest, trailing the third group by exactly ten minutes.

Not enough to catch them unless they slowed down, but enough to feel the pressure of the fifth group closing in behind us.

The order mattered. Some fliers would already be bonded when we entered. Others might be more agitated due to the noise and the bloodshed that had preceded us. Blood was inevitable. Each year, the forest claimed its toll—sometimes from talons, sometimes from the blades of fellow cadets who desired the same fliers you sought. There were no rules in the forest.

The entire outdoor arena was filled with cadets from other branches who gathered to watch newly bonded Riders flying in on their fliers. Zane would watch as I soared in on my bonded dragon, hopefully. My squad moved as a cohesive unit across the frosted grass. Lili led our platoon toward the edge of the courtyard where stern instructors waited, their dark silhouettes stark against the faint glow of the sunrise.

Beyond them, the dark line of Flugblatt Forest loomed. The trees looked ancient and unmoving, holding their own secrets. Somewhere inside, dragons, griffins, and phoenixes would be waiting—some to bond, others to kill.

The instructors began calling out squads in order, each group stepping forward, saluting, and disappearing into the tree line. When the third squad vanished, we were up next.

"Electric's First Squad, to the line!"

My pulse was a drumbeat in my ears as we took our places. Ten minutes. Ten minutes until the forest decides who among us walks out. The whistle was a shrill, cutting sound that made the forest ahead seem definitely quieter.

Our squad stood at the edge of Flugblatt's shadow, the cold air already tinged with the earthy, metallic scent that clung to that place every Bonding Day. Sadie flexed her hands like she was itching for a fight, Lorenzo rolled his shoulders loose, Akira's eyes scanned the tree line, and Jackson adjusted the grip on his spear. Further back, Lili stood with the Rider's Leadership, her posture sharp, hands clasped behind her back, watching our every move.

"Electric's First Squad!" Instructor Quillet barked. "Your window starts now. You have ten minutes before the next squad follows you in. Make it count."

I drew in a slow breath, the weight of the day settling like armor over my skin. Somewhere inside those ancient trees was my flier—a dragon—that was what I wanted. What mattered was finding them before someone else did... or before something killed me.

"Go!"

We surged forward as one, boots hitting the frozen ground in unison before breaking into the scattered, instinctive patterns of a hunt. The forest swallowed us in seconds, the daylight fading under the canopy. The moment we crossed deeper into Flugblatt, our formation began to unravel. The forest demanded it. Paths broke away in jagged directions, narrowing to barely a footpath in some places and vanishing entirely in others.

Akira darted left through a cluster of frost-hung ferns. Jackson vaulted over a downed tree to the right. Sadie slid between two mossy boulders without hesitation, and Lorenzo disappeared into the shadows ahead. In less than thirty seconds, I was alone.

In the back of my mind, Zane's presence pressed faintly at the edges, a steady thrum like the pull of a tide. I knew he wouldn't mean to distract me, but if he felt any flicker of danger, he'd try to interfere—and that was the last thing I needed. I closed my eyes briefly and shoved my mental shields into place. The tether between us snapped silent. The air felt colder without him there, but it was necessary.

The forest breathed around me—distant wingbeats, the low rumble of something significant moving through underbrush, the occasional high, eerie cry that made the hairs on my neck stand up. A gust of wind carried the faint scent of ash and cold metal. My steps quickened.

I slipped between the roots of an ancient pine, my senses straining, as the forest swallowed me whole. Something shifted in the branches above—soft, deliberate.

My breath caught before my eyes when I found her.

Esme.

Silver glinted through the lattice of frost-tipped limbs, her movements fluid but cautious. She stepped from the shadows of an overhanging ledge, and the sight of her hit me like the first breath after being underwater too long. Smaller than the others, her frame was lean and not yet filled out, but every inch of her shimmered with quiet power. Her eyes—icy blue and sharp as cut glass—locked on mine.

Remember me.

The words from Judgment Day echoed in my skull, precisely as she had spoken them to me months earlier, before melting back into the dense forest. I thought of her every single day since. I took a slow step forward, keeping my hands at my sides. The tense air between us felt charged, her gaze sharp and deliberate, measuring and weighing.

A sharp crunch of frost snapped the moment in half.

A tall, dark-haired cadet emerged from the tree line to my left, blade already drawn. "Looks like I'm barely in time," he said, voice laced with smugness.

I shifted to block his path. "Turn around."

"She's unclaimed," he shot back. "You know the rules—first to bond wins. Or are you afraid I'll beat you to her?"

"You try," I said, "and you'll regret it."

His grin widened, but it didn't reach his eyes. "You don't scare me, Blackcreek. And I've waited for this."

We clashed before another word could be said—steel ringing, boots sliding on the frozen ground. He fought dirty, going for joints and aiming to disable rather than test his skill. My dagger bit into his arm. He slammed an elbow into my ribs. I used the momentum to shove him back, keeping myself between him and Esme.

Her wings flexed slightly, feathers of frost scattering to the ground, but she didn't move. She watched. Judging. He lunged again. I caught his wrist, twisted, and slammed him into a tree. My blade was at his throat before he could blink. "This is your only chance. Walk away, or you leave here carried."

He stared at me, breathing hard, then spat to the side. "She's not worth dying for."

I kept my gaze on him until he disappeared, then turned to Esme. She remained on her perch, her head tilting with eyes that seemed to perceive something in me no one else could. She tilted her head once more, her tail flicking faintly through the snow. Suddenly, she spread her wings without warning.

The sound resembled thunder crashing through the forest—intense, sharp, yet quick. She leapt from the ledge in a burst of frost, surpassing the initial row of trees before I fully registered her departure.

Shit.

I bolted after her, boots crunching over frozen roots and patches of snow. My breath tore from my lungs in sharp bursts as I pushed harder, the cold air burning in my throat. Through the lattice of branches, I caught flashes of silver darting ahead—low enough to force me to weave through the undergrowth instead of just watching her vanish into the clouds.

A low laugh—wait, could dragons laugh—rippled through my mind.

"You remembered me. But will you keep up?"

Branches lashed my face and arms, stinging hot lines across my skin, but I kept running. Instinct howled—if I lost her now, she'd vanish, and with her, my chance at the bond.

Esme dipped sharp, weaving between a fallen trunk and the riverbank. I plunged after her, boots sliding down the icy slope. Rocks tore at my palms as I caught myself before the drop.

The river churned black beneath a fragile skin of ice, water rushing fast enough to drag anything under. Esme had already banked toward the far side, wings beating hard, leaving me scrambling to keep her in sight.

"You've got to be kidding me," I muttered, before I sprinted two steps and leapt.

For a moment, I was weightless—the icy wind ripping at my clothes—before I landed hard, sliding into the frost-hardened mud on the far side. My knees jolted, but I was already moving again. Esme glanced over her shoulder mid-flight, and for the first time, I swore there was approval in her eyes.

"Come find me."

And with that, she vanished deeper into Flugblatt Forest, leaving me no choice but to chase her until either I caught her... or I couldn't move another step. The silver light came first—shimmering through the trees like water spilling between leaves. My steps slowed, every instinct on alert, and then the trees opened into the glade. Frost clung to the grass in sparkling webs, but the air was warmer here, humming faintly in my bones.

Esme stood at the far side. Smaller than the great elders, yes, but her presence filled the space, silver scales glinting like she had been born of moonlight.

"You made it." Her voice slid into my mind the same way it had on Judgment Day. *"Now you choose."*

I took a step forward. "Choose what?"

"To take what you want... or turn away."

Movement flickered in the shadows. Two cadets stepped into the glade—daggers drawn, eyes sharp with the kind of hunger Bonding Day always brought.

"I found her first," I warned.

One smirked. "Bonding day's fair game. Let's see if you can keep her."

The first came at me fast, and steel rang as our blades met. The second tried to come in low from my blind side, and I spun—too slow. Pain punched into my ribs, white-hot, as the tip of his dagger slid between the plates of my light armor.

I hissed, shoving him back with my elbow, warm wetness already blooming under my tunic. Not deep enough to drop me. Not today. The one in front of me grinned like he had already won—until I caught his wrist, twisted hard, and drove my knee into his gut. He went down gasping, and I ripped the dagger from his hand in one smooth motion.

The second lunged again, but this time I met him head-on, blades locking before I slammed my forehead into his. He stumbled, dazed, and I kicked his legs out, pinning him with a boot to the throat.

I straightened, breathing hard, the stab wound a throbbing pulse under my ribs. "Not turning away," I said.

Esme's eyes burned into mine. *"Then come to me."*

I crossed the frost-rimmed grass, each step measured despite the ache in my side. When my palm touched her brow, heat poured through me—fierce and endless—burning the pain away until there was only her.

Our eyes locked, and I felt a pulse run from my head to my toes, locking our bond into place. Esme lowered her head just enough for me to reach the ridge of muscle between her neck and shoulder. My side burned where the dagger had been, but I clenched my jaw and hauled myself up, hooking my leg over her sleek body. No saddle. No straps. Just living, shifting muscle beneath me, and a scattering of ridges to hook my knees around.

"Hold on," Esme's voice purred through my mind—equal parts warning and challenge.

Her muscles bunched before we launched. My stomach dropped as the forest floor fell away in a blur of frost and shadow. The wind slammed into me, tearing at my hair and clothes, every movement threatening to pitch me sideways. I pressed my thighs tighter against her flanks, fingers digging into the base of her neck where the scales met softer hide. Her movements were nothing like the experienced fliers—raw, unpredictable, each wingbeat a jolt that rattled my teeth.

Esme twisted midair, banking hard to the left. My body went with her, but my balance lagged, and for a terrifying moment, I was dangling, my right leg slipping free.

"You're not falling, are you?" she teased, but I caught the undercurrent of testing in her tone.

"Not... a chance," I gritted, shoving my leg back over and lowering my weight closer to her spine.

She climbed higher, the air thinning, my eyes watering as cold sliced against my cheeks. Every muscle in my body screamed from holding on, and my wound throbbed in time with my heartbeat. But I didn't let go.

When she finally leveled out, her mind brushed mine again. *"Good. You learn fast."*

Below us, the forest stretched out with endless patches of snow and greenery, leaving the Bonding Day chaos far behind. I wasn't sure whether I had passed her test or if it was only the start, but one thing was clear—Esme wasn't the type of dragon you could tame. She was the kind you had to prove yourself to.

CHAPTER 34

Esme soared all around the campus, weaving high and low. I was quite sure she was trying to make me fall off. However, part of Bonding Day also involved returning safely to the flight field without falling from our fliers. She executed some sharp left and right banks that, thankfully, I had ridden a dragon before. The final step was landing in the outdoor stadium, where we presented our bonded dragon to the Historian for roll call. Knowing Esme was still a young dragon made me a bit nervous during our approach, as we needed to descend lower to land.

"Just because I am young doesn't mean I haven't been flying longer than you've been born..." she snapped into my head.

Fuck. I forgot I needed to work on another mental block.

"Sorry to offend you, I am new to this," I said.

"You should really hold on now."

She moved into a steep nosedive, making my stomach lurch into my heart, my pulse picking up a few notches. My legs were gripping each side of her, my hands holding onto the fleshy bump where her neck met her shoulders. I absolutely couldn't wait to be fitted with saddles. Bareback was an experience, but when she was trying to flip me off, I was actually worried about my life. She lifted almost completely, flipping us around, and went straight for the sky.

"I get it... you can fly..."

"Do you? Do you get it? Actually?" Then she laughed. She actually fucking laughed at me.

"Maybe I should have picked Kekoa—"

She made a growl sound. *"You wound my dragon heart, but point taken."*

She leveled out and circled the college again, gradually lowering. We flew closely over the flight field, where I saw dragons, griffins, and phoenixes standing beside their Riders. We then moved over the stadium wall. On the field, several more fliers were visible, along with some perched on the stadium walls, most of whom appeared to be leadership. I noticed Kim sitting closest to the stage, indicating my dad was likely nearby or up there.

She descended straight down, landing perfectly. I guessed I should never doubt her.

"Do you know what you're supposed to do?" she said with this knowing tone.

"Uh... I am supposed to get your full name, and your parents' names and report it to the Historian who's keeping the roll."

"Yes... and then?"

"Then I will return to you? And we are supposed to go wait in the flight field with the other fliers and Riders until we all come back in for the ceremony at exactly sixteen-hundred."

"Yes, until all of The Aelorian Circle arrives."

"Oh yes, the group of eldest fliers who speak on behalf of all fliers."

"Alright, are you ready? You should go ahead and slide off."

Following her suggestion, I swung my right leg over as she slid her legs out, creating a slide, though a bumpy one. The motion reminded me of the stab wound in my side, which began to throb, feeling as if I were burned. I descended along her leg, clutching my side.

"Are you going to tell me what I need to know?"

"Yes, when you get to the dais," I swore she rolled her eyes.

I started making my way to the dais, walking a little slower. The stab wound was telling me it needed tending soon. All adrenaline had worn off. Zane was pushing on our mental bond. I finally let it collapse, letting him in all the way.

"You're hurt, Auri..." he said.

"Yes, it's merely a flesh wound. I'll be fine."

"Hopefully, the other person can't say the same."

"They live..."

"If they make it back here, it won't be for long. Also, your dragon is a beauty, a beautiful job, love."

I reached the dais where three other Riders were already present, each reporting their dragons' names and lineage for official claiming. I was certain that once a dragon and Rider communicated telepathically, their bond was established—wait a second—then I glanced back at Esme. She exhaled a puff of sulfur air.

"Yes. Yes. You were mine the moment I spoke to you out there. I wanted to see the fight you had in you, to make sure you are truly worthy. Or for you to remember your studies and remember that we only talk to the Rider we claim."

"You're diabolical."

She threw a laugh down our mental bond.

The other three reported their names, and I stepped forward to the dais where Selene sat next to another Historian. She smiled at me, "Name?"

I let out a little giggle, "Auriella Reyna Blackcreek."

"And flier type and name?" the other one asked.

"Dragon and —"

"Esmeraladathoradae,   Daughter   of   Kimraventhrosa   and Korvanleglunga."

"Esmeraladathoradae, Daughter of Kimraventhrosa and Korvanleglunga," I repeated to the Historians. Her mother's name—why did that sound like my dad's dragon's name? I turned on my heels, walking back to Esme. My mind spun in circles. I looked at the ledge to Kim. She stared our way, and I followed her trail back down to stare at Esme. Shock filled my pores.

Holy fucking shit. This couldn't be for real.

My mouth was agape when I reached her.

"Because you currently look to be in a state of shock, I will answer the pounding thoughts that are circling in your head. Yes, Kim, your dad's dragon is my mom." She blew a puff of steam at me. She made a squeaky voice that made her sound ten years old, *"Welcome to the shit show!"*

I didn't even know how to respond to that. She wanted me, and she knew who I was. I closed my eyes, sensing her mental bond that was freely drifting in my mind. I started to construct blocks so she couldn't hear every single thought I had.

She puffed another steamy breath at me. *"You know you won't be able to fully block me out, ever."*

I just blinked my eyes at her. Great, now I had two mental bonds, except this one could read my thoughts unwillingly.

"It's time for us to go to the flight field with others. There are tents there with Healers and Menders."

I started walking towards the vast open gate, and she followed, each step vibrating the ground under me slightly. We crossed through the gate, where many, many other fliers were standing, their Riders with them. I immediately started to look around to see if I could see any of my other wing or squad members. While the Electric Platoon, First Squad, First Flight was my immediate concern, there were many other first-year students in our total wing.

My eyes locked with Thora, who stood next to a beautiful dark blue griffin. I gave her a big smile. As I looked around, it was clear that there were distinct groups or separations of the flier types. Dragons occupied the right side of the field, Griffins covered the first half of the left side, and Phoenixes were on the opposite side. Esme moved into the open space with ease and casually rested her head on her forelegs, her silver scales shimmering in the light.

"Are you truly going to take a nap right now?"

She made this guttural scoffing sound. *"Yes... It will be a while, and you should go to the Healer's tent and stop that awful bleeding."*

"Bleeding that you pretty much caused me..."

"Semantics."

I approached the large open tents on the side, where cadets could find food, water, and get bandaged. I made my way to the tent, where cadets wore baby blue tunics, with a few in black among them. Ophelia saw me and came over, signaling for me to sit down. It felt fitting that she was the one who cared for me during my struggles on the pass in basic training, and also the one who checked on me after my head injury.

"How bad this time?"

"Flesh wound, not bad. I don't need a mender, just some stitches and a bandage."

"I can do that."

In the distance, I saw someone wearing all black walking to the tent. As he got closer, I saw his golden wavy hair and blue eyes beaming at me.

Zane.

"You shouldn't be on the flight field," I told him down our bond.

"And? I actually don't care."

"How is she, and how bad is it?" he said as he approached Ophelia.

"Not bad at all, a few stitches. She's seen worse, as you know."

"You can go now—" I started to say.

"No. I will sit with you until she's done."

Ophelia raised her eyebrows at me and gave me a smirk.

"He's protective. Overbearing. Loving but a mother hen nonetheless," I said.

"Well, it looks like you bonded with a beautiful dragon. One of the few silvers, according to the rumors," she said, changing the subject.

I lifted my chin, pride tugging at my mouth. "Only two silvers, is what we were told."

"What's her or his name?" Ophelia asked.

"Esme is her name."

"That's beautiful, exceptionally fitting."

"She is spicy," I let out a laugh.

They both laughed with me.

Ophelia finished stitching me. She applied a salve on it to aid in faster healing and numb it for a little while. I gave her my thanks and a hug before heading back to the flight field. Overhead, I saw a red dragon flying, doing various maneuvers in the sky that made my heart skip a beat. Sometimes dragons took testing us on bonding day to the extreme. Reds are notorious for testing their new Riders to the limit to see if they're worthy of being a

Rider. The red started descending towards the field, she banked a little to the left, and I could see Lorenzo on its back, holding on for his life. They descended into the stadium field and out of sight.

Zane pressed a gentle kiss on my forehead and returned to the stadium seating. I moved to Esme and stood beside her. She kept her head down but opened her eyes as I approached before closing them again. Several Riders wandered around while some of the fliers lay down like Esme. Others stood nearby, their eyes alert as they looked around. I reached up and scratched gently under Esme's neck before heading down the field to see if I could locate any of our platoon.

As I got closer to the end of the griffins, I spotted Sadie lying against a golden griffin. It was still standing, as she rested against its legs. As I approached, she gave me a big smile and jumped up.

"I am soooooo glad to see you here," she said.

"I am glad to see you—"

She grabbed me into a bear hug, towering four inches over me. It caught me off guard at first before I embraced her back. She let go and stepped back.

"Have you seen any of the others?" I asked her.

"Only Micah," she nodded towards the phoenixes, "He's down there with one of the larger phoenixes."

"Okay, good. I saw Lorenzo flying in on a red dragon. That leaves Akira and Jackson in our group."

"There was so much screaming out there. I could hear dragons roaring, and I could smell flesh burning. It was intense."

"Any injuries?"

"No, I am good. I found Korra within minutes. We locked eyes, tingles ran through me, and she told me to get on and let's get out of here. We were one of the first five or six to land."

"I am glad to hear that. She's stunning."

"What did you get?"

"The little silver, named Esme."

"That's fantastic, but she is so much smaller."

"Yeah, she has some growing to do," I shot her a wink.

I continued down through all the fliers, a few griffins down, and Michalova stood in front of a black griffin that faded into a beautiful gold. He waved his hand at me to come to him.

"Hey! Nice griffin! It's good to see you, my Flight Guide counterpart," I said.

He gave me a wry smile that instantly made my stomach turn. "I saw Jackson get teamed up against, and he went down. One of the dragons incinerated him, I am pretty sure out of mercy, as he wasn't moving."

My heart started racing, my stomach in complete knots.

Gods.

Fuck.

Fuck.

Fuck.

Not another one on our squad. My eyes began to well up with tears. I took a deep breath, telling myself to maintain my composure. There were way too many Riders on this field, and too many of those weren't fans of me.

"Thanks for letting me know." He gave me a nod before I continued on.

I saw Electric's second squad, Vida, standing in front of a mid-size grey dragon, as well as Erik standing in front of a red dragon. Towards the end of the line, I saw Jameson in front of a mid-size phoenix. That accounted for all of Michalova's flight and only left Akira for ours and for all of the Electric platoon.

I headed back toward Esme to wait out the remaining afternoon, eager to spot Akira sooner rather than later. The winter sun sank lower in the gray sky, suggesting it was around fourteen hundred hours. All Riders needed to return by fifteen-thirty. During this period, the bell tolls paused for multiple reasons. First, they forced us to depend on our training to estimate the sun's position. The first bell to toll after we entered the dense forest signaled that cadets had thirty minutes to reach the stadium and check in. It would toll again at the thirty-minute mark to indicate the deadline had arrived. Any cadet still alive and not bonded to a flier faced reassignment to Infantry.

I made my way back to Esme and sat down, leaning against her warm shoulder. She was still resting but kept watch of the bustling flight field. I looked into the expansive sky, observing colorful dragons, graceful griffins, and majestic phoenixes soaring overhead to land in the lively courtyard. I couldn't see most of the Riders because their large flier blocked my view. The few I caught performing sharp, impressive banks, I didn't recognize the Riders.

The bell tolled fifteen times, marking it as fifteen hundred. A jolt of nerves shot through my stomach. I hated losing another squadmate. Our flight had already shrunk to five after Jackson's absence. The only comfort was that during the past thirty minutes, several fliers had arrived, and she might be in the courtyard waiting to identify herself and her Rider. Every few minutes, another flier and Rider walked through the gates of the flight field. My eyes tracked each one with cautious anticipation.

Black dragon, black-gold griffin, grey dragon, phoenix—none of the Riders were Akira.

A large yellow-gold dragon started walking to the flight field, and next to her was the familiar, beautiful face of Akira. Thank the Gods. She passed by, giving me a big smile. I mirrored her back, flashing a large grin. Peace settled within. I let go of the deep breath I was holding.

I hadn't seen any more fliers pass by in a little while, and the Riders coming through the gate were slowing down considerably. Based on the sun and when the last bell tolled, it should be—

DONGGGGGGGGGG. DONGGGGGGGGGGGG.

Long dongs spilled through the air, indicating that no more fliers could fly into the field, and the bonding ceremony would be starting soon.

***

"Hey, I've got news." By the way, all the other Riders on the field perked up. All of their fliers were also telling them something. *"When the bell tolls again, the ceremony will start. Leaders played rock, paper, scissors—and have determined the order. Dragon Wing's four Flight Guides will go through the gate first. Then Feather Wing's, which means it will be you, Michalova Sulivar, Laderra Holmes, and Aeltharion Gaglonda, in that order. Eagle Wing will be the tail. We will go in and stand below the stage. It will be tight in there with all the fliers. The dragons know they need to keep their wings tucked, as they are generally the largest. The rest of the cadets will come in a neat and orderly manner, starting with those closest to the gate."*

She pulled her legs inward and stood completely upright. All the Riders shifted their feet anxiously. The fliers appeared nervous as well. This part of the ceremony was a remarkably sacred moment when the Gods and elder dragons blessed their bonds. We wore distinct marks that connected us to our fliers, solidifying our relationships. Some of us gained new magical abilities, others acquired powerful new abilities, even if we didn't know it yet. The bell tolled sixteen times. It was time.

The four Dragon Wing Flight Guides and their fliers led the way beneath the arch, their steps echoing against the cold stone as though the world itself held its breath. I fell in line behind them, Esme's shimmering silver scales catching the muted winter light. Her head was slightly lowered, wings tucked close to her body, making her appear smaller than she was. Behind me, I heard Michalova's griffin's talons clicking steadily against the stone, each step measured and sure.

The space beyond unfolded in breathtaking scale. The stadium spread out like a carved amphitheater, massive stone walls curving in a circle. Thousands of cadets from every branch filled the tiered seating, their uniforms a wash of disciplined color. They sat in rows upon rows, rising thirteen levels high, separated by the branching stone staircases that divided the sections. Their eyes followed us—some curious, some reverent, some openly envious.

At the far end, opposite the gate, the stage rose above the field. Leadership sat in high-backed chairs carved from dark stone, elevated so that every gaze in the arena fell toward them. The weight of their presence pressed heavier than the crowd's. Generals, Elders, and the council of fliers themselves watched, their faces unreadable masks.

We moved onto the broad, flat expanse of the field itself, fliers finding their places in neat lines. Dragons shifted their massive bodies with disciplined care, griffins folded their wings tightly, and phoenixes glowed faintly in the dim light, as though their feathers drank in anticipation. All of us were standing directly in front of our fliers, between their legs. They towered over each of us.

One by one, the remaining cadets filed through the gates, a relentless stream of boots, talons, wings, and feathers. The air was thick with the scents of scale and ash, oil and leather, feathers and smoke. Every cadet wore the same expression—nerves honed into resolve, eyes fixed ahead, each step a silent promise. By the time the last group entered, the stadium floor was packed from edge to edge, the sound of breathing and shifting wings loud beneath the silence of the crowd.

The bell tolled once, low and resonant, carrying across the arena.

The ceremony was about to begin.

The silence deepened until it felt as if the entire world held its breath. From the raised dais, a tall figure stepped forward, the torchlight catching on the pitch-black of his uniform.

My father.

The murmurs in the crowd died instantly. His presence carried across the field like a blade unsheathed, sharp and commanding. He rested one gloved hand on the rail of the platform, his voice carrying easily without the need for amplification.

"Rider Cadets," he began, his tone clipped but resonant, "today you stand at the threshold of what will define not just your careers, but your lives. Bonding Day is not a pageant. It is not a festival. It is the reckoning of your worth before the Gods, before the Elders, and before the blood of our people."

His gaze swept the rows of us on the field, pausing as if he could see straight through flesh and bone into the marrow of our souls. I forced myself not to flinch when his eyes caught mine.

"Some of you will rise today," he continued, his voice tightening, "forging bonds that will carry you through fire and battle. Others fell. Some at the claws of the fliers themselves, others to rivals too weak to claim their own path without stealing yours. Do not expect mercy. There is none here. There is only the truth. And truth does not care if you live or die."

A hush rippled through the crowd. Beside me, Esme stirred, her silver eyes narrowing as though she tasted the challenge in his words.

Another figure moved forward, broader and less polished but equally commanding. Major General Kamban. He was the one who had harshly reprimanded us for disobedience, bearing his authority with the weight of stone. His voice rang out, less polished than my father's but just as powerful.

"You heard the General," Kamban said, his dark eyes sweeping across us. "This is no child's game. This is blood, sweat, and sacrifice. But make no mistake—those of you who bond today are not just taking on a companion. You are swearing yourself into a pact older than this valley. You will answer to your flier, just as they will answer to you. Fail them, and you fail us all."

He leaned forward, voice lowering into something almost intimate despite the crowd. "I don't care if your flier is a dragon, a griffin, or a phoenix. I don't care if you come from noble blood or from nothing at all. What I care about is whether you prove yourself worthy when the moment comes. Earn your place—or be torn from it."

The two males stood side by side, different in bearing but united in purpose. The contrast was striking—My father, cold precision honed sharp as steel. Kamban, raw force and unyielding presence.

"Ninety-four of you began this path in August. Some of you believed the hardest trials were behind you. You were wrong. After you stood for judgment, only seventy-nine of you remained." My father's voice carried flat and steady, his face unreadable.

A ripple moved through the crowd, but my he pressed on, unrelenting.

"Sixty-eight fliers answered the call—thirty dragons, twenty griffins, eighteen phoenixes. They came not to serve, but to choose. And choose what they did." His voice lowered, weighed down. "This morning, seventy-two of you walked into Flugblatt. As of now... sixty-six stands here before me," he carried on.

"You've learned the truth today. Bonding is not a ceremony of comfort. It is a crucible. Some of you bear wounds that will scar. Some of you bear losses that will never be filled. But all of you who remain... You will carry bonds now that run deeper than blood," Kamban said.

He gestured to the fliers behind them, each massive presence a shadow and a promise. "Your fliers chose you not because you were lucky, but because you are worthy. And now, the Gods themselves and the elder council of fliers will bless these bonds. What you gain today will be your strength, your shield, and—if you are wise—your salvation."

His voice hardened again, sharp as a blade. "But remember, this bond is not a gift. It is a responsibility. Fail your flier, fail your squad, fail your people—and you will not just lose your life. You will damn us all."

CHAPTER 35

A horn sounded low and deep, the call rolling across the stadium like thunder. The elder fliers perched high above answered with roars, screeches, and cries—dragons, griffins, and phoenixes unleashing their voices in unison until the air itself seemed to tremble.

From the far side of the field, the third- and fourth-year Sorcerers marched in. Robes of dark purple shimmered faintly with runic threads, their hands carrying different iron brands. Each brand glowed faintly, three distinct shapes: one carved with a dragon, another with an eagle's head, and the third a bird with small flames erupting from its wings. Each one found a Rider to stand in front of.

Esme shifted beside me, her scales whispering as she stood tall, silver light flickering faintly in her throat as if she already knew what was coming. My heart was hammering so hard that I thought the entire field could hear it.

General Kamban's voice boomed out over us, "By the will of the Gods and the blessing of the elders, let the bonds be forged! Riders, unbutton the top of your tunics!"

The bell tolled once and at once, the Sorcerers pressed the brands forward—onto dragon scale, griffin feather, phoenix feather—and then onto Rider flesh.

The pain struck me like lightning. White-hot iron burned through my chest, branding over my heart, as smoke still curled off Esme's shoulder. I cried out, but my voice was swallowed in the chorus of every Rider and flier screaming, grinding their teeth, enduring together.

And then the world changed.

Light burst from me, silver and sharp, racing over my skin like scales forming out of air itself. At the same instant, Esme blazed beside me, her entire body shimmering like a river of moonlight. The connection roared through me—her heart slamming against mine, her fire rushing in my veins.

When my vision cleared, I saw it.

The cadets around me shimmered in impossible ways—griffin Riders feathered in spectral plumes, phoenix Riders wreathed in red embers, dragon Riders cloaked in faint scales like mine. It was a hidden world, revealed only now that I bore the mark.

Esme's voice echoed steady and proud in my head, *"Do you feel it? This is our shimmer. Only the bonded may see it. In battle, when fear threatens to break you, call it forth. It will harden. It will become armor, no fire, no steel, no claws can pierce, but it is only on your arms and frontal chest, so you're still exposed."*

I pressed my palm against my scorched chest, trembling, but I wasn't afraid. For the first time, I felt whole. Esme's silver fire pulsed with mine, and I knew—whatever came next, neither of us would ever stand alone again.

The burn on my chest persisted, but it felt less like pain and more like something alive. The mark throbbed in time with Esme's heartbeat, each pulse blending into mine until I couldn't distinguish where hers ended and mine started.

Silver shimmer rippled faintly over my skin like scales unfurling in light. I raised my hand, staring in disbelief as it flickered across my arm, shifting and vanishing like a mirage. It was real. It was part of me now.

Esme exhaled, a low rumble that vibrated through the ground beneath my boots. Her silver shimmer rolled across her body, layering over her scales like armor made of starlight. My chest clenched, because she wasn't only beautiful—she was terrifying, and she was mine.

"Now you see," her voice curled through my thoughts, steady and sure. *"The shimmer is not for them. It is for us. Only the bonded may know it, only*

we may wield it. If you are in extreme distress, it will take over. The first time the armor hardens, it will feel quite unique."

I closed my fist against my chest, where the mark still burned faintly, and drew a shuddering breath. "I feel you everywhere," I whispered.

"As it should be."

And in that moment, with the shimmer humming at my skin and Esme's pulse echoing through my own, I knew the bond wasn't only forged—it was unbreakable.

The stadium was alive with glimmer. Now that I bore the mark over my heart, the shimmer was no longer invisible. I could see it everywhere—threading through the other Riders like threads of magic stitched into their skin.

To my left, one of the griffin Riders bared his chest proudly. His shimmer took the shape of overlapping golden feathers, each one edged in copper light. The shimmer reminded me of the griffin at his side—sharp-eyed, predatory, glorious. Farther down, a phoenix Rider laughed with tears in his eyes, his shimmer burning across his chest in fiery plumes that curled and shifted as if they were alive. Behind him, his phoenix shook out its wings, and for a breath the two were mirrors—flame and fire, Rider and flier.

And the dragons—gods, the dragons. Scales shimmered across Rider after Rider, each set distinct. Vibrant reds like little flames, grey scales that gleamed like hammered shields, obsidian black that seemed to swallow the light whole. No two were alike, yet each reflected the essence of the dragon they belonged to.

I pressed my hand over my own chest again, where the spiral of silver-blue still tingled faintly. My shimmer spread from that mark outward in subtle layers of small, delicate scales, silver with faint veins of starlight-blue threading through them. They didn't blaze like the phoenix fire or gleam like gold feathers, but they pulsed with quiet light, almost liquid, shifting like moonlight over water.

I looked back at Esme. She lifted her head, silver eyes fixed on me. Her scales, still small, gleamed with youth, not yet hardened to armor.

She blinked slow, deliberate. Light rippled over her hide, and my chest tightened—the shimmer on my own skin matched hers.

The sight held me. Captivated. Thrilled. Stunned. My breath caught, the thought repeating, circling—the same shimmer, the same light. Mine. Hers. Ours.

"See?" Her voice hummed in my head, calm and sure. *"You carry me with you. My scales are yours now, as yours are mine. That is what it means to be bound."*

I exhaled slowly, feeling my heart hammer under my palm. For the first time since stepping onto the field, I didn't feel small, or wounded, or unworthy.

I felt... claimed.

The shimmer still tingled across my chest when the two generals rose to their feet again. The stadium quieted instantly, thousands of cadets holding their breath as my father and Major General Kamban stepped to the edge of the stage.

General Kamban's voice carried, sharp and commanding. "Today, you are Riders, albeit still a cadet for another three and a half years. Your bonds have been recognized by the Gods, sealed by the elders, and now you carry the mark of your fliers as proof. From this day forward, your lives are not your own—they belong to the bond you swore to uphold."

My father stepped forward, his shadow long under the winter sun. His gaze swept the field of Riders, his tone quieter but no less powerful. "Do not mistake this for triumph alone. Bonds demand sacrifice, vigilance, and a loyalty greater than anything else in this world. Many of you will not live to see the end of your service. But those who do will be legends."

A ripple of unease—and pride—moved through the field. My chest tightened, not only from the brand but from the way his words cut like steel.

As if on cue, the air split with a thunderous roar. The elder dragons wheeled high above the stadium, their wings blotting out the pale light. Their cries rolled over us like storms breaking against the mountainside, answered by the shrill calls of phoenixes and the piercing screeches of griffins below.

Esme's head lifted, silver eyes following the elders. Her chest expanded with a sharp, low sound, not quite a roar but something more profound—like a vow. The fliers were surely talking amongst themselves.

The elders dipped their wings, and one by one, the dragons began to rise. Massive wings churned the air as they lifted back into the winter sky, their silhouettes growing smaller with each powerful stroke. Griffins leapt skyward next, golden and black shapes glinting against the clouds, their screeches trailing like echoes. Phoenixes followed last, erupting into bursts of fire before disappearing into the forest air, embers scattering in their wake.

As they departed, the ground trembled, and the stadium was soon only filled with the faint glow of lingering bonds and the overwhelming silence of thousands watching them disappear. The field was now empty, once alive with wings and fire, but now it lay bare, with flattened grass in wide arcs where dragons, griffins, and phoenixes had stood. The silence felt even heavier, as if the air itself was healing from what had just happened.

Cadets gathered in tight groups, most excited from victory. My squad stayed close, the circle smaller than it should've been without Jackson. We had all survived, but that didn't erase the sense of loss. Esme's absence weighed on me—back with the other fliers in the vale, her voice was now soft and distant, like a fading memory at the edges of my mind. I already missed her presence beside me, though the warmth of the brand on my chest reminded me she was still with me.

I should feel lighter, proud. Instead, my shoulders tensed when the crowd shifted. Cadets made way instinctively, a ripple of silence spreading as two males approached the center of the field.

General Kamban peeled off toward the other instructors, his booming voice carrying as he dismissed groups with crisp efficiency. The other figure, though—he came straight toward me.

My father.

The insignia on his uniform gleamed as if it had been polished precisely for this moment, and every line of his body screamed command. His eyes—cold, sharp, unyielding—locked on me.

"Cadet Blackcreek." His voice carried perfectly, though he didn't raise it. "Congratulations on your bond."

My throat felt dry, but I forced myself to nod. "General."

The weight of his gaze pressed down harder than any battle test. For a heartbeat, I thought—hoped—he might let the mask slip, let something human show through. But it didn't.

"You've done well," he said. Glaring at me, it sounded like a compliment, but I didn't feel it. "Make sure you don't waste what you've been given."

Heat prickled behind my eyes, but I didn't let him see it. "I won't."

He offered only a slight nod, more of a dismissive gesture than acknowledgment, then turned sharply to approach the officers waiting nearby. The tension in my chest eased only when I saw his back vanish into the crowd. I exhaled softly, realizing I had been holding my breath, and finally relaxed my shoulders.

Esme's voice brushed faintly against my mind, low and curious. *"He makes you ache."*

My laugh was soft, bitter. *"Yes. Yes, he does."*

I remained standing there long after he disappeared into the crowd, the impact of his words still echoing vividly in my chest.

Make sure you don't waste what you've been given.

He hadn't always sounded like that.

Once, his voice had been warm. I could still hear it if I tried hard enough—the low rumble of his laugh when he swung me onto his shoulders, the way he used to hum, off-key and distracted, while fixing my wooden practice sword when I split it down the middle. Back then, his armor was just something that hung on a rack, smelling of leather and oil, not this constant barrier between us.

I remember running into his arms when he returned from patrols, how he would lift me effortlessly and say he missed me every day. On nights when Mother was away healing cadets and it was just us, he'd teach me how to braid a rope, whistle through my teeth, and cheat at dice when no one looked.

He had been my whole world.

But at some point between my mom's death and now, he transformed into something different. A wall of steel and authority, with each word carefully chosen and every glance sharp. He still resembled my father, but every time his eyes met mine, it felt as though he'd forgotten how to truly see me.

My chest tightened as I pressed a hand over the brand beneath my tunic, the warmth of Esme's bond a steadying presence. She stirred at the edges of my thoughts.

"He was yours once. Now he belongs to the weight he carries."

I swallowed, blinking against the blur at the corners of my vision. *"Yeah. I... I wish he hadn't given all of himself away."*

For the first time since the ceremony ended, I let myself sit down on the edge of the field, elbows braced on my knees. Around me, cadets celebrated, laughed, mourned—but I stayed still, caught between the memory of a father who used to love me openly and the general who now stood like a stranger in his place.

The edges of the field blurred as memories pulled me backward, but I felt the shift before I actually heard him. Zane's presence always carried heat—steady, grounding, like the earth itself refused to let me spiral too far.

"You're doing that thing again," he said, crouching down beside me. His golden hair caught what little light remained, his eyes searching my face. "The one where you look like you're here, but your mind's miles away."

I huffed a shaky breath. "I was just... remembering. Before everything changed."

He didn't press. He never did. Instead, he eased down to sit beside me, one knee bent, his shoulder brushing mine. For a while, we stayed like that, silent in the afterglow of the ceremony, the stadium's noise muted around us.

Finally, I spoke. "He wasn't always like this, you know. Cold. Untouchable." My throat tightened, but I forced the words out. "He used to laugh with me. Teach me stupid things like rope knots and dice tricks. I'd wait at the door every time he came back from patrols because... he always picked me up like I was the only thing that mattered."

Zane's jaw worked, but he kept his voice low, careful. "Sounds like he traded that part of himself for the general's title."

"Yeah." I rubbed my thumb over the edge of the brand still sore beneath my tunic. "Or it has something to do with my mother's death. I am still struggling to believe that he would hurt my mother."

He finally turned, catching my gaze and holding it steady. "One day, you will get answers, but right now, you've got me. You've got Esme now. You've got your squad. That's more than enough to keep moving forward."

The words settled deep, chasing back some of the cold. I leaned into him without thinking, my temple brushing his shoulder. He didn't move, didn't breathe too hard, like he knew this was fragile and rare. I stayed there, letting his breathing bring me into sync, calming my stirring soul. I was still leaning into Zane when a sharp, familiar voice cut through the hum of cadets in the stadium.

"Auri!"

I pulled back just in time to see Lili darting toward me, practically glowing herself, her braid bouncing behind her. Her grin was so wide it made my chest ache in the best way.

"You did it!" She crushed me into a hug before I could brace. Her arms locked tight enough to make my stitched side flare, but I held on and didn't care.

When she pulled back, still grasping my arms, my eyes fixed on a small detail I hadn't previously seen. Near the base of her throat, a soft shimmer reflected the light, trickling lightly toward her collarbone. It was subtle, resembling moonlight on dark water, only noticeable when I looked directly at it. The shimmer was navy blue, wispy, reminiscent of the shadows cast by her dragon's wings.

"You're shimmering," I whispered, the words slipping out before I could stop them.

Her grin widened, and she tugged at her tunic so I could see more clearly. "So are you. It's—Gods, Auri, it's real. You're bonded. It's so amazing."

My hand moved up toward my chest, fingers lightly touching the spot where Esme's brand still tingled faintly beneath my skin. I hadn't truly seen it reflected back at me yet—not until now, under Lili's glow.

"It's incredible," Lili continued, eyes sparkling. "When they branded us, I swear I felt her settle inside me. Like we are finally... complete. I hadn't realized it would feel that way either."

Behind her, I thought I felt Esme stir faintly through the bond, a pleased rumble in the back of my mind.

Lili's eyes softened as she studied the faint shimmer over my chest and arms. "It feels strange at first, doesn't it? Like you're walking around with a beacon painted on you."

"Yeah," I admitted, fingers brushing unconsciously along my arms. The iridescence shifted when I moved, like silver scales rippling under my skin. "It feels like... everyone can see it."

"They can't. Not unless they're bonded too," Lili reassured me. "Like everyone else, you'll learn to control it over time. Mask it, dim it. Some Riders hide theirs completely—you'd never know they are bonded at all. Others... well." She smirked knowingly. "They let it shine brighter than it should, like a damn peacock strutting in the field."

I huffed a quiet laugh. "That doesn't sound like you."

"Gods, no," she said with a roll of her eyes. "Mine used to shimmer like wildfire when I first bonded. Over time, Veyra helped me rein it in, taught me how to tuck it under my skin when I didn't want every Rider in a mile radius watching me glow like a lantern. You'll get there too. Esme will show you how."

The mention of her name stirred Esme at the back of my mind, a flash of silver warmth pressing against my thoughts. *"Yes. I will teach you."*

My chest tightened, the mix of awe and weight settling deeper. "I don't know if I'll want to hide it," I admitted, softer.

Lili's smirk gentled into something more earnest. "That's your choice, Auri. That's the thing no one tells you—the shimmer is you and your flier. How you carry it is just as much a part of the bond as the brand itself. You'll find your balance."

I glanced at her again, the faint navy shimmer over her chest shifting like hidden wings in the light. Subtle, but strong. Her balance.

Lili's shimmer pulsed faintly as she leaned against me, her grin sharp but her tone soft. "See? You're already glowing brighter than most. Esme wants the world to know she chose you."

I brushed my fingers lightly over the iridescence on my left arm, the scales shifting faintly in the light. It felt... vulnerable, visible in a way I couldn't yet name. Before I could answer, a voice tugged at my thoughts, low and warm.

"Gods, I wish I could see you right now."

Zane.

My heart jolted, the bond I had recently reopened crackling alive like a live wire. I turned my head to give him a look, him still sitting where we had sat moments before, allowing Lili and me a private moment.

He came to stand next to us. "I can't see it, but I know it's beautiful—because it's yours."

Heat rushed up my neck, and I opened my mouth, but no words came out. Lili, of course, smirked and elbowed me lightly. "Careful, Zane. She's still learning how to keep it from glowing brighter when you're around."

His lips curved, but his eyes never left mine. "Good. Let it shine. I want everyone to see."

The weight of his words pressed into me, fierce and steady, and for the first time since the brand seared into my chest, I didn't feel exposed. I felt claimed. Seen.

Esme stirred in the back of my mind, her voice a silver ripple. *"He is not wrong. Your bond is meant to be seen."*

And with both of them watching me, I wasn't so sure I wanted to hide it at all. The three of us lingered in the thinning crowd, Esme's warmth a steady hum in the back of my mind, when another familiar voice cut through the space.

The crowd was fading as Alex located us. His movements were deliberate, and his face was composed yet tense, as if he'd practiced this scene many times and was still uncertain about proceeding.

"Auri." His voice was smooth, but my name carried too much in it.

I smiled faintly, unsure. "Hey, Alex."

His gaze flicked to Zane, only for a heartbeat, before settling back on me. "Esme suits you. I'm glad you made it back in one piece."

"Thanks," I said.

The silence stretched, uncomfortable. Lili muttered something about finding someone and slipped away, leaving the three of us in the charged space.

Zane shifted, tension in the way his arm brushed against mine, but he didn't speak first. He never did, not when it came to Alex.

Alex's jaw worked as he studied us. Finally, he exhaled. "I've been angry. Hell, I still am, if I'm honest. You were—" He broke off, eyes darting briefly to Zane, then away again. "You were my brother for two years. Then she came along, and everything changed."

Zane's voice was quiet, steady. "I didn't plan it. Neither of us did. But I won't apologize for loving her."

A flicker crossed Alex's face—pain, resentment, maybe even a trace of understanding. He dragged a hand over his jaw and shook his head. "I know. That's the worst part. I know you didn't mean to... and I know you'd die for her."

"I would." Zane's voice hit firm, his eyes locked hard on Alex.

For a long moment, they barely looked at each other—two years of friendship stretched thin, tugged almost to breaking, but not snapped completely.

Finally, Alex nodded, the sharpness softening. "I don't completely forgive you. Not yet. Perhaps not in the same way it was before. But..." His gaze flicked to me, then back to Zane. "For her sake—and because she's a

Rider now—I'll try. We all need each other if we're going to survive what's coming."

Zane dipped his head slightly, the closest he'd ever get to a salute between them. "That's enough for me."

The air was still heavy, but different now—less like a battlefield, more like the first tentative step off it. Standing between them, I realized it wasn't about me choosing one or the other anymore. It was about whether the two people I cared about most could find a way to carry this without letting it break them. And maybe—just maybe—they could. Perhaps we all could be friends. Alex and I were always better as friends anyway.

CHAPTER 36

The silence between the three of us still throbbed, thick with things none of us wanted to say out loud. Alex broke it first, exhaling through his nose before forcing a lopsided grin.

"Enough brooding. They've got the celebration set up in the courtyard—platters of roasted meats, honey cakes, and more ale and wine than half of us should be trusted with."

Lili had just stepped back to my side, a spark of her usual mischief flashing in her eyes. "Good, because I fully intend on drinking until I forget just how terrifying today was. Losing my best friend is never an option."

Alex huffed a laugh. "You and half the field, probably. It's tradition—bonding day isn't complete without someone stumbling out of the hall trying to sing the ballads of the First Riders."

His gaze shifted to me, softer. "But you need food in you first, Auri. And rest. You've pushed your body harder than most."

Zane squeezed my hand, voice firm. "We'll go. She's not missing this."

"Good," Alex said, his grin sharpening into something closer to their old camaraderie, if still fragile. "Let's at least walk in looking like we are friends instead of three people trying to murder each other. Deal?"

I couldn't help it—my lips twitched upward, a tiny laugh breaking the heaviness. Awkward or not, maybe that was the first fragile step toward something that wouldn't break us completely.

When we stepped out into the courtyard, the air carried the rich scents of roasted venison, spicy root stew, and the sharp bite of strong ale. Lanterns swung overhead, their warm glow highlighting armor and shimmering marks. The crowd of Riders glittered as if the gods themselves had dressed them for the feast.

That day's courtyard celebrations were for the Riders—bonding day belonged to us alone. The only others present were those who came as companions: siblings, close friends, or lovers, like Zane. He carried himself like he belonged, though I noticed more than one curious glance thrown his way. Let them look.

Long tables had been set up in neat rows, but already the order was unraveling—groups clustered in circles with mugs raised high, songs beginning to rise in half-sung, half-shouted verses. At the far end, barrels were being tapped, the foamy ale poured into clay mugs faster than the servers could carry them away.

"See?" Lili said, nudging me as she grabbed a mug from a passing tray. "Exactly what I promised. Food, drink, and questionable decisions before sundown." She tipped her mug toward me, her faint shimmer pulsing as the lantern light caught her chest.

Zane's hand brushed mine where no one could see, grounding me. "You're pale," he murmured, low so only I could hear. "Eat something before you drink. I mean it."

Alex caught the exchange, his jaw flexing, though he forced a thin smile. "He's right. The courtyard doesn't wait—you'll be three cups in before you realize you haven't touched a plate."

"I'm fine," I said, but my stomach betrayed me with a quiet growl. Lili laughed and tugged me toward the food tables, tossing a teasing glance back at the boys. "Come on, Auri. Before they start bickering like an old married couple."

Behind us, I heard Alex mutter something under his breath. Zane didn't answer, but the silence between them was sharp as a blade.

The celebration engulfed us completely—joyful song, hearty laughter, flickering firelight, and the comforting knowledge that the first-years present had survived where others had not. That night, despite underlying tension, we felt alive, bonded, and close. The courtyard pulsated with life, making the world beyond appear surreal—war, politics, and death couldn't breach the radiant glow of the lanterns. Someone began singing about the first Riders, and by the second verse, half the courtyard had joined in, mugs raised and voices resonating confidently.

I sat squeezed between Lili and Zane on a long bench, a plate heaped with food in front of me. Zane had pushed it toward me before I could protest, and now he was ignoring his own plate, keeping his arm behind me on the bench. Protective. Always protective.

Across from us, Alex nursed his ale, watching me more than he should. His jaw tightened every time Zane leaned close, every time my laugh slipped out when Lili whispered something ridiculous in my ear. He wasn't cruel—he hadn't been since everything broke between us—but the strain was heavy, the kind that made silence louder than shouting.

"So," Alex said at last, his tone just casual enough to fool no one. "How does it feel? The bond. The shimmer. Being one of us now."

I swallowed a sip of ale, setting the mug down carefully. "It feels... right. Like I've been walking half-asleep and finally woke up."

Zane's hand brushed mine under the table, his thumb pressing once against my knuckles. Alex's eyes flicked down, catching the movement. His mug clinked a little too hard against the wood when he set it down.

Lili, sensing the tension, raised her mug high. "To survival!" she declared, loud enough to draw cheers from nearby tables. "To the dead bastards who said we couldn't make it this far!"

The courtyard erupted with laughter, mugs crashing together in messy toasts. For a moment, the sharp edge between Zane and Alex dulled, drowned by the celebration. But even as I laughed with the others, even as I let the ale warm me and the music roll through me, I could feel both of them watching—one with fierce devotion, the other with something quieter, heavier. Regret, maybe. Or forgiveness, he wasn't ready to give. And beneath it all, the shimmer on my chest pulsed faintly, Esme's presence brushing against the edges of my mind, reminding me that no matter what turmoil simmered here, I was not alone anymore.

The courtyard grew louder as the night stretched on, the air thick with the aromas of roasted meat, spiced cider, and an excess of ale. Lanterns hung from the old stone arches swayed in the winter wind, casting moving shadows across the courtyard where cadets sang, shouted, and shoved each other toward the fountain like overgrown children.

Someone shouted "Drink!" from the center, triggering a chant that grew louder with each round of mugs slammed on the wood. A drinking contest erupted between phoenix Riders and griffin Riders, with half the courtyard taunting and the other half betting.

"Gods, every year it's the same," Lili muttered, though she was grinning ear to ear. She tugged at my sleeve. "Come on, you have to at least watch."

Before I could protest, she dragged me closer to the lively circle of shouting cadets. Zane followed, his firm hand at the small of my back kept me steady as bodies jostled and shoved around us. Alex moved with us but hung back slightly, his eyes scanning the chaotic crowd instead of watching the fierce contest. A phoenix Rider tipped backward, unconscious to a chorus of boos. His friends hauled him out of the ring as a griffin Rider opposite him threw his arms in the air in triumphant victory. More mugs clattered on the rough wooden table, frothy ale spilling over in wild splashes.

"You'd beat them," Zane said in my ear, his breath warm against my cheek.

"Would I?" I arched a brow, smiling despite myself.

"You'd drink them under the table and still walk straight."

"You'd have to carry me when I actually didn't," I teased back.

Alex's voice cut through, cool and quieter than the chaos around us. "You really shouldn't. Not with stitches still fresh."

I stiffened, the reminder landing harder than it should've. Zane's arm tensed around me. For a moment, the celebration noise dulled, the three of us caught in a silence heavy enough to smother the air.

Lili, ever the savior, broke it. "Or," she said, "we could skip contests and find warm cider. It's less fun but far fewer hangovers."

We laughed—too sharp, too fast—but it loosened something enough to move again.

Later, I ended up sitting at the edge of the fountain, the chill of the stone seeping through my trousers as I watched Riders dunk each other into the water, shrieking and cursing. Zane leaned against the fountain behind me, his hand brushing my shoulder in that grounding way he always had. Across from us, Alex sat with a mug dangling from his fingers, his gaze unreadable as he watched the flames flicker in the courtyard braziers.

The chaos swirled around us—songs, dares, cadets stumbling arm-in-arm—but between the three of us, it was quieter, tighter. No words could undo what had been broken, but at least that night, amid the celebration, we were trying not to bleed on the cracks.

The courtyard buzzed with laughter, music, and the heat of bonfires, but it all turned sharp when a cadet shoved through the crowd toward me. His words slurred with drink, but his intent was razor-clear.

"You think you're untouchable, don't you?" His eyes burned, the flush of ale making his sneer sharper. "Daddy's little girl. Protected while the rest of us bleed for scraps."

A few heads turned. The surrounding noise quieted down, and conversations stalled into uncomfortable silence. My mouth felt dry. I hadn't said anything to offend him—but it was pointless. It was never truly about me. It was about my last name.

"Careful," Zane muttered at my side, his hand already twitching toward me, ready to step in.

Before I could form a response, my bond mark ignited. Silver shimmer burst across my skin, scales unfurling from my chest outward like wildfire, locking tight against me in a shield I hadn't summoned. Gasps rippled through the nearby cadets. The other Rider laughed darkly—his shimmer flared, unmasked by drink and rage. Grey scales, jagged and stone-like, crawled up both his arms and spread across his chest, pulsing with threatening energy. He hadn't intended to reveal it, but now it bore him completely, his dragon answering my defense with one of its own. The courtyard grew still. Firelight caught our shimmering hues, silver and grey clashing like a fierce storm.

"You see that?" he barked at the crowd, gesturing at me, his eyes wild. "The General protects his own while the rest of us fight to be noticed. She'll never pay the price we do!"

The silver scales on my chest hardened further, searing heat coursing through me as Esme's voice cut into my mind—sharp, unyielding. *"Threat. I will not let him touch you."*

I staggered back, breath uneven, heart pounding as my armor sealed around me. The weight of every eye in the courtyard pressed down. Zane stepped forward, his grip finding my shoulder, his voice low and lethal.

"One more word, and you'll regret it."

But the cadet only bared his teeth, grey shimmer pulsing brighter in the torchlight. For a heartbeat, it felt like the celebration would ignite into something else entirely. The cadet's grey shimmer pulsed like storm light, jagged scales crawling higher up his neck. The courtyard was silent but for the crackle of bonfires, every Rider, every flier-tethered bond holding its breath.

I raised my hands slowly, my silver shimmer still tightly locked across my chest and arms even though I hadn't intentionally willed it. My voice shook, but I forced it to steady.

"I'm not him," I said, searching his eyes. "I'm not my father. Whatever he's done—whatever you think I've done because of him—I don't know what you're talking about. I'm not my dad."

For a flicker, something crossed his face. Doubt. Pain. But it hardened in a heartbeat, drowned by rage and drink.

"Doesn't matter," he spat. "You carry his name. That's enough."

And then he lunged.

His fist slammed into my shoulder, the grey shimmer along his arm scraping sparks against my silver scales. Gasps erupted around us as the crowd surged back, the courtyard exploding into chaos.

Zane moved instantaneously, shoving him off me, his own snarl tearing loose. "Back the fuck off!"

But the cadet only came harder, grey shimmer flaring brighter, his fist cracking against Zane's jaw. The sound of it rang like steel on stone.

I stumbled, heart pounding, with silver armor still fused to my skin. I hadn't summoned it—but it was alive, glowing with every pulse of Esme's fury in my chest. My hand shot out instinctively, hitting his ribs. He staggered, then drove his knee into my stomach, hard enough to rattle my teeth.

The crowd roared. Other Riders began shoving in, some trying to pull him back, others egging it on. Someone threw a cup. Somewhere else, shimmers began flashing in the firelight—gold feathers, red scales, black shimmers—all uncontrolled, answering the madness.

"Enough!" Zane's bellow ripped through the yard, but it was already too late.

The courtyard was a battlefield.

The cadet swung again, grey shimmer striking mine, sparks dancing between us.

My chest felt like fire. Esme's voice in my head like a drumbeat, *"Harden. Survive."* And for the first time—I let it.

My silver shimmer surged outward, locking around me like a second skin. The cadet's blow rebounded off me with a sharp crack, his hand twisting at an ugly angle. He screamed.

The chaos swallowed the sound.

Bonfires cast the courtyard into madness—shimmer on shimmer, Riders against Riders, old grudges exploding as ale and anger fueled the night.

And at the center of it all—I stood trembling, silver armor burning against my skin, knowing there was no putting this back in its box. The fight churned around us, Riders clashing, shimmers blazing in wild, uncontrolled bursts. Ale splashed across the stones, firelight glinting off steel and feathers and scales.

The cadet came at me again, his grey shimmer burning bright down his arms, teeth bared. I barely registered the pain in my gut before instinct had my dagger in hand, the steel glinting pale in the torchlight.

And then—Zane moved.

The mask dropped. For the first time in months, other than in our chambers, his wings exploded outward, massive and black, catching the firelight with a sheen that stole the breath from the courtyard. Gasps ripped through the crowd as space cleared instinctively around him, the sheer dominance of the display forcing bodies back.

The cadet faltered, just a step, and that was enough.

I dropped low, my silver shimmer hard against my skin, and slashed once, twice. The dagger bit clean through the tendon—both of his ankles, giving wet, awful pops. His scream tore the air as he collapsed, thrashing on the stones, his shimmer flickering uselessly.

Zane stepped behind me, wings flared wide, shadows draping across the courtyard. His stance was lethal, protective, a wall of fury and darkness standing guard at my back.

And the noise died.

All around us, the chaos froze. Shimmers dimmed, fists lowered, voices dropped into silence. The only sound left was the cadet's ragged sobbing, cut through by the slow rasp of my own breath.

No one else dared move.

Because at that moment—dagger in my hand, silver shimmer glowing hard across my arms, and Zane's wings stretched out like death itself—I wasn't just the general's daughter anymore.

I was a survivor. I would not fall.

The courtyard went silent.

The Rider lay writhing, clutching at the ruin of his ankles, his cries sharp against the night. My dagger dripped steadily onto the stones. My shimmer burned too bright on my chest, refusing to dim no matter how I willed it, and the strange heaviness in the shadows at my feet made my stomach twist.

Whispers rippled.

The General's daughter.

Savage.

Untouchable.

Zane moved again.

His wings unfurled fully, black and vast, blotting out torchlight until shadows swallowed the courtyard. His voice cut across the silence, low but carrying, edged with authority that brooked no refusal.

"Enough." The word cracked like steel against stone.

Every cadet froze. Some dropped their eyes instantly, others stiffened like they wanted to challenge him—until his wings shifted, the air pressure forcing them half a step back.

Zane took another slow step forward, putting himself squarely between me and the crowd. His gaze swept the ring of cadets, unflinching, daring them to move. "You've all made your point. Now stand down. Before this turns into something none of you will crawl out of."

For a long, tense beat, no one breathed. One by one, cadets lowered their stances. A few muttered curses, but no one stepped forward. The boy on the ground groaned, dragging himself back, blood smearing across the stones.

Zane kept his wings stretched wide until the noise faded into uneasy quiet. When he finally folded them, the courtyard still felt smaller, like his presence alone pressed every cadet into line. I could feel eyes lingering on me, my chest shimmer still too sharp, too alive. I tightened my grip on the dagger, willing the strange pressure at my feet to vanish. It didn't.

Esme's voice brushed faintly against my mind, sly and knowing. *"It's beginning."*

I shoved the thought aside, swallowing hard.

Next to me, Zane exhaled slowly, his sharp eyes remaining fixed on the determined cadets who refused to look away. He commanded them to stand down. He took charge effortlessly as the natural leader he was, though he might dislike hearing it. He was next in line to be the duke, yet he preferred to deny that fact.

And just like that, the balance of the courtyard shifted. Not only around me, but around him. Every cadet there saw it—Zane taking command, his wings dark banners over us both. The courtyard began to thin out, cadets peeling away in hushed clusters, their eyes still darting quickly and furtively toward us. Whispers tangled in the air—about me, about Zane, about the blood still smeared across the stones.

Zane's hand closed firmly around mine, grounding me. His wings remained still exposed until the last of the crowd drifted away. Only then did he pull them back into himself, the air pressure easing.

"Come on," he said, his voice low, roughened by the weight of command, "we should go."

I let him guide me, sheathing my bloody dagger into my thigh sheath. My shimmer refused to fade, the faint glow a reminder that everyone had seen more than I wanted them to. We slipped through the quieter corridors, the sound of our boots echoing against the stone. He didn't speak, and I didn't ask him to. The silence stretched, heavy but safe, his presence cutting through the lingering dread that still clung to my skin.

At my door, he finally stopped. He didn't let go of my hand, just turned enough to study me, his jaw set, his eyes darker than I'd ever seen them.

"You handled yourself," he said, voice steady but tight. "But the next time someone comes for you like that—" His wings twitched, like they might snap open again. "—I'm not sure I'll stop at just guarding."

I swallowed, the weight of his words pressing against the frantic thrum of my heart. "Zane..."

He squeezed my hand once, hard, and then let go. "Rest, you're safe now."

"For now," I murmured. I wanted to protest even more, but something in his gaze stopped me cold. The protective fury that wouldn't bend, not that night. My chest still shimmering faintly in the dark, and the door clicked shut behind him. Only when I leaned back against the wood did I let my breath tremble free. The shadows along the walls flickered strangely, as though they were following me inside.

Esme's whisper brushed the back of my mind. *"Closer now. Much closer."*

CHAPTER 37

ZANE

From the moment I watched her walk into the flight field toward Flugblatt forest, my stomach had been a knotted mess. I wouldn't admit it to her. I didn't know a lot about the Riders' branch, but due to my friendship with Alex and Lili, I knew more than most of the cadets who weren't in that branch. I knew that the bonding day was one of the most profound days for the Riders.

It was why most of the other branches came to the outdoor stadium to watch everything unfold. Like when the first-year Drusearons put on a flight show, the different branches came to watch in awe. Despite the existing conflict among branches, it was set aside when we united to celebrate an important milestone for everyone.

I felt her pain and fear through the bond, along with a flicker of anger, but she had built up all the mental blocks she could so she could focus on her task at hand—securing her dragon.

After what felt like an eternity, I felt her getting closer and closer. I looked up at the sky, watching for any movement. Up ahead, I saw a silver dragon performing acrobatics in the sky, which made my stomach lurch. She descended into the field, and my eyes immediately locked onto Auri. I could see the blood pooled on her tunic, her walk being slightly off. Every few steps, she would grab at her side. I pushed hard through the mental bond, and I felt her letting me in.

Auri's voice hummed faintly through our bond, her words steady though I could taste the edge of pain behind them. *"Yes... It's merely a flesh wound. I'll be fine."*

She lied like she breathed—smooth, practiced—but I'd been linked to her long enough to know when her body screamed despite her mouth not moving. The stab wound in her side throbbed through the edges of her thoughts like an ember. Every step she took toward the dais made my chest burn with the need to go to her, to push through the crowds and throw the bastard who hurt her off the field. But I couldn't. Not here. Not now.

Instead, I stood in the stands, my hand gripping the stone rail until my knuckles ached, watching her every move. When she reached the dais, her name spilled from her lips with pride—Auriella Reyna Blackcreek. Gods, I swore the entire world stopped to listen when she spoke her name. And then her dragon's name.

Esme. Not simply Esme—Esmeraladathoradae, Daughter of Kimraventhrosa and Korvanleglunga.

My jaw clenched as the pieces clicked into place, long before Auri's shock betrayed her expression. Kimraventhrosa—her father's dragon. It was no surprise the silver had chosen her, or why she fought so fiercely for Auri, testing and claiming her with eerie certainty. I almost laughed. Fate had embedded itself so deeply within her that she could never free herself, no matter how much she might want to.

She staggered back from the dais like the words themselves had weight, Esme's steam curling in the air. I could feel her thoughts spilling wild, frantic, disbelief pounding through her skull like a war drum. I wanted to reach for her, pull her into me, shield her mind the way I could protect her body—but she slammed her mental walls up, shutting me out.

That cut deeper than any blade could.

I forced myself to stay still as she crossed the flight field, Esme's silver gleam parting the crowd like water. Fliers rumbled and shifted, their Riders falling into line. The air thrummed with nerves, with anticipation, with the sharp edge of fear no one wanted to name.

As soon as she exited the stadium, I couldn't hold myself back anymore. Rules be damned. My boots hit the ground hard as I crossed the flight field, shoving past cadets who had the sense to get out of my way. She sat there with Ophelia, trying to downplay the wound while blood still stained her side.

"You shouldn't be on the field," she scolded me through the bond.

And? I didn't bother to hide the steel in my answer. I really didn't care.

I stood there through every stitch, every hiss of her breath, my arms crossed, but my body leaning closer to her like I could keep her in place with sheer will. Overprotective? Maybe. Mother hen? She joked about it, teasing. But I saw Ophelia's smirk too, saw the way she knew I wasn't moving until Auri was back on her feet.

Esme's name rolled from Auri's lips—Esme, the silver—and I swore something in me unclenched. Her laughter, her pride, the way she said 'spicy' with that spark in her eye... It was worth every risk, every scar. I had to let her go again, back into the lines of Riders and fliers waiting for the ceremony.

From the stands, I could see everything—the sweep of the amphitheater, the cadence of boots, the nervous flick of wings and feathers, the shimmer of scales catching the light. But my eyes never left her. Never could. The bells tolled again, long and heavy, echoing off stone and soul alike. The last of the cadets filtered in, and the weight of it settled on us all.

That was when he stepped forward—General Blackcreek. Her father.

Despite the distance, his presence pressed like a hand on my throat, his voice cutting through the air sharp as steel. I saw Auri straighten beneath his gaze, felt her thoughts shutter tighter behind her walls. He spoke of reckoning, of worth, of death without mercy. Every word was iron. Every syllable meant to break the weak.

Major General Kamban thundered his piece, raw and brutal, hammering down truth like stone breaking bone. His words had none of Blackcreek's precision, but all of his weight. Together, they carved the field into silence.

Sixty-six left.

My gaze dropped back to Auri, standing proud beneath Esme's silver shadow, blood still damp on her tunic, but her chin high. She wasn't simply standing in the reckoning. She was defying it. And gods help anyone who tried to take her down again.

The silence stretched, heavy as stone, until the bell tolled again.

The air cracked open.

From the ledge above, the elder fliers lifted their heads towards the skies. Their cries shook the bones of the stadium—dragons roaring deep and resonant, phoenixes shrieking in blazing arcs, griffins letting loose sharp, tearing cries. The sound rolled through me, a living storm. Every Rider stiffened beneath it, including the veterans in the stands. Esme stood confident and poised. Auri stood like iron beneath her, her chin high though her hands trembled at her sides.

The Sorcerers entered the field in their plum robes, carrying the brands. Three designs, each seared into glowing iron: a dragon, an eagle head, a flaming bird for phoenixes. They lined the dais, waiting for the signal.

When the bell tolled again, every Rider bared their chest, tunics pulled aside. Fliers lowered their shoulders, flesh exposed. The brands pressed down all at once.

Over a hundred screams filled the air—fliers bellowing, Riders gasping, the sound of flesh searing drowned by the surge of magic that followed. The field lit up. The moment the brands pressed, the entire field erupted. Riders cried out, fliers bellowed in unison. Magic rolled off the ground in a wave, a crackle in the air so sharp it raised the hairs on my arms.

I watched her, my eyes locked onto her. Everything unfolding.

Auri faltered forward slightly, her hand gripping her chest where the iron hit. She tilted her head back, jaw clenched and held back her cry. Gods, she was stubborn and strong, but there was something more. The nearby Riders looked at her—initially at their own chests, then at hers.

But I saw enough. I saw the way her breathing hitched as if she were holding something inside. I saw the way Esme curled protectively around her, silver head dipping low, eyes fixed sharply on anyone who looked too long. I saw the way Auri's shoulders stiffened, as if she were fighting something she couldn't control.

The crowd didn't notice—they were too busy with their own friends, lovers, or siblings. But I saw everything. Every flicker of strain that crossed her face. And I knew, even if I couldn't see what shimmered beneath her skin, that whatever had awakened in her was powerful. Dangerous.

I leaned forward, every muscle tight, every instinct screaming. She needed me. Not right now—not during this ceremony, not in front of the Generals. But soon. Because whatever bond had been formed, it had changed her. And I'd be damned if I let her face it alone.

The magic still hung in the air long after the brands cooled. It clung like smoke, buzzing over the skin, settling deep into the marrow. From the stands, I felt it. But it wasn't mine to claim, not like it was for them. The Riders shifted, murmurs rising across the field as they studied one another. I could see the way they looked—some with awe, some with envy, some with fear. And all of them... all of them seeing something I couldn't.

I hated it. I hated the way their eyes went wide, the way their postures stiffened or softened, the way Auri's chest rose like she held fire beneath her skin. Whatever shimmer had been carved into her, whatever mark now burned across her heart, I couldn't see it. I was blind.

I used to not care about this, nor was it ever relevant to me. When Alex and Lili went through bonding day, we were all first-years, and precisely like today, I watched as the magical ceremony took place. It didn't bother me that I couldn't see the Riders' glimmer, nor did I really care. It was a Rider's thing, and we Drusearons had our own thing.

I saw her clearly. Pink flush spread across her cheeks. Her hand instinctively brushed against her tunic, over the spot where the brand had touched. Esme shifted closer, curling protectively, silver scales catching the faint light of the torches. That dragon watched her Rider intently and challenged anyone else to approach.

My fists clenched in my lap. If I'd been down there, I would've stood the same way.

The bell tolled once more, drawing every gaze to the dais. My stomach tightened as my eyes locked on him. Her Father. Cold, unflinching, as though the ceremony hadn't merely torn through flesh and spirit alike. His voice cut through the stadium like steel.

"You have been chosen. You have been judged. Now you're bound—not only to your fliers, but to the future of this realm."

He paused, eyes sweeping over them, over her. I swore he lingered, just a breath too long, on Auri.

"You carry the weight of our survival in your bonds. Do not falter. Do not fail."

Major General Kamban stepped up beside him, less polished, rawer, his words grinding like stone. "Your scars are proof. Your bonds, your strength. But strength without discipline is nothing. Take this gift, take this power, and remember it is not for you. It is for all of us."

The crowd erupted as the ceremony came to a close. Elders lifted their wings, their voices shaking the night sky before taking off to the Vale, vanishing in the dark like shadows of gods. All the fliers left the field and followed behind.

And me? I sat in the stands, the roar of the crowd crashing around me, feeling more like an outsider than I ever had because I couldn't see it. Because I wasn't one of them. And because every heartbeat told me Auri's world was pulling her further into a place I couldn't follow.

***

The firelight danced against stone, spilling over mugs of ale and flushed faces. Music wound its way through the air, laughter loud enough to echo against the towers. Riders clumped in circles, their fliers nowhere in sight, the bonds fresh but already pulsing between them.

I stuck close to her. Always.

But even here, I felt it—the distance. The way they looked at her was different now, not only because she was the General's daughter but because of whatever shimmer now lived beneath her skin. I couldn't see it, but I could feel the weight of it pressing on the edges of the night.

The courtyard was alive with firelight and noise, but beneath it all, I felt the crackle—tension threading its way between the laughter and ale. I kept Auri close, one hand brushing against hers when I could, a silent reassurance that I was here. Always here.

Then I saw it. The shift. The cadet's stare—hard, bitter, venomous—as he shoved his way through the crowd toward her. His words dripped with poison, not at her, but at her blood.

The cadet came in calling her a daddy's little girl, throwing insults around like she was her father.

My blood turned molten.

Auri lifted her chin, calm, steady, the way only she could. She tried to plead and reason with him, letting him know she wasn't her dad, nor did she know what he was talking about.

But he wasn't hearing her. His eyes burned too deep, too dark. His hand twitched toward his belt. And the courtyard shifted. Riders leaned in. The air thickened. Someone laughed—too sharp. Another shouted something I didn't catch. The cadet lunged, and the whole thing snapped.

My wings tore free.

They ripped out with a force that silenced the courtyard, something shifted with Auri, I couldn't quite see it, but oh fuck I felt it. Gasps filled the air, but my focus was only on him.

He never even saw her move. The flash of steel. Auri's dagger in her hand, a blur of silver in the torchlight as she ducked low. Two sharp strikes, clean and brutal. His scream cut through the night as his legs buckled, tendons sliced, blood spilling onto the stone.

He hit the ground hard. And the world went silent.

Every Rider froze, mugs half-raised, eyes locked on us. Then it happened—like a crack splitting the night—Auri's arms were shimmering with silver scales, and a sense of shadows was all around her. I didn't know how I could see it. I shouldn't be able to, but with our mating bond, maybe I could? I couldn't see anyone else's, though.

The courtyard shifted again. Fear. Awe. Curiosity. And I knew this would change everything. I could feel her magic pulling me, begging me to touch her and use it.

The courtyard was a storm. The cadet writhed on the stone, his screams twisting through the air, blood smearing under his boots as he tried to drag himself upright. Auri stood above him, her dagger still gleaming, her shimmer still hard and clinging to her skin like armor forged from shadows themselves.

Some of the Riders around us leaned forward, eyes wide, hungry for the fight to continue. Others shifted uneasily, clearly calculating what it meant that the General's daughter bled shadows and that I, a Drusearon, had just unleashed my wings during their celebration, on their domain.

The silence was razor-sharp. I stepped forward, wings flaring wider, letting the tips drag sparks against the stone walls.

"Enough!" I yelled again, even louder.

The word echoed, carried not just by sound but by weight. Authority I hadn't yet been granted—but claimed at that moment. My gaze swept across the Riders, meeting eyes that dropped almost instantly.

"This ends here," I said, low but steady, a command rather than a request. I planted myself between Auri and the rest of them, every feather humming with tension, daring anyone to move. "There will be no more blades, no more challenges, no more blood spilled in this courtyard tonight."

The cadet on the ground coughed a laugh, bitter and cracked. "You think you can command us, Drusearon?" he spat.

I bent low, wings curving over Auri like a shield, my stare locking him in place. "No," I said, voice sharp as steel. "But I can end you before you crawl another inch. And so can she."

The courtyard went deathly still again, all eyes watching. Testing. Waiting. And I knew in that silence—I had to seize it. I had to make them believe.

Straightening, I folded my wings in, not all the way, but enough to signal I wasn't about to strike. My tone shifted, steadier, carrying the cadence of command I'd heard from generals and even my father my entire life.

"You all saw it," I said, sweeping my gaze across the Riders. "Strength was demonstrated, lines were drawn, and whether you liked it or not—respect was earned."

No one argued. Not out loud.

The cadet on the ground groaned and tried to crawl away, while a few others finally rushed to help him. I stayed still and silent until he was out of sight. Then, slowly, the murmurs and music began to return, and the chaos eased into a tense quiet. But everything felt different now. Not after this moment, not after Auri's shimmer revealed itself to me. Not after the courtyard went silent beneath my voice.

Her shimmer was fading, but the memory of how it had hardened against her will still haunted me. It had protected her—shielded her—but also unsettled her. I saw it in how her fingers trembled slightly around her dagger, even as she sheathed it, and in the stiffness of her shoulders as she forced herself to stand tall.

She wouldn't let anyone else see it. But I did.

I stepped closer, folding my wings tight until they walled her off from the last curious stares. "Come on, we should go." My voice left no room for debate. She glanced up, ready to argue, but the exhaustion in her eyes gave her away. She only nodded once.

I took her hand—not for show, not for defiance, but because she needed grounding. Together, we pushed through the shifting crowd. A few Riders stepped back when my wings brushed too close, but no one stopped us. Not now.

The academy's corridors felt empty and chilly after the courtyard, with our footsteps reverberating loudly in the silence. She walked beside me, chin raised, acting unfazed. I let her maintain the facade around others, but between us, the truth was clear—her heart pounded, her mind a jumble of emotions: fear, anger, disbelief, all colliding.

When we reached her chambers, I pushed the door open for her. She stepped inside, and I followed, closing it firmly behind us. The silence pressed down, thick and suffocating.

She turned, finally letting her shoulders slump, her guard fall. I caught her before she could even speak, hands framing her face.

"Rest, you're safe now," I whispered, even though both of us knew safety was a lie here. Still, I needed her to hear it.

Her eyes softened, the hardness in her shimmer dissolving completely. "For now," she murmured.

In her chambers, I knew she was safe. I placed the ward myself, and I was damn good at boundary warding.

I stood outside her chambers long after the door clicked shut, palms still burning from her touch. I'd told her to rest, to take all the time she needed, but honestly, it was me who needed space. Space to breathe. Space to regain my control. Because every fiber of me wanted stay inside.

I wanted to pull her against me, press her into the bed, and bury the world outside. I wanted her warmth, her lips, her breath on my neck, her legs tangled with mine until neither of us knew where one ended and the other began.

But it wasn't just the hunger for touch. Gods, if it were only that, I could manage it. It was the hunger born from seeing her fight. From watching her shimmer harden around her like armor, from the flash of her dagger, from the way she didn't hesitate to bleed for her survival. She looked untouchable and wild, and it stirred something profound within me—something darker and more desperate. And that was what frightened me.

Because if I gave in to that craving now, staying in that room might make it hard to stop. I might not be gentle, and she was injured. Part of being branded meant, unless it was life or death, Riders shouldn't get mended until forty-eight hours after, to ensure the scar remains on their chest.

So, I remained in the hallway, jaw clenched, struggling with myself just as she had struggled with that cadet. I reminded myself she needed rest. That she was still reeling from the fight, from the brand, from the weight of her father's words. But the truth was—my restraint wasn't for her. It was for me. Because loving Auri wasn't just about wanting her, it was about craving her fire... and knowing one day, if I wasn't careful, it might burn me alive.

I forced myself to walk away from her door before I gave in and took her in every way I wanted, knowing she wouldn't stop me. Her restraint was worse than mine. My boots echoed down the stone corridor, each step dragging the ache in my chest along with me. If I wasn't able to hold her in my arms that night, then I needed another way to burn the fire out before it consumed me. I knew exactly where to go.

The sparring ring was dimly lit with torches hissing softly along the weathered walls. Eli stood there, leaning against the railing with that familiar, easy smirk that hadn't changed since childhood. He had always been quicker than me and sharper with his blade, and he knew it.

"You look like you're about to snap," Eli said as I stepped into the circle. He straightened, tossing me a dulled training sword. "Lucky for you, I'm in the mood to break something."

I caught the sword in one hand, rolling the grip in my palm, feeling the weight. "Good. Because if I don't bleed this out, I'll go mad."

His brows raised just slightly. "Her again?"

I didn't answer. I didn't need to. He knew me too well.

Eli grinned, feral. "Then fight me like you'd fight the thought of her."

I swung harder than I should have, pouring all my frustration, craving, and unmet desire into each hit. Eli responded equally, sparks flying as our blades collided. He pushed me back, but I managed to shove him off, sweat already trailing down my back.

"You're sloppy," he barked, laughing between sidesteps. "She's in your head, Zane."

"She's always in my head," I growled, pushing forward, slamming my weight into him.

He staggered, regained his footing, then smirked. "Good. Hold onto that. Let it sharpen you, not drown you."

We kept at it until my arms burned and my lungs heaved, until the sting of each strike dulled the storm inside. When we finally broke apart, panting and grinning like idiots, I felt the fire inside me settle—not gone, never gone, but contained.

Eli slapped my shoulder as we left the ring. "Better?"

I sheathed the dulled sword, shaking the sweat from my hair. "For now."

However, the truth was that sparring was only a temporary solution. No fight, no bruises, no blades could quiet the deeper hunger. The one that belonged to Auri alone.

CHAPTER 38

I tugged my jacket tighter against the chill as my wing and I cut across the courtyard toward the dining hall. The first rotation on breakfast always meant the place was quiet, the air sharp with the scent of wood smoke and the promise of coffee. My stomach growled, eager for food.

Then I saw him.

Initially, my mind tried to tell me he had just collapsed. Maybe he fainted from exhaustion or hunger. But the stillness felt wrong. Too wrong. He lay sprawled across the courtyard stones, eyes open and glassy, staring into nothing. His neck bent at an impossible angle for a living body. Blood pooled beneath him, but it was the wound that truly froze me.

His chest was ripped open, not by blade or claw, but seared—blackened. The mark wasn't clean. It crawled out from his sternum in burned veins, curling the fabric of his uniform like parchment too close to flame. The edges still smoked faintly, a sickly scent burning the back of my throat.

Gods.

Gasps and screams erupted around me as everyone froze, boots scraping on the stone. No one dared to step closer. I couldn't look away. I had seen death before—training mishaps, brutal falls, cadets pushing themselves too hard on the mountain. But this—this was no accident.

My bond stirred uneasily in my chest, like both Esme and Zane sensed my distress.

"Gods," someone whispered. "Who would...?"

My hands trembled at my sides. Whoever had done this hadn't just killed him. They left him here, in the open, as if they were saying, *"I'm here, and no one is safe."*

No one moved at first. The courtyard held its breath. Then the whispers started.

"Was it sabotage?"

"Training accident, it has to be."

"No—no one dies like that."

I took a step back, my boots scraping stone. My pulse thundered in my ears. This wasn't training. I knew it down to my bones. Someone had done this.

"Clear the courtyard!" an instructor barked from across the yard, but his voice actually cracked at the sight.

The cadets shuffled, but no one tore their eyes away. His gaze, glassy and fixed, looked like it still tracked us. The smell of burnt flesh clung to the air, thick and sweet, sinking into the back of my throat until I wanted to gag. Behind me, a girl bent double and vomited. Another voice trembled through a prayer, the words sharp against the silence.

Zane appeared at my side, his shoulder brushing mine. His jaw clenched hard, eyes gone dark with fury. I knew that look—he was already scouring the crowd, ready to fix blame. And gods help whoever he chose. "Don't," I whispered. My voice sounded foreign in my own throat.

He didn't answer, but his hand brushed against mine, steadying me in a way he wouldn't admit aloud.

Professors rushed in, robes sweeping the floor as they forced us back. One dropped beside the body, two fingers pressing against the cadet's throat. His stillness told the truth—he was gone. Another professor scattered powder in a ring around him, muttering low and fast, the words laced with urgency. Not to save him. To contain whatever lingered.

"Back to your chambers," the instructor snapped. "Now."

But no one moved. Because we all knew the truth, whether they said it aloud or not, this wasn't an accident. It wasn't training.

Someone killed him.

And they wanted us to see it.

We didn't go to breakfast. We didn't go anywhere.

"Back to your chambers," the instructor roared again, voice raw with something that wasn't solely anger—fear. "Now! Move!"

The courtyard erupted into chaos with boots pounding and cadets stumbling into each other as we were herded like livestock. I followed, my legs feeling as if they were carved from stone. My eyes kept darting back to the body until the professors formed a tight circle around it, obscuring it from view. Lockdown. Morning lectures canceled. No drills, no training. Only the hollow echo of our own thoughts filled the quiet chambers.

I went to the seventh floor to check on my flight. The halls were chaotic. At first, no one spoke. We had all seen death before, but not like that—left in the open as some twisted message.

"They said accident," one of the cadets muttered, voice thin.

"Accident?" I snapped before I could stop myself. "Did you see his chest? That wasn't a blade or a fall. That was—" I cut myself off, throat closing.

"That was what?" someone challenged, eyes wide, desperate.

There was no answer, only the image of those blackened veins crawling from his sternum.

"It was murder," another whispered.

The word silenced the chamber. Murder. Once spoken, it clung to the walls, impossible to scrape away.

I finally made it to my own chamber after encouraging everyone to get into their rooms. My mind kept replaying the way his eyes were empty, how his body had been left in the courtyard like a warning. The person who did this wanted us to be afraid. And it was working.

I'd been sitting on the edge of my bed for what felt like hours, staring at the same knot in the floorboards, replaying the courtyard again and again. The boy's eyes, the blackened wound, the way the professors closed ranks around the body as though shielding us from the truth.

A sharp knock rattled the door. I jolted upright. No one should be visiting during lockdown.

"Auri," Lili's voice hissed through the wood. "It's me."

I rushed across the room and swung open the door. Her braid was half-loose, and her cheeks were flushed as if she had run here. She moved to come inside but hit the invisible barrier and bounced back. She looked shocked, but I reached out, grabbed her arm, and pulled her in. I closed the door behind her.

"What are you doing?" I whispered, heart hammering.

"We are gonna come back to *that*, but I had to tell you." She wrung her hands, pacing once before stopping in front of me. Her eyes were wide, fierce with a secret that wanted out. "This isn't the first cadet they've found."

The words landed like a punch. "What do you mean?"

Her throat bobbed. "It's the fourth. Four bodies, Auri. The others were... removed before anyone else could see. Found quick and quietly. But this one—" she shook her head, voice dropping to a whisper, "they couldn't hide it. Too many of us were already in the courtyard."

Pure cold washed over me. "Four," I repeated, as if I said it out loud, it would make sense. It didn't.

"They keep saying it's on a need-to-know basis." Lili's mouth twisted, bitter. "But how long can they keep lying to us? Pretending it's simply an accident when it's murder?"

I braced against the edge of my desk, knuckles white. "Why tell me?"

Her expression softened, but her voice cut sharply. "Because if someone's hunting cadets, you may be in their sights. You stand out, Auri—your bloodline, your mark, your bond. You're exactly the kind of target they'd choose. And you're my best friend, like the only sister I have."

She gripped my hand for a heartbeat, urgent and warm. "Be careful. Whoever this is, they're not finished."

"I will, I always have my daggers on me."

"Now—what the fuck was *that*?"

"What?"

"The ward that didn't allow me to enter."

"Ahhh. Zane."

"Protective much?" She raised one of her eyebrows.

"As a third-year you don't have a ward on your room?"

"You've been in my room... no."

"Well... I have people trying to kill me, and I have been kidnapped."

'That's true I guess."

"Anybody that I want in here, can come in."

"Okay. I guess that helps me feel a little better about your safety."

"You should ward *your* room."

"Yeah... I should. Be safe, little savage, I got to go."

"Always."

And then she disappeared, the door clicking shut behind her, leaving me alone with the truth.

Four dead.

And the promise of more.

The walls of my chamber felt like they were pressing in on me. My thoughts kept circling the same dark truth. Four dead. Not one. Four.

I closed my eyes and reached for him. *"Zane?"*

His presence brushed mine almost immediately, steady and warm in the way his voice rarely was. *"Yes, my Anam Cara"*

"You knew. You knew this wasn't the first cadet. Why didn't you tell me?"

Silence. For a moment, I thought he blocked me out, but then his voice slid in, low and heavy. *"Because knowing doesn't change anything except worry you more than you do. You think I want that for you?"*

"Don't lie to me," I pressed, pacing across my room. *"Lili told me. Four cadets. Four, Zane. Who were they?"*

A sigh rippled through the bond, tired, weighted. *"Two were Shapeshifters. The other two were Infantry. Different wings, different branches. No pattern anyone can trace."*

The air caught in my lungs. *"And the professors are covering it up."*

"You saw what happened this morning. Multiply that by the entire academy and it unravels fast. Chaos, riots... squad members turning on each other. No one survives that."

My pulse thundered, my bond sparking hot. *"So, we simply pretend? Pretend we're not waiting for our tragic death?"*

"I don't like it either," he admitted. His voice softened, brushing against me with a warmth that cut through the chill of my chamber. *"But pretending doesn't kill you. Knowing too much might."*

I sank onto the edge of my bed, clutching my knees. *"So, what do we do?"*

For a heartbeat, his presence pressed closer, almost like his hand against mine. *"We survive,"* he said. *"We keep our eyes open. Whoever's doing this... they'll make a mistake. And when they do, we'll be ready."*

His certainty settled in me like an ember, not enough to burn away the fear, but enough to keep me from breaking under it.

And I couldn't shake the thought. What if I was next?

The bell finally tolled, signaling the end of the lockdown and announcing that it had been lifted. My stomach clenched with hunger. I spent hours confined in my chamber with no breakfast, surrounded by silence and the echo of Lili's warning that haunted me. Our floor was filled with other cadet leaders, so fewer of us rushed out of our rooms. I imagined the seventh-floor erupting into chaos.

The dining facility was already packed when I slipped inside, the noise jagged and uneven. No laughter, no casual chatter—a buzz of whispers, sharp enough to cut skin.

"They said he was an asshole anyway."

"Got what came to him."

"Always thought he was cruel in sparring."

I froze in the doorway for a moment, listening.

They weren't talking about what happened or who could've done it. They were talking about the cadet himself—the one who'd been sprawled across the courtyard with his eyes wide open and that blackened wound across his chest.

"He used to trip people in the obstacle course for fun."

"Broke a first-year's arm and laughed about it."

"My squad hated him."

The words slithered around me as I moved toward the food line, each one making my skin crawl. Relief. That was what I heard under fear. A twisted kind of satisfaction. It chilled me more than the body had.

If someone was truly out there killing cadets and everyone believed only the cruel deserved it. How long before they decided I should be on that list? I clenched my tray tighter, keeping my face blank as I sat next to Zane. His jaw was tense, his eyes steely, and he ignored the whispers as if they were mere buzzing flies.

But I could feel his bond brushing against mine, tense and alert. He'd sensed it too. Everyone was hungry and afraid.

And some of them—gods help us—were almost grateful.

I stepped into the sparring gym with Professor Gile. Today it was all of our platoon, a platoon from the Drusearons, and a group from the Sorcerers. The air felt different. Charged. Paranoid. Usually, sparring was sharp and competitive. Cadets were eager to prove themselves. Not today. No one wanted to turn their back.

We lined up in pairs for sparring. No call-outs today. My palms were slick, the steel of the sword tacky in my grip. Across from me, my opponent's eyes kept darting past me, scanning the rows, like he was waiting for someone else to strike him from behind.

"Focus," Professor Gile snapped. "Begin!"

Steel clashed. Boots scuffed. But every swing was half-hearted, tentative. Blades that should've been quick and clean—dragged, slow, as if no one dared to push too hard.

"Pathetic!" the Gile roared, weaving between lines of cadets. "You think the enemy will hesitate? Again!"

My opponent lunged, sloppy and late. I sidestepped easily, heart pounding harder than the fight warranted. It wasn't him I was afraid of. It was the whispers in the mess hall, the smoldered wound on that cadet's chest, the idea that someone among us could be watching, choosing who "deserved" to die next.

Somewhere down the line, two cadets went at each other too hard—panic bleeding into fury. One's blade slammed into the other's ribs with a thud that made everyone freeze. The cadet doubled over, coughing, spitting blood into the dirt.

Every face I looked at carried the same question in their eyes—*what if I'm next?* I clenched my sword tighter, chest burning. This wasn't training anymore. This was fear, raw and dangerous, spreading through us like rot.

***

After dinner, half of my wing gathered in the small practice gym of the Alpha Wing, restless and too tense to stay in our rooms. It smelled of sweat and old leather. A few of us pretended to stretch, others tossed practice blades back and forth, but no one was really training. The air buzzed with whispers.

"They say it was a shifter," one cadet muttered near the wall, voice pitched low but carrying in the quiet. "Figures. Can't trust their kind."

"Shit..." another snapped. "Those Historians are some of the weeeeeirdest."

"Maybe it's Sorcerers," a third cut in, bitterness sharpening their tone. "They've got the magic for it. That burn on his chest. It looked cursed to me."

I braced against the stone wall, heart sinking as the words spread, sharp as daggers. Every name thrown, every branch accused, only twisted the room tighter.

"Infantry. Sorcerers. Shifters. Maybe Riders." Someone laughed harshly. "Gods, maybe it's one of us in this very room."

The noise rose all at once—voices overlapping, accusations flying, fear bleeding into anger. Boots scuffed on the mats as cadets squared off, teeth bared.

"For fucks sakes," I hissed, louder than I meant to. My voice cracked through the noise, pulling a dozen eyes to me. My stomach lurched, but I held my ground.

"We're turning on each other and whoever is behind this is laughing," I said, forcing my voice steady. "You think they want us strong? No. They want us to be afraid, divided. Keep pointing fingers, and we'll hand them exactly what they want."

The room fell into a tense silence. No one answered. But no one argued either. From the far corner, Zane's eyes met mine. Dark. Fierce. Proud. Although the whispers died down, I knew the damage was done.

Fear had already sunk its claws in.

CHAPTER 39

The indoor stadium classroom was always cold in the mornings, the kind of chill that seeped into your bones while you waited for the professors to begin. I trudged in with the others, still heavy with the ache of yesterday's training.

I froze completely.

There were already three professors present. Their robes were pushed up at the sleeves, their hands covered with gloves, and their faces bore serious expressions. One knelt in the middle of the aisle, scrubbing vigorously at a dark stain on the stone floor. Another quietly muttered precise words that shimmered faintly before fading into the walls. For a moment, I found it hard to breathe because I recognized those stains, knew what they concealed, and understood who was involved.

My stomach clenched fiercely. The boy I saw sprawled in the courtyard a day earlier was a stranger to me. But this one... I knew him too well. The Rider cadet whose sneer echoed in my mind. The one I had wounded across the Achilles tendon days ago, who limped away cursing my name. Who directed hatred at me? He was no longer here.

Dead.

The professors worked faster, scattering powders and scrubbing away the last traces. By the time the rest of the class filed in, there would be nothing but a faint metallic tang in the air, the kind that would be explained away with a lie. An "accident." A "disciplinary removal."

But I knew better.

My breath came shallow, my palms slick as I forced myself to my seat, forcing my face into something unreadable. Around me, cadets whispered nervously, catching the edges of what happened but not daring to name it.

My bond shivered in my chest, unsettled.

Two shifters, two Infantry, and now a Rider. The message was clear. No branch remained safe. I clenched my fists in my lap, my pulse pounding. Whoever this killer was, they had not only left another body behind. They left it here, where all of us would walk in and see what awaited us.

I couldn't keep my hands still. I laced my fingers together, unclenched them, and clenched them again. Every creak of the old seats made me flinch, and every whisper felt like it was aimed straight at me. Because I had cut his Achilles tendon, everyone remembered it. He swore he would pay me back for it, spat my name like a bitter curse. Now he was dead.

What if they thought I had a hand in this? What if the professors already suspected? The thought gnawed at me, tightening like a noose.

At the front of the room, the professors finally straightened from their scrub work. The floor was clean now, the stain vanished as though it had never been there. But the smell lingered, metallic and sharp, sticking to the back of my throat.

Professor Melamora cleared her throat, her voice carrying over the restless cadets. "Due to recent... incidents, the college will be enacting stricter measures." Her eyes swept the room, daring anyone to challenge her. "Earlier curfews will be enforced. Chamber inspections will be conducted without notice. We will start by having every wing, every platoon, and every squad conduct morning and evening formations, where every cadet will be accounted for. Morning formation will happen at zero-six hundred, evening formation at eighteen hundred. After evening formation, every cadet will be released to their rooms. The college will be receiving various second lieutenants from outposts to help enforce and monitor the situation."

A ripple of unease swept through the seating.

Professor Fogg stepped forward, "You will continue your training as scheduled. Fear is a disease, and it will not take root here. You are not children, don't cower in the shadows."

"What about winter leave?" A Healer cadet shouted from the middle row.

Professor Pascal turned to face the cadet. "Winter leave will still happen. This year, no cadet will be allowed to stay on the premises unless they are incapacitated or have explicit permission. We have six days before Winter Solstice and seven days before cadets go home for two weeks. Leadership is still trying to determine if we will be having our annual winter celebration."

The chamber erupted—gasps, whispers, hands clutched over mouths. The thought of losing even that one bright spot sent shockwaves through the cadets.

But I couldn't join the chorus. My thoughts churned too fast, too dark.

Winter leave. Inspections. Daily formations. Rules meant to cage us in. None of it would stop the fact that someone was hunting us inside these hellish walls.

***

The tension followed us out of the indoor stadium classroom like a storm cloud. No one spoke as we filed into Professor Vindex's lecture hall, twenty-two first-years from the Feather Wing shuffling to their seats with shoulders hunched and eyes flicking nervously to the door. The air felt brittle, like the faintest spark could shatter it.

Vindex stood at the front, his black robes spotless and crisp, his brown hair neatly tied back in a severe knot. If these deaths rattled him, he showed no sign of it. He looked down his sharp nose at us as if daring anyone to break rank.

"Eyes front," he barked, and the mutters died instantly.

"You all have bonded to a flier, which means you will start channeling anytime," he began, pacing the dais. "Some of you have been preparing diligently. Others—" his gaze swept the room, lingering long enough to make stomachs drop, "seem to think channeling isn't a big deal. It is."

The word cracked like a whip.

"Getting your unique ability is part of bonding with a flier. It is a unique power that ties you and your flier together. If your power doesn't manifest in the next week, it could manifest at home. Over the next week, we will be hammering down on what that could look like, what that could mean for you, what that could mean for your family."

A nervous murmur rippled through the room.

Vindex slammed his hand down on the lectern, silencing it. "Control. Precision. Restraint. These are what would keep you alive. You will train harder, focus longer, and sacrifice more in the coming week. You will master the ability, or the ability will master you."

My chest tightened sharply. The shimmering energy inside me roused anxiously, as if it had heard the warning and disliked it. I pressed my palms firmly against my knees to ground myself.

Vindex's gaze swept the hall once more, sharp as a blade. "Do not mistake my words for threats. They are truths. Most of you have simple magic, like lighting candles, amplifying your voices, shutting doors, feeling magic, creating wards, creating small wind paths, making small water ripples, or imbuing runes, to name a handful. Some of you didn't have any magic until you bonded."

Vindex went on to remind us of information we learned in the beginning but may have forgotten, "Fliers have the unique ability to control the flow of power to you, which means they can seize the power flow if they sense you will burn out. Fliers are fickle creatures, and some of them don't like when their Riders are being used or are out of control. Do *not* mistake this and believe that your flier will stop you from burning out, especially in the first year of your bond. Fliers can be cruel in a way. They test your powers, patience, and control."

The bond mark on my chest ached in response. I felt Esme tingle at our bond, something I was still getting used to. *"I would not let you burn out for the fun of it. I might let you fall off me for the fun of it."* Followed by laughter.

She. What.

"That's not nice."

"I will catch you, offfff courseeeee, after I let you think I won't."

"Well, you just told me your plans... sooooooo."

"Shit."

"For the next week, while you are still here, lectures for the newly bonded Riders are changing," Vindex announced.

The class shifted nervously, some of them not prepared for this news. Luckily for me, Lili had already told me that right after bonding, our schedules would be changing, focusing on our magical abilities and flying.

He continued, "You will continue to have your typical first class—current events, that will not change. That is where you are given the most update information concerning happenings around the—"

"Like the murders?" a Rider from second squad interrupted.

Vindex rotated on his heels, making this awful noise come from his boots as they scraped the stone floor. "I know that what happened is alarming, Cadet Vidacovik, and we professors and the leadership are alarmed. Since neither I nor most professors know much more than you all, we will not be spending class time pondering all the what ifs."

He walked back to the front of the class and turned around. "Each wing will be staying together, in the same cohort, for the following week. There will be no days off for the weekend. This means there will essentially be three cohorts that will be rotating. As I said earlier, everyone will report to the stadium classroom first. For your wing, the second hour will be with me. The third and fourth hours will be on the flight field, with Professor Hildegard. All three wings will have lunch together. Your fifth hour class will be with Professor Duft, which is your wielding teacher, so new to you all. Your sixth hour will be Professor Bhatta, to finesse your knowledge on the flier you've bonded with. Seventh- and Eighth-hour courses will be with Professor Yan, who is also new to you. She is our amazing, magical leather worker. You will spend that time working on saddles for your fliers."

"After which, it will be dinner, mandatory formation, then all cadets are required to report to their chambers for the night. Are there any questions?"

Everyone just stared at him, almost afraid to say anything, to ask anything. All in shock by the parameters he just laid.

"Are the stricter rules normal or ..." Micah asked.

"The updated schedule *is* normal, but the formation and staying in chambers isn't."

"How does one get home for the holidays? I presume we can't leave our fliers?" Landon Bosmini shot out.

"As someone who didn't have Rider parents, that is a fair question. Riders and fliers who are separated for longer than a week become extremely weak, with their unique ability becoming diminished. The flier going into a state of depression. That has only happened a few times. With that said, next week will be strenuous, focusing on powers that manifest and the ability to fly. Everyone will be required to do some basic maneuvers without falling off," Vindex said.

"And if we fall off? It was clearly stated that we shouldn't remain during this leave."

"Well, I hope you don't live super far, because it may be a long train ride. Just as you arrived here, you would have to walk to the nearest town and get on a train. Your flier will fly overhead the entire way. Either way you get there, your flier will not be able to remain with you, unless you're going to an actual fort or vastly close to one. They will drop you nearby and fly to the nearest lair or if you are near a vale. There are some areas where the lairs may be too far, in which case your flier will find a forest nearby to stay. Typically, non-military Fae are not used to fliers, and it alarms them."

All of our faces were fixed on him, eyes wide, like he had just dropped a damn bombshell on us.

"Now, in the five years I have been here, we have not had that happen. Most of your fliers performed more dangerous maneuvers while you were without a saddle, and you made it alive to the ceremony."

The sigh that swept through the room. Seriously, why did he stir things up? I arrived by train from Zion Outpost, where my dad was stationed. Over the past two years, he was rarely home, busy traveling between strongholds and forts. It wasn't a long journey—where would I go? Damn. Zane. We were also bonded.

"They also can't be separated for an extended period without their power diminishing."

What Professor Vindex said about mated Faes rang back into my head. Zane and I would need to discuss this soon. Thankfully, he had a nifty little secret way to get in and out of my room without anyone suspecting a thing. For now, I really needed to focus on class and all the information being presented.

"Let's bring it back to your magical abilities. We practiced creating a light orb and controlling it. Today, we will add a little more ante. In front of the class, there are twelve-inch-tall logs. You will get one and place it in front of you. You will then cast your orb directly above the log, precisely one inch above it, not two, not less than one. I want you to be able to hold it there for at least ten minutes. If you are a cadet who recently gained magic through channeling, you will come to the front and start with some basics. Because of the delay in magic, your channeling usually comes much later than the others."

Chairs scraped as a handful of students shuffled forward, their faces tight with embarrassment. The rest of us lined up to grab our logs. When it was my turn, I bent and lifted one into my arms, the bark was rough beneath my fingers, the weight grounding me as I set it down on my desk.

Ten minutes. One inch. Control.

My bond mark throbbed faintly, a pulse in time with my heartbeat. Esme stirred. *"Ten minutes? Pfft. I could hold an orb over this log for ten days."*

"I'm not you," I shot back, biting down on a laugh.

"Exactly," she said. *"That is why you will struggle, and why I will laugh when you do."*

I rolled my eyes before closing them, slowly summoning my power as Vindex taught us. Light formed in my palms, flickering like a loosely controlled force.

One inch, I reminded myself. Not more. Not less. I exhaled slowly, lifting the orb toward the log. The shimmer gathered hotter than I meant it to, the orb in my hands growing until it wobbled like a bubble about to burst. My palms were already damp, the log below me taunting with its silent demand: one inch, steady, ten minutes.

I lowered my hands carefully, guiding the orb down until it hovered over the log. Too close. It dipped and brushed the bark with a sharp hiss, leaving a scorch mark.

"Damn it," I muttered under my breath, yanking the light back up.

"Control," Vindex's voice snapped across the room like a whip. He didn't even look up from pacing the aisles, but I felt his eyes on me anyway. "Not brute force. You can't panic, control it."

Magic pulsed in my veins, wild and eager, as if it wanted to prove him wrong by blasting the log to splinters. I clenched my jaw. No. Not the time. I wasn't losing to a piece of wood. I tried again. That time, the orb shuddered and sank too low, bumping against the log before collapsing into sparks. Groans of frustration rose around me as other cadets lost their focus too—tiny bursts of light popping like firecrackers across the room.

Esme's laughter flickered through the bond, smug and unhelpful. *"You're overthinking it. It's a log, Auri. Not the end of the world."*

"Easy for you to say," I hissed back. *"You're not the one about to humiliate yourself in front of the entire wing."*

Her warmth rippled through me, calmer now. *"Stop thinking like a normal Fae. Think like me. Balance. Breath. Patience."*

I swallowed hard, rolled my shoulders back, and pulled the shimmer up again. Slowly this time. Carefully. The orb reformed in my palms, smaller, steadier. I guided it downward until it hovered—shaking, fighting me—exactly one inch above the log. My breath caught.

It held. One second. Two seconds. Three seconds.

The tremor smoothed as I matched my breathing to Esme's presence, in and out, steady as wingbeats. The ache in my bond mark eased, replaced by a slow, glowing thrum.

I had it. Finally, I had it. Across the room, logs hissed and popped as cadets lost their focus, curses flying under their breath. But I kept mine there—one inch, steady, unwavering. And for the first time since the body in the courtyard, I felt something like pride.

CHAPTER 40

Our cohort moved to the next class, boots echoing down the stone corridor as we filed toward the flight field. Some of the fliers were already there, their massive shapes sprawled across the packed dirt, wings rustling like restless sails. Others thundered down from the cliffs in pairs, their arrivals shaking the ground beneath our feet.

My chest tightened when I caught Esme's familiar silhouette, her sleek body coiled and proud, silver-blue eyes fixed on me the moment I stepped into the sunlight. Our bond mark flared in response, warm and insistent, and I couldn't stop the small smile that tugged at my mouth. Knowing she was mine, and I was hers.

Professor Hildegard stood at the edge of the field, his white braid snapping in the wind, with arms crossed over his chest. Dressed in riding leathers, his posture conveyed strict discipline.

"Wings in formation!" he barked the instant he saw us. "Simple drills today. Nothing fancy, yet. You'll be using generic fitted saddles until Professor Yan completes your custom sets. Your task is simple—practice launches and basic maneuvers. Nothing more."

Several cadets exchanged nervous glances.

Hildegard's sharp eyes narrowed. "If you can't manage a clean takeoff with the simplest of equipment, you don't belong here, and your fliers chose poorly. Consider today your first step in proving you're worthy of the wings you bonded."

Assistants brought out racks of plain leather saddles, rough and utilitarian compared to the elegant ones I'd seen in the upper wings. My hands itched at the sight. Fitting one of those onto Esme felt like dressing her in rags.

Esme rumbled in my head, amusement coloring her tone. *"Oh, I cannot wait to throw you off in front of everyone."*

I nearly choked. *"What?"*

"Nothing. Nothing at all," she sang, our mental bond pulsing with her laughter.

Professor Hildegard's whistle snapped the cohort to attention. "Pair with your flier. Saddle them. Mount cleanly. We'll start with vertical launches—straight up, straight down. If you cannot manage that, you will sit the rest of the day."

My stomach flipped. The moment I'd been waiting for since I got there. Unlike most of these cadets, Kim's mother flew with me often. Reminding me that Esme and I needed to have that conversation about Kim being her mother.

The saddles were heavier than they looked, the stiff leather awkward in my arms as I wrestled one free from the rack. It smelled faintly of oil and smoke, nothing like the sleek, supple gear the second- and third-years used. Generic, functional, ugly.

Esme crouched low as I approached, her tail swishing with ill-hidden amusement. *"This looks ridiculous,"* she drawled, lowering her head to eye the saddle, *"did someone stitch this together from scraps?"*

"Don't start," I said, fumbling with the girth straps as I hauled it onto her back. "I can barely keep my hands steady."

"I could throw you off just by shrugging."

My fingers slipped on the buckle. "You wouldn't dare."

Her silver eyes gleamed, and she didn't bother to deny it.

Around me, the field was alive with noise—cadets grunting as they heaved saddles into place, fliers rumbling or snapping at each other, Professor Hildegard's sharp voice cutting across the chaos like a whip. "Tighten those girths! If I can see daylight between strap and hide, you'll be eating dirt in ten seconds!"

She straightened her leg, giving me a ramp to climb up and mount onto the saddle, a nice advantage to having a dragon. Although some dragons forced their Riders to climb up them. My legs pressed too far apart, the leather creaking under my weight. Esme shifted deliberately, just enough to make me grab at the pommel with a yelp.

Her laughter rippled through my chest. *"Oh, this will be fun."*

"Cadet Blackcreek!" Hildegard's voice snapped across the field. "Eyes forward, back straight, hands off the horn. You cling like that, and you'll never learn balance."

Heat flushed my cheeks. I straightened up, letting go of the pommel. My stomach twisted with the sudden realization of how high I was—and we hadn't moved.

"Feather Wing!" Hildegard whistled. "Vertical launch. Straight up. Straight down. Clean and controlled. On my mark... three, two, one—launch!"

Esme clenched her muscles and jumped. The ground sped away in a dizzying blur, and the rush of air hit me so forcefully that I lost my breath. My stomach churned, and every instinct told me I wasn't supposed to be that high or moving that fast. I doubted Kim had ever launched herself that forcefully.

"Hold on," Esme purred. *"Or don't. I'll catch you. Eventually."*

I locked my jaw and forced my hands to stay at my sides, away from the pommel. My thighs burned as I crushed the saddle between them. The wind roared past, my pulse hammering so hard it felt like it might crack my ribs.

Esme rolled her wings, and we dropped. My stomach lurched into my throat. Breath tore out of me in a ragged gasp. Gods, we were falling—plunging like a stone. Every instinct screamed at me to grab the pommel, to claw for control that wasn't mine. Hold steady. Don't panic. *She knows what she's doing. She knows what she's doing.* I repeated it, but the words rattled thin against the terror flooding my chest.

Straight down. The ground rushed toward us, too fast, too close. My scream tore loose before I could stop it.

At the last possible second, Esme flared her wings and landed with bone-jarring force. My teeth rattled, my body trembling.

But I was still in the saddle. Still alive.

Professor Hildegard's voice cracked across the field. "Better than I expected, Blackcreek. Worse than I wanted. Again!"

He whistled a shriek again, and the field exploded into movement.

To my left, Sadie leaned low over her golden griffin, Korra, her braid whipping behind her as they launched with a grace that made my stomach twist. Korra's wings flared in perfect rhythm, their descent so smooth it looked like they were dancing.

Show-off.

Two lanes down, Akira and her yellow-golden dragon, Orix, weren't as polished. Orix sprang too hard, his wings beating so violently the air around him churned into a miniature storm. Akira's curses carried all the way across the field as she clung for dear life. They landed with a stumble, Orix bellowing in frustration.

Professor Hildegard's sharp voice cut in. "Control the launch, Cadet Faraday! You let him do the flying."

Lorenzo's red dragon, Syth, was all brute power—launching so high, so fast, the other cadets gasped. For a moment, it looked like perfection. Then Syth plummeted back down like a stone, slamming into the ground hard enough to rattle teeth across the field. Dust plumed around them. Lorenzo staggered on top of the saddle, pale and wheezing.

Micah and his phoenix, Sera, were a story entirely different. The phoenix launched in a burst of searing flame that made the air shimmer, her wings trailing fire. The crowd of cadets oohed as Sera hovered, flames curling harmlessly off her body, Micah grinning like a natural in the saddle. Their descent was flawless, feather-light.

I grit my teeth, determination sharpening in my chest. If he could make it look that easy, so could I.

Farther down, Thora and her dark blue griffin, Sylivia, moved with icy precision. Their vertical was clean, crisp, clinical—perfect lines, no wasted motion. Hildegard gave a single approving nod.

Then Erik mounted his red dragon, Sylari. The beast roared, wings snapping wide as they shot upward with terrifying speed. But halfway through the climb, Sylari did a dramatic dip, like a bucking horse. Erik yelped, sliding sideways in the saddle. Only a desperate grab at the pommel kept him from being flung into the dirt. They slammed down hard, Sylari snarling in fury.

The cadets nearest them scrambled out of the way. Erik's face was white as chalk, his hands trembling onto the pommel.

"All of you, again!" Hildegard barked, pacing the sidelines with fire in her eyes. "Do not waste your flier's strength with sloppy form. They will not tolerate it forever."

Esme's laugh rippled through me. *"Sloppy form,"* she said, *"I think we looked spectacular."*

"We looked like we were falling to our deaths," I snapped, adjusting my grip.

Another shrieking whistle came. The field erupted once more.

That time, I forced myself to breathe with Esme's rhythm, to match her pulse with mine. The launch was smoother—less screaming, more balance. The descent wasn't perfect, but it was better. My thighs burned, my hands ached, but when we hit the ground, I was still upright, still holding steady. Progress.

Around me, some cadets were improving. Others weren't. But one truth settled heavy in my chest—this wasn't just about drills. Hildegard was right. If we couldn't master this, we wouldn't survive what came next.

Feather Wing was loud as always, regardless of whether half of us were seconds away from puking our guts out from the verticals.

"Gods, Lorenzo," Sadie called, yanking off her riding gloves after his third crash landing. "If you hit the ground any harder, they'll start charging admission."

"Funny," Lorenzo wheezed, brushing dirt from his leathers. "I didn't see you up there doing barrel rolls."

Korra gave a sharp shriek that sounded suspiciously like laughter.

Akira groaned as Orix flapped too aggressively again, sending dust storms across the line. "I swear he's trying to dig us both a grave."

Micah stretched, leaning smugly against Sera's fiery flank. The phoenix preened, flames shimmering harmlessly across her wings. "Maybe you should ask Sadie for pointers. Korra's practically a feathered ballerina."

"Maybe you should choke on your own smoke," Akira snapped back.

Thora rolled her eyes, tightening Sylivia's straps with clinical precision. "At least your fliers try. Some of us don't get the luxury of drama. Isn't that right, Sylivia?"

The dark blue griffin blinked slowly, like she couldn't be bothered to dignify the chaos with a response.

Then Erik stomped over, pale and shaken after nearly being bucked into the afterlife by Sylari. "If anyone tells my mother about this," he said, "I'll say you pushed me."

That made everyone laugh. Even me. Which felt strange, considering my hands were still trembling.

Esme's silver-blue eyes swiveled toward me, her voice rich with smug amusement, *"Tell him I'll happily push him if he needs proof."*

"Don't tempt me," I thought back, biting a grin.

Professor Hildegard's whistling cut the laughter short. "Enough chatter! Feather Wing, you'll be running paired launches. I want synchronization. Takeoffs, vertical climb, descent. If one of you hesitates, both of you will eat dirt."

"Guess we'll find out who's dead weight," Sadie said, swinging onto Korra's back.

"Not me," Micah sang, vaulting onto Sera in one graceful move. Flames licked harmlessly at his boots.

"Oh, this is going to be a disaster," I whispered.

"Correction," Esme said smugly, *"this is going to be fun."*

Professor Hildegard whistled loudly again. "Riders, get ready. Your fliers don't need my instruction—they were born knowing how to fly. You are the ones who need discipline. If you cannot stay in the saddle, you are useless to them. Understood?"

A ragged chorus of "Yes, Professor!" followed, though a few voices cracked.

"Sadie and Akira. You're first."

Korra preened her wings like she was about to walk a stage, then crouched low. Orix, Akira's yellow-golden dragon, yawned wide enough to show every daggered tooth before launching without warning. Akira squealed, clutching the saddle as Orix twisted sideways mid-climb just to see if she'd fall. Korra followed in perfect, smug arcs, wings slicing the air like golden blades.

Sadie sat proudly and balanced, not budging an inch, while Akira flailed so hard she almost lost a stirrup. From above, Orix let out a roar that rippled through the sky so loud I felt it in my chest.

When they landed, Akira slid halfway off and glared up at him. "You're an asshole." He then blew a sulfur breath at her. Gross.

Korra shook her feathers, flicking dust onto Akira's boots like punctuation. Sadie smirked, "Don't blame him for testing your grip."

Hildegard didn't so much as twitch. "Lorenzo and Erik. Up."

Syth launched straight up like a shot, wings tucked tightly before flaring open in a dizzying spiral. Lorenzo's jaw clenched so tightly his teeth threatened to crack. Meanwhile, Sylari took Erik on a wild sideways climb, banking into sharp, aggressive turns that made him swear loudly enough for the entire wing to hear.

Both dragons landed smoothly, like the whole thing had been choreographed. Their Riders, however, looked green around the edges. Lorenzo slid down stiff-legged, knees shaking. Erik hung on to Sylari's neck long after the landing, pale as death.

Micah snorted. "Pretty sure Hildegard said stay in the saddle, not claw your way off your flier like a drowning rat."

"Eat flame," Erik said, still clutching Sylari's neck.

"Riggins and Blackcreek," Hildegard said.

Micah vaulted onto Sera, bursting upward in a flare of fire. Esme's stardust eyes gleamed as she crouched, her body thrumming with restrained power. Sera's heat shimmered over the line, sweat breaking instantly on my brow.

"Ready, little Rider?"

"No," I shot back, heart hammering.

"Perfect," she purred, and launched.

The force slammed me back in the saddle, wind ripping through my hair. Esme climbed vertically, faster than I could blink. My stomach lurched, the ground a blur beneath us. Then she tipped sideways, rolling once, twice—deliberately throwing my balance. Sera danced through the sky like pure flame incarnate, Micah holding steady, his grin infuriatingly smug.

"Esme!" I shouted, clutching hard, the straps biting into my palms.

Her laughter flooded the bond, wild and wicked. *"Prove you deserve me."*

I locked my thighs, gritted my teeth, and forced my body into her rhythm. My muscles screamed, but I held. By the time she leveled out and spiraled down to land, my entire body shook with adrenaline. I slid off, boots hitting the dirt hard. My legs wobbled but didn't buckle.

Esme's eyes glittered, her voice smug in my mind, *"spectacular."*

When the last pair arrived, half of Feather Wing looked like they were about to vomit, while the others tried to hide it. Saddles squeaked as cadets dismounted, their boots dragging in the dirt, faces pale and sweaty. The fliers shook off the fatigue, looking confident and shiny, as if none of this had required any effort.

Professor Hildegard stalked the line, his boots crunching in the gravel. His gaze swept over each of us in turn—lingering on Akira's frizzed braid, Erik's trembling hands, the dirt still smeared across Lorenzo's cheek.

Finally, he spoke. "Your fliers flew flawlessly today. Every stumble, every near-fall, every scream—" his eyes flicked to me, sharp enough to make my stomach twist, "—was on you. Do not forget it."

No one dared move. The griffins crouched low, feathers slicked tight, like they respected him enough to listen.

Hildegard crossed his arms. "If you thought today was hard, enlighten yourself of the notion now. This was nothing but a warm-up. Tomorrow, we add maneuvers—dives, banks, and speed runs. Your fliers will push you harder. Some of you will eat dirt. I don't care. You either keep up or you don't belong here."

Sadie muttered something under her breath that made Akira snicker. Hildegard's head snapped their way like a hawk, and both of them went stiff.

"You think this is a joke?" Hildegard's voice was like steel grinding against stone. "Every second in the saddle is a test. Fail, and you're not just humiliated—you're dead. Or worse, your flier is."

Silence pressed heavily on us. Micah's smug grin faltered.

Then Hildegard straightened, his expression unreadable. "Dismissed. Eat. Rest. Tomorrow, you'll need it."

I exhaled, realizing I was holding my breath.

Esme's low rumble of laughter filled the back of my mind, *"he likes me."*

"He terrifies me," I thought back.

"Both can be true," Esme said, her eyes gleaming as she stretched her wings, *"wait until tomorrow. I haven't even started having fun yet."*

By the time Professor Hildegard barked 'dismissed' my legs were jelly. The trek to the dining hall felt longer than any march, every step reminding me of muscles I didn't know I had.

Esme peeled off toward the cliffs, her voice smug in my head. *"Eat well, little Rider. Tomorrow I'll shake it out of you again."*

"Can she hear herself?" I muttered, earning a curious glance from Sadie.

Feather Wing claimed the tables near the back of the mess. Trays clattered, boots scraped, and the smell of roasted meat and stale bread thickened the air. Most of us slumped into seats like corpses-in-waiting.

Sadie dropped her tray with a loud clank. "If I survive this week, someone owes me a medal. Or at least boots that don't smell like griffin sweat."

"That's optimistic," Akira groaned, collapsing beside her. "Orix nearly rolled me straight into the dirt. Pretty sure my left arm's longer than my right now."

"Good thing you didn't have my dragon," Lorenzo muttered, pushing food around his tray. "Syth would've launched you into the stratosphere just for the entertainment value."

"Correction," Erik said, still pale from Sylari's antics. "He would've launched me into the stratosphere. Then eat you for dessert."

That earned a round of tired laughter, the kind cadets use when they were too sore to manage anything louder.

Micah leaned back, balancing his spoon across his fingers like it was a weapon. "Honestly, you lot make it sound worse than it is. Sera and I could've gone another ten rounds."

"Because she carried you," Thora cut in, her voice sharp as her griffin's talons. "We all saw it. She practically gift-wrapped that landing while you sat there grinning like a prince."

Micah's grin only widened. "And didn't it look flawless?"

Akira chucked a crust of bread at his head. He caught it mid-air, popped it in his mouth, and winked.

For a moment, it almost felt normal. Almost.

Then the whispers started.

"...wasn't just an accident. You know it wasn't."

"...fourth one dead, now fifth..."

"...professors can scrub stone, but they can't scrub the truth."

The laughter died off. Trays scraped quietly.

Sadie lowered her voice, glancing down the length of the table. "Word is, the one they found this morning wasn't the first Rider. Making it two, now. Two Riders died in a week."

My chest tightened. I forced myself to chew, though the bread tasted like ash. Around us, the mess hall buzzed with the same rumor, each retelling darker than the last.

"They're targeting branches."

"No, they're targeting personalities—he was cruel, remember?"

"Doesn't matter. None of us is safe."

I caught Zane across the hall, coming in to sit with his wing. His eyes met mine for a single heartbeat, dark and unreadable, before he looked away.

The unease in the room spread like a stain, impossible to ignore.

After lunch, Feather Wing dragged to Professor Duft's wielding class. The room smelled of chalk and ink, the walls lined with shelves of rune-etched tomes. Duft herself stood straight at the front, her hair pinned in an impeccable bun, her voice carrying like steel through the air.

"None of you has manifested your specific ability yet," she began, "but that does not mean you are powerless. It means you are unprepared."

She paced slowly, hands clasped behind her back. "When your ability does surface, it will not ask if you are ready. It will pour through you without restraint. Some of you will create storms. Others will warp air, stone, or flame. A few of you will bend magic itself. Whatever it is, if you are careless, you will kill yourselves or those standing closest to you."

The room went still. Every cadet locked on her words.

Duft's gaze narrowed. "You should not experiment on your own, should it manifest while you are gone. Uncontrolled power leaves bodies in its wake. Do not mistake your family's home for a training ground. Gifts are often brought out in times of distress, so try not to allow yourself to be in distress."

Her sharp certainty chilled me. How the hell could we decide whether we ended up in a stressful situation?

"If it can be so dangerous, why are they sending us home when manifestation is likely?" A cadet shot out.

"Usually, students can stay, and many faculty members encourage first-year Riders to remain on campus. Most of them do."

She gestured toward a series of diagrams chalked across the board—energy flows, runes, containment circles. "Once you manifest, you will be taught containment, precision, and restraint before anything else. Until then, you drill the fundamentals. Meditation. Control of power. Don't channel. Nothing more."

She stopped, her eyes sweeping the room like daggers. "Consider yourselves warned." By the time she dismissed us, the silence in the hall was heavier than it had been all day.

Professor Bhatta's classroom was on the third floor of Alpha Wing, a long stone chamber with narrow windows that let in more shadow than light. The walls were bare except for a massive tapestry of a dragon in flight, its wingspan stretching nearly the length of the room.

Bhatta himself stood at the front, tall and broad-shouldered, with hair gone silver at the temples and a voice that carried like gravel over stone. He didn't waste time with introductions.

"You've bonded," he said, scanning us with a soldier's sharp eyes. "That means you will be around fliers on an almost daily basis. There are some rules you need to drill into your head."

He paced slowly, boots thudding against the floor. "First rule: never step too close to a flier unless you are their Rider. Not even if they seem calm. Not even if you think you're safe. They don't like it, and they don't forgive it."

Uneasy glances flickered between cadets.

"Second rule: never rush a Rider when their flier is close. The flier reads it as a threat. I've seen wings snap ribs before a cadet can draw a breath. Worse—I've watched a dragon turn someone to ash. Don't test it."

The air in the classroom seemed to thin, tension pressing against us. My bond mark prickled, and Esme's low, satisfied hum brushed my thoughts, *"at least he understands courtesy."*

"Third rule." Bhatta stopped at the center of the room, his voice dropping low. "Fliers speak to no one but their bonded Rider. There are some very, very rare occasions when this doesn't apply. For instance, on Judgment Day, when you all took a tincture."

A couple of cadets laughed nervously. Bhatta's gaze cut to them, cold as a blade. Silence snapped down again.

"But fliers do speak among themselves. Constantly." His eyes flicked to the tapestry, the woven dragon looming above us. "They can relay messages from one Rider to another if they choose. Don't count on it being reliable—or flattering. They are not couriers. They are creatures with wills of their own."

He folded his arms, letting the silence stretch, his presence heavy as iron.

"These rules will not be found in your handbooks. They are truths written in blood. Break them, and it will not be the professors who punish you."

A shiver traced my spine. Esme's amusement rippled through me, sharp and smug. *"I would never break your spine, little Rider. Not unless you annoyed me terribly."*

I clenched my jaw. *"You're not helping."*

When Bhatta dismissed us, the scrape of chairs against stone echoed like thunder. We filed out in silence, the weight of his words pressing heavier than any saddle. Rules written in blood. The kind you didn't get second chances on.

I rubbed absently at my bond mark as we left the wing, the ache faint but steady. Esme's presence pulsed warm at the edge of my thoughts, smug as ever.

"Do you really talk with the other fliers that much?" I asked, keeping my tone casual.

"Of course," she said, almost bored. *"It keeps things entertaining while you humans shuffle about like ants."*

"Do you ever... talk to your mom?"

A pause. The brush of her mind was colder than before. *"Not often. We are not close enough for that. Fliers need to be decently close to each other to communicate. And she is busy..."*

Her voice quieted, sharp edges blunted by something I couldn't quite name. Loneliness? Resentment? I couldn't tell.

"I would rather talk to you," she added. A flicker of humor returning to her tone. *"You are far more entertaining when you panic."*

I rolled my eyes, but my chest felt warm in a way I didn't want to think about too hard.

The scent of oiled leather and hot metal hit me the moment we entered the outdoor stadium for Professor Yan's class, which wasn't quite like a class. All around were racks of straps, buckles, and tools that gleamed under the sun. Long worktables stretched on the side near the benches, already laid out with measuring cords, chalk, and thick parchment sheets.

But none of that held my attention.

It was the silver dragon standing in the courtyard, scales catching the light like hammered moonlight. Enormous—easily double Esme's size, their wings folded. Its head alone was longer than a cart, and when her gaze swept the room, every cadet went still.

Silvers were rare, and being bonded to one was awe-inspiring. Seeing a second one at the same time.

Esme stirred, a ripple of distaste coloring the bond. *"Don't stare."*

"She or he is incredible."

"She knows. We are incoming."

Professor Yan, small and wiry beside her dragon, clapped her hands. "Eyes front. This is Araceli, my bonded dragon. She will be serving as a model today for those of you measuring dragons. Her size is... unusual." Yan's smile was wry, her dark eyes flicking toward her dragon with pride. "Most of you will not require this scale, but the method remains the same."

From the opposite side of the room, a golden griffin strutted in, feathers glinting with bronze undertones. At his side walked a broad-shouldered male with kind eyes and sun-darkened skin—Professor Yan's spouse, though not a professor himself—a Rider, nonetheless.

"This is Daren and Klythe," Yan announced. "They'll demonstrate measurements for griffins and phoenixes. Their skeletal structure is similar enough that the process translates."

All of our fliers landed in the stadium, shaking the ground. Klythe fluffed his wings, sending a ripple of golden feathers scattering across the ground. A few cadets bent to snatch one up before Bhatta's voice in their memory stopped them cold.

Yan gestured to the fliers. "Your task today is simple. You will record preliminary measurements for your fliers: wingspan, neck girth, torso length, and saddle ridge. These will guide the custom fittings for your first real saddles."

Esme's silver dust eye swiveled toward me, a low rumble vibrating in my chest. *"If you make me look smaller than I am, I will bite you."*

"Good thing I am small, making you already look taller," I shot back.

Her laughter rolled through the bond, low and sharp.

Professor Yan clapped her hands again, her silver dragon's scales flashing. "Collect your cords, chalk, and parchment. You'll begin with torso length, then wingspan. Daren and I will correct your form."

She moved to the side table, her spouse already laying out a coil of cord across Klythe's golden back. "And before you ask—yes, I am a Rider. No, I do not ride often anymore. My gift manifested as a metallurgist. I can bend, shape, and strengthen metal, which makes me far more useful here, ensuring your saddles don't split in the sky. Consider me semi-retired, but don't think for a moment I've forgotten how to keep you all in line."

That earned a nervous laugh from a few cadets.

I gathered my cord and chalk, Esme crouching low so I could scramble up her shoulder. She rumbled under me, *"Measure carefully, little Rider. Leave nothing out."*

"Stand still," I said, bracing across her broad back as I chalked her shoulder ridge. "This isn't a competition."

"Everything is a competition," she purred.

Across the room, Akira yelped as Orix flicked his tail deliberately, knocking the chalk from her hands. "Gods, hold still!" she shouted, scrambling to retrieve it. Orix's booming chortle rattled the stone walls—that was definitely a laugh.

A few cadets snickered until a sharp crack echoed—the sound of Korra, snapping her beak dangerously close to Micah's sleeve when he drifted too close.

"Watch it!" Sadie barked, jerking Micah back.

Klythe ruffled his feathers, golden eyes flashing with predator pride. Daren gave a patient smile. "Griffins don't like strangers in their space. Quick reminder—don't test them. Their tempers are sharper than their beaks."

Micah muttered something under his breath but gave Sera a quick pat, the phoenix's feathers shifting in what looked suspiciously like smug agreement.

Meanwhile, Lorenzo's dragon, Syth, sprawled across the floor with deliberate weight, forcing him to climb halfway up the beast's forelimb to reach the neck cord. "You're doing this on purpose," Lorenzo grunted.

Syth rumbled, eyes gleaming.

Thora and Sylivia, by contrast, were immaculate. The dark blue griffin stood statue-still while Thora measured her wingspan, the chalk lines neat and perfectly aligned.

Sadie groaned when she saw it. "Of course they're perfect."

"Of course we are," Thora said, not even looking up.

I rolled my eyes, then stretched across Esme's spine to pull the cord tight. My arms trembled, but I got the mark down cleanly. She shifted just enough to jostle me, and I slid an inch sideways with a gasp.

Her laughter shook through me. *If you fall, I'll let the griffins peck at you first.*

"You're the worst," I shot back, chalking her last mark with a shaky hand.

Professor Yan moved between us, her keen gaze sweeping over our work. She paused by me, fingers brushing the chalk line on Esme's shoulder. "Not bad. Next time, tighten the cord higher across the ridge. Precision matters—half an inch off here, and you'll feel it every second in the sky."

I swallowed hard and nodded.

Yan straightened, her silver dragon shifting behind her, the ground trembling with each slight movement. "Remember, today is about patience. Your fliers are testing you, not failing you. The sooner you learn to read their moods and adapt, the sooner you'll stop ending up on your ass."

She looked around the room, sharp as a blade. "And tomorrow, we begin cutting leather. If you thought today was difficult, just wait."

I shook my head, but my eyes kept drifting back to Araceli, her silver scales glinting with every slow breath. Rare. Beautiful. Powerful in a way that felt untouchable.

I wondered what secrets Esme's bloodline might hold.

CHAPTER 41

By the time Professor Yan dismissed us, my arms ached from stretching cords across Esme's back, and chalk dust clung to my leathers. Feather Wing trudged out together, trading jabs about who had the most uncooperative flier. The fliers themselves had already returned to the Vale, leaving us lighter but somehow lonelier as we crossed into the courtyard.

The laughter died at once.

Gasps rippled through our ranks. My chest squeezed tight as my eyes found what silenced us.

A cadet hung against the pale stone of Alpha Wing, suspended by shimmering cords of magic. Her arms stretched wide, her boots swung two feet above the ground, and blood dripped from her chin in a slow, sick rhythm.

Harlyn Cowens. Infantry.

Recognition struck like a blade to the gut. Months earlier, she challenged Sadie in the sparring rings and nearly killed her, stabbing only millimeters from her heart. She didn't just humiliate Sadie—she relished it.

Now she hung lifeless, head tilted at an unnatural angle.

Beside me, Sadie went rigid, the color draining from her face. Her fists clenched at her sides, knuckles white, but she said nothing.

Akira swore softly, her voice shaking. "Gods... they did this in broad daylight."

Micah stopped dead, a tray of tools slipping from his grip, the clatter ringing too loud in the silence. Thora's griffin wasn't there, but I could almost imagine Sylivia's feathers slicking tight in predator stillness.

Whispers broke like cracks in ice.

"Another one."

"Infantry this time."

"She deserved it."

"No one's safe."

My skin crawled, every hair prickling. The shimmering cords that held Harlyn flickered faintly, not rope or chain but something conjured—something wrong.

Esme's voice slid through my mind, colder than I'd ever felt her. *This is deliberate. Calculated. Whoever did this wants you all to watch.*

Boots thundered behind us—professors and lieutenants sweeping in, shouting orders, throwing up wards to shove cadets back. A shimmering barrier sealed the courtyard in moments, cutting us off from the body, but the sight of it was already burned into our eyes.

I couldn't breathe.

Because this wasn't an accident, it wasn't a warning gone wrong. It was a choice. And whoever picked Harlyn Cowens had done it in the open, daring the rest of us to wonder—Who was next?

The courtyard filled fast, cadets pouring in from every wing and floor, their boots thundering across the cobblestones. Voices rose, high and panicked, whispers turning sharp as blades.

"Who is it?"

"Infantry—look, it's Harlyn Cowens."

"She's strung like a trophy."

"Gods, how didn't the towers or patrol see this?"

The press of bodies made it hard to breathe. Some craned their necks for a better look, others shoved forward as if daring the barrier to let them through. The wards shimmered brighter with every cadet that pressed close, humming with restrained force.

"Back to your chambers!" Lieutenant Gray's voice cracked across the courtyard like a whip. Professors fanned out behind him, their faces grim, their gestures sharp as they forced the crowd back. "Move! Lockdown until further notice. No exceptions."

The orders rippled outward, swallowed by a tide of cadets resisting. Fear made them stubborn. Nobody wanted to turn their back on the sight of Harlyn hanging limp against the stone.

Professor Melamora strode forward, eyes flashing, her tone colder than the night air. "Do as you're told, or I'll have you dragged there myself."

That broke the standoff. Reluctantly, cadets shuffled back, peeling away in stiff, uneasy lines. The barrier shimmered one last time before sealing tight, cutting off even the faintest glimpse of Harlyn's dangling form.

The walk to my chamber was a blur. My body moved, but my mind stayed rooted in the courtyard, in the steady drip of blood on stone. By the time I reached my hall, the smell of food clashed harshly with the memory. Mess stewards had been ordered into the halls, dropping canvas sacks onto tables for cadets to snatch on their way to their rooms.

I pulled mine open and blinked. Inside was a hunk of hard bread, a wedge of cheese, and a tin cup already half full of watered juice. Simple. Practical. The kind of thing you'd hand a soldier on campaign in the last century. It tasted like ash in my mouth.

Around me, cadets grumbled as they accepted their rations, the noise a low, restless growl. A few cracked bitter jokes—about prison fare, about the professors chaining us in our rooms next—but none of it stuck.

Not with the image of Harlyn burned into our eyes.

Esme's voice brushed the back of my mind, quieter than usual. *"Eat, little Rider. You'll need your strength. Whoever strung her there... they're not finished."*

And I knew she was right.

The canvas sack sat forgotten at the edge of my desk, its contents—bread and cheese—untouched. I sat cross-legged on my bed, staring at the wall. The image of Harlyn strung against Alpha Wing burned so deep it pulsed behind my eyes every time I blinked.

"Zane?"

His voice slid in, low and steady, like dark water. *"I'm here. I'm always here."*

I hesitated, fingers knotting in my blanket. *"She wasn't just killed. She was on display. Whoever this is, they're... escalating. First, the courtyard. Then the classroom. Now strung up like a warning sign. They're not hiding anymore."*

A long silence stretched before his reply. *"You're right. This isn't just killing. It's performance. Whoever's doing this wants us afraid, wants us watching."*

"It's working," I admitted, pressing my palm to my chest. My bond mark thrummed faintly with unease. *"Everyone's jumpy. Sadie hadn't said two words since we saw her. What happens when cadets start turning on each other?"*

"They already are," he said. *"I've heard the whispers. Branch against branch. Wing against wing. It's tearing at the seams."*

I shut my eyes and leaned my back against the wall. *"Winter break can't come soon enough."*

The thought slipped out before I could stop it, and the silence on the bond shifted.

"Where are you going?" Zane asked.

My stomach tightened. I didn't know. I had been pondering the thought for a few days. Knowing, we couldn't be separated for long.

"I don't... know." The words felt small. *"My father's house isn't home. It never has been. Not since... I swallowed hard. Not since my mother died. He wouldn't care if I came or not. I don't have anywhere else. He surely won't be there. And what about us, our bond, our powers?"*

The bond hummed warm, steady. Zane didn't rush his reply. *"Come with me."*

My breath caught. *"What?"*

"To my family's palace. It's not perfect. It's... complicated. But it's safer than going back to your father's. And you wouldn't be alone."

The offer settled between us, heavy and bright all at once. I mean, it was what I wanted, deep down, but also the thought terrified me. He had a lot of siblings, and his father was the fucking duke for goodness sake. Not to mention I killed his brothers, Zane's uncles.

And then the image of Harlyn slipped back, the dread in my chest easing just enough for me to breathe.

"Think about it, you deserve somewhere that feels like home, Auri. Even if it's only for two weeks."

The bond was quiet for a long stretch, but my chest wouldn't loosen. My thoughts spun too fast, words tumbled out before I could stop them. *"What if I manifest there? At your palace. In front of your family. In front of your father. None of you Drusearons channel raw power—you don't know what it's like. What if my power breaks loose? What if I destroy something? What if I hurt someone? What if I make your family hate me before they even know me?"*

Zane's reply was steady, like iron wrapped around fire. *"We'll deal with it. Together. If you burn a hall, we'll rebuild it. If my father hates it, well he hates it. You won't be alone, Auri. Not in this. Not ever again."*

I pressed my palm hard to my bond mark and forced myself to believe it. Another thought burned hotter than the rest, one I refused to say aloud until now.

My voice shook. *"What about... what I did to your uncles?"*

The silence that followed nearly broke me. My throat closed, but the words wouldn't stay buried.

"You know... what happened..." Tears started to blur my vision, hot and unwanted. *"I killed them both, Zane. How do I face your family with that? How do I walk into your father's house when I've spilled Drusearon blood?"*

His answer cracked through the bond, fierce and unyielding. *"You don't apologize for surviving."* His voice dropped, sharp as a blade. *"The one who touched you deserved death the moment he laid hands on you. And the one who shielded him deserved it the moment he chose to stand between you and justice. You didn't kill them for being Drusearons, Auri. You killed them for what they did."*

My breath hitched, the tears slipping free. *"But your father—"*

"My father," Zane cut me off, his temper bleeding through the bond, *"is not a god. He is a duke. And as far as I know, he believes your father was the one responsible, not you. He doesn't know what happened to you, and if he*

did and he didn't punish him by death, then I wouldn't want to associate with him."

The conviction in his voice broke something loose inside me, leaving me raw and trembling. I curled deeper into my blanket, the ache in my chest sharp and sweet all at once.

"You make it sound simple."

"It is." His thought struck fierce, hard-edged. *"It is when it comes to you."* The next pulse came softer, gentler, almost breaking at the edges.

For the first time since seeing Harlyn strung up, my breath came easier. The fear didn't vanish, but it eased—like a shadow pushed back by firelight. I wanted to believe him. Gods, I wanted to. I knew deep down if I didn't want to go, he would go with me wherever I chose—but I didn't want him to sacrifice the holiday with his family. I also didn't want to be away from him, especially not for two weeks.

CHAPTER 42

The tension in the stadium classroom was already sharp when Feather Wing filed in. Still, it snapped taut the moment Professors Melamora, Fogg, and Pascal entered together, their faces saying there wasn't anything good to announce. Behind them was a group of second lieutenants. I scanned each of them fast. As my gaze fell on the last one, my eyes widened, and my stomach dropped.

Fuck. This can't be happening. I dropped my head quickly, hoping he didn't notice me either. We had only released some steam together a few times before I left for here. Maybe he wouldn't remember me.

Melamora stepped forward first, her dark purple robes whispering against the floor, her expression carved from stone. "Due to the recent... incidents, leadership is taking precautionary measures."

Fogg crossed his arms, his deep voice booming in the vaulted space. "All students—except first-year Riders, all Wing Commanders, Executive Officers, and Platoon Leaders—will be leaving the campus today."

A wave of shocked gasps rolled through the benches. My stomach dropped.

Professor Pascal raised a hand for silence, his tone clipped but clear. "You have until fifteen-hundred hours to get off the campus grounds. Extra trains have already been arranged in Chalahana, with departures at ten hundred, twelve hundred, thirteen-thirty, and fifteen hundred."

A cadet from the back shouted, "So we're being thrown out?" Melamora's eyes flashed. "You are being sent home—for your safety. You all were being sent home in six days anyway. There will be no further debate."

The room broke into whispers and protests anyway.

"What about winter solstice celebrations?"

"What if we don't have anywhere to go?"

"They can't do this!"

Professor Fogg slammed his palm down on the lectern, the crack silencing half the room. "You will obey your orders. If you do not have a place to go, you can see one of your professors who will help arrange something for you."

Pascal stepped in again, calmer but no less firm. "Except for the first-year Riders, the rest of the lectures have been cancelled for you to go and pack your bags for leave." His eyes swept the rows of first-year Riders, landing on me for a fraction of a second. "Those of you who remain... will not be idle. You are expected to continue your training, and you will be watched. The remaining cadet leadership will need to assist your cadets in their departure. This evening there will be a leadership meeting after the campus is closed, this will include the first-year Flight Guides who will remain."

The words sent a shiver down my spine. Melamora's gaze raked across the hall, daring anyone to speak. "Dismissed. Begin preparations immediately."

The room erupted.

Cadets scrambled for the aisles, some furious, some frightened, some pale with relief. Shouts and questions tangled together, boots pounding down the stairs. A few already ran for their chambers, desperate to pack.

I sat frozen in my seat, heart hammering. In the span of a breath, half the academy was being scattered, sent home early. Had this ever happened before?

Leaving the rest of us—the ones with fragile bonds that needed to be tended to before we could leave. The ones that had fragile magic manifesting within our skins, waiting to explode. Extreme duress was enough to trigger it, which made me believe that some of us would be channeling quicker than we should.

And what if the murderer wasn't someone who was being ordered to leave? That would leave our small group to pick from. What if it *was* a Rider? No, it couldn't be. A flier wouldn't allow it.

The benches scraped and thundered as cadets poured toward the exits, a storm of panic and outrage.

"They can't just throw us out!"

"What about exams?"

"Gods, I don't actually know if my family is home yet"

"Good riddance, I'm not staying here to be strung up like the rest."

"I hope this shit is figured out before we get back."

Feather Wing moved together, swept in the tide of bodies funneling toward the doors. I tried to match their pace, but my legs felt heavy, my chest tight with a panic I couldn't quite name. Everyone leaving—the noise, the fear, the tension—it was like watching the college splinter before my eyes.

As I started to move with my wing, I saw him approaching. Shit. I almost forgot about him with the professors turning our world upside down.

"Hey Auri!" he said.

Damn it. I knew Zane would be joining me soon.

I turned to him "Hello, Lieutenant McGrath."

"Ahh c'mon you know you can call me Orrin."

Sadie, Lili, Micah, and Thora had all stopped, noticing that I had stopped. Gods this could go to shit fast.

"Ah, who's your friend?" Sadie asked.

"Someone I knew from Zion Outpost."

He gave them all a smile then said, "hmmm a little more than just knew."

Micah cringed and locked his eyes behind me. I didn't need him to say anything to know Zane was approaching—

A hand interlocked with mine. Orrin's eyes dropped down to our hands.

"Oh, I see. I guess asking if you wanted to throw some drinks back and have some fun is out of the question," Orrin said. He was so fucking cocky.

My cheeks rushed with flaming heat, heart beating faster. I am sure everyone around us could see my bright red cheeks against my pale skin. Anger coursed down the bond, and it wasn't mine.

"Yeah... no. She will not be having any fun with you," Zane said. His voice steady, cold, calculating. No one here would guess that his anger was surging between us.

"Sorry. No disrespect. I'll see myself to my duty," Orrin said.

"See you around," I said.

"Yeah... I am also going to go, this is not the conversation I am staying for. I have witnessed this *way* too many times," Lili said.

"Wow. Thanks..." I said.

She turned and headed out. Sadie, Micah, and Thora took that opportunity to also leave.

He didn't say anything at first. Just pulled me into him, his arms closing around me in the middle of the storm. His chest was solid against mine, the steady thrum of his heartbeat grounding me when everything else felt like it was unraveling.

"You know, I am not a possession. I have a past, as do you."

"Sorry if I overstepped. You are happy to get drinks with him, but the fun he was insinuating won't be happening. And yes, I am aware we both have a past. I have to see yours every day."

"I have never hidden that I was wild before... You and I are real. So very fucking real. I would never do anything to disrespect you. No one will have my eyes the way you do. You have to trust that."

"I will try to do better and give you that autonomy. Sometimes my jealousy takes over. I never had a problem with sharing before, but you... I don't want to share. I love you, Auri."

"I also don't want to share, the thought of another female swooning you makes me nauseous."

"Well as you said, no one will or has ever had my eyes the way you do."

The flood of cadets shoved past us, their voices echoing down the halls, footsteps pounding down each side of the hallway. It already felt different. Thinner. Unsteady. Like the bones of something hollowing out from the inside. And I couldn't shake the thought that we'd just been left behind in a game no one else wanted to play. After what felt to be a hundred heartbeats, he let go of his grip on me. He rested his lips onto my forehead, both of us soaking in the moment before we carried our day on.

"It will be chaotic today, but I will find you. Stay safe, my Anam Cara."

"I love you, Zane."

***

By afternoon, the campus felt half-dead. Chamber doors gaped open, shutters banging as cadets hauled trunks down stairwells. The echo of hurried boots and carriage wheels still carried from the outer gates as Feather Wing trudged onto the flight field.

Professor Hildegard was already waiting, broad-shouldered, arms crossed, his pale hair bound in a tight braid that snapped in the wind. His voice carried across the field like a whipcrack. "Mount up. No excuses. The sooner you learn to fly, the sooner you can leave the ground when danger finds you. Today, we test your grip and your stomach. You can use your pommel. We will work on core strengthening when you all return."

Esme crouched low as I cinched the saddle straps. Her silver eyes glittered with anticipation, her amusement curling through the bond. *"Tight banks. Tight circles. Excellent. I'll enjoy this."*

I groaned, *"I was afraid you'd say that."*

He whistled, which had to be part magic, making my head twitch.

Feather Wing launched in a storm of beating wings and sparks. Sera blazed, Micah laughing like it was the greatest day of his life. Korra cut arcs sharp enough to shear the wind, and Sadie pressed low, fierce and steady. Orix dove into wide spirals that tightened without warning, forcing Akira to cling like a ragdoll.

Esme soared straight before banking hard left without warning. My stomach lurched, the world tilting. My grip slipped on the pommel, teeth clacking together as I fought for balance, thighs screaming with the strain.

"Hold," Esme urged, laughter bright in my head. *"Feel the pull. Lean with me, not against me."*

I tried. Gods help me, I tried. The circle narrowed, the ground rushing closer as she carved another brutal arc. My braid whipped loose, eyes watering, but that time I found her rhythm, body flowing with the turn instead of fighting it.

"Closer! Tighter!" Hildegard roared from the field, his voice cutting through the thunder of wings. "If you can't bank a circle, you'll never survive a dive under fire! Again!"

Sylari bellowed as Erik nearly toppled sideways, clinging with both hands. Lorenzo cursed so loud that half the wing laughed when Syth's bank slammed him against the saddle horn.

Thora and Sylivia, naturally, looked carved from perfection—circles clean, seamless, mercilessly precise.

By the fourth lap, my lungs burned, arms ached, and thighs shook with every shift of pressure. Esme's exhilaration only climbed, her joy fizzing through me like lightning, a stark contrast to my trembling muscles.

When Hildegard finally whistled again, I sagged forward, every muscle screaming.

"Better," Hildegard barked. "But not enough. Not yet. Remember that, if you find danger while flying home, you need to be prepared for your dragon to get you somewhere safe, and quick. See you all tomorrow."

Esme rumbled smugly beneath me as I slid down her shoulder, legs wobbling when I hit the dirt, *"you'll thank me later."*

"For the bruises?" I groaned.

"For the wings," she purred.

The dining hall felt hollow without the upper years. The clatter of trays echoed too loudly against the stone, and empty tables stretched like broken teeth. Unusually, Feather Wing's usual noise was also muted, and cadets hunched close together, voices low. No one lingered long.

The afternoon passed in Professor Yan's workshop. Chalked measurements turned into leather cuts. The stiff hides spread across the worktables. My fingers ached by the end of it, but for once the work was almost soothing—something steady in a world gone unsteady.

Professor Yan and her spouse moved tirelessly from bench to bench, correcting grips, trimming edges, reminding us that every stitch mattered. She swore that our own saddles would be done soon, and I almost believed her.

CHAPTER 43

Second Lieutenants kept first-years in the courtyard. Flight Guides, Wing Commanders, Executive Officers, and Platoon Leaders were led to the administrator's building. My chest tightened when they told us to report to the large conference room, where important decisions were made and punishments were enforced.

The space was stark and cold, with a U-shaped table dominating the center, wrapping around like an arena. At the far end, a wide table stood alone, accompanied by two enormous chairs carved from dark oak. We filled the open seats, and some stood along the walls.

At the head sat General Blackcreek—my father—and beside him Major General Kamban, their uniforms immaculate, their expressions carved from stone. The air thickened just seeing them there, command radiating like a pressure you couldn't escape.

Brigadier General Scullin, the male who oversaw the Rider branch, leaned forward in his chair, sharp eyes cutting across the room as though daring anyone to meet them. He wasn't alone—other brigadier generals lined the table, representing the branches I didn't know well enough to name. Infantry, Healers, Historians, Shapeshifters, Sorcerers, and Drusearon—faces I'd only seen from a distance, all gathered under one roof.

Professor Melamora stood near the left side of the table, dark purple robes contrasting against the pale stone wall, her presence cold as iron. Professor Pascal sat closer to the right, his hands folded on the table, his posture deceptively relaxed, but his eyes sharp.

The weight of them all, gathered here at once, pressed heavily on my chest. This wasn't a lecture. This wasn't another curfew, another list of restrictions. This was a council.

The hush that fell over the room when my father stood was absolute. Every scrape of boot leather, every cough, every nervous shuffle stopped. His presence alone pressed like a weight on my chest. My father didn't need to raise his voice to command silence—he carried it in his blood.

"We are past the point of whispers and speculation," he said, his tone sharp enough to cut. "Six cadets murdered. Three strung up in public as if this campus were a stage. If this continues, the campus itself will collapse from within."

My stomach twisted. He spoke as if we were nothing but numbers on a ledger, assets to be lost.

Major General Kamban leaned forward. "The question is whether we're facing an outside infiltrator... or a predator among the cadets themselves."

"Among them," Brigadier General Scullin snapped, his voice like gravel. "Who else could move so freely? Who else could silence six cadets without being noticed?" His sharp gaze swept the room, lingering on the Rider leaders.

Professor Melamora adjusted her cuffs, speaking in a cool tone. "If it is a cadet, they are highly skilled. That alone should give us pause. These murders are not random. They are calculated."

Pascal's reply was softer, but no less firm. "Fear is spreading faster than we can contain it. Sending the cadets home will slow the panic. But it will not stop the killings."

My father raised a hand, and the room fell silent again. His pale eyes cut across us, merciless. "Speculation wastes time. We need the truth."

I stiffened in my chair.

"My gift," he continued, his voice level but cold, "is classified." He let the word linger, heavy. "And today you will learn it and keep it classified. I can see what others have seen. Hear what they have heard. If necessary, feel what they have felt. I will use it. Every cadet who remains on this campus will be subject to interrogation."

A ripple of unease shuddered through the room, low gasps and muffled protests.

Zane went rigid at my side, his jaw tight. I kept my face blank, though my pulse hammered so hard I thought it might split me open. Alex and Lili both shot each other a look, then looked at me at the same time.

I was the only cadet present who wasn't in shock. I knew my father could read memories. He would interrogate me as a teen, way too often. Honestly, probably for good reason, I was a little unhinged. If contact had been made, he would see everything since I've been here. A hard swallow was forced down.

Fuck.

He would learn about Zane and my bond, and he would be aware of the letters my mom wrote to me. He would learn that Zane's dad was part of a mutiny... Fuck.

My father's gaze swept the room once more, daring any of us to challenge him. "I will find the truth. One way or another."

I clenched my fists in my lap, my nails biting crescent moons into my palms. Because for the first time, I realized the murderer might not be the only threat waiting for me on this campus.

The silence didn't hold long.

One of the Brigadier Generals stood, his voice taut with anger. "With respect, General, memory reading is a violation. We're not criminals to be dragged through like archives."

"Sit down," Scullin snapped, his chair screeching as he half-rose. "Six cadets are dead. We don't have the luxury of privacy."

Murmurs broke like sparks across the room, cadets shifting uncomfortably, others bristling with fury. A few brigadier generals glanced at one another, uneasy.

"Quiet!" My dad said in a voice that shook me to my core. "According to MCOE 1.5.1, any interrogation methods may be used with cadets or officers when a threat is present, at the discretion of the General. As a reminder, I am the *fucking general!*"

I hadn't seen him this angry or riled since someone attacked me. My heart pounded so hard I thought it skipped beats.

"Zane," I pushed through the bond, my pulse loud in my ears. *"He can't do this. Not to me. If he touches me—"*

"Breathe," Zane cut in, his voice was low and firm, steady as iron. *"Don't let him see fear. That's what he looks for. That's what he presses into."*

"You don't understand," I shot back, my nails bit harder into my palms. *"He's done it before, when I was younger. He's gonna know about us. About my mother's letters. About your father—"*

"Stop." His word struck through the bond like a blade, but his presence stayed steady, wrapping around the panic clawing at my chest. *"If he finds out about us, it's okay. He may already know, because he is bonded to one of the most powerful dragons, who is the mother of your dragon. As for my dad, we need to get rid of that thought before he starts touching. Build the biggest wall you have. And if he tries to harm you... Well, it will be the last thing he does."*

I risked the smallest glance at him. His jaw was still tight, but his eyes—dark, unyielding—burned with promise.

The silence after my father's outburst was suffocating, the words *I am the fucking general* still echoing off the stone walls like a lash. The brigadier generals shifted uneasily, exchanging sharp glances.

Major General Kamban cleared his throat, his voice calm and measured. "With respect, General Blackcreek, the regulation does not dismiss the consequences. Memory reading is invasive. If you push too far, you risk breaking the minds you intend to protect."

Scullin snorted, slamming a fist against the table. "Six cadets were already broken—in blood. I'd rather lose a little trust than lose more bodies strung up by dawn."

Professor Pascal leaned forward, his tone quiet but cutting. "And when cadets realize their thoughts are no longer their own, that their memories were weapons for leadership to plunder—what then? Fear will no longer come from a murderer in the shadows. It will come from us."

A ripple of agreement moved through the room, low and nervous.

"Fear already comes from us," my father snapped, his gaze cold and merciless. "That is the point. Order comes from fear. Without it, we have chaos. And chaos is where killers thrive."

"*Zane,*" I whispered through the bond, fighting to keep my expression still, "*he'll tear me apart if he looks too closely. I can't bury everything. Not the bond. Not your father. Not—*"

"*Stop spiraling.*" Zane's voice pressed hard into me, steady and fierce. "*Build the wall. Stone by stone. Let me anchor it if you can't. I'll keep you steady.*"

"*What if he sees you, too?*"

"*Then let him.*" His reply was sharp as a blade, his bond wrapping around mine with iron certainty. "*If he touches you, he won't get what he expects. I'll be there, pressing back. He won't take anything I don't allow. I'll push out the memories of you sucking my cock—*"

I choked out loud, and everyone shifted their eyes to me. My cheeks turned seven shades of red. "*Fuck Zane!*"

"Sorry." I dropped my gaze to the table. There wasn't an excuse to throw out that came to my mind.

At the head table, Melamora finally broke her silence, her voice smooth as silk over steel. "Then perhaps, General, we can compromise. Limit the interrogations to cadet leadership alone. If there is rot, it will be most evident in those closest to the command. Spare the first-years until necessity demands otherwise."

My father stared at me. I felt like he could see right through me. He straightened himself and looked around the room. "First off, this isn't a negotiation, not a compromise. Every cadet in this room *is* in leadership, which is why I ordered this meeting. Furthermore, no one will know that I have used my gift on them, because I am *that* good. I am informing you all. These cadets and anyone who didn't know just got briefed on classified information. I am reminding you that MCOE 1.1.3 states that any member of the military who shares classified information with anyone who does not have the clearance will be punished by death. This is your warning, in that regard."

Professor Pascal cleared his throat, as if he were almost afraid. "Clearly, we will not be talking you out of this. How do you want to proceed with this little mind violation?"

My father shot a look at him. "Well, first off, I could have done it, without you knowing, making it truly violating. Secondly, we will do it momentarily. Lastly, anything I may or may not see will not be shared with anyone who doesn't need to know, unless you, of course, are murdering cadets for fun. After I make sure everyone in this room is honorable, I will discuss the next steps."

I swallowed hard, forcing my eyes down to the table so my father wouldn't see the panic rising in me. My cheeks still burned from Zane's earlier comment, and the weight of my father's pale gaze remained..

At the front of the room, Brigadier General Scullin shifted impatiently in his seat. "Then let's get on with it. The longer we sit here debating, the longer the killer remains at large. If the General has the means to find the truth, I say we let him."

Professor Melamora's jaw tightened, her voice like polished steel. "You speak as if memories are infallible. They are not. They warp. They twist. They can be weaponized and misinterpreted. Reading them is no less dangerous than ignoring them."

Pascal added, quieter, "And yet here we are." His gaze cut toward me for just a fraction of a second, sharp and knowing. "We'll see if the General is as precise as he claims."

My father's voice cut through the room again, unyielding. "Precise enough." He scanned the table once more, then he leaned back against the table with the poise of a male who already owned the truth. "Does anyone have anything to share before we begin?"

Everyone was silent, lips pursed, staring at him. It's not like we can argue with him. He was the General of the military after all.

Every muscle in my body wanted to bolt, but Zane's hand slid across beneath the table, his fingers brushing mine, a grounding weight against the chaos.

"Stay steady," he whispered in my head. *"No walls crack unless we let them."*

"You don't know my dad. He is powerful." And if he pulled too hard—if he pushed too deep—every secret I carried could unravel.

Chairs scraped as everyone shifted, stiff with dread, but no one left. My father made it clear that this wasn't optional. One by one, he moved around the U-shaped table.

He didn't rely on theatrics. He simply stepped behind a cadet, placed his hand on the crown of their head or along their temple, and closed his eyes. The room held its breath, waiting. The cadet flinched, stiffened, sometimes gasped—but never for long. After a minute or two, my father moved on, his face unreadable and his voice sharp. "Next."

Each time, he found nothing—no killer, no confession, no guilt. Yet fear kept growing.

By the fourth cadet, sweat beaded on foreheads, knuckles whitened against the table. The brigadier generals who demanded these interrogations sat with uneasy expressions, as if witnessing the process felt far more invasive than they expected.

When he reached Zane, I had to bite the inside of my cheek to keep from trembling.

My father's hand settled against the side of his head, his pale eyes shutting as the silence grew heavy. Zane's bond presence flared immediately, sharp and molten, wrapping tight around mine like a shield.

"Stone walls," he whispered through the bond. *"He won't take more than I give him."*

I felt the pressure immediately—a tug in the bond, like a current trying to pull me under. My chest tightened as panic clawed at me. Zane put up a block, which also shut me out. It felt strange to sense him tugging at me through Zane.

The pressure shifted. It stayed but redirected and forced through paths I couldn't quite trace. Zane held it steady, offering him something but not everything.

My father lingered longer than he did with anyone else. Abruptly, he lifted his hand. He stayed silent, making a sharp, unreadable expression as his mouth tightened for a moment before he turned to me.

My heart nearly stopped.

When he pressed his palm to my head, the world narrowed. The cold weight of him pushed inside, searching and peeling back layers of thought like pages torn from a book.

I built every wall I could. I pushed everything down—Zane, the letters, the shimmer twisting in my chest, the mutiny. I tried to think of Esme's wingbeats, saddle straps, chalk lines on leather—anything else, anything ordinary.

He overpowered me. I felt him brush deeper, pressing harder.

Zane was there in the bond, anchoring me, steady as stone. *"Focus on me. Just me. Nothing else."*

I clung to him and pushed every thought toward his voice, his presence, his hand brushing mine under the table. My father slowed and faltered as he probed—redirected. He lingered longer with me, his jaw tightening, his expression flickering the same way it did with Zane. Then, finally, he lifted his hand.

Silence followed.

He gave no accusation or declaration of guilt.

He only flashed that sharp expression—a twitch of his mouth, a narrowing of his eyes—as if he brushed against something he couldn't quite identify.

"Next," he said.

I let out a breath I didn't realize I held, my hands shaking in my lap.

"We blocked it out, he didn't see it..."

"We think we did," Zane said, his own steadiness carrying a darker edge now. *"But he knows we're hiding something. That's why he made that face."*

I swallowed hard, my pulse still thundering in my ears.

He hadn't found the murderer, but he found enough.

When my father circled back to the front of the room, silence felt thick enough to choke on. He folded his hands behind his back, his expression unreadable as stone.

"You all passed," he said at last, his voice echoing across the chamber.

Every one let out a collective exhale, tension breaking in uneven gasps.

One of the brigadier generals from the Healer branch, I guessed, leaned forward with narrowed eyes. "You claimed you could take memories without detection. Yet everyone here felt it. Why?"

My father's mouth twitched faintly without a smile. "I wanted you to know I was digging. All of you threw up shields—as I expected. That forced me to break through. When I pressed hard enough, people felt the intrusion. I meant for the discomfort to happen."

Scullin grunted, leaning back in his chair. "Well, congratulations, General. You've put the fear of gods into all of us in one sitting."

"That's the point." My father's reply came flat, his gaze steady and cold.

Another general—Infantry branch, this time—snorted under his breath. "Gods, imagine what a hug from you feels like. No wonder your generals walk straighter than fence posts."

A ripple of low laughter skittered around the table, sharp-edged and uneasy.

He didn't twitch. "Which brings me to our next step. This leadership group will serve as a filter when the rest of the cadets return from winter break. They will not know it is happening. But I will touch each one of them—preferably when welcoming them back. A hand to the shoulder, a handshake, a hug. Enough contact to see what I need." His pale eyes swept across us. "If there is rot, it will be cut out before it spreads."

My stomach twisted. I flicked a glance at Alex and Lili across the table—both stiff, both pale, their gazes locked on my father as if they didn't dare blink. They stared at a stranger, not someone who had been like their uncle for most of their lives. They knew what this meant, too. We all became his net, whether we wanted to or not.

"Before that," he continued, his voice carrying an edge of finality, "I will speak with the first-year Riders in the courtyard. Briefly. I will be eliminating them before they leave. That will happen shortly."

The air thinned, and every Rider cadet glanced at one another. My pulse hammered against my ribs.

My father straightened, his gaze sweeping the room. "Dismissed."

Chairs scraped back in a rush as cadets and officers moved with speed toward the doors, none lingering.

"Except Cadet Blackcreek and Cadet Braegon," he added, his voice like a blade through the din. His eyes fixed on us—Zane and me. "Stay behind."

My stomach dropped. Lili shot me a knowing glance—the one I knew too well, when he dismissed her to scold me. The last chairs scraped back, the final cadets filed out, and the heavy doors thudded shut, sealing Zane and me inside with my father.

He leaned back in his chair, studying us in silence. Then, to my shock, his expression shifted slightly—softer.

"Congratulations," he said, his voice low and steady. "On the bond. On the mate. I'm... glad you finally know, Auri. That you found him."

Heat climbed my neck. My pulse jumped, my cheeks betraying me before I could compose myself.

Zane's hand brushed mine beneath the table, steady.

But my father wasn't finished. His pale green eyes narrowed, glinting like ice. "You're hiding something else. At the end of the day, I don't care—not right now. What I do know is that neither of you is the killer. Not intentional killers, at least." His gaze lingered on me for a moment longer than comfort allows, then slid to Zane.

The stare that followed could split stone. It stayed cold, unrelenting, as if he were weighing Zane's soul piece by piece.

"You." His voice dropped lower, edged in steel. "You dare to throw that filth into my head—an image of my daughter, *my daughter*—" His jaw tightened, and his eyes cut to me, catching the way my face burned hot again.

"Fuck," I said.

Zane, to his credit, didn't flinch. He met that gaze head-on. "You went digging where you weren't wanted," he said. "I defended myself. I defended her. I won't apologize for that."

The silence that followed was enough to shatter glass.

My dad stared at him. "You are free to go, Cadet Braegon, or should I say the Marquess of the Veil of Vultures."

Zane stared back. Shock rippled through our bond, but his face stayed iron, steady against that cold stare. "Respectfully, I am not fucking leaving, sir."

And then—shockingly—my father inclined his head. Not much. But enough. "You protect her, *that*—I respect, never stop."

I blinked, my throat thick. I never thought I'd hear that from him.

My father's attention slid back to me, his voice dropping lower. "I saw the letters. You've read them. I know."

The floor tilted under me. My mouth went dry.

He nodded once, deliberate. "I swear to you, Auri—I had no part in your mother's death. But yes... she was murdered. And I will avenge it. I have sworn as much."

My chest tightened. My breath caught like a sob I refused to let free.

"Your mother and I once loved each other, but we weren't meant for each other. We stayed together, but not truly. Only for you. But I did care for her. And I will not let her killer walk free."

The room spun, my mind reeling. For the first time in years, I didn't know what to say to him. Zane's hand tightened around mine under the table, grounding me as the silence stretched.

For the first time, my father gave me something I never expected. Not control. Not commands. Only the truth.

He stood up, nodded to us, and walked out.

The door shut behind us with a thud that rattled through my bones. I couldn't move for a long moment. My legs felt rooted to the floor, my lungs too tight for air.

Zane's hand stayed on mine, firm, grounding. "Auri—"

"He knew," I whispered, my voice raw. "He saw the letters. He knew I read them." My throat closed around the words. "And he confirmed it. She didn't just die. She was murdered."

Zane's eyes softened, though his jaw stayed tight. "You've always known it in your gut. He only gave a voice to what you already felt."

"That doesn't make it easier," I shot back, tears stinging my eyes. I dragged my sleeve across them before they could fall. "I wanted him to deny it, Zane. I wanted him to say I was wrong, that I made it up, that she—" My voice broke. "But he didn't."

Zane didn't argue. He only pulled me in, his arm strong around my shoulders, letting me press my face to his chest until my breaths eased.

When I finally straightened, his eyes searched mine. "You heard the other part, too. He's vowing to avenge her. Whatever else he is... that promise, I believe."

I nodded faintly, though my insides still twisted. "Believing him doesn't mean trusting him."

Zane's mouth ticked up at the corner. "Good. Don't trust him. But take the truth where you can."

We walked in silence until the heavy doors opened to the winter air. Voices drifted from the courtyard below—cadets murmuring, restless, boots crunching on stone.

And there he was.

My father stood in the center of the first-year Riders, towering in his immaculate uniform, every line of his posture commanding. His eyes swept the crowd as he clasped shoulders and gripped forearms, pulling cadets in with the false warmth of a commander welcoming his troop.

As soon as Lili and Alex locked eyes with me, they headed towards Zane and me. Their eyes said exactly why they were coming. They were disappointed and had questions. Lili grabbed my wrist and pulled me back to the wall. Zane and Alex followed suit.

"Why the fuck didn't you ever tell us about that little fucking gift your father has?" Lili said. Her voice was low and seething. Her cheeks were rosy colored, her eyes flaring at me.

"I couldn't." My eyes dropped to the ground. I felt like I betrayed them.

"You're our best friend..." Alex said.

"Yes, and he is my father. As you saw by his little party trick, he would know if I told you."

"You could have told us without telling us," Lili said.

"If it makes either of you feel better, she also did not disclose this to me," Zane said.

"No, actually it doesn't, but I am not surprised, we dated for years. Clearly, I was clueless." Alex said.

"It is a classified ability. Could. Not. Tell. You. Now you know."

"After he dug through my head," Alex said.

"She is right, though. She really couldn't tell you. Just as you guys aren't allowed to share that with anyone else," Zane said.

All four of us turned to focus on my father as he went around the courtyard talking with other cadets. A few looked proud, straightening under his attention. Most looked nervous, glancing away as soon as his hand touched them, as if they sensed the same chill I did.

Esme stirred faintly in my chest, her rumble curling with sharp amusement. *"Your father plays with kindness, but every touch is a blade. They don't know he's cutting through their thoughts even as he smiles."*

My stomach turned as I watched him lean close to a boy from Dragon Wing, clapping him on the back as if he were proud. To everyone else, it looked like encouragement. But I knew better.

Zane's hand brushed mine again, his voice steady through the bond. *"We'll keep our walls up. Together. He won't take more than we allow."*

I swallowed hard and nodded. But the truth hung heavy in my chest as we stepped into the crowd. My father didn't just mingle with the first-years. He dissected them. From the courtyard's edge, I tried to blend in, but my eyes never left him.

My father moved slowly through the first-years. His presence unsettled the cadets. He clasped forearms, pulled cadets briefly into embraces—a firm hand on a shoulder, a measured pat on the back. To onlookers, it seemed like encouragement, pride. But I knew every touch was a blade. Every smile, a mask.

Cadets straightened under his attention—some hid nerves, some faked approval, some masked dislike. They had no idea what happened to them, what he scraped from their minds as his pale eyes flicked, narrowed, and released.

I crossed my arms, forcing my expression neutral, my stomach twisting tighter with every handshake.

Esme hummed faintly against the bond. *"They line up for him like sheep for shearing. None of them even sensed the blade."*

When he finished with the last cadet, he lingered a moment longer in the circle, his gaze sweeping over them. Then, as if nothing had happened, he glanced to Major General Kamban, who waited with the other officers. My father gave him a subtle nod—barely there.

But I caught it.

So had Kamban.

His jaw eased, his arms loosening behind his back. A silent exchange, but clear as spoken words. Not this group. My father casually joined Kamban, and they walked off. Relief rippled through the first-years, though they didn't know why. Some began to whisper to each other, the tension breaking. A few even smiled, thinking they'd just been inspected and found worthy.

I stayed silent, my pulse still heavy in my throat. Because I knew better, it wasn't mercy. It was a violation.

He would sift through them all, sooner or later.

And when he finished, there would be no secrets left at all. None of them knew they should shield their minds.

CHAPTER 44

By the time my father left the courtyard, the weight in my chest hadn't eased. Even with his absence, the air still felt too thin, too sharp. Featherwing didn't linger in the shadows the way I wanted to. Sadie looped an arm through mine, tugging me toward the edge of the crowd. "You look like you saw a ghost, Auri. Come on. We're still alive. Let's act like it."

"I mean, I have seen three dead people in the last three days. Soooo— I don't think acting like it means I can breathe again," I muttered, but I let her drag me anyway.

Micah appeared on my other side, a grin plastered across his face. "Did anyone else see it earlier? Professor Hildegard nearly got squished by Orix earlier when Akira couldn't get him to stop banking in circles. It looked like Orix drank a little too many times."

Akira shoved him from behind, scowling. "He listens, just... selectively."

"Selective?" Lorenzo snorted, striding up with his usual swagger. "He nearly flattened half the practice field! The only thing he listens to is his own ego."

"Like Rider, like flier," Thora muttered, earning a chorus of snickers from the group.

Even I cracked a smile, the knot in my chest loosening a little. For a moment, it was just us again—bickering, teasing, then laughter.

Esme stirred in the bond, her tone rich with amusement. *"You humans mock each other endlessly, yet it makes you closer. Strange. But... not unpleasant."*

"Hmm, I somehow feel like fliers are just as equally mean, just based off of you," I shot back at her, shaking my head.

Zane drifted closer, his shoulder brushing mine. He didn't say anything, but the warmth of his bond wrapped around me, steady and reassuring. For the first time all day, I felt my lungs fill completely. The murders and threats weren't forgotten. But for this sliver of an evening, Featherwing was together, alive, loud—and maybe that was enough.

We should've gone straight back to our chambers. That's what the orders said, anyway. But instead, most of Featherwing and Zane ended up shuffling in the small practice gym, the smell of leather and chalk dust thick in the air.

Micah produced a bottle from his satchel with a grin that made me want to roll my eyes. "Found this little treasure in the Healer's wing storage closet. Pretty sure it was meant for tinctures, but, well—what's medicine without a little fun?"

"Pretty sure that's called malpractice," Sadie muttered, but she still reached for the bottle first.

Lorenzo snatched it out of her hands. "If anyone's going to test this for poison, it should be me. I'm already halfway invincible." He tipped it back with an exaggerated flourish—then immediately doubled over, coughing.

"Invincible, huh?" Thora deadpanned, arms crossed. "Looked more like you swallowed a wasp."

"It burns," Lorenzo rasped, wiping his mouth and shoving the bottle toward her. "Your turn."

Akira snatched it instead, sniffed, and winced. "Smells like turpentine." She drank anyway, then hissed through her teeth. "Tastes like turpentine, too."

Micah was rolling with laughter. "Oh, this is so much better than drills." He raised the bottle high. "To Sandorg—may it not implode before we return."

"To Sandorg," Sadie echoed dryly, taking the bottle to take her swig like it was penance.

The bottle made its rounds, each of us coughing, wincing, or swearing in turn. By the time it landed in my hands, my stomach already hurt from laughing at the others.

Esme stirred faintly in the bond, her voice sharp with disdain. *"You all willingly ingest liquid that tastes like paint. You're all mad."*

"Maybe," I thought back, *"but it beats thinking about cadets hanging from walls."*

She huffed but didn't argue.

I tipped the bottle and nearly choked on the burn. "Gods above, this could strip rust off armor."

Zane took it last, his face blank as he downed a full swallow. He set it down calmly, cleared his throat once, and said, "tastes fine."

We all groaned.

"Show-off," I muttered, my face still burning from the alcohol.

"Bro, I've told you before, but you are feral," Alex said.

Micah flopped onto the mat, arms spread wide. "If we survive history, murderers, and flight training it'll be because of this bottle."

"Or it'll kill us first," Lili added flatly.

"Either way," Lorenzo wheezed, clutching his chest, "at least we'll die laughing."

And for the first time in days, we all forgot about what was surrounding us, and were present in the moment. The bottle had just made another shaky lap around the circle when the gym door creaked open. We all froze, like kids caught with our hands in the grain barrel.

Second Lieutenant Renwick leaned against the doorframe, arms crossed, expression somewhere between bored and predatory. His eyes swept over the bottle, over Lorenzo's flushed face, over Micah lying starfish on the mat.

"Well," he drawled. "If this isn't the picture of discipline."

My stomach plummeted. Oh shit. I wasn't even sure if he could discipline us, since we weren't technically under his chain of command. He could run and tell any of the professors or the generals, but instead of ratting us out, Renwick walked in, boots clicking against the floor.

He reached into his coat, pulled out a battered silver flask, and held it up with two fingers. "Trade?"

The silence broke all at once. Micah shot up like he'd been struck by lightning. "Gods bless the campus, you're our favorite officer."

Renwick smirked, kneeling and plucking our half-empty bottle from Lorenzo's limp hand. He took a swig without flinching, then grimaced. "Gods, that tastes like varnish. Where'd you even find it?"

"Don't ask," Sadie said flatly, though her lips twitched.

Renwick poured a generous splash of his flask into the bottle. "Now this is fine whiskey. If you're going to break the rules, at least don't poison yourselves in the process."

The smell hit immediately—warm, smoky, worlds better than the sharp burn from before. Lorenzo lifted it reverently. "Sir... you're a saint."

"Saints don't drink with cadets," Renwick replied dryly. "Luckily, I'm no saint."

We laughed, too loud, too long, the kind of laughter that only came when fear had been riding you for too many days straight. Even Thora cracked a grin, and that alone felt like a minor miracle.

When the flask finally reached me, I took a cautious sip. The burn was still there, but it was smoother this time, heat rolling down my throat instead of clawing. "Better, but not great," I admitted.

Renwick joined in like he was part of the group, lounging against the wall with his flask in hand, tossing out sharp quips that had us laughing louder than we should've. I took everything in around me, from Lorenzo trying to juggle the bottle. Alex pretended to duel a training dummy with a broom handle. Renwick's gaze lingered on Thora, and she smirked back at him. I could see where that was going. I was that drunk female before.

By the time the bottle was empty, the two of them were sitting next to each other, making inappropriate jokes that made her cheeks pink and had him grinning like a wolf.

"Are we watching Thora flirt?" Sadie muttered under her breath.

"I didn't think she knew how," Akira whispered back.

The next thing I knew, we all staggered out into the hallway because, well, we were drunk. Whose idea was this anyway? Renwick was walking shoulder-to-shoulder with Thora, the two of them laughing under their breath like conspirators. Micah tripped over his own boots twice, Lorenzo sang something horribly off-key, and even Sadie was biting her knuckles to keep from cackling. Alex and Lili were walking arm and arm, balancing each other, something I had seen them drunkenly do more times than I can count. Zane was walking poised, like he was completely unfazed.

We must have looked like utter chaos tumbling through the stone corridors. Which is exactly when Corson stepped out from a stairwell, arms folded, his face like thunder.

"What in the hells is this?" His voice cracked like a whip.

We all froze. Even Renwick, who blinked once before straightening his coat. Like his rank didn't supersede a Wing Commander.

Corson's eyes narrowed, his gaze flicking from the empty bottle dangling from Lorenzo's hand to Thora's pink cheeks to Renwick himself. "Lieutenant. Cadets. Rooms. Now."

No shouting. No punishments. Just that voice, sharp enough to slice us in half.

"Yes, sir," Renwick said smoothly, tucking the flask back into his pocket, winking at Thora as Corson turned away.

She rolled her eyes—but the faint smile tugging at her lips gave her away. The moment Corson's boots clicked out of earshot, the dam broke. We collapsed into each other, choking on giggles, trying to muffle them as we stumbled our separate ways down the hall.

"Best night," Micah wheezed, clinging to Lorenzo's shoulder for balance.

"Worst hangover incoming," Sadie muttered, grinning, nonetheless.

"I am sure our fliers will make us all regret this while flying tomorrow," Akira chimed in.

Thora grabbed Renwick and tugged him along, whispering something in his ear. Something told me they were about to enjoy themselves a little too much. I shook my head, my stomach aching from laughing too much. For a little while, at least, the worries of what was happening didn't bother me. It just felt like home. Zane grabbed my hand, and—

Darkness swirled us.

Lights flashed, and we were in his chambers.

"Wow... I am a little too tipsy for all that spinning."

He let out a laugh. The most wonderful, perfect sound ever.

"I admit, I am a little tipsy myself. I haven't roved before while drinking and was really hoping I didn't fuck it up." He laughed.

Still holding onto my hands, he stepped back a little and looked me up and down, as if taking me all in. I felt electricity swirling in my toes.

"You are so absolutely stunning, have I told you that lately?"

I let out a little giggle. "Every day, but tonight your eyes are screaming it too."

He pulled me closer, letting go of my hands, then reached behind me, gripping my ass, pulling me up into his arms. I wrap my legs around him tightly, our kissing started out slow and sensual before it turned into feverish and demanding.

"Hmmm, what should I do with you tonight?"

Nothing came out, and I wasn't even sure what to say. Everything? That sounds greedy, of course, he'd obliged if I'd asked. His lips felt amazing as they traced down my neck. Alcohol made everything feel a little warmer.

"Hmmm?" he asked again.

"Whatever you want..." I let out, before throwing my head back, letting him suck on my neck, just enough to make my body crave more, crave him, but not enough to leave a mark.

"Oh, Auri, I don't think there are enough days in our lives for all the things I want to do to you, and you to me."

My skin responded with goosebumps, and wetness spread between my legs. He moved to his bed, gently placing me down on the edge. He motioned to pull my tunic and tee off, then he moved to pull my leather pants down slowly. I pushed myself up, and he had already gripped his tunic and pulled it off. I started to pull his leather pants down, letting him free.

"Let your wings free too," I whispered to him.

He obliged, letting them free. I came to a stand, inches from him. I reached my arm over his shoulder, touching a little spot that I knew drove him crazy. I could feel his cock dancing between us. He let out a grunt. He wasn't even touching me, and I already felt so very turned on, warmth rushing over me. Wetness filled in between my thighs.

"I've never came that way, but if you don't stop—oh fuck I might," he growled at me.

Before I could pull my hand away, he grabbed me and twisted me around. He gripped my hips and pushed me forward onto the bed. I pulled my knees onto the bed. He rubbed his hands down my back, doing idle circles on my ass. I let out a little moan, his touch alone did everything to me. He reached down, pushed my knees apart, spreading me wider.

He trailed his fingers from the inside of my thighs to the center. Moving his finger from the top of my clit down one side, so slowly. Gods, he hadn't even entered me, and I was at the threshold. He moved his finger up the other side, tracing every crease of me. I could feel the wetness building, just before he plunged two fingers in.

"Gods, Auri, you are soaked...all for me," he whispered with a low grunt.

"If you keep playing around—"

He pulled his finger out, swiped it up, doing a quick circle on my clit, and I let out an uncontrollable moan. He pulled his fingers down, plunging them in again, then took them out, bringing them to his mouth, tasting me.

"So sweet and so tangy, like strawberries," he moaned.

He moved his body closer to me, while also pulling me towards him. He dropped his knees, bringing his dripping and excited cock to me. He slowly entered, we both moaned in unison. He kept the slow pace, moving in and out slowly.

"I love watching you quiver on my cock" he moaned through the words.

Every moan he made brought me closer and closer to the edge of explosion. He reached for my chest, pulling me back against him, still moving in and out, my hips responded with his rhythm. He gripped my nipple with his right hand while moving his left hand around to my clit.

"I won't last much longer, if you do that," I moaned.

"I am not gonna last much longer, either way, cause fuckkkkk, this is so good."

He rubbed my clit, doing a few circles, bringing me to the point where I was about to lose all control. Then he came to a complete stop and pulled himself out. I wanted him back inside immediately—the need coursed through me.

"Hmmm... I think I want you on top, so I can see how perfect you are when your world explodes."

He moved to the bed, pulling me on top of him. I straddled him, kissing him, without bringing him inside of me. We both needed a little cooldown, even though my body was screaming for him to be back inside. I knew that if I pushed him in too soon, we would both explode after just a few moments. Being on top for me was one of the quickest ways for me to orgasm, well, and him feasting on me.

After a few moments, which felt like an eternity, kissing him, feeling my intensity go down some, I moved to enter him, slowly lowering myself, teasing just the tip for a few thrusts.

"Oh, fucking gods, Auri!"

Just what I wanted, teasing him just the way he had done to me. He reached his hand to my nipple, rubbing it slowly between his thumb and finger, and gods, if I didn't want to let it go right then.

I finally lowered myself all the way, taking every bit of him inside of me. Fuck this felt so amazing, euphoric.

"Oh fuckkkkk." He moaned out.

I moved my legs up on each side, planting my feet flat on the bed, maximizing his depth inside of me, grinding back and forth. His grunts got more intense and deeper. He was so close. I was so close. He was still holding my tit, every minute or so, rubbing my nipple. His other hand firmly gripped my hip. Both of my hands were on his chest, gripping him, trying not to dig my fingers in too hard. I had a habit of gripping whatever was in my hands with every bit of grip I had, often leaving marks. I tried to reach for pillows when that happened, but—

"Oh gods, Auri, I can't... hold it... back"

He let out a roar that shook the windows. His sounds and our movement triggered me to explode right behind him. Letting out a mixture of fucks and moans, thank the gods the room had a ward on it. Just as I thought, I gripped onto his chest with a death grip, leaving small punctures from my nails. I collapsed onto his chest, moving my legs out. Both of our breathing was ragged, our pulse racing. We lay there holding each other, because no matter what, we had each other.

CHAPTER 45

Morning came too fast. The bell tolled six times, each clang like a hammer to my skull. First-year Riders and leadership were the only ones in the dining hall. We were informed that all first-year Riders would report to the flight field. The cadet leadership, minus the Flight Guides, would be discussing plans.

All of us first-years shuffled onto the flight field, but Featherwing looked like we'd been dragged through the stables backward. Micah wore his headache plain, squinting at the pale winter sun like it was trying to kill him.

Sadie kept muttering under her breath, "never again, never again." Though she still walked straighter than most of us.

Lorenzo looked ready to vomit on his boots, and Akira had the hollow-eyed stare of a woman bargaining with the gods.

Thora, infuriatingly, looked composed. Only the faint tightness around her mouth betrayed her. Micah shot her a look and let out a large laugh.

Professor Hildegard was waiting, arms folded, expression tight. His voice cracked across the field, far too loud for anyone with a pounding head. "You are Riders. You will learn to fly, whether you drank yourself sick or not. And yes, it's that obvious."

Lorenzo groaned audibly.

Hildegard's gaze snapped at him. "Be inconvenienced again, Cadet Carnethon, and I'll have you running laps until you can't stand."

Lorenzo snapped upright, trying not to sway. "Yes, sir."

Hildegard's eyes swept over all of us, merciless. "From today until you leave, your only duties are flight training and saddle completion. You will not waste time in classrooms when you need to learn this before you can leave. Flight field. Saddle making. Nothing else."

That actually perked Sadie up. She straightened, her eyes sparking. "So, no lectures?" she whispered to me.

"No lectures," I muttered back, rubbing my temple. "Just falling to our deaths."

Our fliers all landed in the field, so many more than when it was just Featherwing. The ground shuddered like an earthquake each time they landed. We all walked to our fliers and mounted.

"You're sluggish," she teased as I scrambled onto her back, head throbbing. *"Last night did not serve you well."*

"Neither did your sarcasm," I shot back, gripping the pommel.

"I want everyone to go up and do four laps around the entire campus ground," he shouted across the field.

She launched, wings beating hard, dragging me up into the icy morning air as my stomach lurched. Below, Micah was screaming something incoherent as Sera rolled him into a spiral, and Lorenzo was already half dangling out of Syth's saddle.

Sadie's laughter carried even over the wind, sharp and merciless. "Gods, we're pathetic!"

"Speak for yourself," I shot back at her.

One by one, fliers landed back in the field. I felt like my teeth rattled from the drastic landing Esme did. I was pretty sure she wanted me to puke.

"Today's lesson," Professor Hildegard barked, pacing the flight line with his arms behind his back, "is survival. Every Rider falls. Whether you live through it depends on your flier—and on you trusting them to catch you."

My stomach dropped. Where was he going with this?

"Since all of you are out here, each wing will be doing different maneuvers. I have asked for some aid, just in case you and your flier have ill timing. Given our current status of losing cadets left and right, we have been ordered to reduce training deaths. There are twelve Drusearon cadets and twelve Riders still on campus who are joining us. Some of them are perched in the towers, some are flying around, and some will be down here.

There are also some of the professors who are Riders or Drusearons that will be assisting us."

"I have a really bad feeling about this," Thora spouted out.

I looked around, trying to find Zane. *"Where are you?"* I finally said down the bond.

"I am in tower one, sitting on the ledge, your favorite thing to do. Watching you look like you're facing death. Trust your dragon first and then know I'll be there before you can blink."

"You will be fine. They are here to catch you if your flier doesn't. Dragon Wing will be doing spiral maneuvers. Eagle Wing will be doing sharp banks and practicing dropping and raising in the sky. Which leaves the little drunken rebels, doing my favorite part. Your fliers will be turning upside down, you will drop, and then they will fly below you to catch you. You will probably not land on the saddle the first couple times, and your flier may end up grabbing you with their talons and throwing you back up there. We will rotate when you have mostly mastered your task."

A groan rippled through Featherwing, half misery, half terror.

Micah sputtered, gripping Sera's pommel tighter. "Sir, with all due respect, I don't think I should be making life-or-death choices while still drunk."

"Excellent," Hildegard said without missing a beat. "Then maybe you'll learn faster."

Sadie snorted. Akira muttered something in Orix's ear that sounded a lot like a prayer. Lorenzo actually went pale, which was impressive considering how flushed he still was from last night.

"First up!" Hildegard bellowed, pointing at Micah. "Since you volunteered."

Micah's face went slack. "That was not volunteering!" But Sera was already launching into the sky with the kind of speed that made my stomach lurch just watching. Micah's voice echoed across the field. "This is a bad ideaaaaaaaaaa!"

From above, she spun upside down, and he let go. For a split second, he flailed wildly, arms and legs pinwheeling as the wind yanked him downward. Then Sera tucked her wings and dove, flames streaming from her tail, and snatched him midair with terrifying precision, throwing him onto his saddle.

Micah's scream of terror turned into something closer to hysterical laughter. "I'm alive!"

The rest of us groaned.

Sadie was next, and she slid off Korra with infuriating grace, arms tucked to her sides as she plummeted like she'd done this a hundred times. Korra swooped and caught her so smoothly that she was laughing by the time she landed in the saddle perfectly.

"You're insane," Akira muttered.

"Thank you," Sadie called back sweetly.

One by one we went. Lorenzo clung until Hildegard shouted at him to let go, then dropped, screaming curses the entire way until Syth snapped him up, leaving him green in the face and retching. Akira fell gracefully, Orix caught her with her landing right behind the saddle, and she moved into the saddle with ease.

Then it was my turn.

"This is insane," I told her.

"So is flying," she said, and then tipped her body hard.

The world dropped out from under me. For one terrifying heartbeat I was free-falling, air tearing at my braid, ground rushing up far too fast. My scream ripped free before I could stop it.

Then Esme's shadow engulfed me. Her claws closed with terrifying gentleness around my waist, and she flung me back into the saddle like I weighed nothing. I collapsed forward against her neck, panting, my heart hammering loud enough to drown out everything else.

"See?" she purred. *"Perfect trust."*

"Perfect heart attack," I muttered, gripping the pommel with white knuckles.

Professor Hildegard didn't look impressed. If anything, he looked bored, like watching us scream our lungs out was the most predictable thing in the world.

"Pathetic," he declared once Lorenzo finished dry-heaving over Syth's wing. "You'll never survive if you can't fall without looking like hatchlings shoved from a nest." His gaze swept the line of us, sharp as a blade. "Now, you all will fall together instead of one by one."

A collective groan rippled across the field.

"Remember there are cadets who fly themselves, as well as professors who can or have a flier. They will catch you if needed. You can catch each other if it's needed, but for the love of fucking gods, do not put yourself in danger to catch another cadet when we have capable fliers that can do it better."

I felt Esme's dark amusement curl through the bond. *At least it will be entertaining.*

Micah went sheet white. Sadie elbowed him. "Relax. If Korra doesn't catch you, maybe Esme will. Just don't flail like last time. You looked like a cat dropped in a barrel."

Micah groaned. "I am going to die."

Lorenzo, still pale and wiping his mouth, raised a hand weakly. "Sir, permission to sit out on account of imminent organ failure?"

Hildegard's expression didn't shift. "Denied."

He whistled loudly, sounding us off. Esme vaulted skyward under me, her wings snapping open with a rush of air. Around us, twenty-one other fliers launched, the sky filling with beating wings, screeches, and shouts of Riders trying not to panic.

"All at once!" Hildegard bellowed from the ground.

The signal came, and twenty-two bodies dropped like stones.

The screaming was immediate. Micah's voice cracked into something between a shriek and a laugh. Sadie actually whooped on her way down, Korra diving neatly after her. Lorenzo shouted, "gods help me," before Syth snatched him up mid-fall, only for him to promptly vomit over the side.

"Ugh, disgusting!" Akira yelled as Orix banked to avoid the spray.

Halfway down, one cadet from the Fire Platoon second squad started tumbling sideways instead of straight, arms flailing. Their dragon missed the first grab, and for a horrifying heartbeat it looked like they were done for—until Professor Quillet's dragon darted in, claws hooking them out of the air with terrifying precision.

"See?" Hildegard's voice roared from the ground. "You are only as strong as your trust. Fail, and someone else must clean up your mess!"

By the time Esme scooped me back into place, my stomach was somewhere near my boots. Micah was laughing hysterically, Akira was still swearing at Lorenzo, Sadie was grinning like a lunatic, and three cadets were retching over the sides of their fliers.

Hildegard surveyed the chaos like a warlord surveying his battlefield. "Fly up and drop again!"

And we did, for over forty minutes. My stomach was so turned, I was surprised I hadn't puked like the others. I watched so many cadets not make it back on their fliers, with Drusearons or Riders dipping in to grab them before they hit the ground. I knew I'd seen Zane at least twice grab a cadet. Thankfully, I didn't need saving, nor did anyone in my flight. In the last ten minutes, we all landed on our fliers in the saddles successfully.

Hildegard ordered each wing to swap maneuvers. We ended up flying around, doing quick drops and rises in the sky next. Nothing too extreme, which allowed my stomach to settle some. This was the flying I missed on the rare times Kim flew me. For once, I was the one who looked graceful in the sky.

This part was more about flying with our dragons, feeling comfortable on them, and flying for periods of time without breaks. When we all flew home, if everything went well, it would be a straightforward flight without any maneuvers. However, if something arose or we found ourselves in hostile territory, we needed to know how to handle the flights our fliers would need to make to get us somewhere safely.

Finally, after what felt like hours, we heard the long whistle beckoning us back. We all turned and flew back to the field, landing and making the ground shudder once more. When I slid down her leg, I felt the consequence of flying for hours, especially on a poor-quality saddle. Both of my glutes screamed in pain, my legs wobbly from the position and vibrations of Esme.

Hildegard stalked the line like a general surveying a battlefield, his boots crunching on the frosted ground. His eyes raked over us—sixty-five of us first-year Riders all sweat-soaked, standing with wobbling legs but still standing.

"I may be hard on you," he said at last, voice booming, "but you all have made me proud. You've completed a week's worth of training in four days. We have never had to push training this hard, and you all did it."

There were collective sighs, like a room finally letting go of a held breath.

"I am confident in every single one of you to fly home tomorrow. Professor Yan has informed me she and her leather workers have finished every one of your saddles." A sharp grin twitched at his mouth. "Though, knowing Yan, I suspect she had some witchy help."

That even drew a few tired laughs.

He continued, pacing slowly. "Now, your fliers will hunt for their meals. You will go eat yours. After lunch, you will report back here for saddle fitting and adjustment. Depending on how quickly we finish, you may have some downtime before dinner. Don't waste it."

Micah leaned toward me and muttered under his breath, "If downtime doesn't involve lying face-down on a mattress, I'm revolting."

I snorted, but Hildegard's gaze snapped to us instantly, sharp as a blade. We both straightened like guilty children caught stealing sweets.

Unimpressed, he went on. "After dinner, you will gather in Professor Vindex's lecture hall. It is the largest available, and we'll need it. We will review flight plans home. The twelve remaining Drusearon cadets will also be present, as they will be flying home as well, some of them on the same flight plan, and I expect cooperation."

His gaze swept over us one last time, and despite the pain in my legs and the ache in my spine, I felt something stir in my chest. We weren't perfect. Gods, half of us were still green-faced from vomiting out of the sky. But we'd survived. We'd flown. And tomorrow, we'd fly home. Well, I would be flying to Zane's... my stomach churned at that sudden reminder.

***

We breezed through lunch, most of us starving from hours of riding, not to mention most of us puked out our breakfast somewhere in the sky—well, not me, of course, but I was still starving. As soon as everyone finished, we headed to the flight field. All the leadership was preparing to leave, finishing last-minute meetings, which would make the return process go smoothly.

The flight field was cold, but the air smelled of fresh leather in the bitter wind. Tables were crowded with saddles—rows and rows of them, dark, gleaming hides stitched and tooled. They almost looked like works of art. Professor Yan stood in the center, her silver dragon standing directly behind her—over her, actually. Her scales shimmered like diamonds. I was mesmerized for a brief second. Daren lingered nearby with his golden griffin, both beasts watching with unnerving sharpness as we filed in.

Yan's gaze swept over us, sharp as a knife, though her mouth curved faintly in pride. "Every stitch, every strap has been checked. These saddles will carry you through the skies for years to come. Treat them as an extension of yourselves. Neglect them, and you neglect your life."

All of our fliers were lined up in the field, waiting for the final part of the day. Some of them were preening their feathers, some of them looked like they were utterly bored, almost asleep.

"Your last name is etched into the side of the saddle. It won't be visible when you are riding—in case you come across enemies, but it is there for when you store your saddles in the tack room, or if your flier returns without you. Please approach, find yours, and then saddle your flier."

We all walked forward to the tables. The saddles were in alphabetical order, so I quickly found mine at the beginning of the pile. I ran my finger across the "Blackcreek" that was etched into the side. It was a stunning piece of work. I picked it up and carried it to Esme, then started cinching it down.

"Too tight," Yan muttered, adjusting one buckle, smacking my hand lightly when I reached to help. "Hands off. Learn to watch before you ruin my work."

Heat flared in my cheeks, but I stayed put, watching her trim the strap until it lay flat and smooth.

Esme's hum rumbled through the bond. *This one respects the craft. I like her.*

"That makes one of us," I thought back.

Across the room, Lorenzo tried to mount Syth with his new saddle and promptly slid off the other side, hitting the ground with a grunt. Half the room erupted in laughter.

"Shut it!" he barked, rolling to his feet, though even Syth looked amused, a low rumble vibrating through the red dragon's chest.

"Perfect fit," Thora drawled, deadpan as always.

By the time all sixty-five saddles were strapped, Professor Yan and Daren walked around checking our handiwork, making slight adjustments as they went, praising some and critiquing others. Luckily for me, not only was I used to Kim's saddle, but I also rode horses, which had much smaller saddles, but saddles, nonetheless.

"You all will mount and fly around the campus for at least an hour. You need to stay within the campus airspace, but you may practice whatever maneuvers you want. Test the saddles. If anything—and I do mean anything—feels off. A cinch, a buckle, a ring, a pommel, anything feels off, let's take care of it today. You fly home tomorrow, and don't want your saddle to fail then."

"Oh, she said whatever maneuvers we want..." she sent a full laugh down the bond.

I am so fucked. I might not have puked earlier, but lunch might see itself out. Esme launched like she'd been waiting all day to show off, her wings snapping open with a thunderclap.

"Whatever maneuvers we want," she repeated through the bond, smug delight dripping from every syllable.

"Esme—please," I begged, already gripping the pommel tighter. "I just got used to my lunch staying where it belongs."

She rolled to the side without warning, the world flipping upside down, my braid smacking me in the face.

"Parvaiz above—" I choked, clinging for dear life.

Her laughter rang bright and merciless. *"You should see your face. Pure terror, it suits you."*

Across the skies, chaos reigned. Micah was already shrieking as Sera performed a corkscrew dive, his voice echoing over the rooftop. "Whyyyyy does she like thisssss?"

Sadie whooped gleefully as Korra skimmed so low over the field her talons kicked up snow.

Lorenzo looked like he was praying as Syth climbed high, then abruptly dropped in a vertical plunge that had him screaming obscenities.

"This isn't testing the saddle, it's testing my digestive system!" he bellowed as they leveled out.

From the ground, Yan and Daren craned their necks, shouting corrections up at us like furious parents. "If you puke, puke away from the leather!" and "Check the buckles, don't just scream at them!"

Esme, of course, chose that moment to snap into a steep dive, my stomach hurtling into my throat as the wind tore at my eyes. Just when I thought I'd hurl, she pulled up so sharply I nearly kissed her neck.

"Esme!" I gasped, half laughing, half gagging. "This is not funny!"

"It's hilarious," she corrected, smug as ever.

By the end of the hour, the sky was littered with cadets—some grinning ear-to-ear, others hanging limply like half-dead ragdolls. All of our saddles stood the test of our wild fliers. At least four had landed early, one clutching his stomach, another pale and trembling.

Esme landed with a triumphant snap of her wings, lowering herself so I could slide off. My legs hit the ground like wet noodles, and I grabbed her foreleg for balance, groaning.

Micah stumbled past, his face green. "I really hope they don't do this to us tomorrow..."

"We absolutely will not. It's only fun when we're training. Trust me, we all get a good laugh—well, except Korra, she's a quiet one," she shot down the bond before taking off.

Sadie smirked, still glowing with adrenaline. "Speak for yourself. That was the best hour of my life."

I groaned again. "I hate you."

CHAPTER 46

Our downtime before dinner turned out to be actual downtime, except we weren't allowed to venture beyond the courtyard. Even though my father had cleared everyone, we were still being watched unless it was lights out. Tables had been brought in so we could sit and talk.

Lili, Alex, Eleanor, and the other Platoon Leaders walked into the courtyard, drawing everyone's attention. "All Flight Guides, come with us," Eleanor announced.

Michalova, Laderra, Aeltharion, and I—along with the others from Dragon Wing and Eagle Wing—stood and moved toward them, exchanging quick glances. We followed them into Dining Hall One, where the rest of cadet leadership already sat. Scullin and Kamban were present as well.

"Thanks for coming in," Kamban said. "Everyone in this room has been read in and is aware of what will occur when cadets arrive back. Cadets are due on January fifth. Everyone here returns on the third. We'll go over perimeter details to ensure every cadet is vetted."

Scullin stepped up beside him. "Does everyone understand? Questions?"

Silence stretched a few heartbeats.

"Alright then," Scullin said. "Rider cadets and Drusearon cadet leaders report to Captain Vindex's room. The rest of you—the only train coming through tomorrow arrives at zero-nine hundred. Don't miss it. Dismissed."

We filed out to the courtyard where cadets clustered at tables or stood in groups. Corson strode in front of us.

"Riders, listen up—we're going to Vindex's classroom. It's time to discuss flight plans—"

"I thought we were doing that after dinner?" a Rider from another wing cut in.

"We were," Corson said, "but we have time now. Dinner is in an hour. After you eat, pack and be ready to leave at zero-six hundred." He motioned to the Alpha side, and we headed in.

All eighty-nine of us—sixty-five first-years, twelve Rider cadet leaders, and twelve Drusearon cadet leaders—packed into Professor Vindex's classroom. It was large, but with all of us, it felt full. A wall-sized map of Yebel hung at the front. My gaze drifted, as it always did, to Winterhand Stronghold—then slid northeast to Ashwynd, where Zane's family lived, where the duke of the Veil of Vultures lived.

Professor Hildegard stood poised at the front. Of course, he was helping organize. Flying was his domain. "We're breaking this into sections by destination province. Once your plan is set, you can head to the dining facility." He turned to the map and tapped Veskonia, the southeastern province. "If you're going to Central or West Veskonia, eastern Esten, or Fort Dasyn, come forward."

Eighteen cadets stepped up. He held out a quill pen. "Circle your destination unless you're bound for Dasyn."

Three were from Feather Wing—two of those to Dasyn—seven from Dragon Wing, five from Eagle Wing. One by one, they marked villages. Six were going to Dasyn. Most others aimed for border towns, which made sense. Veskonia had more Shapeshifters, and deep Veskonia could be less welcoming to other Fae. Kalona, a coastal fort with a Shapeshifter majority, remained heavily guarded, and nearby towns were friendlier. The beaches were spectacular. It had always been one of my favorites to visit.

Hildegard worked their routes, pairing them into travel groups—some splitting only near the end. He reminded everyone that forts, outposts, and encampments had Riders or Drusearons on air patrol and had already expanded their patrol zones to support returning cadets—standard for leave periods. Once they had their orders, they filed out. Seventy-one of us remained.

Hildegard circled a finger over the map. "Northern Veskonia and south-central Eastvwyth?"

Fifteen cadets stepped forward—only one Drusearon. Michalova and Lorenzo were part of this group. Two would go to Coastal Camp Echo, including Robert. If I could be a fly on the wall when he got home... it had come out that his "Rider father" wasn't his father. That affair explained why the tincture didn't work for him. The rest of the villages were scattered across the region. The lone Drusearon headed for Mid-Eastvwyth. Hildegard reviewed their plans and gave a sharp reminder not to fly directly over the fliers' vale—no need to stir tempers.

"Next up, western Esten or Cliana?" he called.

Fifteen stood—eight to Cliana, seven to Esten. It was oddly grounding to see where classmates actually called home. Many still had at least one parent in uniform, forever moving. Micah circled Whisper Outpost on the Esten/Cliana border.

Lili and Alex marked Zion Outpost, the same as my father this rotation—another border post. Three cadets were bound for Lakish Outpost on the coast, with a planned stop at Zion.

"If you're going to Glonia—or any towns between the college and Glonia—step up," he said to the forty-one still seated. Nineteen moved, leaving twenty-two for the Veil of Vultures.

"Anyone bound for the far north—Winterhand Stronghold or beyond?" he asked the Glonia group.

Four raised hands. "Rejoin the Veil group—you'll travel with them." Thora and Akira were two of those. They returned to us with two from Eagle Wing.

He ran the Glonia plans quickly—six to villages beyond the mountains. Several to Fort Nemlina in central Glonia, the third largest post on the continent. One to Hallowford, a large city south of the river on the mountainside. Hildegard shifted that cadet to our Veil group—it made more sense for the route.

Finally, our turn. Sixteen Riders and eleven Drusearons—including Zane—gathered at the front. The Veil of Vultures sprawled across most of Yebel's north. Some of us would fly east, others west. Zane and I would go to Ashwynd, a large city north of Winterhand Stronghold on the far western side.

"This is the largest cohort—maybe I should have started with the Veil," Hildegard said with a quick chuckle. "We've got four to Winterhand and one to Hallowford. Who else is headed west, toward Ashwynd?"

Remus, Oliver, Eli, Sadie, Landon, Nikolai, Arya, Zane, me, and four more raised hands together. A surprising concentration of leadership.

"Two, four, six, eight, ten, twelve, fourteen, sixteen, eighteen—eighteen of you," he counted. "That's a lot of bodies in one path."

"Staggered departures, like years past?" Nikolai Corson asked. As a fourth-year, he'd done this before.

"Yes," Hildegard said, rubbing his jaw. "Normally, the week prior, everyone submits destinations and preferred companions. We pair groups of two to five with timed departures. Given the circumstances, we're condensing on the fly."

He pointed to the four going to Winterhand and the Hallowford Rider. "You five will fly together, stop in Hallowford, then the four continue on. Depart at zero-five-thirty. Winterhand's air-patrol will extend almost to Hallowford. If you run into trouble, your fliers will call for assistance."

He scanned the remaining thirteen of us. "Let's do Mooring, Haladega, Corson, Devins, Bosmini, and Blackcreek."

"Respectfully, sir, Blackcreek and I will remain together," Zane said before Hildegard could name the second group.

Hildegard narrowed his eyes, forehead creasing.

"You can switch me with Mooring," Zane continued, "which keeps the same balance—four Riders and two Drusearons. And one group doesn't need three Wing Commanders. Too many cooks in the kitchen."

"Reason?" Hildegard asked, still glaring at him like he was a thorn in his side.

"She's my partner, and we're going to the same location. If you have further questions, direct them to General Blackcreek." Zane's tone carried so much authority it made my heart skip. He met Hildegard's stare head-on, daring him to push back.

"Alright. Then we'll do Braegon, Haladega, Corson, Devins, Bosmini, and Blackcreek. Haladega and Corson will be in charge as Wing Commanders."

He went on to explain that the remaining seven would form the second group. Ours would depart at zero-five-forty-five, theirs at zero-six-hundred. We were to follow the river north to the town of Blackmere and rest there. Once the second group arrived, we would continue east.

There was a vale between Winterhand Stronghold and Ashwynd where our fliers would stay when not in use. We were discouraged from flying beyond transit, though.

Esme grumbled down the bond, *"Pshhh. We'll be exploring."*

I smiled faintly.

Hildegard assured us patrol coverage would be strong in the region. He also gave return plans, since many of us were expected back early. We'd fly home in slightly different groups.

One cadet voiced what I was wondering. "Why not put us in the groups we'll be returning with?"

"That's a fair question," Hildegard said. "Among you, thirteen, there are four Wing Commanders—two Riders, two Drusearons. Then, there is an Executive Officer, three Platoon Leaders, and one first-Flight Guide. That makes nine returning early. Which leaves four first-year Riders. If we grouped strictly by return schedule, those four would fly there alone. I'd rather their first real journey home include experienced leaders."

It made sense. None of us wanted new Riders flying solo if it could be helped. There would be plenty of cadets already traveling alone.

Our group was dismissed, leaving the last cohort to go over their plans. My stomach rumbled. Food and sleep—those were the only things I wanted before tomorrow's long flight.

Zane walked behind me, his hand light at the small of my back. The gentle touch grounded me. I hadn't realized how tense I was until I finally exhaled. He rubbed up and down my spine, sensing it. Gods, he was the best.

***

Dining Hall Two was already full when we slipped inside, noise rattling the rafters. With most of the campus emptied, Riders claimed the space like wolves with a carcass—loud, restless, ravenous.

Trays clattered. Voices overlapped. Laughter rang sharp, more relief than joy. Training was done. Saddles fitted. Departure close. Feather Wing grabbed a table at the center. Micah piled his tray so high it hid his face—until Lorenzo "accidentally" jostled his elbow and half of it toppled.

"You menace!" Micah wailed, clutching his bread roll like it was his last meal.

"You'll live." Lorenzo grinned, snagging a potato while Micah was distracted.

Akira groaned, shoving her tray between them. "If you two start another food war, I swear by the God of Wymond I'll throw you both out the window."

Sadie lifted her goblet high, smirking. "To Wymond—may they save us from Micah's whining!"

The table howled. Even Thora cracked a smile before hiding it behind her mug.

Around us, chaos spread. At Eagle Wing's table, someone pounded a rhythm, cadets slamming cups in time. Dragon Wing roared back with a call-and-response that rattled the hall until even the professors gave up silencing it.

Esme rumbled in my chest, amused. *"Your kind sings like carrion birds fighting over scraps. Yet... it stirs something."*

"It's called tradition," I thought back, grinning.

Zane slid onto the bench beside me, his arm brushing mine. He didn't join the shouting, but the corner of his mouth curved faintly as he watched.

"Enjoying yourself?" I teased.

"Not really." He dropped his voice so only I heard. "But I like seeing you laugh."

Heat rushed to my cheeks. I ducked, spooning stew before anyone noticed. For a heartbeat, tomorrow didn't exist. Tonight, we were loud. Reckless. Alive.

***

The noise still rang in my ears when I closed my chamber door later. I packed clothes beside the med bag my mother had given me. My body ached, my stomach was too full, and my head still buzzed with laughter. Esme was already settled in the vale. I collapsed onto my bed with a groan.

"You look dead."

I nearly jumped out of my skin. Zane sat at my desk, shadows clinging like armor. Far too comfortable for someone who'd broken into my room.

"You could warn me," I hissed, hand on my chest.

"I could," he said flatly. "But this was priceless. I've got a dark streak."

"You're insufferable."

His smirk softened as he leaned forward, elbows on his knees. "Tomorrow," he said quietly. "You'll meet my family."

My stomach clenched. "Ashwynd. The duke. Your siblings. Fuck, that's a lot. I might need a refresher."

"My father's informal with family. My mother will love you. Names are Aeliana, Theodora or Thea, Arkin, Helena, Adrian, and Elizabeth. Don't be nervous. I'll be holding your hand."

I laughed harshly. "Nervous? Zane, your father is the Duke of the Veil of Vultures. Your family lives in a city named for ash and wind. Mine lives in secrets and lies. Meeting them isn't going to be easy."

His expression softened more, shadows yielding to warmth. "They'll see you as I do."

"I hope so."

He leaned closer, voice dropping low, the bond carrying it like a vow. "Tomorrow they'll know. You're mine. You belong with me."

My breath caught. For once, I didn't argue. I only whispered, "And if they don't approve?"

Zane's jaw flexed, storm-dark eyes steady. "Their approval doesn't matter. But I doubt it'll be an issue. One last thing..."

"Yes?"

"There may be... possibly... a painted picture of you in my room."

I blinked. "What?"

"Don't panic. My aunt had precognition. She knew you were coming—knew I had a mate. She drew what she saw. I kept it as a reminder that my true love was out there, waiting."

"I... don't even have words."

"You just spoke some." His laugh was nervous, boyish.

I stared at him, floored. Why hadn't he told me before? Not bad—just overwhelming.

"Do I get to stay in your room?"

He held my gaze, sharp as steel. "Do you not want to?"

"No, I do. I just didn't think it was allowed."

"We aren't married, so technically... but my whole family knows about the vision and the drawing. They'll know who you are. They won't object."

"They're going to recognize me?"

"Very likely."

"Oh, this is going to be weird."

"It won't. They'll be glad I found you. My greatest fear was finding you too late—when we were old."

I snorted. "That's funny."

"You and Aeliana will have plenty to giggle about. She'll arm you with stories about me."

I laughed softly, easing. "Back to what I was getting at... if we're in the same room—"

"I'll be fucking you. Every. Single. Night."

"Is the picture going to be staring at me?" The ridiculousness broke me into laughter. Tears streaked my face. He laughed too, harder than I'd seen.

"We'll turn it around. Or move it elsewhere."

He chuckled, then pulled me into his lap, kissing my hair and cheek. The simple gesture melted me further.

"I want more," he whispered, "but we need sleep. Tomorrow will be long."

"Would you have normally roved?"

"Actually, yes. But not the full distance. I have destinations I can rove to, like the cavern outside Blackmere.

"Then why not—"

"If I can't take you, I'll fly beside you. Esme wouldn't approve of flying alone. And it would expose my ability too easily."

"He is right—that would not happen." She purred. Always interjecting.

"How long is the flight?"

"Eight to nine hours. Mixed group means we fly at the slowest pace—probably Sadie's griffin. After six hours, even Remus and I will slow. Blackmere's about five hours in. Your Wing Commander's dragon is fast, but he's used to pacing mixed groups."

"Got it. Long day. We'll get there around two or three."

"Enough time for a nap." He winked. "And a shower."

"A napppp and a showeerrr," I repeated, mocking his emphasis.

He laughed, which made me laugh harder. He lifted me to the bed, and we curled together, my ear on his chest, memorizing every beat of his heart.

CHAPTER 47

The morning arrived far too fucking fast. They started knocking on doors at zero five hundred to wake cadets. Dining Hall Two opened for early meals before departure. Everyone watched the grandfather clock, ensuring plenty of food and time for last-minute packing.

The campus remained cloaked in shadow as we started gathering on the flight field. Breath steamed in the cold dawn. Professors were stationed around the field, checking groups and departure times. Boots scraped frost, leather straps creaked, and low, restless rumbles from eager fliers filled the air.

Esme's silver-blue eye swiveled to me the instant my steps reached the clearing, wings stretching wide with a ground-shivering snap. *"Are you ready, my little Rider?"*

Movement around us continued with quiet efficiency. Sadie muttered at Korra, who snapped her beak at Cassia Mooring's braid. Zane's golden hair already looked windswept, posture calm as if nothing unusual unfolded. Corson worked with his red dragon, securing gear. Landon stood beside him, giving neck scratches to his phoenix. Remus and Zane looked like they could be relatives, though Remus stood taller by several inches and had longer, wavy blond hair.

Other Riders moved around us, groups preparing, things tucked into saddlebags. Drusearons checked that knapsacks were secured. Micah yawned while tightening Sera's cinches. Lili gave alternate scratches to Veyra.

A hard swallow, reality hit—flying wasn't exercise. We were headed home.

Or, whatever counted as home.

Hildegard's voice carried over the field, less bark and more steel. "Zero five forty-five departures, you have five minutes before you take to the sky. Remember your route. Stop at Blackmere. Wait for the second group to join you. Do not deviate. If something feels wrong, trust your fliers."

Esme crouched low, anticipation rumbling while I swung into the saddle. Leather pinched, unfamiliar yet properly fitted. Churning nerves tangled with leftover stew. Fingers curled round the pommel, thighs clamped tight. The other three Riders mounted. All of us made final adjustments. Zane stood below, and Remus waited on the far side of Corson's red dragon.

"Fly safe," Jameson called as he tightened another strap.

"Try not to puke on anyone again," Sadie shouted at Lorenzo, who had only groaned and made a half-hearted hand gesture in response.

"I love you, Auriella!" Lili yelled a few fliers over to me.

"I love you, too!" I yelled back.

"Aw, so heartwarming, going to make Zane jealous." Eli snapped. He was in the group behind us.

It had been the perfect send-off—chaos, laughter, and nerves tangled together.

"You're off!" Hildegard stated, pointing to our group.

Esme surged forward, wings slicing the air as we leapt into the gray dawn sky. The ground fell away, the campus shrinking beneath us.

We left, and I couldn't pin down how to feel. Nerves twisted tight in my gut, but excitement pulsed right beside them.

Cold air bit hard above the tree line, wind slicing through my jacket, stinging my cheeks raw. Beneath me, Esme's wings beat in steady rhythm, each downstroke driving us higher until the campus shrank into a shadow behind us.

Our group drew together fast. Zane drifted close, his silhouette black against the pale sky, every glide smooth as if the wind itself bent for him. Landon came in with his phoenix, flames licking her wingtips, trails of heat shimmering across the currents. Corson's red dragon held lower, crimson scales flashing with what little sunlight broke through. Remus, like Zane, flew alone, his Drusearon wings stretched wide and steady. Sadie's griffin cut sharp, Korra's shriek splitting the air and sending a flock scattering from the trees below.

Micah hadn't been with us this time, but his absence meant quiet.

"Remind me," Sadie called over the wind, her braid whipping behind her, "why exactly are we flying in the frozen-ass dawn? Couldn't we have waited for the sun to come out?"

"Less likely to be targets, but more importantly, so we arrive during the day, and before dinner." Nikolai barked back, his dragon snorting steam. "Arriving at Forts at night as a drift, makes everyone edgy."

"Less likely targets?" Landon wheezed. His phoenix banked hard, fire trailing in her wake. "Yeah, sure. I'm a flying torch. Real subtle. No one's ever gonna notice me up here."

"Agreed," Sadie laughed. "We could probably see you from across the continent."

Esme rumbled in my head, *"he's not wrong. He burns like a beacon. Though, that's the choice she makes. At least I am elegant in my shadow."*

"Elegant?" I shot back. "You nearly dumped me on the ground thirty minutes ago."

"Gracefully," she corrected, and I could feel her smirk.

"Wing Commander Corson—" I started.

"While we are away from campus, I am simply Nikolai to you," he shot a look at Sadie and then Landon, "you two as well."

"Alright—Nikolai—where are you from?"

"Where. Are. We. Going?" He said with such confusion, as if I was expected to know his origins.

"So, from Ashwynd?"

"Yes, on the outskirts, but yes. Ror—Zane and I actually grew up together."

I shot a look at Zane. *"You never told me that."*

"I mean if I told you everything, it would take months and months... there's entirely too much."

"He almost called you Roarke."

"That he did, and yes, he knows."

"Clearly, you didn't know. Over the last few years, we haven't been as close, been busy in different branches both leading, but I will always be a Drusearon at heart."

I think my eyes bugged out of my head. Holy shit, he was one of the few Drusearons that had been born with mixed Fae parents, leaving him without wings.

"Wow... yeah, I didn't know, and I didn't know that either."

He shot me a smile and looked forward. Nikolai's composure was always maintained with discipline. A more relaxed version hadn't been witnessed before. Countless questions were held back about his missing wings, curiosity stifled to avoid prying. Landon had also been a Drusearon, born without wings, whose mother was a Sorcerer.

The wind tore at my braid as we leveled out into steady flight. The horizon stretched wide and pale, the world below nothing but a smear of frost-tipped trees and the winding river we were following northwest.

"Formation's sloppy," Remus growled, his voice carrying easily across the space between us. His broad black wings flexed once, shifting into position like it was the easiest thing in the world. "If this were a real patrol, we'd already be attacked."

"Thank you for the encouragement," Sadie shot back, patting Korra's neck as the griffin shrieked loud enough to make her point. "Always inspiring."

"Better harsh truth than a funeral," Remus said.

"Gods, you two sound like my parents," Landon groaned, his phoenix flaring a plume of gold fire that arced across the sky. "And before you say it—yes, I'm still single, no, I don't need the lecture."

Nikolai's laugh rolled out across the air, low and sharp. "Still single because no sane female wants to spend her evenings smelling like burnt feathers."

"Better burnt than brooding," Landon shot back, tilting his phoenix into a cocky half-roll. "Tell me, Nikolai, do you practice looking like a storm cloud, or does it come naturally?"

"Natural talent," Nikolai said, without missing a beat. His dragon's wings beat once, hard, sending a gust that rocked Landon sideways.

Sadie cackled. "Oh, that's rich. The Wing Commander is taking cheap shots."

"Not cheap," Nikolai said, his grin flashing. "Instructional."

I bit my lip to hide my laugh, tightening my grip as Esme banked lazily into their draft. She rumbled along our bond, *this is what Riders do—fight, boast, compare scars. Always trying to prove who has the sharpest tongue.*

"And you're enjoying it," I thought.

"Immensely."

Zane hadn't said much, but I felt his presence steady in the bond, calm and watchful. He moved a little ahead of us, wings stretched wide, the early light sparking across their dark span.

"Silent as ever," Nikolai called toward him, his tone edged with familiarity. "Not going to join in? Or do you think we're beneath you, as usual?"

Zane hadn't turned. "I think you all waste too much breath."

That earned a chorus of groans and laughter, and Sadie nearly choked on it. "Gods, he's impossible," she said, shaking her head.

But her grin told me the same thing Esme had already whispered in my head—this had been the rhythm of a drift. Rough edges, sharp tongues, and trust woven through it all.

The wind cut sharply across my face, Esme gliding smoothly and effortlessly beneath me. We'd been flying steady for a while when Remus's voice rang out over the air, loud enough to cut through the roar of wings. "Formation. Arrowhead. Now."

My stomach dropped.

That word was last heard months ago in a chalk-dust classroom, diagrams arranged neatly on Bhatta's board. Arrows and dotted lines were drawn, nothing resembling this moment—no sky, no wind, and no real lives placed in the balance.

Nikolai's dragon angled cleanly into place beside Remus, the red scales gleaming in the pale light. "Zane and Remus on point," Nikolai shouted back, his voice cutting across the slipstream. "Sadie, you're behind Zane, center right. Blackcreek, rear right. Landon, center left. My dragon will hold the rear left."

Sadie laughed nervously, gripping her pommel. "To be clear—I'm not actually steering anything. If Korra decides she wants to perch on a chimney, that's on her."

"Pray she doesn't," Nikolai barked.

"Not comforting!" Landon shouted from behind, his phoenix scattering sparks as it beat its wings harder. "You know I've only ever seen this drawn in ink, right? Never done it in real life?"

"None of you have," Remus said. "That's the point. Now shut up and hold your damn places."

Esme rumbled beneath me, *"he acts like this is difficult. I know exactly where I belong."*

"Great," I thought. *"Shame I don't."*

The fliers had done the work—Korra tucking in neatly behind Zane's dark wings, Sera's golden fire settling into the rear center, Esme slid sharply to the left of Sadie without hesitation. I clung to the saddle, heart hammering, terrified I'd somehow ruin it even though I hadn't actually been the one flying.

And then I felt it.

The air shifted. Suddenly, the sky seemed... smoother. Our six fliers cut through the wind like one creature, the arrowhead shape slicing the currents apart.

Sadie let out a low whistle. "Oh. Okay. That actually feels... kind of incredible."

"Efficient," Remus said, his tone clipped but approving.

"Sexy," Landon crowed immediately.

"Idiotic," Nikolai shot back, though his dragon's wings twitched as if amused.

Zane said calmly and steadily. "Hold your lines. Save your jokes for the ground."

Which, naturally, had only made Sadie snicker harder. "Is he always this... dominating?" she shot at me.

I gripped the saddle tighter, unable to stop the grin that tugged at my mouth, saying nothing.

Maybe we had merely been passengers strapped to predators who knew better than we did. Maybe this had been the first time I'd actually felt what Bhatta's neat diagrams meant. It had been quite impressive to fly and be a part of a drift. It had been a glimmer of the future, the one very far away.

We held the formation longer than I thought possible, six fliers slicing the wind in perfect rhythm. My nerves began to ebb, replaced by something steadier, almost exhilarating.

Zane's voice cut across the air, calm but carrying. "Blackmere ahead."

I squinted into the distance. At first, it had barely been a smudge along the riverbank, smoke curling thin and gray into the pale winter sky. The outlines sharpened—wooden rooftops huddled close together, a spire poking above them, the wide gleam of water splitting the land in two.

The fliers adjusted without needing instruction, banking into a gradual descent. The air grew heavier, the river scent sharp and cold in my lungs.

Sadie whooped as Korra tucked her wings for a sharper dive, feathers flashing silver in the light. "Finally! If I don't get off soon, I'm going to be one with this saddle."

"Better than falling off it," Remus called back dryly, his voice a low rumble.

Landon's phoenix flared with a streak of fire as they leveled. "Remus, has anyone ever told you you're a joy to fly with?"

"Yes," Remus said. "And they were lying."

Everyone let out a chuckle. Nikolai's dragon rumbled in amusement, a sound that vibrated through the air as they dipped lower. "Enough chatter.

Eyes on the ground. Follow the river curve—we'll set down in the clearing south of the bridge," Nikolai commanded.

The river widened beneath us, dark and glassy, flowing fast between its banks. Wooden barges dotted the current, their crews pausing to stare upward as wings blotted out the sun. The closer we got, the more faces tilted skyward—villagers spilling from doors.

Esme's wings flared wide, rippling snow over the patchy fields, a landing made in a rush of displaced air that rattled nearby trees. I clung to the saddle to as she crouched low, steady as stone beneath me. The others thudded down around us, one by one. Nikolai's dragon shook her wings, and snow scattered across the ground. Korra was seen stalking forward, feathers ruffled with predator's grace, drawing delighted squeals from watching children before they darted behind their parents. Zane and Remus set down last, wings folded in perfect unison, each standing poised in silence.

The villagers gathered in a cautious half-circle, whispering among themselves. Some bowed their heads. Others crossed their arms tightly.

"Lovely welcoming committee," Sadie said, sliding down Korra's side.

"Better stares than arrows," Nikolai said, his tone edged but amused.

Esme's eyes swiveled toward me, bluer and sharper, *They look at us as if we are gods."*

I rubbed her neck as I slid stiffly down. Legs wobbled as boots struck frozen earth. The saddle creaked solidly behind me.

Blackmere wasn't home. Simply a stop on the journey. Yet, after hours above the ground with nerves stretched thin, the scent of woodsmoke and fresh bread drifted from the village was salvation. Once we dismounted our fliers, they launched into the sky, hunting for their own meals in the woods—deer, panthers, whatever could be caught. Riders clustered together, walking into town as a close group.

A few heads turned, a couple of children pointed skyward, then life in the little town carried on. Buckets were hauled from the well. Carts creaked along the cobblestones. Smoke curled from chimneys.

"Everyone here is nice. This is a common stopping ground for fliers and Drusearons. There is some small shopping if you want. The little shop in the center has delish fresh-baked bread and thick soup that we all drool about…”

“Bread?” Sadie perked up immediately, Korra’s feather still tangled in her hair. “Gods, why didn’t you lead with that?”

“Because I wanted to see which of you would faint from hunger first,” Nikolai said dryly, then started down the cobbled lane without waiting.

We followed in a tight group, boots crunching over patches of ice, our breaths puffing in the cool air. The shop hadn’t been much—a squat stone building with a painted sign of a loaf and a ladle swinging gently above the door. But the smell that hit us when we pushed inside nearly knocked me flat—yeast, broth, and roasting meat, warm enough to melt the frost from our coats.

The female behind the counter didn’t so much as blink at us, just pointed to a chalkboard and asked, “beef or root vegetable?”

“Both,” Landon said, already fumbling for coins.

We crowded the small space, leaning against walls and benches, cradling steaming bowls and fat sandwiches wrapped in paper. The bread was crusty and warm, the soup thick and spiced, the meat salty and tender.

Sadie bit into hers and made a sound that turned more than a few heads. “This is better than the Fall Solstice dinner.”

“Blasphemy,” Landon said through a mouthful of bread. “But accurate.”

Even Remus was eating in silence, a gesture as close to praise as any could receive from him. No attention was drawn to our group—no gawking villagers, no fearful whispers. Only good food was served, warm air warmed us, and a quiet hum drifted through a village where wings had been witnessed overhead too often to impress any longer.

Esme’s bond had grown faint in my chest, content and distant. *“You eat. I hunt. We both return full.”*

“I really don’t want to hear about your hunting while I am eating.”

I tore off another hunk of bread and dipped it into the broth. For a moment, it was easy to pretend we were just travelers, nothing more. Just hungry cadets in a river town for lunch.

By the time we finished, we scraped the bowls clean, and only crumbs remained of the sandwiches. The shopkeeper didn't linger over us—just collected our empty bowls, set them aside, and went back to kneading dough as though Riders and Drusearons eating at her counter was the most ordinary thing in the world.

Nikolai wiped his hands on his napkin and stood, voice clipped. "On your feet. We leave as soon as the others arrive."

We filed out into the crisp air, the cobbled street slick with frost. The sky above had already begun to dim to a bruised gray, with smoke from the chimneys. It hadn't been long before the second group appeared at the far end of the street, boots crunching on ice, breath misting in the cold. Mooring led them, her pale hair stark against the dark of her cloak. Oliver and Arya flanked her, with Eli just behind, his stride deliberate and steady. Three younger Riders followed, looking flushed from flight, eyes bright with the lingering rush of it.

"Look who finally caught up," Sadie called, smirking.

"Someone has to keep the rear safe," Eli shot back smoothly, though his grin betrayed the sting of the long flight.

Oliver clapped Zane's shoulder as they passed. "Family feast tonight?"

"Of course, my mom will be excited to host us all again," he said.

Nikolai gave them the faintest nod. "Eat. Rest. Don't dawdle."

And that was it. No lingering. No long goodbyes. Just two groups of Riders passing one another.

We turned down toward the river, our boots crunching in unison, the path widening into open ground. Ahead, the fields gave way to the frozen bend of the Blackmere, glittering silver in the late morning light. Beyond it lay endless dark trees and the long stretch north.

Esme's presence thrummed warm against me, her voice amused, *"you have eaten. I have hunted. Now we fly, my little Rider."*

I pulled my flight coat tighter against the wind as we neared the clearing where the fliers were already waiting, wings folded, eyes sharp.

Our rest was over. It was time to retake the sky.

We left Blackmere with the sun overhead, the river flashing silver beneath, fliers pushed toward the west, and mountains as a destination. Air brought sharpness, cold pressing into lungs, refusing release. The early flight offered an open sky and steady current. Further west, conditions shifted, and less forgiveness was found.

Mountains rose, jagged stone crowned with snow, ridges stark in noon light. Air was funneled in bursts, crosswinds striking without warning.

Esme moved forward, wings spread wide, as more effort was required to counter the gusts. My thighs burned from keeping my seat in the saddle, and leather creaked as air pushed sideways.

Silence replaced laughter and jokes. Sadie was pressed low over Korra, griffin feathers flattened in the pass. Landon's phoenix no long held flames on her wings. Zane and Remus maintained the lead, wings cutting through turbulence. Nikolai's dragon matched their pace, sharp banking and keen observation.

Below, ravines cut the mountains, shadows swallowing ground. From above, cracks in the world revealed beauty.

Esme's voice brushed through the bond, low and particular, *"Eyes forward, little Rider. The air is treacherous here. Trust me."*

I forced a hard swallow down, gaze fixed on Zane's silhouette ahead. He didn't show any falter in the strong gusts. The flight northwest was long but steady. Westward flight proved shorter, but it demanded every resource—wingbeat, breath, and focus. Silence had consumed us.

Sunlight reflected off the snowcaps, and the air thinned as the passage through the mountains deepened. The wind howled, pushing against wings, the cold clawed as we flew through.

"Stay tight!" Nikolai barked, his dragon banking sharply against a gust. "Keep your spacing, don't drift!"

Esme surged beneath me, wings driving hard. I pressed low against her neck, heart hammering. Sadie and Landon had been on each side, their griffin and phoenix cutting steady lines—until the crosswind hit.

Screaming wind came down the ridge, delivering brutal force to our fliers. Esme skidded sideways, her claws scraped stone. Korra's shriek was heard, narrowly avoided tumbling into me.

And then—Landon's phoenix folded.

"Daphhhhneeee!" Esme shrieked through the bond.

The red-orange phoenix screamed as the gust tore its wings inward. Landon pitched forward in the saddle, hands clawing for the pommel, but the strap snapped like a string.

"Landon!" I shouted. My voice was lost to the wind.

The phoenix tumbled, fire sputtering. Landon's scream tore across the mountains as he fell—first tangled in flames, slowly gone in the abyss below. His body shattered on the rocks far beneath us, a smear of color against the snow.

The phoenix's death cry followed. Wings crumpled, body blazing, it struck the cliffs in a burst of fire so bright the world went white.

Then silence.

My breath caught. My stomach heaved. I wanted to dive after him, but Esme's voice cut sharp through the bond, *"do not break, he is gone. We will mourn his loss later."*

"Focus, Auri. We will stop as soon as we can." Zane spoke to me.

"Hold!" Remus thundered, his black wings steady as stone. "Keep formation, or you'll join him!"

We held. Gods, we held. The pass funneled narrower, each of us flying while trying to hold our composure, holding the line.

Then—light.

From the ash below, fire was whirled upward, swirling into a new form. A red phoenix was released, wings spread wider and brighter than anything witnessed before, its cry split the sky like a trumpet. It was lifted on a column of heat, rebirth achieved in flame and glory.

But the saddle was lost.

And Landon was gone.

The phoenix circled once, a keening note sent out that left hollowness behind. Wings were tucked, and a dive sent westward. The bird was swallowed between the peaks—a streak of fire erased by the horizon.

"She will rejoin us once she mourns her Rider," Esme reassured me.

The silence in the drift had been heavier than the wind.

I clenched the pommel until my knuckles whitened, blinking hard against the sting in my eyes.

Landon was gone.

Daphne would mourn him for the rest of her years.

At last, we were spat from the mountains. Wind eased, stony walls slipped behind, and a broad sweep of pale sky opened above. Our group was left forever altered.

An orange-golden blaze was seen rising behind—Daphne soared, slicing through cold air with haunting, terrifying grace. Her cry rang out, high and mournful. Intense grief poured through her voice.

She slipped quietly back into formation, the molten glow of her feathers casting a shadow across the silent group. No words were spoken, but every gaze flicked her way, to the space Landon once filled.

Esme's hum rumbled low in my chest, *"the phoenix knows. She will stay with the drift, but the Rider is gone."*

We flew on in heavy silence, the air biting colder with every wingbeat. Finally, Nikolai's dragon angled down toward a clearing on the mountainside—a patch of hard snow cut with dark stone, barely wide enough for all of us to land.

"Down," he barked, his voice low, clipped. "We stop here."

Descent was made, one by one. Snow crunched beneath Esme's claws, and sharp, cold air forced through my boots as we reached the ground. My legs wobbled as exhaustion and a chest-tightening weight combined. Korra landed next, and Sadie slipped down stiffly, her face pale and determined. Remus's black wings were folded as he stood nearby, tall and silent. Zane landed on the frozen ground, his expression hardened, unreadable.

Daphne landed away from the group, talons pressed into icy snow. She spread her wings wide, flames flickering through crisp air, then folded in, embers fading. Her golden eyes appeared full of sorrow. She emitted pain that we all felt across the field.

We all stood in silence. Only breath and the faint crackle of phoenix fire broke the stillness. Zane came up behind me and wrapped his arms tight around me.

After what felt like several minutes, Sadie broke the silence. "I can't believe—" She'd stopped, jaw clenching hard. "He was just here."

Nikolai's gaze was sharp, but not cruel. "He knew the risks, we all do. Death doesn't negotiate. It only collects."

"That doesn't make it easier," I said, my voice rougher than I meant.

Zane ran his arm down mine, grounding me. He hadn't said anything, but the bond pulsed warm, steady. He knew just what I needed without saying it. It was more than I could ever ask for.

"Ashes don't ask, they simply remain," Esme said.

We sat in silence a while longer, the phoenix's glow casting long shadows across the snow. Landon was gone. But Daphne was still with us, flames now embers, soaring because that was what she was born to do. We had only been bonded with our fliers for a short time, but the bond nestled deep within Rider and flier.

Nikolai ordered us to carry on, not wanting the group behind to close the gap. Sadie and I mounted our fliers, and the formation shifted gradually. Zane and Remus stayed in front, guiding the group. Sadie settled far left, my position was set in the middle left, Nikolai took the middle right, and Daphne was on the far right. This time, Nikolai didn't give any command. Esme relayed the order from Nikolai's dragon, Inna.

Remus maintained his quietness. When he broke his silence, surprise jolted through me. "We are thirty minutes out, we will land on the east outskirts of the city. Afterwards, your fliers can go above the skyline, and head to Ashen Vale."

"I can be back there quickly, if you need me," she purred to me.

"I am sure that Zane won't let anything happen to me."

"He better not, or he will be a toasted bat."

"ESME!" Sometimes she really caught me off guard.

There was a stable on the outskirts of the city, where we could obtain horses to ride into town. However, Zane told me, we would either fly or rove. Nikolai revealed that he lived near where we were landing, and he would simply walk to his father's home.

Sadie lived on the west side of Ashwynd in the countryside, so instead of her getting a horse and traveling so far, on the way to Ashen Vale, Korra would drop her off on the other side. The primary goal was not to bring the fliers into the middle of the city. They were accustomed to Drusearons flying in and around, but definitely not large fliers.

"We're approaching!" Zane announced.

We all dived low at the last moment, trying not to bring attention to us. My stomach felt like it was trying to become one with my heart. Esme's talons landed with perfect grace, throwing a dust of snow in our wake.

"Rate your ride five stars or the next landing won't be so gentle," she purred.

I choked a laugh out. She caught me so off guard with that. The other Riders whipped their faces to me. I reached up and rubbed the scales on her neck.

"She told me to rate my ride five stars, or the next landing won't be so gentle. So, everyone knows, I give Esme ten stars!" I told them before giggling more, and they all chuckled.

She stretched her leg forward. I threw my right leg over and slid down her massive tree trunk of a leg. Zane was there with his hand stretched out. I grabbed his hand, and he pulled me into his arms.

"Welcome to your new home, my love, my Anam Cara, my Auri," he caressed down the bond.

My eyes locked onto his, *"I am soooooo nervous."*

"Pep talk time, my little Rider—they will love you, you are amazing, and funny. If someone doesn't love you, then something is wrong with them." Esme purred down the bond.

As I turned to give her a look, she shot into the air with Korra, Daphne, and Inna. Sadie gave all of us a wave as she rose into the sky.

"Hey Nikolai, as you know, you are always welcome to the welcome home dinner," Zane said.

"Yes, I'll see how my pops is doing." There was a sense of sadness when he'd said that, suggesting there was much more to all that. He looked at me, "Cadet, behave and do us Riders an honor in the palace."

"Geez, Nik, don't scare her before I get her home," Zane bantered.

"Ah, it's not too bad. I'll more than likely be there, I have to go into town to let Landon's parents know anyway."

"Yeah... It's always rough when it's one of us."

I looked between both of them, worried I may be in over my head. Nikolai gave a nod and headed off down a dirt road. Zane, Remus, and I were the only ones left on the field.

"Of course, Remus, you are always welcome, but I know your parents would bury you if you didn't have dinner with them tonight. We're going to head out. You know where to find me."

"As always, I am sure I will stop in. Be safe," he said. He sprang his wings out wide and took off.

"And it's just you and me now," Zane smirked.

"That it is," I smiled.

"Do you want to go straight to the palace, or do you want a tour?"

"Can we do a short tour on the way there and then finish the tour maybe tomorrow? I am exhausted."

"Anything for you."

Zane's arms slid around me, firm and steady, before his wings unfurled with a snap that stirred snow from the ground.

"Hold on," he murmured against my ear.

"I already am," I whispered back, though my pulse had been a drum in my throat. He'd never actually flown with me, though he roved me several other times. I imagined it would be similar to flying with Esme.

With a single beat of wings, he rose in the air. My heart skipped. Difference and similarity blended. Only his arms held me. The ground dropped away, the wind cut sharply, and we soared low over Ashwynd. The city unfurled beneath us like a living map. Cobbled streets twisted among rows of stone buildings, and smoke curled from chimneys. Carriages were driven over frozen ruts, iron-rimmed wheels striking sparks from the stones. Merchants' calls rang out from patched awnings, bread, wool, and roasted chestnuts were offered to the city.

Children shrieked below, playing in the snow with each other. They briefly looked up before going back to their games. Most others on the ground hadn't paid any mind to us, and we hadn't been the only ones in the sky.

Zane's mouth brushed my temple as he spoke low, guiding my gaze. "The south quarter is filled with tradesmen, workshops. The loudest place in the city is always awake. Beyond that, there is the train where boxcars are unloaded from dawn to dusk."

We banked slightly, and the main square opened beneath us, a vast expanse of stone framed by tall, uniform facades. A frozen fountain glittered at its heart, icicles catching the late afternoon light. The smell of baking bread and coal smoke rose even this high.

And then I saw it.

The palace. His home. His family.

It sat on a rise at the far end of the square, not gleaming or delicate like a storybook. Heavy stone walls loomed, black and gray, built like a fortress. Guard towers bristled at the corners, each manned with knights, their halberds gleaming. The iron gates at the front stood tall and uncompromising, already flanked by knights who scanned the streets with sharp eyes.

My breath caught. "That looks... less like a palace and more like a fortress."

"That's because it is," Zane said. His chin rested lightly against my hair. "My father doesn't build for beauty. He builds for survival. What you see down there—that's what keeps the Veil standing."

The weight of it pressed on me, heavy as the stone itself. And yet, with his arms tight around me, the beat of his heart steady against my back, I breathed.

Because whatever waited beyond those walls, I wouldn't face it alone.

The closer we swept toward the rise, the more the city noise dulled beneath the beat of Zane's wings. The palace loomed larger with every second, a fortress of black stone and iron.

"Ready?" he murmured against my ear.

"No," I whispered, clutching his arm tighter. "But go anyway."

He laughed softly, the sound curling warm against my skin, and angled us down. His wings spread wide, catching the air as we descended past the outer towers, landing in the formal yard. The guards stationed there tracked us, halberds gleaming, but none moved to intercept.

Zane lifted one hand from my waist, casual as anything, and gave them a sharp, easy wave. Recognition flashed in their eyes. The tension eased instantly and they saluted back. One sheathed his sword again.

We stood in the large formal yard in front of the palace. It was stunning. Everything was covered in snow and ice, but it was clear that the groundskeepers had done a good job maintaining everything. Towers ringed the inner court, banners snapping from their heights—black cloth embroidered with a silver Drusearon, wings spread wide. Troops lined the yard, their eyes snapping to us. No one spoke. No one questioned. They only saluted.

Zane's arm stayed firm at my back as he guided me forward. "Welcome to Ashwynd Palace, Auri," he said low, his voice steady, even as the fortress seemed to swallow me whole.

My chest tightened, my nerves tangling. But I nodded, stepping forward with him.

And there was no turning back.

Figures started running toward us, toward him.

I certainly hoped they would like me.

"If not, I'll be there to swoop you away, but they will." Esme purred.

CHAPTER 48

"ZANE!"

Six figures broke from the far archway, their footsteps echoing on the stone as they moved closer. Aeliana reached him first, her golden-blonde hair whipping loose from her braid as she slammed into him with enough force to jostle me back a step.

"Finally!" She laughed, breathless. "Do you know how boring this place has been without you?"

Zane actually staggered, catching her with a grunt, smiling faintly. "Aeliana..." His eyes flicked toward me, steady, proud. "Meet Auri."

Aeliana's gaze cut sharply to me, and for a heartbeat, the world stilled. Her eyes were so much like Zane's—they narrowed, then widened. The realization hit her who I was.

"It's her."

My mouth went dry. "Hi."

Aeliana stepped closer, studying my face like she'd known me all her life. "You found her before you turned old and crusty. And she's just as beautiful as Auntie said."

I could feel the heat rushing to my cheeks—thankfully, they were already red from the cold. Before I could find words, the others piled in.

Theodora, tall and poised in her haste, folded her arms but smiled warmly. "So, you finally brought her home. About time."

Arkin, broad-shouldered and grinning, elbowed Zane hard enough to make me wince. "She's real. Gods, I thought you and Auntie were bullshitting us."

"Arkin," Zane warned, though his mouth twitched.

Helena, all sharp eyes and restless energy, circled me like she was already sizing me for sparring lessons. "She doesn't look like she'd put up with your brooding."

"I don't," I said before I could stop myself. Helena barked out a laugh.

Adrian, gangly but quick with a boyish grin, gave me a dramatic bow. "Welcome to the madhouse."

Elizabeth, the smallest, peeked around her siblings, wide-eyed and clutching the hem of Theodora's coat. "She's pretty," she whispered, shy as a bird.

My face burned. I had no idea what to say to any of them, their energy sweeping me up before I could catch my balance. And then the crowd shifted.

The air seemed to change—sharper, heavier—as the duke and duchess stepped into the courtyard.

The duke of the Veil of Vultures, Zane's father, was as imposing as the palace itself, his black cloak edged in silver, his pale eyes cutting through the chaos with a single sweep. Beside him, the Duchess moved with quiet grace, her dark hair streaked with silver, her expression softer but no less commanding. Zane definitely favored his father, while his mother had been beautiful beyond words, but I could see where Zane got his attractive stoic features.

The siblings all turned toward him, their smiles dimming a little, like they were also unsure of how this would go.

Zane's hand pressed against the small of my back. *"He's really amazing, past his eyes of death,"* he murmured down the bond.

My heart was racing, knees weak—as the duke's gaze settled right on me. Every fear and worry ran through my mind like a toddler on sugar. How would he react to my name? Would he know who I was? Would blame be given instantly? Zane's anger was triggered when the pieces finally fell into place. Gods, this could end so fucking poorly. I felt my panic rising, the weight of his gaze pressing like stone. For half a heartbeat, my breath was lost.

"Breathe, Auri... your anxiety is overwhelming me, and I am not close," Esme said.

Suddenly, training—and instinct—took over.

I stepped forward, dipping low into a bow, my braid sliding over my shoulder. "Duke Braegon. Duchess." My voice steady though my knees trembled.

Silence stretched.

When I dared to lift my eyes, the duke of the Veil of Vultures had been studying me with that pale, merciless stare I'd come to dread at the college. But there was something different now—not cold calculation, but something quieter.

"Rise, young lady," he said. His voice had been deep, commanding, but there had been no edge to it. "No need for formality here. You are welcome."

The knot in my chest loosened just a fraction. I straightened slowly, my pulse hammering in my ears.

The Duchess stepped forward, her presence softer but no less powerful. She reached out, taking my hand between hers, her eyes warm in a way that startled me.

"Zane's Anam Cara," she said, the words carrying like a blessing. "We have waited for you far longer than you realize. This is your home as much as his."

Heat pricked the back of my eyes, unexpected and sharp. Gods, I hadn't known how much I needed to hear that until the words wrapped around me. Zane's hand brushed mine again, grounding, steady. The bond thrummed with quiet pride, with relief.

"Father. Mother. This is Auri—Auriella Blackcreek."

I braced myself—for questions, for narrowed eyes, for disbelief.

But none of that came.

The duke inclined his head, expression as implacable as stone. "Hello, Auri."

I blinked, waiting for the other foot to drop. "Hi!" It was all I could get out.

The siblings shifted behind us, grinning like this had been the most ordinary thing in the world, as though bringing home a soulmate had been no more remarkable than bringing home a friend. My pulse was still a storm, but for the first time, I hadn't been sure if I was afraid—or simply overwhelmed.

The courtyard was still buzzing with the siblings' chatter—Helena already asking if I could spar, Arkin trying to convince me that he and Zane once flew off the roof of the armory on a bet, Elizabeth tugging at my sleeve like she wanted me to follow her.

The duke lifted his hand, and the noise died instantly.

"You all overwhelm her," he said, his voice low but leaving no room for argument. His pale eyes swept the six of them. "Go. Give your brother space."

They hesitated—only for a breath—then scattered like a flock of birds, some throwing quick smiles back at me as they went.

When the last of their footsteps faded, the Duchess turned to Zane, her hand still warm on mine. "Show her around, give her the ins and outs like it's hers too." Her gaze flicked toward me, kind and steady. "And see her settled in her chamber."

Zane hadn't flinched. His hand was still holding mine tightly. "She'll be with me, in my room."

The words hung heavy in the winter air.

The Duchess's brows lifted, and for a heartbeat, I thought she might object. The duke's pale eyes narrowed slightly, weighing the words, the bond, the meaning.

But neither spoke against it.

At last, the duke inclined his head. "So be it."

The Duchess's mouth curved into the faintest smile. "It seems the choice is already made."

Heat flushed up my neck, and I dropped my gaze, my pulse roaring. I wanted to vanish into the stones themselves. But Zane's bond pulsed warm and steady, an anchor against the storm.

He guided me forward, past the guards and through the marble French doors, his hand firmly holding mine, like he never wanted to let go. Inside the palace, the air felt thicker, every hall echoing with weight and history. I wasn't just stepping into Zane's world anymore. I was stepping into his life.

The palace swallowed us as soon as we went through the doors, its vaulted ceilings rising higher than I expected, the corridors echoing with every footstep. Zane walked steadily at my side, his voice low and calm as he pointed things out.

"That hall leads to the old armory. Still in use, though mostly for drills now. The eastern wing holds the archives—endless shelves of dust and secrets. Tomorrow, I'll take you to the temple where the statue of the seven Gods are. It's carved from a single block of obsidian, older than the palace itself."

I swallowed, overwhelmed by the scale, by the history pressing in from every wall. "That sounds... terrifying and beautiful."

"You'll see," he promised, his mouth curving faintly.

We turned another corner, climbing a staircase lined with heavy tapestries. He led me down a quieter hall, away from the bustle of maids and guards, until we reached a set of carved double doors.

His chambers.

When he pushed them open, I froze.

It hadn't been the size that stopped me—though the room was vast, lined with shelves and maps, a hearth already lit with a low fire. It was what hung over the mantel.

The painting.

My own face looked back at me from the canvas—softer, but undeniably me. My long blond braid, the tilt of my emerald eyes, the set of my jaw—every detail captured by a hand that didn't know me.

My chest tightened, my breath catching in my throat. Although Zane told me it existed, seeing it was different. Seeing me in this room, painted years before I'd ever stepped inside, was like standing on the edge of something endless.

"I told you," he said softly. "It is undeniably you, and like you, it is a beauty."

I couldn't speak. I could only stare at the girl in the painting, at the ghost of myself that lived in his world long before I arrived.

I tore my eyes from the painting at last, my chest still tight, my throat aching with things I didn't know how to say.

Zane drew me closer, his hand warm at the small of my back. "I know it's all overwhelming," he murmured. "Just... be here. With me."

The fire crackled low, throwing soft light across the chamber. The weight of the day pressed down all at once—the flight, the mountains, Landon's death, the palace, his family, that painting. My body felt heavy, like the stone walls themselves seeped into my bones.

"I don't think I am ready to mingle," I admitted, my voice small.

"You don't have to," Zane said. "Not yet."

He led me toward the wide bed draped in dark furs, the smell of cedar clinging to the heavy blankets. I hadn't protested when he pulled me down beside him, his arms wrapping firm around me, anchoring me in the storm.

My back pressed to his chest, just as it had every night I'd fallen asleep in his arms, his breath steady against my hair. The bond between us hummed, warm and sure, tugging the knots loose in my chest.

I felt safe. I was safe. Sure, there were unknowns, but I was safe. My eyelids grew heavy despite the weight of what waited for us tonight.

"Rest," he whispered, pressing a kiss to my temple. "We'll face them together."

The palace could rage, his family could question, and the dinner could turn into chaos. But wrapped in his arms, exhaustion won.

And I let sleep take me.

By the time Zane and I entered the dining hall, it was already chaos. The long table stretched beneath glittering chandeliers, flames from a dozen candelabras flickering against polished silver and crystal. Footmen weaved between chairs with trays of steaming platters—roasted game hens, spiced root vegetables, bowls of broth that smelled like heaven itself.

But the food was the background. The noise came from his siblings.

Arkin had already been halfway through a dramatic retelling of some "harrowing duel" in the training yard, gesturing so wildly that he nearly elbowed Theodora in the face. She hadn't flinched, only rolled her eyes and kept sipping her wine. Helena was arguing with Eli about whether griffins or dragons made the better war mounts, both of them getting louder and louder until Elizabeth squealed for them to shut up. Aeliana tried to keep some order, but her presence couldn't quiet them all at once.

"Gods," I said under my breath, hovering at the threshold, "this makes the dining hall look peaceful."

Zane chuckled, his hand at the small of my back as he guided me forward. "Welcome to dinner at Ashwynd, I told you it was chaos at home."

The moment they noticed us, six voices overlapped.

"About time!"

"You nearly missed the soup."

"Don't sit next to Arkin—he spits when he talks."

"Do sit next to Arkin—I want someone else to suffer."

"She looks nervous. Stop staring at her."

"She is nervous, look at her face!"

Heat rushed to my cheeks. I opened my mouth, but nothing came out.

"Enough," the duke's voice cut through the din, calm but carrying. Instantly, the siblings quieted, though smirks lingered on their faces.

The Duchess rose slightly, smiling at me. "Come, Auri. Sit. Eat. Let the noise wash over you—it always does."

I let out a shaky breath, sliding into the seat beside Zane. Across the table, Aeliana caught my eye and winked, as though to say welcome to the family circus. The footmen poured wine and passed platters around. Conversation roared back to life—questions hurled at Zane about the college, sly jabs at each other, debates over politics and war tactics thrown in between bites of bread. And somehow, through the chaos, I found myself laughing. The nerves hadn't vanished—but maybe, just maybe, I could survive this.

The meal had already been a blur of sound and motion by the time I had a plate in front of me. Arkin kept reaching over people to grab food that wasn't his. Elizabeth had been sneaking candied nuts into her pocket when she thought no one was looking, and Adrian had been loudly insisting that Drusearons could outfly griffins.

"Blasphemy," Nikolai said into his wine, and the table erupted again.

I found myself smiling, actually laughing, despite the knot in my stomach. It felt... chaotic, but familiar. Like Feather Wing in the dining hall back at the college, just louder and with better food.

Helena leaned across the table, her sharp eyes catching mine. "So, Auri," she said, voice deceptively light, "what was it like the first time you felt the bond with Zane? Did you know what it was?"

My fork froze halfway to my mouth. "I—" My chest tightened. That hadn't been something I really talked about.

Before I could find an answer, Aeliana chimed in, smiling but with that same piercing look. "Your father is—General Blackcreek, right?"

Every sibling fell silent, their eyes locking on me. Zane's hand settled on my thigh, steadying me.

"Yes... he fathered me." Their stares lingered, heavy in the pause that followed.

Elizabeth broke it with a sudden burst, her eyes wide and bright. "Did you really fight a Rider in training and cut both of his Achilles?"

"Lizzie!" Theodora hissed, scandal sharp on her tongue.

"What?" Elizabeth blinked back at her, all innocence. "It happened."

Zane's hand brushed mine under the table, steadying me, though his jaw was tight. *"Don't let them shake you,"* he murmured down the bond. *"They're testing, but not in the way you think."*

Arkin leaned back in his chair, grinning wolfishly. "Don't worry, we prefer you to be able to hold your own. Gods, we know you need to, to survive this family..."

Laughter rippled down the table again, the noise surging back, almost enough to hide the thrum of unease still in my chest. Almost.

By the time the main platters vanished, my stomach already ached with fullness—but the feast didn't care. Trays rolled in one after another:

sugared tarts, candied nuts, custards laced with cinnamon, and a tower of spun sugar that caved the instant Arkin jabbed it with his fork.

Elizabeth squealed. Eli's laughter boomed across the table. Hands shot in from every side, grabbing, swiping, voices rising in shouts over the last tart, accusations flying as plates emptied faster than they could be defended.

"Gods above," I said, ducking as a sugared almond flew past my head. "Do you always eat like this?"

"Only when the food is good," Helena grinned, licking sugar from her fingers. "Which means always. How are we supposed to eat?" She raised an eyebrow at me.

"I... I don't know. I am an only child, and every royal dinner I have eaten at was quiet with light conversation."

Almost all of them roared in laughter. I hadn't thought what I'd said was that funny.

Aeliana leaned toward me, her smile deceptively sweet. "So, Auri, what about your childhood?"

My chest tightened. "I moved around frequently. I grew up with two best friends, who are also twins."

Eli chimed in, his eyes bright. "Is it true your magic was diminished by your parents?"

I shot Zane a look.

"He didn't tell me. I heard the rumor around campus. I guess people thought it was interesting that the General gave his daughter the tincture."

My cheeks flushed hot. "That's... true."

The room quieted for a moment, just long enough for the duke's voice to cut across the table. "How did that feel? You have magic now, though?" His pale eyes fixed on me, not unkind but heavy.

The air thickened. My fork shook slightly in my hand. "I was upset. There was a lot hid—shielded from me. I felt like I needed to catch up on something I should have known. I don't have my unique ability from Esme yet."

The Duchess leaned forward, her voice softer. "And do you feel safe with Esme? Truly safe?"

I blinked, startled by the question's intimacy. "Yes. Including when she is... testing me. Especially then."

A small, knowing smile touched the Duchess's lips, and she leaned back again.

Before the silence could stretch, Helena pounced. "All right then, tell us—first crush? Don't say Zane."

I nearly choked on my wine. "What?"

The table erupted with laughter again, Elizabeth banging her spoon against the table and chanting, "First crush! First crush!" while Zane groaned beside me, pinching the bridge of his nose.

I buried my face in my hands, half-laughing, half-dying inside. This family would eat me alive.

"Yeah... we're not going there. I draw that line," I said.

The table was still roaring with laughter, Elizabeth banging her spoon, Arkin mock-groaning about my "mysterious taste in males," when Theodora leaned forward, her smile a little too sharp. She had been mostly quiet during dinner.

"All right," she said, her tone casual but her blue eyes cutting straight to me. "One more question, Auri. Tell us—how does it feel to be General Blackcreek's daughter... and know he killed the uncles of your mate?"

The laughter collapsed into silence so fast it left my ears ringing.

My chest went cold. My fork slipped against the plate with a scrape. Every sibling stared now—some curious, some guarded, some clearly enjoying the spectacle. Nikolai's smile vanished. Eli stared at his plate in disbelief. Oliver, who had remained quiet, stared at me with pity.

I opened my mouth, but nothing came out. Gods, how did she know that?

Before I could form a single word, Zane's chair scraped back hard against the floor. His hand closed over mine, steady but iron-strong.

"That's enough," he said, his voice low, dangerous, the kind of tone that stopped even Arkin mid-breath. His eyes swept the table, dark and burning. "You've had your fun. You've got your questions. She answered more than she owed."

He looked at his parents, his gaze sharp yet respectful. "With your permission, we'll retire. It's been a long journey."

The duke inclined his head, expression unreadable. The Duchess's smile had been faint, but I caught the approval in her eyes.

Zane hadn't waited for further comment. He pulled me gently to my feet, his arm sliding around me as he steered me toward the doors.

Behind us, the siblings already erupted back into whispers, their voices carrying sharp undercurrents of curiosity and speculation. But I didn't look back. Because my heart was still hammering with Theodora's words, and my biggest fear came alive on the first day we were here. I knew I had to address this because they would wonder. There would be more questions.

The door to the dining hall closed behind us, muting the roar of voices. My lungs ached like I had held my breath the whole meal. Zane hadn't spoken. His arm stayed around me, guiding me through a side corridor lit by flickering sconces, until we reached the quiet of his chambers. Only then did he let out a long, sharp breath, dragging a hand through his hair.

"They shouldn't have asked that," he said, his voice low, taut with fury. "Not like that. Not at dinner. Gods."

I leaned back against the door, my stomach still twisted. "How could they even know? Theodora—she asked it like she was certain."

Zane crossed the room in two strides, catching my hands in his, his eyes locking on mine. The bond pulsed hot and steady between us.

"They know things they shouldn't. They've always been too sharp for their own good. But listen to me, Auri—" his grip tightened, *"—you don't owe them anything. No explanations. Not pieces of yourself. Not now. Not ever, unless you want."*

The heat in his voice startled me. He hadn't just been protective—he was livid.

I exhaled slowly, trying to let his steadiness bleed into me. "I just don't think learning the real truth will benefit them either. Learning one of their uncles raped someone, raped your mate."

He hadn't said anything, just pulled me into a hug.

"Your sister practically gutted me with one question."

"Theodora's blades are always sharp." His thumb brushed over my knuckles, gentler now. "Don't feel like you can't throw the dagger back... metaphorically, of course."

For a while, we just stood there, wrapped in the silence of the chamber, the fire crackling low in the hearth. His arms around me, the hum of the bond steady, the tension of the hall fading little by little.

Then—a knock at the door.

Not hurried, not soft. Deliberate.

A voice followed. "Lord Zane. The duke requests your presence. Both of you. In his study."

My stomach plummeted.

Zane's jaw flexed. He pressed a kiss against my temple before drawing back, his hand still in mine.

"Then we don't keep him waiting," he said.

Through the bond, I felt a shimmer of worry. I hadn't thought this conversation would be happening today, but it's better to get it over with.

The duke's study had been all dark wood and heavy velvet curtains, the fire snapping low in the hearth. I braced myself for cold silence, for his pale stare.

Instead, the first thing I saw was him.

My father.

General Blackcreek, my father, sat at ease in one of the duke's chairs, a glass of amber liquor in his hand. Not a prisoner. Not a guest. Comfortable. At home. The duke sitting next to him was sipping on his own glass.

My breath stuttered. Zane stopped short beside me, his shoulders tightening like steel.

"Good of you to join us," the duke said, his pale eyes flicking between us.

I hadn't been able to move. Couldn't breathe. "What—" My voice cracked. "What is he doing here?"

My father swirled his glass, the liquor catching the firelight. "Relax, Auri. If I meant you harm, you wouldn't have walked through the door." His gaze had been sharp, too sharp. "Though, you should know… the two of you haven't been nearly as clever as you think."

Zane stepped forward, jaw locked. "What's that supposed to mean?"

My father's smirk hadn't reached his eyes. "The mutiny you were trying to hide." He lifted his glass in a mock toast. "You didn't block it out well enough. I saw the edges. You need practice. You both do."

My stomach twisted. Cold sweat prickled the back of my neck.

"Shit," I choked out.

He shook his head slowly. "That's not what we really call it anyway… We call it," he looked at the duke, "the Resurrection of Yebel."

The words hung in the air, heavy and dangerous, like a curse released into the room. Zane's hand was still holding mine, his grip iron-hard, but I'd barely felt it. My father leaned forward, his voice lower now.

"Your mother was close, Auri. Too close. She pieced together more than anyone realized. But she didn't get everything right. And when she brought her questions to the wrong ears…" He exhaled slowly, eyes sharp as glass. "I watched her die in front of me. By the King's own hand and I had to pretend I didn't know a damned thing, or he would have killed you, killed me, killed…"

The floor felt like it shifted under me. My knees locked to keep me upright, my chest burning with the weight of it.

And then—everything shattered.

The firelight guttered as shadows ripped free from the corners of the room, streaking like black lightning across the walls. They twisted, coiled, alive—wrapping cold around my arms, sliding across the duke's desk, lashing upward.

One struck like a serpent, curling around my father's throat and hoisting him from his chair. His glass shattered when it hit the floor, his face pale with panic as he clawed at the darkness.

"Auri!" Zane's voice was ragged in my ear. "What are you—"

But I hadn't been doing anything. My heart hammered, my breath ragged in my chest, and still the shadows poured from me, endless and furious, answering some instinct I hadn't known I had.

My father's strangled sounds filled the room. "Shhhaaa—doowsss" he gasped out.

The duke surged to his feet, his pale eyes wide for the first time since I'd met him. "Gods, help us," he breathed. "A shadow summoner."

His gaze locked on me, sharp with awe and terror all at once. "There hasn't been one in centuries."

And then the room went still—every flame guttered low, every breath caught, the weight of my power choked the air.

I stared at my own hands, the shadows writhing around them like they'd been waiting for this moment.

And for the first time, I had been more afraid of myself than of anyone else.

Everyone in the room looked at me—like they were petrified of me.

ACKNOWLEDGMENTS

This book would not exist without the love and support of so many people.

First, to my husband, James—thank you for your patience, encouragement, and for always believing in me, even when I doubted myself.

To my children and grandchildren, whose laughter, questions, and resilience remind me every day why stories matter. You are my greatest inspiration.

To my friends—thank you for cheering me on, listening to my endless ramblings about dragons and Riders, and pushing me forward when I wanted to stop. Your encouragement carried me through every draft.

And to my lifelong love of books—for being my escape, my teacher, and the spark that ignited this dream in the first place.

Finally, to **every reader** who picks up *Black Wing and Shadows*—thank you for stepping into this world with me. I hope it brings you wonder, escape, and a little piece of magic.

ABOUT THE AUTHOR

J. L. Rosenauer is a fantasy author who loves letting her mind go wild and spill onto a keyboard. When she's not writing, you may find her floating down the river and spending time with her family. She lives in Missouri with her family, where she proudly answers to both "Mom" and "Gigi," roles that inspire her belief that every generation carries a story worth telling.

Throughout her life she has endured hard challenges and writing has been a powerful outlet for her. Black Wing and Shadows is her debut novel.

www.ingramcontent.com/pod-product-compliance
Lightning Source LLC
Chambersburg PA
CBHW060602300726
48975CB00005B/1423